Gravity

Sarah Deming

MAKE ME A WORLD
New York

MAKE ME A WORLD is an imprint dedicated to exploring the vast possibilities of contemporary childhood. We strive to imagine a universe in which no young person is invisible, in which no kid's story is erased, in which no glass ceiling presses down on the dreams of a child. Then we publish books for that world, where kids ask hard questions and we struggle with them together, where dreams stretch from eons ago into the future and we do our best to provide road maps to where these young folks want to be. We make books where the children of today can see themselves and each other. When presented with fences, with borders, with limits, with all the kinds of chains that hobble imaginations and hearts, we proudly say—no.

Text copyright © 2019 by Sarah Deming
Jacket art copyright © 2019 by Malin Fezehai

All rights reserved. Published in the United States by Make Me a World, an imprint of Random House Children's Books, a division of Penguin Random House LLC, New York.

Make Me a World and the colophon are trademarks of Penguin Random House LLC.

Visit us on the Web! GetUnderlined.com

Educators and librarians, for a variety of teaching tools, visit us at RHTeachersLibrarians.com

Library of Congress Cataloging-in-Publication Data
ISBN 978-0-525-58103-1 — ISBN 978-0-525-58104-8 (lib. bdg.) —
ISBN 978-0-525-58105-5 (ebook)

The text of this book is set in 11.2-point Goudy Old Style MT Std.
Interior design by Jaclyn Whalen

Printed in the United States of America
November 2019
10 9 8 7 6 5 4 3 2 1

First Edition

In memory of

Trendon "Tray" Franklin Grant
(1992–2012)

&

Michael Davon Hayden Jr.
(1993–2014)

Dear Reader,

No fighting! Playgrounds and classrooms and school gyms across the world post signs that mark one of the primary injunctions of childhood. Parents and teachers and administrators all join in common chorus.

But there are things worth fighting for, and fights worth having.

Gravity Delgado is a young woman, a fighter, who must discover which fights are the important ones.

It seems sometimes that young adult literature is streaked with heroines. There are underestimated leaders who discover that they have real power. There are observant, unnoticed introverts who discover conspiracies. There is also a disturbing trend of bedridden sleeping beauties who wait for quirky princes to discover them, all the while trading sarcastic bon mots.

Gravity Delgado is none of these. She knows that she is a fighter. She has been fighting since she was born. The question for Gravity, and for so many of us today, is not whether or not to fight, but what is worth fighting for.

Sarah Deming, a writer and Golden Gloves champion who splits her time between writing about boxing and coaching and mentoring young people at the gym in East Flatbush that inspired Gravity's environs, gives us a new kind of heroine in the landscape of young people's literature. Gravity can take a punch; she can knock you out. But her biggest fights aren't in the ring—they are with herself.

Christopher Myers

MAKE ME A WORLD

Prologue

Because the gym had no address, it was impossible to enter into a GPS. The first time Gravity tried to find it, she got lost in the housing projects in Brownsville. Nobody she asked—the policeman, the boy on the bike smoking weed, the lady with the baby carriage—had heard of a boxing gym called PLASMAFuel Cops 'n Kids.

Brownsville was one of the roughest neighborhoods in Brooklyn, but Gravity was not afraid. She was tall for her age and dressed in jeans and a hoodie, and the good part about being half Dominican and half Jewish was that you could pass for different things in different places. She never quite fit in, but she never stuck out too bad either.

On her second trip, she found a dead-end street that sloped downward to a basement entrance of the projects. Above the door, the brown brick wall was painted over with a mural of smiling cops holding boxing gloves and bald eagles. Because it was the lowest place around, all the Styrofoam clamshells, used condoms, and broken headphones people had tossed out their windows were gathered into a drift before the door.

An electric gate blocked the entrance, and a handwritten sign, duct-taped to the front and wet with rain, read "Gym Closed for Funneral." Gravity reached out to touch the sign and got zapped with an electric shock that sent her flying backward onto the seat of her jeans. Cans of cat food clattered out of her way, and a feral tabby peeked out from under a nearby dumpster and hissed. Gravity hissed back.

The third time she showed up, one of those Access-A-Ride vans was pulled up at the end of the street. An old man rolled off, pulled a dustpan and broom off the back of his wheelchair, and cleared away the rubbish that had accumulated before the gate.

Gravity hurried down the street so she could help him, but he was done before she got there. She watched as he replaced the broom and dustpan in his saddlebags and pulled out several cans of gourmet cat food, which he opened with trembling hands and set down on the sidewalk.

She cleared her throat. "Mr. Thomas? I'm Gravity Delgado. I want to learn to box."

Because Gravity recognized him now. The wheelchair had thrown her off, but the huge hands, callused over the knuckles and gnarled like roots, were unmistakable. She had first seen them in an internet video on how to wrap hands, and she had fallen into a kind of rapture as she watched them wind strips of gauze around a young boy's knuckles. She had searched the comment thread until she learned that the coach's name was Jefferson H. Thomas III. When she'd googled him, she had found an article in the *Daily News* that named this gym and, incredibly, said it was free to train.

He ignored her, fishing a boxing glove keychain out of his fanny pack and raising the electric gate. Gravity wondered if he might be hard of hearing until he grunted over his shoulder, "Careful with the gate. It electrocutes you when it rains."

Gravity stood in the dark entryway of the long, rectangular space awhile, waiting for him to tell her what to do. The basement air was thick with sweat and leather. It reminded her of the smell of the karate dojo where she used to train as a little girl. She remembered the rush of breaking her first board, the thrill of making her first sparring partner quit.

As Jefferson H. Thomas III zipped around the gym, turning on the flickering overhead fluorescents, details of the room within emerged slowly: fight posters, newspaper clippings, and champions—everywhere, photos of champions. A polished mirror at one end reflected the nine heavy bags stretching in neat rows between the two raised rings.

The old man grunted and pointed to a little table beside the door, which held—alongside a jumble of used mouthpieces and half-empty PLASMAFuel bottles—a logbook with neat columns for boxers' names, weights, and the times they arrived and left the gym.

Over the logbook hung a sign:

COPS 'N KIDS GYM RULES

ALL BOXER'S MUST SIGN IN, NO EXCEPTIONS!

NO SAGGING!!!

NO SPITTING

NO HORSE PLAY

NO CUSSING

NO KISSING

NO KICKING THE BAG'S

NO LOITERING, IF YOUR HERE, YOU MUST TRAIN!

MOUTHPIECE AND HEAD GEAR MUST BE WORN AT ALL TIMES
WHEN SPARRING

FLUSH COMMODE AFTER USE

These rules were like the Jewish holidays: observed by only a small fraction of the population. Gravity bent to sign her name, noting as she did that the previous day's page had been filled out in a chaotic fashion. Some entries were complete, like "Kimani Browne, 230 pounds, 3:10–5:30 PM," which was written in the neatest handwriting Gravity had ever seen, and some kid called Lefty (aka $outhpaw) signed his name in Gothic lettering with one of those art markers that write in liquid silver. Others kids left things blank or scrawled in a way that was totally incomprehensible. Someone had written "THE GREATEST" in huge letters across a whole line.

"Come here," barked the old man. "Bring that stool."

Gravity picked up the wooden stool next to the door and walked across the gym to the old man's wheelchair. She was expecting him to ask her if she had boxed before (she hadn't, but she would have been a black belt in karate by now if her mom hadn't been too cheap to pay the testing fees) or why he should train her (she had taken a photo of all the trophies she had won in different sports), but instead he just pointed to a high shelf where a round timer sat, flashing its green work light and counting down from 4:00.

"Change that bullshit to a three-minute round," he commanded. "Boca don't know shit about boxing. Tell me how you train boxers to a four-minute clock when they only fight threes?" He shook his head. "That makes slow starters."

Gravity didn't understand what he meant or why he was so angry, but he did not seem to require any comment from her. As she climbed up onto the stool and reached for the buttons on the bell, he launched into a long list of this Boca person's bad qualities, including never cleaning the bathroom, never refilling the watercoolers, hoarding gauze, stealing other people's boxers, playing annoying Mexican music, and—alarmingly—leaving floaters in the toilet that were "bigger than Butterbean."

The last image made Gravity so uncomfortable that she wobbled on the stool and had to reach out to steady herself against the wall, but it was papered three-deep in advertisements for PLASMAFuel, which slipped off, sending her careening backward onto the dirty cement floor. The stool clattered into the nearest ring post, shattering.

She bounced back up, ignoring the pain in her tailbone, and stared at the broken stool. Her mother's voice, high and harsh, echoed in her imagination: calling her a klutz, saying she could not be trusted with nice things. Gravity closed her eyes, trying to banish the shame.

Gravity broke everything sooner or later: letters on keyboards, zippers on jeans, countless pieces of Auntie Rosa's pottery. She'd had to quit orchestra after she sat on her viola, and she got suspended from fourth grade for breaking a boy's nose.

She opened her eyes at the unexpected touch of the old man's hand on hers.

"It's not how many times you go down," he said. "It's how many times you get up."

His teaching rippled through her mind, and her mother's voice went away. She committed the words to memory. She would think about them later when she meditated.

She had started meditating in the anger management classes Auntie Rosa paid for after she broke that boy's nose. Even after the course was over, she had kept meditating, because it made her feel more calm. It wasn't enough to train your body: a warrior's most powerful weapon was her mind.

When the old man pulled the dustpan off his wheelchair

again and started pushing in the broken stool, Gravity tried to help, but he shook her off with a look so fierce that she backed away.

"How old are you?" he demanded.

"Twelve."

"Hmm. Tall for twelve. Long arms, too. What do you weigh?"

"The last time I went to the doctor, I was a hundred and six pounds, but I think I grew since then."

He squinted at her as he dumped the shards of wood in the trash can. Then he rolled over and reached out to grab her arm. She held still and waited to see what he would do.

Up close, he looked even older. His USA Boxing cap hid the hair on his head, but his eyebrows were like fat white caterpillars, and he had little white hairs coming out of his nose and ears. Rivers of wrinkles flowed through his deep brown skin from the corners of his eyes and mouth, disappearing into the folds of his neck. His thick lips were fixed in a perpetual scowl, but it was not a mean scowl, like the ones on the faces of Gravity's schoolteachers. It was the kind of scowl you make when you have been concentrating very hard for a very long time on something you love.

"How tall are your parents?" he asked.

"Mom says she's five six, but I think she's really five three."

He did not ask about her father, just looked at her sadly for a moment and then nodded. He felt the bones of her wrist. He examined her feet. He poked her in the ribs, making her cough.

At last he said, "You'll most likely be a lightweight when you're grown."

He pulled something out of his fanny pack that Gravity had only seen before in YouTube videos. It was called a cassette tape, and it was the way they played music in the old days. The old man slid the cassette tape into an ancient boom box that sat on one of the ring aprons, and James Brown began to holler.

Before Gravity could ask him what "lightweight" meant, a boy about her age blew in on a bicycle. He was small, dark, and handsome. Gravity recognized him as the boy from the internet video whose hands the old man had been wrapping, but there was something special about him in person that no camera could capture. Narrowly missing the tips of Gravity's sneakers, he did a wheelie around one of the heavy bags and bounced back down with a whoop in front of Coach Thomas's wheelchair.

The old man yelled, "No sagging!" and cuffed the boy across the forehead, knocking off his Steelers cap.

The boy didn't seem to mind. In fact, Gravity got the feeling that he enjoyed the attention. He slid off the bike and made a show of hitching up his jeans, but they immediately rode down again. As he bent to retrieve his cap, Gravity tried not to look at his boxer shorts, which were printed all over with little hearts, or the smooth inch of warm brown skin just above.

He caught her looking, winked, and said, "Hey, shorty. They call me D-Minus 'cause I'm all you need."

"Hah!" the old man scoffed. "We call him D-Minus 'cause he's as lazy as the day is long. Talent like that, it's a goddamn shame."

D-Minus adjusted the Steelers cap atop his fade with elaborate care.

"Hi," she said, extending a hand. "I'm Gravity."

He gazed at her hand, his deep brown eyes unreadable. Then he looked her over, from her frizzy brown hair to her scuffed Nikes and back up again. Gravity felt herself blush. She let her hand drop to her side, where it clenched into a fist.

"*You* wanna be a fighter?" he asked.

Was it her imagination that he leaned into the word "you"? As though he was amused by the thought of her wanting to box. As though she didn't belong in his gym. Gravity felt a flare of anger go off inside her, the way it did sometimes before she broke things on purpose.

She said something she had never said out loud before: "I want to be a *champion*."

She waited for him to laugh at her, but he didn't.

He just nodded and said, "I feel you, shorty."

Then he reached out and softly took her hand. Humming along to James Brown, he moved it through a complicated sequence of choreography. The Cops 'n Kids secret handshake was always evolving. At that moment, it was a double pound, backhand, fist bump, finger wiggle, and pop-and-lock dance move that made Gravity feel kind of silly. She executed it to his satisfaction on the fourth try.

D-Minus smiled, and Gravity felt a little dizzy.

In boxing, one punch can change a whole fight. D-Minus had a smile like that. It was like the sun coming out from behind the clouds.

He motioned for her to follow him up the stairs and into the smaller of the two rings, which had a faded yellow canvas and blue ropes with white stripes that said "NYPD." He asked her which hand she wrote with, and when she said her right, he told her she was "orthodox." That meant she had to stand with her left foot forward.

He showed her how to keep her guard up: elbows in tight to catch body punches and hands against her cheeks to block

8

head shots. Coach Jefferson H. Thomas III sat next to the ring and served up commentary in a booming voice that carried over the music and the bell.

The jab was a straight punch thrown with the lead hand. D-Minus moved her left arm to its fullest extension, keeping her elbow in tight and turning over her knuckles at the end. The hardest part was remembering to bring the hand back to her face immediately, instead of leaving it there like they did in karate.

D made her jab in a line going forward and backward. Then he had her add the right cross after the jab, in a combination he called the one-two. Coach Thomas kept blowing his whistle and pointing at her feet, and she would realize with dismay that they were way too close together, or too far apart, or just plain wrong.

The round timer divided everything into slices of work and rest. For three minutes, the light atop the clock was green and you had to keep punching. A warning bell rang when ten seconds were left. Then the light turned red and you could rest for one minute and talk to people.

And the gym was filling up with the coolest people. As they passed her, everybody reached their hands in between the ring ropes to shake hers. Even Boca was friendly. Gravity was not sure what she had been expecting, but certainly not this short, bald coach with a scar running down one tan cheek and a goofy smile. He walked in with a pack of Latino boxers in red tracksuits that said "BOCACREW" on the front and "#NoNewFriends" on the back, including Lefty (aka $outhpaw), who looked like a sexy vampire and dressed like a rap star. Lefty had thin braids that zigzagged across his head like lightning bolts and tattoos of guns across the backs of his hands.

When she told him her name, he threw back his head and sang, "Gravity . . . is working against me! And Gravity wants to bring me down!"

She laughed. He had a really good voice.

"I'm surprised you know that song," she said.

"I'm full of surprises," he told her, smoothly vaulting onto the apron to adjust her elbows.

He leaned in close as he did it, and she could feel the warmth of his body and smell his cologne. It wasn't sleazy, but it wasn't *not* sleazy either. She glanced across the gym at D-Minus. All these cute boys paying attention to her made Gravity feel pleasantly nervous. Like she wasn't just some skinny tomboy in her cousin Melsy's hand-me-downs. Like she was somebody who deserved attention, somebody who belonged.

Coach Thomas set a pair of tiny dumbbells on the apron and told her to repeat the drills with the weights in her hands.

"They're too light," she objected.

He laughed one of those old-people laughs that turn into a cough at the end. Then he rolled across to the larger ring on the far side of the gym, which had red, white, and blue ropes and a blue canvas with a PLASMAFuel decal in the middle, spattered with bloodstains.

D-Minus was inside that ring now. He had changed into a spectacular pair of leopard-print trunks with gold fringe and was shirtless, his trim abs gleaming. He grinned as his combinations snapped out, sometimes right on the beat of the James Brown and sometimes in obedience to an inner rhythm of his own. Gravity could have watched him all day long. Somehow, she just knew that he would do it: he would be a champion one day. That made her believe that she could too.

Next to D-Minus were several of the boxers from the Bocacrew, including Lefty, throwing furious combinations as Boca yelled out commands. Gravity was a little scared of the fighter called Monster. He was the biggest, darkest man in the room, with arms that were thicker than Gravity's legs. Oddly, though, he wore pink satin trunks and a *Powerpuff Girls* T-shirt. He seemed to be Coach Thomas's fighter, but when Boca gave his boxers water, he gave some to Monster, too, while Coach Thomas watched, glaring.

The tiny dumbbells didn't feel so heavy at the beginning, but by the time she had done four rounds, it was hard to keep them to her cheeks. By the time Coach Thomas finally let her put them down, her shoulders ached and sweat dripped down the handles of the weights.

He said, "You don't complain. That's good."

She felt a rush of pride that he had praised her. "Thank you, Mr. Thomas."

"Call me Coach."

Just then, the door swung open and a pack of tall white men trooped in, speaking a strange language. They wore blue-and-yellow tracksuits that said "UKRAINE." In the middle of the group were two kids: a big boy whose face was hidden behind a fringe of blond hair and, trailing behind him—

"A girl!" Gravity exclaimed. "Look, Coach, it's another girl! Can I fight her?"

The men stopped and shook Coach's hand. The tallest among them, who looked like a shaggy bear, pointed at Gravity and said, "How much she weigh?"

Coach chuckled. "It's her first day, Kostya."

"I want to fight her," Gravity said quietly.

"You're not ready," said Coach.

The girl looked at her and smiled, but it was a funny kind

of smile, like she knew something Gravity didn't know. She had two stubby blond braids and wide blue eyes and creamy skin with pink patches over the cheeks. The sleeves of her tracksuit came past her hands, making her look like a little kid.

"I'm a hundred and six pounds," Gravity announced. "How much do you weigh?"

The girl laughed and said, in a loud voice, "I fight at ninety-five. But I ate a big breakfast."

Gravity could tell Coach was annoyed, but he would be happy when he saw how good she could fight. She said to Kostya, "I won't hurt her. Since she's so much smaller than me."

All the men laughed.

Kostya said, "We just do four rounds. Sveta work with her nice and easy."

"She doesn't even have a mouthpiece," Coach said.

"I do too!" Gravity cried. "I still have one from karate!" She had bought it for the kumite they were supposed to have for their black belt, but then her mother said they couldn't afford the testing fee, so she never got to fight.

"Please?" she whispered to Coach. "She doesn't look so tough. I fought *way* bigger girls before. In third grade, I beat up a fifth grader!"

"Svetlana's been boxing since she could walk," he said.

"Please?"

Coach frowned, but he looked at Kostya and said, "Three rounds."

Gravity was so happy she wanted to jump up and down, but Coach told her to shut up, sit down, and give him her hand. He produced a long strip of soft yellow cloth and, just like in the video, looped it over her thumb and between each

12

of her fingers. His hands moved rhythmically, making a pad over her knuckles and weaving X's across the back of her hand.

Gravity's mind got quiet. The wraps felt snug but not too tight, like her favorite pair of jeans. It made her feel safe, and it reminded her of something. Cousin Melsy called it *déjà vu* when you felt like you'd done something before. She said it had to do with ghosts. Gravity shivered.

"Be still," Coach said.

Be still. That was it. Her dad used to say that when he brushed her hair in the morning.

He would sit on their old burgundy couch, and Gravity would sit at his feet and lean back against him, and he would hold her hair by the roots so it didn't hurt when he brushed out the tangles. He said Gravity had curly hair like a Dominican girl and that her mom didn't know what to do with it. She had forgotten all about that.

He would fix it with colored rubber bands he produced from the pockets of his jacket, where he kept the butterscotch candies she loved. He did Gravity's hair like that every single morning for seven weeks. The seven beautiful weeks she remembered her father, between his sudden appearance at her eighth birthday party and his equally unexplained departure. Gravity shivered again.

"I said, be still," scolded Coach.

She blinked and searched the old man's face: the permanent frown, the smushed-up nose of an ex-boxer, the tiny scar at the corner of one eye. No, he didn't look a thing like her dad. Maybe it wasn't *déjà vu*. Maybe it was the opposite.

Time is strange. Three minutes can seem like three hours if you're shadowboxing with hand weights, or three seconds if you're talking to a cute boy. And even though round one always comes before round two, sometimes you get a feeling from the beginning for how things will end. When Coach Thomas wrapped her hands that very first time, Gravity somehow knew that he would do it again and again. She would get her hands wrapped—and, later, wrap them herself—so often that she would come to feel a little naked without it.

Coach yelled across to Boca, who coached Svetlana, "Sixteens?"

Boca nodded.

Coach held a sixteen-ounce sparring glove open for her, and Gravity pressed her hand into the opening. Her palm sank into the warm lining, torn in places from the kids who had worn it before. He steadied her elbow against the arm of his wheelchair and tightened the laces, then wrapped them around her wrist and swiftly tied them off. He held out the other glove. She pushed in.

"You go at the next bell," he said. "Three things: Keep your hands up. Move your head. And jab."

D-Minus appeared and said, "Who Svetlana sparring?"

Coach inclined his head toward Gravity. D's eyes widened in shock.

"I'm a good fighter!" Gravity said, exasperated. "I can *beat* that girl."

D-Minus laughed so hard he fell down on the floor. That made Coach laugh too. It even made Gravity smile a little, although she knew they were laughing at her.

D-Minus got back up, readjusted his Steelers cap, and spoke to Gravity in the kind of voice she used when her little brother put metal in the microwave: "Shorty. Listen. Homegirl is a *regional champion*. And in Russia they fight *bears* and shit. If she had caught the flu, broke up with her

14

boyfriend, *and* got hit by a bus on the way to the gym, your ass would *still* lose."

That made Gravity angry, but she didn't say anything.

He shook his head and said, "Just don't make her mad."

"Hush," said Coach. "Get that girls' cup. It's on the top shelf behind the toilet paper."

D trotted off to the large locker bank against the back wall, which had been spray-painted with a mural of Jefferson "The Truth" Thomas as a young boxer, underneath a plaque that read "Happy Eightieth Birthday, Coach!" All around the mural were clippings of the champions the old man had trained, since way back in the day. Gravity wanted her photo up there too.

"Here," D said, handing her a big red thing that she didn't know what it was.

"It's a female abdominal protector," said Coach. "Put it on like shorts."

D-Minus helped her find the place to put her legs and steadied her as she pulled it over her sweatpants. Coach rolled behind her to adjust the Velcro, and D-Minus pulled a headgear over her head. She felt like a NASCAR in the pit.

"Can you see?" D asked.

She said, "Yeah," even though the forehead hung low over her eyes, but D-Minus noticed this and tightened the top laces.

Coach rinsed her mouthpiece over a bucket and slipped it in her mouth. She climbed into the big blue ring. Word had gotten out about the sparring, and all the fighters and trainers and dads in the gym had gathered around to watch. Svetlana, bouncing in her boxing boots in the opposite corner, looked meaner than she had before, her upper lip stretched by the mouthpiece. Gravity looked down at her worn-out trainers, wishing she could afford boxing boots. When her mother's voice sprang up, saying she always ruined nice things, she silenced it by murmuring, through her mouthpiece, Coach's three commands: "Keep your hands up, move your head, and jab."

The bell rang, and Svetlana skipped into center ring, holding out her gloves. Gravity touched them. That was like shaking hands.

Gravity had missed with three shots before she realized there was something different about the way the other girl was standing. It felt like she was looking at a mirror image of herself. Svetlana stood the way Lefty did; she was a southpaw.

"Jab!" yelled Coach.

Gravity tried, but Svetlana parried and slapped her with a short right hook. It hit her temple, dizzying her. Kostya yelled something in Ukrainian.

"Sorry," said Svetlana.

Gravity shook her head. Why was she apologizing? She ran at Svetlana, trying to hit her hard, but the other girl just spun off to the side. Gravity chased, throwing a one-two, but Svetlana blocked the jab with her elbow, slipped the right, then hit Gravity in the stomach. Gravity froze for a moment, unable to breathe.

"Good one!" yelled Boca.

Before she could recover, Svetlana swooped in and landed four more light taps. Gravity came back with a hard right hand to the place where she thought Svetlana's head was, but Svetlana's head wasn't there anymore.

Gravity dropped her hands, panting, just as Kostya called time. It had only been sixty seconds—kids fought shorter rounds than adults—but she could not remember ever having felt so exhausted.

D-Minus beckoned her over to where he stood on the apron. He squeezed water in her mouth and said, "Keep your left foot outside her lead foot. Aim at her body."

Svetlana got even faster in the second round. Gravity spent the first thirty seconds just chasing her, at one point tripping over her sneakers and dropping to her knees.

D-Minus yelled, "One! Two! Three!" like he was counting a knockdown.

She got up, cheeks burning. When she looked over at Svetlana, she thought she saw a slight smile cross the other girl's lips.

"Hands up!" barked Coach.

Before she could obey, Svetlana dashed to her and peppered six shots into the padded part of her headgear. All the Ukrainians cheered.

Just then, she heard a deep voice in her ear: "Come on! Don't let her do that."

It was Monster, bending over the top rope. He was so tall that he didn't even need to stand on the ring apron to talk to her.

"Go on." He put an enormous hand on her back. "Hard right hand to the body. Sneak it in."

Gravity decided she was going to land one shot, just one. She pretended to throw the right hand at Svetlana's head. When Svetlana lifted her hands to block, Gravity got low, putting everything she had into one right hand to the open place between the elbows. When it landed, Svetlana let out a tiny "oof" of pain that made the whole thing worthwhile.

Kostya called time.

Gravity looked down at Coach, who smiled and raised a fist, but when D-Minus gave her water, he said, "That was stupid."

"What do you mean?" she asked him.

He just shrugged. "You'll see."

When Kostya called time in and the real beatdown started, Gravity remembered what D-Minus had said before about not making Svetlana mad. The first punch that hit her with full force felt like a hard roundhouse kick, and she almost went down.

At first the gym rats oohed and aahed but then they got quiet. Somewhere in the middle of it, Svetlana landed a looping left to the tip of her nose that made her eyes tear. Red droplets spattered to the canvas.

"Easy!" thundered Coach.

Svetlana froze and said, "Sorry. You okay?"

This time, it didn't make Gravity mad. She nodded, and when Svetlana extended her gloves, she touched her own to them. For the last thirty seconds or so, Svetlana barely threw any shots.

When Kostya called time, Svetlana hugged her and then sat in between the ropes to make space for Gravity to climb out. Gravity looked back and saw her blood spattered on the PLASMAFuel decal, a shade lighter than the older stains. Svetlana's brother, Genya, helped her down the stairs, and Boca appeared with a damp towel and cleaned her face of blood.

Coach didn't say "I told you so," just unlaced her gloves. Even D-Minus seemed disinclined to crack jokes. The vibe in the gym was calmer, as though someone had taken a lid off a boiling pot and let off the steam. As Gravity made her way across the gym floor, many of the fighters softly touched her glove. Despite her miserable performance, the sparring seemed to have made them accept her more.

The boys changed in a large, foul-smelling locker room behind the shadowboxing mirror. Gravity glanced in as she passed and saw a half dozen boys slap boxing amid piles of stinking handwraps and moldering plastic suits. The girls changed in a tiny closet with a piece of paper taped to the door that read "Any Man Caught In The Girl's Room Will Be Kicked Out From The Gym Period Point Blank End Of Story No Questions Asked."

It smelled nice inside, like pine trees. A mirror, broken and fixed with duct tape, leaned against one wall. The opposite wall was covered with cool fight posters of female boxers, mixed with pictures of nearly naked male athletes from *Sports Illustrated* and beefcake shots of a young Mike Tyson. Svetlana was already in there, in front of the sole locker in the room. When Gravity walked in, she nodded, turned her back, and started spinning the dial of her little combination lock. She had unbraided her hair, and it spread across her back in golden waves.

As Gravity changed, trying to shield her naked body, she watched Svetlana strip and scrub herself fiercely with baby wipes. She didn't seem at all uncomfortable changing in front of Gravity in such a tight space.

Svetlana put on a purple lace bra and matching panties. She spread a towel on one of the milk crates, sat down on it, and began inspecting her toenail polish.

"You can keep stuff in my locker if you want," Svetlana said without looking up from her toes. "I asked Boca to put another one in for you, but he said you'd probably give up soon."

Gravity didn't know what to say. It was nice of Svetlana

19

to share her locker, but what Boca had said made her mad. She was never going to give up boxing. And the next time she fought Svetlana, she would win.

"My combination is thirty-six–three–one."

"Thanks."

"Don't tell the boys." Svetlana shot her a look that was fiercer than any she had given her in the ring.

"I won't."

"It's Sugar Ray Leonard's record. If you forget, just look it up on BoxRec. He's my favorite fighter."

"What's BoxRec?"

Svetlana looked at her like she was crazy. "You don't know *BoxRec?*" She produced her cell phone, which was the same light purple as her underwear and had rhinestones on the back, and pulled up the website, which listed the records of every boxer you could think of.

While Svetlana applied makeup in the cracked mirror, Gravity sat on the milk crate looking up Muhammad Ali, Marvin Hagler, and some of the female boxers whose posters were on the wall, like Belinda Laracuente and Lucia Rijker.

Certain entries had special notes by them—like for the night Muhammad Ali first won the heavyweight title in Miami, it said, "Liston retired on his stool citing an injured shoulder. After this fight Cassius Clay changed his name to Cassius X and then Muhammad Ali. 1964 Fight of the Year—*Ring Magazine.*"

"Sometimes there's mistakes in the records," Svetlana said. "Like it says my dad was seven and one, but he was really eight and one, because he had a pro fight in our country before we came here."

"Wow." Svetlana sure knew a lot about boxing. "It must be nice to have a dad who's a boxer. And who works out with you and stuff." Gravity ignored the pang of envy at the thought of what it must be like for Svetlana and Genya to have a dad like that. To have a dad at all.

But Svetlana made a face. "Sometimes I wish we could leave him at home. He's always getting on our cases." She spritzed herself with perfume, and the changing room was so small that Gravity felt some settle on her, too. It smelled like green apples.

Svetlana said, "I hope Boca was wrong."

"About what?"

"About you giving up. It's nice to have another girl in the gym."

Gravity smiled. "Thanks."

Svetlana took her arm like they were best friends, and they walked together out of the changing room. Out on the gym floor, there was some kind of ruckus. Two of Boca's little nephews were running around, screaming, wearing lucha libre masks. Monster was chasing them around the heavy bags, arms extended, making zombie sounds. Lefty was doubled over in laughter.

D-Minus yelled from across the gym, "Yo, Gravity! Watch!"

He and Genya were balanced on the ropes of the big ring like professional wrestlers, their arms raised overhead.

"No horseplay!" hollered Coach.

But it was too late. D-Minus did a front flip off the ropes, the fringe on his trunks streaming. He landed directly atop Boo Boo, the gym's top-ranked light heavyweight, who was doing medicine ball exercises in the center of the ring. D-Minus popped back up, unscathed, but Boo Boo writhed on the canvas making terrible sounds.

"Oops. My bad," said D-Minus, shrugging.

"That's boxing," said Boca, calling the ambulance.

"That's boxing," said Coach. He made D-Minus drop and give him fifty push-ups.

"That's boxing," whimpered Boo Boo, whose broken clavicle made him miss the Olympic Trials.

But Gravity never missed a single day for the next four years. No matter how tired or stressed or PMS-y she felt, she schlepped there on the subway right after school. If Mom was acting crazy and Melsy couldn't babysit, she dragged her little brother, Tyler, along. Gravity liked it better at the gym than at home.

By the time she turned sixteen and won her first Golden Gloves, Gravity was undefeated at 19–0 with seven knockouts. And Coach was right: if she ate right and ran every day, she could just make lightweight.

BOXINGFORGIRLS.COM
YOUR ONLINE DESTINATION
FOR THE BEST IN BOXING WRITING

Carmen Cruz, Independent Journalist

January 12, 2016

Meet the Fighters of PLASMAFuel Cops 'n Kids

BROOKLYN, N.Y.—As we lead up to the Summer Games, *Boxing for Girls* has been traveling across the country to scout out America's top contenders for Rio. Our first stop was this free community gym, founded to combat gang violence in the Brownsville section of Brooklyn by retired NYPD sergeant Giovanni Rizzo in partnership with energy drink giant PLASMAFuel.

"PLASMAFuel is delighted to support these elite warriors," said brand ambassador Andre Vázquez. "Nothing quenches their ferocious thirst like an ice-cold PLASMAFuel."

Head coach Jefferson H. Thomas is an imposing octogenarian who claims a 97–12 (80 KOs) record as a professional heavyweight and once sparred the great Joe Louis. Thomas has trained over 200 national champions, most notably 1984 Olympic gold medalist Leon "Too Fine" Hines.

"I'm from the old school," Coach Thomas said. "None of this dancing around and wrestling bullshit you see nowadays. My fighters come to fight."

His output has slowed in the last decade, but he has two strong contenders for Rio: male bantamweight Demetrius "D-Minus" Saint-Amand and female lightweight Gravity "Doomsday" Delgado, both making their debut this year in the elite division. By winning the PAL Nationals, Delgado

23

already earned her spot in this year's Women's Boxing Olympic Trials. Saint-Amand hopes to earn his at the Men's Olympic Qualifier. Both tournaments will be held concurrently next month in Spokane.

Also coaching at Cops 'n Kids is Benavides "Boca" Velez, recently featured in the Netflix documentary "Bloody Noses." Originally from Puebla, Velez represented Mexico in the Pan American Games. His impressive stable includes superheavyweight Kimani "Monster" Browne; middleweight Gennady "The Ukrainian Bear" Mamay; Gennady's sister, featherweight Svetlana "She-Bear" Mamay; and lightweight Esteban "Lefty" Perez, all of whom begin their road to Rio in Spokane.

Since featherweight is not an Olympic weight for women, Svetlana Mamay has chosen to move up to lightweight, where she qualified for Trials via the Women's National Golden Gloves. This makes Cops 'n Kids the only club in the nation sending two competitors to the Women's Olympic Trials, both in the same weight class! So far, Delgado and Mamay have never faced each other in competition, but a meeting in Spokane seems inevitable.

"Gravity and I have been sparring since we were kids, and we know each other's styles very well," Mamay said. "It will come down to who wants it more."

"A fight is different than sparring," Delgado said. "I like Svetlana a lot, but there's no friends in the ring. She never should have moved up to lightweight."

Chapter One

Sweat sloshed in the folds of Gravity's plastic suit as she jogged past the Cyclone roller coaster. She ran the Coney Island boardwalk six mornings a week at five-thirty. It was the most peaceful part of her day. Nobody was out except a few other joggers, a couple of homeless people, and the seagulls.

She was terribly hungry this morning, and her scalp ached from the tight cornrows Melsy had put in last night. To distract herself, she conjured the faces of the women she would fight at Trials: decorated national champions like Paloma Gonzales, strong women twice her age like Aaliyah Williams.

But first, *Svetlana*. Gravity would show her old friend what a mistake it was to challenge her. She turned around at the Wonder Wheel and lengthened her stride, her breath making steam in the cold February air.

Her body felt strong and lean. She had weighed 133.6 that morning, naked, after taking a hot shower and pooping. Subtracting the 0.4-pound inaccuracy of Mom's scale, and the fact that, between the plastic suit and the Albolene she had smeared on to open her pores, she would sweat off at least a pound and a half on the jog, this meant she could have a little water and a PowerBar for breakfast, a salad without dressing for lunch, and a chicken breast for dinner. If all went well, she would make 132 easy in Spokane without having to spit or jump rope.

Rio.

Rio.

Rio Olympian.

She chanted the words in her mind as her sneakers hit the weathered wood and the tips of her braids slapped her shoulders. The sleeping amusement park gave way to rows of shuttered hot dog stands and beach bars. She pulled her boxing glove keychain out of her sports bra and sprinted down the side street that led to their apartment complex, making a 6:30 mile going home. Tyler was in one of his moods, and she didn't want him to be late for school again.

When she opened the door, he jumped up from the couch, the video game controller still in his hand, and picked up the nagging where he had left off.

"Why did you take so long, Gra Gra? I'm hungry! I was waiting and waiting."

His eyes reflected the television screen on which he was playing his favorite video game, *Hell Slayer 3*. He had been up all night playing and had dark circles under his eyes.

Gravity felt her temper rise.

"Ty Ty, I've told you a million times. I have to run in order to be an Olympian. You're a big boy now. You could have made yourself a bowl of cereal."

"There's no milk!" he yelled.

"There is! I checked the fridge last night."

"Is not!"

Gravity stalked into the kitchen. There were three roaches crawling over the counter, and she got one with her left hand

and one with her right but missed the third. She washed her hands, threw open the refrigerator door, and pulled out the carton of milk to show her brother, but she could tell from the weight of it that it was completely empty.

Fucking Mom!

Gravity smashed the milk carton down on the counter. One of the juice glasses in the dish drainer toppled over and broke. Tyler began to cry.

Who does that? Who takes a completely empty carton of milk and puts it back in the refrigerator to deceive her children? If Mom had thrown it out or left it on the counter, Gravity could have bought a new one on the run home.

She closed her eyes and began to count backward from one hundred. The heat slowly abated. When she got to eighty, she opened them.

Tyler had followed her into the kitchen and was staring at her. His pudgy face was covered with tears and snot.

"Are you okay, Gra Gra?" he asked.

"Yeah. Sorry."

"You broke a glass."

"I break everything."

He stuck out his lower lip. "There's no milk."

"I know."

His nostrils began to tremble, and another tear rolled down his wet cheek and fell on his Spider-Man pajamas. "I *hate* when you run. You take so long I think you aren't coming back."

Gravity's anger evaporated and guilt flooded her. How could she get mad at Tyler? It wasn't his fault everything was so fucked up.

"Come here, baby," she said.

He shuffled over and hugged her around the waist. Her plastic suit rustled and a little river of sweat dripped down her legs. She kissed the top of his head, wrinkling her nose at the smell. She scratched away a fleck of dandruff from his scalp.

"When's the last time you took a bath?" she asked.

"Don't 'member."

She glanced at the clock.

"Well, take one tonight. We're going to eat cereal with water today, okay? It's yummy like that. I don't have time to go to the store."

Or much money, either. Mr. Rizzo would probably give her some pocket money for Spokane when she saw him at the gym, but it wasn't like Mom would have thought to leave them cash. And she hoarded that EBT card like it earned interest. Sometimes Gravity wanted to shake her mother and ask if she thought Gravity and Tyler were plants or something that grew off water and sun.

There had been a time when their mother had cooked dinner every night. Steak with broccoli. Brisket with barbecue sauce. Best of all, her homemade challah bread, which was so buttery and moist it tasted like cake. Gravity salivated, remembering its sweet smell. But that was a long time ago.

She watched her little brother think over the cereal-and-water proposition. Stubbornness ran in the family; she had learned through trial and error that she couldn't make Tyler do anything he didn't want to do.

"Okay," he said at last.

She shook some frosted cornflakes into a bowl for him, then poured a little cold tap water into the carton of milk and shook it up before pouring it on. She put the bowl on the table, but Tyler carried it back to the couch, where he unpaused his game and kept playing while he ate.

She let him. Tyler could never sleep when Mom was out all night, and that game was the only thing that kept him from worrying.

She took off her plastic suit in the shower and watched with satisfaction as salty water flowed down the drain. Her abs looked pretty good. She didn't have the kind of build like D-Minus, where you could see the cuts, but when she got down to fighting weight, her belly got flat and tight. Unfortunately, her butt got flatter too. Her boobs, which were small to begin with, basically went away.

When Mom was being extra mean, she said Gravity would never have a boyfriend, because boys liked girls with curves, and nobody wanted a girlfriend who was taller than him. But Auntie Rosa said she was built like a runway model and that, when it came to having boyfriends, it was good to be a late bloomer.

She got dressed in front of her trophies. They were in a case Coach had given her, which she used, along with a big tapestry, to divide her half of the bedroom from her brother's. She had the trophies in size order, with the championship belts in the back and her pride and joy, her New York Daily News Golden Gloves necklace, glittering from a hook in the front.

She ran a finger over the little boxer on top of the trophy she had won as the outstanding female boxer at the Police Athletic League Nationals. She liked how you could tell the little golden boxer on top was a girl. Most of the time, they just stuck the same figure on top of the boys' and girls' trophies. The PAL Nationals had been the first tournament in which she was eligible to compete as an adult, and she had been shocked at how easy it was. Just like Coach said it would be.

Gravity wanted to be like Vasyl Lomachenko, who won two gold medals and got the Val Barker Trophy for being the outstanding boxer of the Olympic Games. He only lost once in the amateurs, and he kicked Selimov's ass in the rematch. Gravity would be just like that, only she planned to never lose at all. And after she won her Olympic medals, she would go pro and retire undefeated, like Floyd Mayweather. Then she would have lots of endorsement deals and be on TV and everything.

She took the necklace off its hook and felt the pair of gloves heavy in her hand. Of all the accomplishments in her life, winning the Golden Gloves was the greatest, and just holding the necklace in her hands made her feel like there was nothing she couldn't do. She only wore it out on very special occasions, because she was scared of losing it.

The little gloves were so beautiful: gold set with a diamond and textured to look like leather, with lettering across the front that said "Daily News Charities Inc." and an inscription on the back that said "2016 Golden Gloves 132 lb women champion." She closed her eyes and pressed the gold to her heart, feeling grateful and calm.

As she hung the necklace back up, she met her own eyes in the mirrored back of the trophy case. She and Tyler had the same eyes—Mom said they got them from their dad—small and squinty when they smiled and such a dark brown you couldn't see the middles. Gravity had learned from experience that she could intimidate a girl in a staredown if she gazed right through her and thought cold thoughts.

She found Tyler asleep on the couch in the living room

with the game controller and empty cereal bowl in his lap. A death march was coming out of the television, which flashed with the words "YOU GOT SLAYED." It was very hard to wake him up and even harder to get him into his school clothes. She made him eat a PLASMAFuel caffeine gel on the way to the bus stop so he wouldn't fall asleep in school.

Chapter Two

Gravity walked from Ty's bus stop to her school. It was about a mile, which gave her a chance to stretch out her legs and burn a few more calories. Lots of people neglected walking as a part of cross-training. Plus, it was good for anger management.

As she turned onto Neptune Avenue, a text came in from Mr. Rizzo:

Good morning, champ. Make sure you buy the Daily News today.

She fished through the bottom of her backpack until she had scavenged enough change, then stopped at the bodega across from school. The guy who owned the bodega was a big sports buff. When she learned that he was from Yemen, she had asked if he liked "Prince" Naseem Hamed, and ever since then they had been friends. Sometimes he gave her free sandwiches.

She leafed through the *Daily News* to the sports section in back.

"Hey, look, Hamza!" she said.

She didn't usually like photos of herself, but this one was fierce. It was an action shot from her Golden Gloves finals victory. Her body was twisted in full extension from the right cross, sweat flying off her like rays of light. She was baring her mouthpiece at the other girl, who had slipped the right but was about to eat a huge left hook. You could see the hook coming from the way Gravity's elbow was cocked.

Hamza read the caption aloud in an impressed voice: " 'Coney Island Teen Is a Knockout Queen: Gravity Delgado, right, will compete in the Women's Boxing Olympic Trials next week in Spokane.' "

"It's all about my gym and how we have so many people going to the tournament," she explained. "There's me and, you know, Svetlana." Hamza nodded solemnly. Gravity had complained to him at length about Svetlana's moving up to 132. "And then there's four guys trying to qualify for the Men's Trials. D-Minus, plus three of Boca's fighters."

Hamza reached below the counter and put on the Cops 'n Kids cap she had given him a few months ago. "I will wear it when I watch the livestream," he vowed.

"Thanks, Hamza."

"I know you will prevail." He slid another copy of the paper across the counter. "Here. Take an extra for your coach."

"Thanks!"

She trotted across the street to school, past a pack of boys hanging on the corner in a cloud of skunky smoke, blue do-rags beneath their baseball caps and blue bandannas trailing from their jeans. Gravity stood up to her full 5'9", and they let her pass with one slow whistle. She kept her eyes on her school.

Gravity did not fight in the streets anymore. At her age, street fighting could get you killed, like D-Minus's big brother, Tray. That second time she had tried to find Cops 'n Kids, when it had been closed for a funeral, had been the day of Tray's service. Tray wasn't gang-affiliated, just in the wrong place at the wrong time.

She was grateful every day that Tyler got bused to a nice

yuppie elementary school in Park Slope. Auntie Rosa had helped Gravity do the research and hook everything up. Ty was really sharp when it came to computers and math, so she wanted him to be in an environment where he could focus. After she won her gold medal, she would send him to a good college and get them a nice house somewhere like Connecticut. She wouldn't let Mom live with them, but they would go visit her once a month.

Gravity shrugged off her bag and put it in the scanner, nodding hello to the school safety officer. It was a little depressing to have to go through metal detectors, but after that, William Grady High was an okay place. It was a vocational school that was supposed to prepare you for the real world. Gravity liked working with her hands, and she wanted to have a Plan B to support Tyler in case boxing didn't work out.

Her favorite conditioning guru, Rick Ross, said that Plan B stood for "Plan Bullshit," and that true warriors should never let the possibility of losing enter their minds. But Rick Ross didn't have to give Tyler cereal with water in it. A boxer's career could end at any moment due to injury; Gravity needed something to fall back on. She had tried out computer repair and automotive before settling on culinary. It was a little more interesting, and sometimes you got to take food home.

Culinary lab that morning was torture because she was so hungry. They were making chicken potpie for the teachers' lunch, and the room was filled with the smell of baking pastry. She waited until the teacher's back was turned and popped in a piece of sugar-free gum, which she chewed ferociously, imagining it was food. At least she was assigned to the group peeling carrots. Raw carrots were not that tempting.

At lunch, a couple classmates who had seen her picture in the paper came up to congratulate her. There were less girls than boys at Grady, but they had a pretty good women's basketball team and Gravity always sat with them. Once in a while, they would come out to Cops 'n Kids to cross-train, or she would go to their practice and play a little ball.

She drifted in and out through her afternoon classes, dreaming of being in the ring with Paloma Gonzales, who had won lightweight bronze in London and was considered the favorite to win the Women's Trials. Gravity could not wait to show all the sportswriters how wrong they were.

Paloma was a boxer-puncher who did everything pretty well, but Gravity didn't see anything that special about her, except how pretty she was. She got more press than any of the other boxers, including Sacred Jones, and Sacred had won middleweight gold in London. That made Gravity mad.

She tried to hold on to the anger to keep herself awake. It was hard not to fall asleep in school after getting up so early to run. Her favorite teacher, Ms. Laventhol, was especially nice and never said anything when she nodded off in earth science. Once, she had let Gravity sleep through her entire class. When she had woken up, it was a whole different group of students and a whole new teacher.

Today it was easier to stay awake, because Ms. Laventhol was doing a unit on physics, and Gravity kept hearing her name mentioned as one of the four fundamental forces and waking back up.

When the buzzer sounded, ending final period, she felt her heart lift. School was a little like boxing: You did your best to protect yourself at all times and go the distance. In the end, you got saved by the bell.

Chapter Three

Gravity listened to Rick Ross's latest podcast on the hour-long subway ride to the gym. It was about how athletes should try to make themselves into a "luxury brand." This wasn't Gravity's favorite episode; she preferred the stuff about performance, but it was good to learn about the business aspects, too. There was more to boxing than what went on in the ring.

Rick gave a whole example about designer watches. He said that even if you thought you couldn't afford an expensive watch, really you couldn't afford *not* to have one, because people judge a man by his watch. He didn't say what they judge a woman on.

Gravity frowned. The only fancy thing she owned was her Golden Gloves necklace.

Thinking of those little gold gloves cheered her up, as always. You couldn't buy them in a store but had to win them. In Gravity's opinion, that made them better than the most expensive diamonds.

She broke into a trot when she turned onto the dead-end street that sloped downward to Cops 'n Kids. She couldn't wait to hear Coach's congratulations about the *Daily News* article, and she was really hoping he would let her spar.

The gym was hopping when she got there, Boca's Mexican brass band music blaring out of the speakers, and boxers on every heavy bag. She didn't see Svetlana, which suited her just fine. Lately, Kostya had been taking her and Genya to Smiley's Gym more and more.

Gravity made the rounds, shaking hands, starting on Boca's side of the gym. Nobody did the secret handshake anymore. At some point, D-Minus had announced that secret handshakes were for kids, and everybody had stopped doing them. Gravity kind of missed it.

Boca didn't seem too happy about the article. Mr. Rizzo had scanned it and posted it on Facebook, but Boca hadn't liked it or shared it. Probably he wished one of his own fighters had gotten the photo. Gravity made sure to act humble and say that it wasn't an article about her but about all of them. Boca grunted and asked if she wanted to get a few rounds in with Boo Boo.

"Sure!" she said.

She waved to Boo Boo, who was shadowboxing in a plastic suit and sweats. Boo Boo was 12–0 as a professional now and training for an upcoming bout at the Barclays Center. Boca had made him drop down to super middleweight. This was a constant struggle, because Boo Boo's mom owned the best soul food restaurant in Brooklyn.

"Hurry up," Boca told Gravity. "We'll put you in first, before the boys."

Monster, who was wearing pink trunks and a *Buffy the Vampire Slayer* T-shirt, gave her a hug and asked her how she liked the photograph. Something about the way he said it made her take out the paper again and examine the caption. In tiny letters, it said "Photo by Kimani Browne, Special to the Daily News."

"Wow, Kimani!" she said. "It's my favorite photo ever. You're getting really good."

He shrugged. "Andre Vázquez got me this great lens. And you're easy to photograph. You look so intense when you fight."

"Thanks, Kimani!"

She was the only one in the gym who called Monster by his real name. She still remembered the day, back when he was Coach's fighter, that she had asked him to reset the round timer. As he reached a long arm upward, she had remarked that she sure wished she were tall enough to reset the bell without a stool.

"Be careful what you wish for," he replied.

Later on, while they had shadowboxed in front of the mirror, he told Gravity that sometimes it was hard being so big and dark-skinned. He said that when he got onto a subway car or crowded elevator, he could see the fear in people's eyes. That was why he always wore pink clothes and T-shirts with friendly things on them.

"I wish everybody would stop calling me Monster," he had said, throwing a fearsome right hand at his reflection.

"What do you want us to call you?" Gravity asked.

He said shyly, "How about King?"

Boca, who had approached just then to give Monster water—he was already trying to lure him away from Coach—laughed and said, "Yeah. King *Kong*, maybe."

Gravity had tried calling him King, but it never took off, so she just called him Kimani. You couldn't fight gym nicknames. If they stuck, they stuck, and a lot of times they were mean, like the great pad man they called Fatso, or racist, like the kid they called Fósforo, Spanish for "matchstick," because he was so dark and skinny. All things considered, she was pretty lucky everyone stuck with Gravity.

When she said hello to Lefty, he made her blush by

38

bowing down to her about the newspaper article and teasing her about signing a modeling contract, but D-Minus just touched his fist to hers without comment and kept on shadowboxing.

D was like a cat: he rarely came when you called or gave you love when you wanted it. She watched as he threw a blindingly fast six-punch combination. Today he was wearing one red Adidas boot and one blue one, blue camouflage trunks, and a red beanie with a huge pom-pom. He made it look like the next big thing. Monster had told Gravity that D-Minus was the only person in their gym who looked better photographed in color than in black-and-white.

When she got to Coach, he was busy wrapping the hands of one of the old maintenance men from the building. As he worked, Coach grumbled about Boca's music and how dirty he had left the gym yesterday. Gravity kissed his soft, wrinkled cheek and waited for him to bring up the article.

The maintenance man asked a question about jabbing form that Coach answered as thoughtfully as if he were talking to a champion. She smiled. Boca never would have done that. He never paid attention to anyone until they started winning. Even if they had won in the past, he would give them the cold shoulder if they slumped. But Coach would train anybody. As long as you listened and didn't talk back, he gave you everything he knew, for free.

She pulled out the paper and set it on the ring. "I brought you a copy. You know, for your wall?"

She indicated the area over by his locker bank. She wished he would hang a picture of her up there. He had lots of D-Minus's clippings but nothing about her.

Once again, she admired the mural of Coach as a young boxer. Whoever had painted it had done a really good job. It showed him in gloves and trunks, bare-chested and scowling, with "Jefferson 'The Truth' Thomas, Marine Corps Heavyweight Champion" painted across the bottom in cool graffiti lettering next to his record: "97–12 (80 KOs)."

They didn't make records like that anymore. Coach had been fighting back in the 1950s, when Rocky Marciano ruled the heavyweight division. If you wanted to make Coach mad, all you had to do was bring up Rocky Marciano. He would get a look on his face like he had just sucked a lemon and talk about all the great black heavyweights who could have beaten Marciano in their prime. But boxing was racist, and Coach had retired in disgust after one too many unfair decisions. It made Gravity angry just to think about it.

When Coach made no move to take the newspaper from her, Gravity opened it to the page with her photo, saying, "See? 'Coney Island Teen Is a Knockout Queen'?"

"I saw it."

She frowned.

The maintenance man said, "That's you in the *Daily News*?"

"Yeah."

"Well, I'll be damned. You look great!"

"Thanks!"

"Go hit the bag," Coach told him. When he'd gone, he told Gravity, "Fifteen minutes of rope."

"But I told Boo Boo I would spar him, and Boca said to hurry."

He gave her a look. "Oh, so is *Boca* training you now?"

She sighed. "I just thought we could—"

"Keep your goddamn hands up!" Coach bellowed across the gym at D-Minus. He looked back at her and said, "Sit your ass down."

She sat. He snatched the newspaper off the apron and held it up in front of her. The paper rustled slightly from the trembling in his hands.

"Tell me what you see."

"I see a picture of me," she said defensively. "A *good* one."

"Why is it good? Because you got your hair done? Because you can see your little muscles?"

The disrespect in his tone hurt. It was true that Gravity liked the way the tips of her braids looked, flying out from under the headgear—Melsy had braided in blue extensions to match the color of her trunks—and she liked the racing stripe of muscle in her calves.

She said, "You can tell I'm winning. That's why it's good."

"Look at your feet," he said, stabbing a finger at the paper. "Did I teach you to stand with your feet like that?"

She hadn't really noticed that before. She must have thrown the right hand with such force that she had stepped forward so her two feet were square.

"And look at your left!"

She looked. "I was about to throw a hook. You can tell from the way my shoulder is."

He snorted. "Shit, everybody in the motherfucking *Barclays* can tell. Might as well hold a press conference. Ladies and gentlemen: PLASMAFuel Cops 'n Kids is proud to announce that Gravity Delgado is about to throw a left hook!"

D-Minus snickered. He had quit shadowboxing and edged closer to them, in typical catlike fashion. Sweat dripped down the stripy muscles of his abs to disappear into his baby-blue boxers. Gravity looked away. Someone ought to tell him to pull up those trunks. It was distracting.

"And look how low your right is coming back," Coach

41

went on. "If she'd countered with a good hook, she would've knocked you out."

D-Minus said, "Don't hook with a hooker, hooker."

Gravity said, "She *didn't* have a good hook, though. And if she did, I would've blocked it. Or, you know, adjusted."

"Hmph. You would have *adjusted!*" Coach pounded on the arm of his wheelchair. "In *here* is where we make adjustments. In the *gym*. You are not a slick boxer. Your game plan can't be to adjust."

D-Minus shook his head sadly. "You ain't slick, G."

She leapt up and tried to knock off his pom-pom hat, but he slipped, stuck out his tongue, and said, "See?"

Sometimes he made her want to hit below the belt.

"Sit your ass back down," Coach thundered.

Gravity sat on the apron, her face burning. She looked down at the pink Adidas boots that Mr. Rizzo had given her a year ago. They were starting to get a little hole on one side. She wiggled her pinky toe until it poked through.

Why couldn't Coach and D give her any credit? Couldn't they at least act happy for her for *one day*?

When Coach spoke again, his voice was gentle.

"You can *beat* those girls in Spokane, Gravity. *All* of them. I have high hopes. That's why I'm hard on you. Do you hear?"

For some reason, that made her sad. She looked back up. He was peering at her intently from beneath his bushy eyebrows. Coach had more boxing information inside his skull than there was on all of BoxRec. Gravity felt it all there, behind his bloodshot eyes.

A wave of calm spread through her. How could she have gotten mad at him for expecting the most from her? He was her coach. She didn't want to be one of those divas who argued with their coaches. Nobody could train alone, not even Floyd Mayweather.

She said, "I'm listening, sir."

"Good." He counted off on his gnarled fingers. "You have sharp eyes. You see the openings. You're not too fast but you have good timing. You have heavy hands and you throw your punches with bad intentions."

D-Minus said, "You *do* hit hard. For a girl." He winked at her. To Gravity's intense irritation, she felt herself blush.

Coach went on, "The girls from now on will be stronger. Slicker. More experienced. You can't beat them if you make mistakes." He picked up the paper and shook it at her. "You can't beat them fighting like *this*. You have to rise to your potential."

"I will," she promised.

"I know you will." He patted her on the shoulder. "Remember, you're not just representing me, you're representing Brownsville."

Gravity grinned. She joined D-Minus in reciting the motto of Brownsville, Brooklyn: "Never ran, never will."

Boo Boo approached in his usual respectful manner. "Coach Thomas? Boca asked for three rolls of the good gauze. He said we're ready for Gravity, and he wants D for Lefty."

Coach rooted through his ancient trainer's bag, grumbling under his breath. He handed the gauze to Boo Boo and said, "Ask him for four rolls of the good tape. Tell him she'll be right there, and we're tech sparring only. I don't want anybody hurt before Spokane."

Whenever their gym competed in tournaments, Coach and Boca presented a united front. To outsiders, they were all Cops 'n Kids, the winningest team in New York (except when Smiley's Gym pulled off the occasional upset). But all the boxers knew the truth: The two great coaches always sat at a distance from each other. They communicated through gifts and messengers, like rulers of rival kingdoms.

Gravity hopped off the apron and went to change and wrap up. She pulled on her headgear and cup, slipped in the mouthpiece, and let Coach lace her into sparring gloves. She didn't need to warm up for Boo Boo; he always took it easy on her.

When the bell rang, they trotted out and touched gloves, then he hung back and let her get her rhythm. Gravity took the first round to work on feints. She managed to sucker him twice, once with this stutter step D-Minus had taught her where you fake to the body and pop up to the head, and once with this really flashy move she got from watching vintage Sugar Ray Leonard. She couldn't believe it landed.

Boo Boo laughed and took out his mouthpiece to say, "Yo, G, that was slick!"

D-Minus came up on the ring to give her water, and the way he grinned at her confirmed what she felt inside. She was peaking, getting things off on Boo Boo that she never had before. As the rounds went on, she worked on keeping her feet in good position to show Coach that she was taking his critique to heart. He said a real boxer didn't need to stop and set but was always in position to punch. After five, Boca waved her out, and she saw that Genya was the next one in. His sister sat on the ring apron wrapping up while Kostya yelled at her in Ukrainian.

"Hi, Sveta."

"Hey," Svetlana said without looking up.

Kostya shook her hand a little too hard.

The tension between Gravity and Svetlana had intensified

after the *Boxing for Girls* piece had come out. But Gravity had no regrets. What she had told Carmen was the truth: Svetlana never should have moved up to her weight.

Gravity headed to one of the heavy bags, where she pounded away steadily for six rounds. D-Minus took the double-end bag next to her and worked with furious speed. Coach rolled over to watch, keeping up a steady stream of instruction in his scratchy voice: "That's it, baby. Jab the man. Jab. Now throw that right hand. Now right back on the jab."

The way Coach said "jab" made you feel like you could cut someone, and the way he said "right hand" made you feel you could drop them. And when he called her baby, Gravity felt like nobody in the world could beat her.

After she was done, Gravity reluctantly pushed open the door to the girls' room. Svetlana looked up from her locker and nodded. Her eyes looked red-rimmed from crying.

There were two lockers in there now. Gravity had shared Svetlana's for about a year until, one day, Tray's old locker had appeared next to it. Some people might have gotten creeped out by inheriting a dead kid's locker, but Gravity didn't mind. D's big brother was a good spirit to have on her side. She left up all his stickers, and sometimes she touched the *Dragon Ball Z* one for luck. She did that now, before turning to Svetlana.

"You okay?"

Sveta sniffed. "Yeah."

Sometimes Kostya was really hard on her and Genya. Or maybe it was some drama with Boo Boo. The two of them had been dating since the start of the school year, but Sveta didn't talk to Gravity about that stuff anymore.

"You all packed for Spokane?" Gravity asked.

"Yeah."

Svetlana pulled her jeans up over her hips, and Gravity noted the slight bulge above the waistband and the way her bra straps cut into the fat of her back. She wasn't in elite competitive shape at 132.

Gravity changed quickly, keeping her eyes on the wall of fight posters. Gravity and Svetlana had slowly added to it in the last four years, supplementing the beefcake shots of Tyson with glossies of a shirtless Floyd Mayweather, Amir Khan in a tuxedo, and Sergio Martinez silhouetted against the sunset.

But Gravity's favorite was the poster of Sacred Jones in front of Kronk Gym in Detroit. Sacred was probably the best female boxer in the world. She had won a gold medal in the London Olympics and would be at Trials in Spokane. She was built like a sprinter, with thick legs that gave her great punching power, but it was her mental strength that made her unbeatable. Gravity wanted to be teammates with her someday.

Gravity struggled to think of something else to say to Svetlana. The tiny room felt more claustrophobic than usual.

"I heard the casino out there has a really good buffet," she said.

"Stop it." Svetlana slammed her locker and turned to face Gravity. To her surprise, Gravity saw tears on her cheeks.

"Stop what?"

Svetlana sighed and pressed her hands to her temples. "Just *stop* it. Stop trying to pretend you're my friend."

Gravity felt her stomach lurch. "I *am* your friend."

"You're so *arrogant* sometimes."

Gravity looked down at the floor. She wasn't arrogant. She was just confident. There was a difference.

"Fuck! I have such a headache," Svetlana said, plopping down on the milk crate and clutching her head in her hands.

Gravity pulled out a packet of Advil and offered it to her. "Thanks."

"Want me to go get you some PLASMAFuel?"

"Nah. I hate that shit."

They both laughed, and everything felt okay between them. Then the tense silence descended again. It made Gravity sad.

"I'll go get you some water."

Svetlana hadn't even talked to her about the weight change, had just shown up on the lightweight brackets at the Golden Gloves Nationals, a tournament she knew Gravity was skipping. It was a stupid move. She usually fought at 125 or 119, which meant she could have cut down to 112, the lightest of the women's Olympic classes. It would have been hard, but she could have done it. Gravity would have helped her.

Now it was too late. She was going to get destroyed at Trials.

Gravity trotted out for water onto the gym floor, where Monster was in the large ring sparring a visiting heavyweight, a tall white man in a tank top that said "Italia." Andre Vázquez, the PLASMAFuel rep, leaned against the ropes, eating gummy worms and offering inane advice. Andre was involved in Boo Boo's management and always came sniffing around the gym in his flashy, too-tight business suits when one of Boo Boo's pro fights was approaching. He was pushing up on Monster now too, hoping to turn him pro after the Olympics.

She watched the sparring for a moment, taking in the

visiting Italian's unusual style. He kept his left arm extended stiffly, as though he was holding a shield.

Kostya said, "European style. Very good. He win bronze in London."

Gravity didn't like the style, but it was effective. Monster was getting frustrated and kept swatting at the Italian's lead glove like an angry bear.

Gravity trotted back into the girls' room. She handed the water bottle to Svetlana, who pressed it to her temples.

"Thanks. Is Boo still sparring?"

"No, Kimani's in there now with this Italian. He's kinda getting schooled." It seemed dumb to make Monster spar a stranger right before the Olympic Qualifiers.

Svetlana said, "That European style is confusing if you're not used to it."

"How do you beat it?"

Svetlana gestured with the water bottle. "Take control of the rhythm. You can't let that lead hand distract you. They're really the same as any other opponent."

"Like southpaws!" Gravity said.

Svetlana gave her an odd look. "Yeah, I guess."

Gravity remembered the exact moment when Svetlana's left-handed stance had ceased to bother her. It'd happened the third time they sparred. Ever since, Gravity had been in control.

Svetlana knew so much about boxing. Kostya had been taking her and Genya to the gym since they were toddlers. Gravity was always trying to make up for lost time by watching classic fights on YouTube and reading books on training. Still, knowing and doing were very different things. Gravity sometimes imagined that everything she knew about boxing was a big iceberg, and everything she could execute was the tiny bit that peeked out of the water. Too many people focused on *knowing* more, building up the huge, sunken part of their game that no one ever saw. It was much better to focus on rising.

Gravity sat down on the other milk crate, squeezing her legs to one side so they would not touch Svetlana's. She said quietly, "I'm sorry you think I'm arrogant."

Svetlana sniffed. "You're sorry I *think* you're arrogant? Or you're sorry you *are* arrogant?"

"I'm sorry for whatever it is that's making you so mad."

Svetlana shot her another look. Part of Gravity wanted to lock in and stare Svetlana down, but she forced herself to look away. There would be time for that. It wasn't Gravity's fault that she was better than Svetlana. She trained harder and wanted it more.

She stood back up. "Okay, then. I guess I'll watch the sparring."

Svetlana said, "Okay."

Out on the gym floor, the heavyweights had finished and were standing in front of the mirror taking selfies together. D-Minus and Lefty had taken their place in the ring and were in the middle of a furious exchange of body punching. It was like changing channels on the radio from something slow and serious to one of those tracks that get the whole club jumping. Coach and Boca were posted up at opposite corners, barking instructions.

Mr. Rizzo had arrived too. Gravity went and hugged him.

"I loved what they wrote in the *Daily News*," he said. "You looked real good in that photo."

"Thanks!" Gravity glowed with pride. "I can't wait for the Trials."

"You'll do great out there. Here."

He pressed some bills into her palm. It felt like at least a hundred dollars.

"Thanks, Mr. Rizzo!"

It had taken Gravity years to figure out that Mr. Rizzo owned their gym, because he acted so humble. She didn't like cops, but he was different. He was the only person Gravity had ever met who was equally nice to everyone, no matter where they came from or what they could do for him.

They both turned to look at the ring as Boca yelled, "That was *way* south of the border!"

Lefty was backing up to the ropes, bent over in agony. D-Minus wore an expression of exaggerated innocence. All the men in the gym made sounds of sympathetic pain.

Boo Boo said, "Damn. D straight up hit him in the nuts."

"That was fucked up," said Genya.

Kostya muttered something in Ukrainian.

D-Minus had always had something against Lefty. Gravity had never figured out what it was. Maybe he was just jealous because Lefty was such a good rapper. His latest $outhpaw track had over a hundred thousand likes on SoundCloud.

Lefty recovered and the sparring finished uneventfully. As the two boxers climbed out of the ring, Gravity felt a ripple of excitement pass through the gym. She turned and saw that her cousin had arrived. Melsy was wearing her hot-pink vegan fur, big gold earrings, and white jeans that fit her like a second skin. She held a green juice in one hand and Tyler's wrist in the other. Some new kid whistled under his breath.

Monster said, "Chill. That's Gravity's fam."

Melissa was the most beautiful girl Gravity knew. She wasn't just biased because they were cousins; everybody on Instagram thought so too. Melsy had flawless light brown skin, huge dark eyes that stared into your soul, and a tiny body that was all softness and curves. Auntie Rosa was really artistic, and Melsy had inherited her mother's talent when it came to styling. Gravity loved her new hairdo: shaved on the sides, ironed flat so it hung to her butt, and streaked with electric blue. It made her look like an anime heroine.

Melsy clacked across the gym floor in her high-heeled booties, dragging Tyler, who looked sleep-deprived and grouchy.

"Hey, cuz!" she said in her high, squeaky voice. "Hello, Coach Thomas."

Gravity inhaled deeply as she kissed her cousin's soft cheek. Melsy always smelled like honey. It was some kind of lotion she used.

"Hello, young lady!" said Coach. He turned an amused look on Tyler. "Hey, champ! When are you learning to box?"

Tyler shrugged. "I don't like to fight. Except zombies."

Coach chuckled and ruffled Tyler's hair, which, Gravity was relieved to see, Melsy had washed.

"I made you a kale smoothie, cuz!" Melsy said. "I read this article in *Men's Health* about how kale is great for performance."

"Why you read *Men's Health?*" said D-Minus. He stuck close to Gravity whenever Melsy came in.

Melsy gave him a look. "Health is very important to me and my cousin. And you *know* that if men discover something important, they're not about to tell *us*."

She pressed the foul-smelling concoction into Gravity's hand. Behind her back, Tyler pointed at it and shook his head, eyes wide with fear. Gravity was extremely touched that her cousin had operated a blender, a behavior that was quite unusual for her, but drinking the smoothie was out of the question.

51

"Melsy," she said, gently placing the glass back in her cousin's hand, "this looks *so* good! But liquids weigh a ton. I have to be super careful about my weight."

Melsy offered the smoothie to D-Minus, but his desire to flirt only went so far.

Gravity kissed Coach goodbye. He fixed her with his Jedi gaze, and Gravity felt mysterious energy levels rising within her. She thought about all the great champions he had coached. D-Minus with his heart and flash. "Too Fine" Hines with the jab to end all jabs. She thought back farther, to Coach's own days sparring Joe Louis. All of that was her legacy.

"You make that team now, you hear?" he told her.

She grinned. "Yes, sir."

"My cousin's about to beat some girls' *asses*," Melsy said.

A slow smile spread over Coach's face, revealing a thousand wrinkles. He said, "I do believe she is."

A wave of certainty washed over Gravity, like the calm gratitude she always felt when she clasped her golden gloves to her heart. She thought of the ring out there in Spokane, waiting for her. The girls. The crowd. Her hand raised in the air for everyone to see.

She would need to put in a new hook in her trophy case. Soon her gloves would have a gold medal keeping them company.

Chapter Four

As they left the gym, Melsy took a sip of the smoothie and froze, staring into the glass with a look of shock. Gravity laughed and showed her the sewage drain where they dumped the spit buckets. Melsy slowly poured the contents down it, muttering angry things about *Men's Health*.

Gravity took advantage of the moment to block off a nostril and blow out some snot.

Melsy raised her perfect eyebrows. "Do you do that in the gym?"

"Of course." Gravity repeated the process with the other nostril. "It's great because you don't even need to take off your gloves."

Melsy shook her head. "And you wonder why that fine boy isn't trying to get with you."

"What boy?" Gravity asked, even though she knew who Melsy meant.

"You know who I mean."

Gravity blushed. She herded Ty into the backseat of the Ark, moving aside some paintbrushes and a bolt of fabric to make room for him and making sure he was buckled in. He fell asleep immediately.

Gravity called Auntie Rosa and Melsy's car the Ark. It was a big LTD the color of old pennies, filled with at least two of everything, mostly from Auntie Rosa's various art projects. It had a wonderful smell inside from the sticks of palo santo she burned to dispel the smell of the engine fumes, and Melsy's dad, who passed through once in a blue moon, had installed a really good sound system with bass so loud it could set off other cars' alarms.

"The gym isn't about sex, Melsy," Gravity said as she slid into the passenger seat.

Melsy put the key in the ignition. "*Everything* is about sex, cuz."

They drove silently through Brooklyn for a while and then Melsy said, "So? What's the plan with D-Licious?"

Gravity frowned. "My only plan is winning the Olympic Trials."

"But I thought *he* was going too!"

"He is. It's the men's qualifying tournament at the same time."

"So?"

"So what?"

"So . . ." Melsy spoke slowly, as though explaining something to a child. "If he wins, he'll want company. If he loses, he'll want sympathy. Either way, you need a fabulous outfit. I wish you'd stopped growing so we could still share clothes."

Gravity laughed. "My height is my biggest asset. Coach says long, tall fighters like me and D and Leon Hines have the best power."

"That boy D is tiny!" Melsy said.

"Not for bantamweight. He's real tall for his weight and has way longer arms than me. He's got a perfect boxing body." She stopped, aware that Melsy was giving her one of those I-told-you-so looks. "First you get the money, then you get the honey," she said, quoting one of Coach's rules. "Besides, I don't feel any kind of way for Demetrius."

But when she said his real name, Gravity felt an ache in the middle of her chest. She pressed a hand to her heart and glanced over to see if her cousin had noticed, but Melsy's eyes were on the road.

By the time her cousin had pulled into their apartment complex, Tyler was so deep asleep that Gravity was unable to rouse him. Melsy offered to help carry him upstairs, but she had a long drive home to Washington Heights, and Gravity wanted to save her from the sight of whatever state Mom was in. She slung Ty across one shoulder in the fireman's carry and called the elevator.

There were no lights or sounds from behind their apartment door, which was a relief, since it meant Mom was still out. Opening it just a crack, Gravity reached inside to flip the light switch on, then slammed the door shut again. She opened and shut the door three more times, slamming it as loudly as possible.

Cockroaches liked it quiet and dark. If you walked right into Gravity's apartment at night, it looked like a horror movie. If you gave them some advance notice, it just looked like a regular roach convention.

Tyler only grumbled a little as she laid him in bed and took off his sneakers, wrinkling her nose at the smell of his socks. She licked her finger and rubbed a spot of mustard off his shin. How did he get *mustard* on his *shin*? Boys were a mystery.

That made her think of D-Minus, and she pulled out her phone and went on Instagram. He had put up a new shot from his Golden Gloves finals win. She smiled and hit Like. D-Minus was in midair, leaping with joy right after the decision was announced.

The caption read: "MAN I'M SO BLESSED THANK

YOU TO EVERYONE WHO SUPPORTED ME THRU IT ALL NO MATTER WHAT I LOVE YOU I LOVE MY TEAM NOW I'M ON MY WAY TO SPOKANE TO WIN MY SPOT IN TRIALS #COPSANDKIDS #PLASMAFUEL #LEGENDARYCOACHTHOMAS #FATSOTHEPADMAN #THEREALDMINUS #FUTURE WORLDCHAMP #THECROWNPRINCE #NODAYS OFF #MYLIFE$TYLE."

He had tagged pretty much everyone in the gym except for her, which shouldn't have hurt her feelings at this point but still did. The boys almost never tagged her, even though she always tagged them and liked their posts. It was like she was invisible. They never tagged Svetlana, either, but Svetlana didn't train as hard as Gravity or love boxing half as much.

She went to do the one thing that always cheered her up: taking her golden gloves off their hook in her trophy case and pressing them to her heart.

Except her necklace was missing. At first she thought it might have fallen off the hook and gotten lodged somewhere, so she took all the trophies out and ran her hand over the ledge behind them, but it was gone. So were the two P.C. Richard gift certificates she had won for Knockout of the Night and for being champion, which she had been saving until she could make up her mind on the perfect thing to buy.

Before she knew what she was doing, she had grabbed the PAL trophy—the one she loved the best—and smashed it into the wall. The little golden boxer broke off the top and the wall broke too, fragments of dust drifting down from the jagged edges of the hole. That was when her mother came home.

Gravity could tell her mother's condition by the sounds she made when she walked in. The best was the thump when she was so drunk that she just hit the floor. Then all Gravity had to do was drag her to the couch. Worse was the giggling and off-key singing of her goofy-drunk and chatty phase. This might have been cute from Melsy or Svetlana but not from a grown woman who was supposed to be watching out for you and your eight-year-old brother.

In this mood, Mom would cuddle Gravity and tell her stories about all the men she'd had sex with, although she always called it schtupping, which made it sound disgusting and cheap. Afterward, the images were burned into Gravity's mind. Her mother fucking that creepy man who owned the 7-Eleven. Giving some guy she'd just met a blow job in the bathroom of Applebee's.

Worst of all was the time she had told Gravity about her abortions. She had gotten two in between Gravity and Tyler and one since. Mom said abortion was a great invention and that it didn't hurt at all.

It hurt Gravity, though. She tried not to think about whether they had been boys or girls, who the fathers were, or what it would have felt like to be the eldest of five.

Tonight's loud door slam, jingle of dropped keys, and muffled cursing indicated that Eileen Berman was in the worst stage of her intoxication. This happened when she drank her way past tipsy but not all the way to unconscious and got stuck in the toxic rage in between. Whenever this happened, she would always find a way to pick a fight. Gravity would have liked to just leave, but she was afraid for Tyler, so there was nothing to do but wait it out.

"Graaaa-vity!" her mother shrieked.

Gravity had asked her mother many times why she had

given her such an unusual name. Her mother always replied vaguely that she thought it was a pretty word. She never spoke it that way, though. She made it sound like a curse.

"Graaaa-vity! Where the hell are you?"

She barged into Gravity and Tyler's bedroom. She must have gone right to the bars after work, because she was still in the scrubs she wore as a home health attendant. There was a greasy stain over one breast; Gravity couldn't tell if it was food or puke or what.

Somehow, though, she still looked stunning. Her dyed red hair and perfect ivory skin gave the impression of a much younger woman. She stood up very straight and moved through the world like a displaced Disney princess. Gravity would never be as beautiful as her mother. She would have known that herself, even if Mom hadn't told her so all the time.

"What the fuck did you do to my wall?" her mother yelled, staring at the hole.

"What happened to my golden gloves?" Gravity asked quietly.

The alcohol came off her mother in waves: a thick, slightly sweet odor that made Gravity want to retch.

"Ungrateful parasite!" her mother shouted. "You break everything you touch!"

"My gloves," Gravity repeated. "They were hanging right here. And two gift certificates. What did you do with them?"

Her mother shook her head like a wet dog. Gravity couldn't be sure she had even understood. Sometimes when she was this drunk, she mistook Gravity for other people.

"Feeding and growing, feeding and growing, that's what a parasite *does*!" As her mother spoke, she worked herself up to a more fevered pitch. "It *uses* its host! It *breaks its host down*! Then it moves on to somebody else."

Gravity dug her fingernails into her palms. She was sixteen now, a grown woman. But somehow her mother always had the power to make her feel small. She could hear her brother stirring on the other side of their bedroom, and she willed him to stay down.

"Did you *sell* the necklace, Mom? Did you trade it for alcohol?" Gravity knew it was useless to try to get real information from her mother when she was this far gone, but she could not stop herself. "I *won* that fair and square. You had *no right* to take it."

Her mother's voice turned mocking. "I won *this* trophy, I won *that* medal, I'm a *box*er, I'm a *cham*pion." She laughed. "You're not shit."

Gravity hated the sound of her mother's laugher. She wondered dimly if there had ever been a time when she had not hated it.

When she heard her mother say, "You're a selfish pig just like your father," she turtled up, covering her face and ribs with her arms. The hitting always started after Mom got onto the topic of Dad. Gravity didn't bother slipping; that only made Mom madder. She just let her mind go quiet and took the beating. It didn't hurt that much anymore.

There was a man Gravity saw sometimes when she did her morning roadwork. His name was Curtis, and he sold kites on the boardwalk. Once, she had stopped to talk to him, and he had let her hold the string of a red-and-gold dragon. They watched it climb, the spool spinning out and the string pulling against her hands like something alive.

Curtis had told her, "A kite is a form of defense against evil."

Gravity went there now, floating on a string with the red-and-gold dragon, far from the hands of her mother.

Curtis had said, "The spirit is what keeps you alive. We're just passing by. This is just a learning experience."

It took a long time, but finally the blows slowed down and then they stopped. Gravity stayed still and counted to ten. When no more came, she lifted her head.

Her mother was swaying on her feet, her hair disheveled and damp. For a moment, Gravity was scared she was going to vomit, but she didn't.

"What did you do with the necklace?"

Her mother fixed her with hate-filled eyes and said, "Nobody wanted it, so I threw it in the ocean."

A funny memory came to Gravity then: her mother, very pregnant with Tyler, tearing up a cable bill and throwing it in the ocean.

Dad was gone by then, but Mom was still keeping it together. She had declared that TV rotted the brain and they were going to save money by going without it.

Except it was a windy day, and the ragged pieces of paper kept getting blown back onto the sand, and Gravity was running around, snatching all the pieces up and throwing them into the waves. And they were laughing together, she and her mother, so hard it hurt. And when all the paper was gone, Mom put both of Gravity's hands on her swollen belly and told her, "Being a mother is the most important job in the whole world."

And they had sung the Shema together, there on the beach with their hands on Tyler. Mom had taught Gravity lots of Hebrew prayers, but she said the Shema was the best one, because most prayers were for special days but the Shema was for every moment of your life.

Gravity came back to the present. She studied her mother's

face. It seemed incredible that she had ever sheltered them inside her body, that they had ever prayed together, that Gravity had ever been young enough to think tearing up a bill would make it go away.

Her mother spun on her heels like a tiny supermodel and fell down. Gravity left her there on the floor.

When she got into bed, she found Tyler there, tears running down his cheeks.

"Hey, shhh," she said.

She cradled him in her arms, stroking his head and rocking him. After a while, his sobs died down.

"What's a parasite?" he asked.

"Like a cockroach."

He sniffled. "Mom's the cockroach, not you."

"I know."

"Can we see the pictures?"

"Yeah."

She didn't need to ask what pictures he meant. She reached underneath her mattress for the old composition notebook in which she'd hidden the photographs of their father. She should have put the gift certificates in there too.

There were three pictures, worn out and curling around the edges. She had scanned them so they could look at them on her phone, but Tyler preferred to hold them in his hand. It was the closest he had ever gotten to their father. The first image was of Gravity as a newborn, swaddled in a yellow blanket in the crook of Dad's arm. She had a full head of dark hair and was red-faced from crying, her mouth open in a wail.

"Why was I crying?" Tyler asked, gazing at the photo in wonder.

61

"I don't know," she said, stroking his cheek. "Babies cry a lot. Maybe you were hungry, or maybe you needed your diaper changed."

"'Cause I pooped!"

She laughed. "Yeah, maybe you pooped."

He squinted at the picture. "I don't think I pooped. Because then I would smell bad, but it doesn't look like I smell. Dad is smiling."

"He's smiling because he loves you so much."

Their father was young in the photo, probably not much older than Gravity was now. He was very handsome, whip-thin, with long hair twisted into curls and a skinny mustache above his grin. He looked delighted by the thought of being a new father. She wondered, as always, what had gone wrong.

"Here you are at the zoo," she said.

It was a good thing Gravity had been such a tomboy, because the clothes she was wearing in the toddler pictures could easily pass for a boy's, and her hair was short and curly, just like Ty's was now. All you could see was her back, but their father was in profile, kneeling next to her, so you could see his laughing eyes again. His hair was buzzed short now and he had gained a little weight, but he had the same skinny mustache. They were looking at turtles. Gravity had always liked turtles.

Tyler yawned. "What was Dad's favorite animal?"

"The lion. He said it was the king of the jungle." She smiled, remembering her father's exact words, not from that zoo trip but from a nature show on Channel Thirteen they had watched together during his brief reappearance after her eighth birthday. "He said the lion had a good hustle, because the lionesses did all the hunting, and all the lion had to do was eat, nap, and make cubs."

"Did Dad love us both the same?"

She looked at Tyler in surprise. That was a new question. "Yeah, of course. Why?"

He snuggled close to her. "It's just sad that you're not in any of the pictures. I thought maybe you and Dad were fighting."

She smiled. "No, I was just shy. Look, here you guys are on the couch."

It was the old burgundy couch. This was right before Dad left the first time, so she must have been about two and a half, but she still looked enough like Tyler that you couldn't tell the difference. She was sitting in Dad's lap with a video game controller in her hand, and he was bent protectively over her, pointing at the TV, which you couldn't see. But Gravity wasn't looking at the television; she was looking up at her father, and her dark eyes—the same eyes as his, the same eyes as Tyler's—were overflowing with adoration. It almost hurt to look at that photo. She wished she could remember what it had felt like to sit in her father's lap, to feel so protected.

"What game was I playing?" Tyler asked, as he always did.

She replied, as always, "I can't remember."

Chapter Five

When Gravity got to the gate at LaGuardia, there were a dozen fighters sprawled in the chairs and over the floor, some wearing warm-up suits identifying them as Metro champions and some still in pajamas. The rest of the airline passengers eyed them with varying degrees of alarm as Boca and the other adults patrolled the perimeters, yelling at kids whose music or trash talk exceeded a certain threshold of volume and vulgarity.

Gravity settled on the floor in front of Fatso, who was listening to Koranic chanting while leafing through a magazine. As always, Fatso was the best-dressed man in the room. Today he had on a button-down shirt with suspenders, pinstriped slacks, and two-toned alligator shoes. He must have ordered his clothes from special stores to get sizes that big.

"Hey, baby," he said, pulling out one of his earbuds and holding out a hand. "Book."

She gave him her USA Boxing passbook. As he tucked it into his trainer's bag, she glanced at the open magazine. It was an old copy of *Black Belt*, open to an article about spinning back kicks that Fatso had highlighted and underlined.

"How much you weigh?" he demanded.

"One thirty-two even." She had gotten up extra early

and squeezed in one last run, then eaten a little oatmeal and scrambled egg whites.

"Good girl. Get some rest. We board in half an hour." He put the earbud back in and kept reading.

Fatso looked a lot like the Notorious B.I.G., except fatter and more athletic. He had been Coach's fighter back in the day, and now he passed through Cops 'n Kids once in a while to hold focus mitts for the boxers. You wouldn't think it to look at him, but he was the best pad man in New York. He made money training rich businessmen, but every so often he flew to Vegas to work with MMA fighters or Hollywood to train movie stars. He always flew first class, because he needed the room.

Since Coach was too old to travel with her and D-Minus, Fatso went to the really important tournaments with them to make sure they had a good chief second. Boca looked out for them too. Despite their differences, Coach trusted Boca to corner for his fighters, but this would be out of the question in Spokane, since Svetlana was competing for the same slot.

Gravity snoozed until it was time to board. There were always a few boxers who were nervous about flying. This time it was Monster, who had not been on a plane before and was asking Lefty if there would be a lot of turbulence.

Lefty said it wouldn't be that bad, because this was a big plane, unlike the little planes that flew to Vieques, the Puerto Rican island he was from. He told a story about the worst turbulence he had ever experienced, and Monster looked like he was going to cry. Gravity tried to change the subject by telling Monster that there would be cool movies, and if the seat was too small for him, he could walk up and down the aisle to stretch his legs.

But D-Minus said, "Your heavy ass better *stay* in that seat. If you move around, you'll throw off the weight balance. Plus, you'll scare the stewardesses."

"Don't worry," she told Monster. "Flying is safer than taking a cab. It's probably even safer than boxing."

"Not safer than boxing *you*," D-Minus said.

She ignored him.

Fortunately, D had a seat in the front of the plane, and she was in back next to Svetlana, which might have been awkward except that Sveta slept all the way to Spokane. Gravity never slept on planes. She lifted up the blind on the window so she could watch the runway speed by and then watch the houses and cars get smaller and smaller as they rose into the air.

Gravity loved to fly. She had always loved it, from the very first trip she took, at age five, with Auntie Rosa and Melsy. They had flown to Santo Domingo for the ninetieth-birthday party of Mamita Grande, her great-grandmother on her father's side. Soon after, Mom had cut off ties with Dad's family, but that party was a magical memory, from the beautiful flight attendants who had fussed over Gravity and Melsy to the cousins who greeted them at the airport with fresh-cut sugarcane. Ever since then, she had associated flying with sweetness and adventure.

The Vision Quest was a quick ride in the rental car from the Spokane airport. It was the first time Gravity had ever been in such a fancy hotel. The lobby had a big urn of water with lemons in it and a mural about the history of the Kalispel Tribe, the Native Americans who ran the hotel and casino.

Gravity and Svetlana went to check in at the table that said "Women's Boxing Olympic Trials." Paloma Gonzales was leaning against it, laughing theatrically as she chatted with two of the USA Boxing bigwigs. When Gravity and Svetlana approached, she shot them a look and said, "There's so many novices this year! I feel like I don't know anybody!"

"We fought before," Svetlana said.

Gravity cringed. If she were Svetlana, she wouldn't want to relive that memory. It had been an all-women's card in Paloma's hometown of Sacramento. Gravity had wanted to go too, but Coach nixed it because he said the organizer was a sleazebag who would set her up to lose.

Paloma looked Svetlana up and down and said, "You always remember the women who beat you but never the ones you beat."

Svetlana went pale, and then she said something that took Gravity entirely by surprise: "You'll remember Gravity Delgado, then. She's winning this whole thing." Sveta turned back toward the registration chair, muttering, "You better fuck that bitch up, G."

"I will," Gravity promised.

Gravity was touched and relieved. This was the first double-elimination tournament either of them had ever competed in. It promised to be the most grueling of their careers and would be easier to get through if they weren't beefing.

The kindly old lady in charge of registration told Svetlana that her request for a roommate had been approved and she would be sharing with Wendy Li, a nice middleweight from Long Island. Gravity felt irritated, because she hadn't known it was possible to request a roommate.

"Gravity Delgado, we have you with Chantal Thompson," the old lady said.

Gravity nodded. Chantal was a flyweight from Cincinnati. They hadn't spoken much, but she seemed okay.

Gravity and Svetlana exchanged a brief, awkward hug, and Gravity rode the elevator up to her room. Chantal had already been there and had lined up all her things in neat rows, leaving Gravity half of every shelf. The crisp white sheets of Gravity's queen bed were tucked so tight she had to wriggle inside them like a worm. She fell asleep immediately and dreamed she was in the ring.

Chapter Six

After breakfast the next morning, Gravity and Fatso elbowed their way to the front of the crowd buzzing around the lobby bulletin boards. The USA Boxing bigwigs had met in a sealed room that morning and conducted the draw for both the Women's Trials and the Men's Qualifier. Gravity scanned the sheets until she found the women's lightweights.

Number one seed Paloma Gonzales was at the top of the bracket. Aaliyah Williams, seeded second, was at the bottom. Gravity found her name in the middle, and her heart sank when she saw the name next to hers: Svetlana Mamay.

"It's a lucky draw," Fatso said. "You'll beat Svetlana easy tonight and be fresh for Paloma tomorrow."

Gravity sighed. Just a few days ago, she had been so eager to fight her old friend, but Svetlana's kindness had changed the way she felt.

"I know," she told Fatso. "I just wish I didn't have to."

Gravity heard something behind her. She turned around to meet Svetlana's pale face and wide blue eyes. Gravity could tell from her wounded expression that she had overheard the conversation with Fatso. Sveta spun around, blond braids whirling, and took off toward the elevators.

Gravity stood frozen, watching her go. She wanted to chase her, to explain. But what could she say?

Fatso put a heavy hand on Gravity's shoulder and said, "Fight starts the minute you know who you're fighting." He smiled a strange kind of smile that left his eyes cold.

"Well played!" said a lilting voice.

They both turned to see a beautiful woman in a skirt suit studying them through tortoiseshell glasses. Gravity was bad at telling adults' ages, but Carmen Cruz could have been anywhere from thirty to sixty years old. Her long black hair was untouched by gray, but there was a worry line in the middle of her forehead and deep wisdom in her onyx eyes. She held a reporter's notebook in one hand and a glass of champagne in the other.

"I'm so happy you're covering the tournament!" Gravity told her. "Your blog is the best thing on the internet about boxing."

"*Gracias, boxeadora,*" Carmen said, inclining her head. "Perhaps you would consider granting me an interview. Mustafa, hold my drink so I can give the young lady a business card."

Gravity looked at Fatso in surprise. She had never heard anyone use his real name before. Even his wife called him Fatso.

Fatso eyed Carmen's champagne with distaste—Gravity had heard him deliver many lectures on the evils of alcohol—but he held its stem while Carmen withdrew a card from a silver holder and passed it to Gravity. It was printed in shiny black letters that looked like they came from an old-fashioned typewriter:

Carmen Cruz
Independent Journalist
San Diego, Bogotá, and Beyond
mobile: (917) 555-0184
email: carmen@boxingforgirls.com

Gravity turned the card over and examined the back, which bore a list of all the weight classes in amateur and professional boxing, in both pounds and kilograms. It was really useful! She slipped it carefully into her pocket.

"What do you think of the draw for my weight?" Gravity asked.

Carmen spread her hands, and the light from the hotel chandelier sparkled off the large emerald on her finger. "The estimable Mustafa was correct when he said it was a lucky draw. Of course, the draw is less of an issue in double elimination, but one never wants to find oneself in the challengers' bracket. It is an uphill battle back." She retrieved her champagne.

When Carmen spoke, the sentences came out rapidly, in fully formed thoughts, as though they were already written down in her head. It was impressive. "You will beat Svetlana Mamay with ease. Paloma will, of course, defeat poor May Okamura. You and Paloma will have a magnificent semifinal battle for the right to face whoever emerges victorious from the lower half of the bracket, most likely Aaliyah Williams. Fatigue will, as always, be a factor."

"I don't know about that, Carmen!" Fatso said. "That girl Luz is tough. She might mess around and beat Aaliyah Williams."

A red-faced older man interrupted with, "Luz Ortega is gonna win this whole gosh-darn thing!"

Carmen took a sip of her champagne and remained silent, which increased Gravity's confidence in her predictions. In boxing, it was usually true that the less someone spoke, the more they knew.

With a ding, the elevator doors slid open and D-Minus and Genya tumbled out, sopping wet from the hotel pool

71

and wearing nothing but underpants and flip-flops. They swaggered over to the bulletin board, but the smiles froze on their faces when they saw Fatso, who grabbed them by the napes of their necks. Gravity tried not to look at D-Minus's briefs, which were royal blue with red stripes and very form-fitting.

D-Minus said, "Yo, Fatso, watch the hair. We gotta peep the draw."

"Not dressed like that you don't. Go to your room and put on some clothes."

"It is a tough draw for the young men from your club, Mustafa," Carmen said, gesturing to the billboard. "And, of course, theirs is single elimination, so the draw is vital. I see that Gennady here drew the rising Junior Olympic champion, Jack Riebel, who beat him in their last encounter."

"I'ma spank Jack," Genya said.

Carmen looked Genya up and down, from his dripping blond fringe to his flip-flops.

"He's better than he looks," Fatso said.

It was true that Genya did not look intimidating. He had even less muscle definition than his sister and resembled an oversized, pimply Justin Bieber. But it took guts to be the only white boy in their gym, and you couldn't judge fitness by what someone looked like. When they all did uphill sprint intervals on the treadmill, Genya was the only one who never got gassed.

Carmen continued, looking over her notes, "Demetrius Saint-Amand comes in fourth seed at bantamweight and has easy prelims, but he will collide with the extremely tough Tiger Biggs in the semifinals, a bout he must win if he is to qualify for Trials. Any comments? Have those two ever fought before?"

D said, "We fought once."

The way he said it, you didn't need to ask whether he had won or lost.

"Demetrius was only eleven," Fatso said. "Finals of the Silver Gloves Nationals. We're much stronger now."

"And was it a stoppage?" Carmen asked, scribbling away.

D-Minus looked at her with outrage. "Ain't *nobody* ever stopped D-Minus."

She smiled as she wrote. "I see. And you're, what, sixteen now?"

"Yeah," he said, craning his neck to see what she was writing. "But I date up to forty."

"What a character!" Carmen said to Fatso.

Fatso rolled his eyes. "Tell me about it."

Chapter Seven

The preliminary rounds of the tournament were battled out in a huge, airy sports center about ten miles from the hotel. Three rings ran simultaneously, while boxers, coaches, officials, and family members sat in the bleachers like armies with their banners. Sacred Jones and her fast and flashy Kronk crew mingled with the Cincy Youth, bright in their purple and gold. The D.C. Headbangers were eating peanuts out of the shell as they swapped gossip with the Philadelphians. Gravity saw Miami Cubans, Texan brawlers, Wichita slicksters, and Angelenos in trunks like the Mexican flag.

The warm-up for Svetlana went smoothly. Gravity had switched off the part of her that remembered all the good times they had shared and how Svetlana had always had her back. She stayed grimly in the present moment.

Fatso, magnificent in an enormous burgundy-and-cream tracksuit that said "Brooklyn Boxing," was working the pads with panache. He smacked her gloves harder than usual so that her punches made a louder sound and Svetlana, who was within earshot, would be afraid.

D-Minus was enjoying the drama of this matchup between teammates. He had a ten-dollar bet riding on Gravity with Genya and had been trying unsuccessfully to get Gravity and Svetlana to pose for a face-off he could Instagram. Failing that, he was running back and forth between the two camps, irritating everyone with obvious lies about the trash Gravity and Svetlana were talking about each other. When he reported that Svetlana had said she was going to send Gravity back to the Dominican Republic in a coffin, Fatso said, "Enough!" and ripped the cell phone out of his hand.

D-Minus complained loudly. Apparently, he had given the number out to several female flyweights and could not remember which one had invited him to her room.

"You'll get it back after the fights," Fatso said.

D-Minus accused Fatso of cockblocking and stalked off.

Gravity watched in silence as the decision was announced for the bout before theirs—Kaylee Miller had won an upset—and then she ducked through the ropes and bowed in turn to each of the judges. Across the ring, Svetlana stood with her back turned so Boca could adjust her headgear. She looked so small and vulnerable that Gravity felt a shiver of pity.

She gathered her anger like armor, remembering the first time they had sparred, when Svetlana had made her bleed in front of everyone. She willed Svetlana to become every girl who had ever bullied her on the playground or mocked her in the lunchroom for being too skinny, too tall, too poor, too Dominican or not Dominican enough, for her hand-me-down clothes and bad temper and the gap between her two front teeth.

Fatso pulled her forehead against his and whispered, "She's already beat mentally."

Gravity said, "I know."

Girls were crueler than boys. It was a piercing kind of meanness, like a stiff jab. All those sexist men who opposed women's boxing because they said they didn't like to see females hurt ought to spend one day as a woman and see how much hurt was involved. Like Gravity's old rabbi, who had actually called her into his office one day and tried to convince her to quit boxing with some bullshit about Eve being made from Adam's rib to be protected.

After that, Gravity quit synagogue. She didn't need to go to a special building to pray. Nobody had ever protected her in her life, except maybe Coach and Mr. Rizzo. And if God didn't want her to box, why would He have made her so good?

She got down on one knee in the blue corner, rested her forehead against the padded post, and recited the Shema. She asked God to protect her and Svetlana from injury, to make the judging fair, and to allow them to perform up to their potential. Gravity never prayed for victory. She didn't want any unfair advantage, and she figured God had better things to do than interfere in sports.

Gravity had never given Svetlana her real stare before, and her friend looked startled when they met at center ring. She tried to hold Gravity's gaze but faltered, blinking and turning away to look at the referee. Gravity felt something click into place inside her.

When the bell rang, she did not shuffle forward in the boxing stance but sprinted straight at Sveta, trapping her in her own corner. She let fly a lead right so wild that it missed and hit the ropes, but the elbow connected with the padding over Svetlana's forehead, knocking her back. Since the ref didn't call it, Gravity kept on punching.

You fight different ways for different people, and she did not need her best game here, just her toughest. She felt her arms windmilling rather than flying tight and straight, but she pressed on, making it a brawl. Svetlana had never had much heart for that.

Gravity took a half step back to give herself room. Svetlana's guard might have seemed tight to someone in the back row of the bleachers, but up close it was a sieve. Gravity saw all the holes in her defense, lit up and sparkling like video game gold.

When the bell made its triple chime—there were multiple rings, so each ring had its own distinct sound—Gravity was shocked. The three minutes had flown by.

Ring time was different than real time. Sometimes it seemed to speed up, and sometimes it slowed down. Some fights she could remember afterward in precise detail. Others faded away, leaving behind only isolated impressions: momentum shifts, words spoken in the corner, big scoring blows.

Gravity waved away the stool and stood up during the one-minute rest. She was too hyped to sit.

"Good round," Fatso said.

He pulled out her mouthpiece and passed it down to D-Minus, who had weaseled his way into her corner, as he often did. You weren't supposed to be able to corner unless you were a registered coach with USA Boxing, but that didn't stop D-Minus. He reached out for Gravity's ankle and said, "Hey, G, throw the lead right, left hook! She wide open when—"

"Hush!" said Fatso. "She's doing just fine."

He gave her water silently, then laid one of his broad palms against her chest and told her to breathe. Gravity loved that about Fatso. When you were in your zone, he didn't try to get up in your business.

Midway through the third and final round, it stopped being about Svetlana at all. It was just something Gravity had to do. That was when she doubled up the straight right hand. The first one was fast. The second snapped back Svetlana's head and made her eyes widen.

The referee jumped between them. He turned to face Svetlana and held up a finger.

"One! Two!"

Svetlana tried to argue, but he kept counting.

It was a standing eight! She had hurt Svetlana bad enough for the referee to stop the action and count.

It was like having all her birthdays at once. It was like all the bad things that had ever happened to her were erased with a big eraser. Gravity bounced from foot to foot in the neutral corner. She wanted to do it again.

When the referee gave the signal, Gravity leapt out and drilled Svetlana's nose with another lead right. This time Svetlana did not even argue the eight count but took it, head lowered. Two lines of blood dripped over her upper lip, spattering red stars on the canvas.

Gravity grinned and smacked her gloves together, but the referee was leading Svetlana to her corner, where he conferred with Boca and the ring doctor.

It was a third-round stoppage. Gravity knew she should have been happy, but this win was different, because it was against her friend. She felt a kind of dread take hold of her stomach as the full weight of what she had done to Svetlana sank in.

She stood in the center of the ring with the referee, holding his hand. Out in the crowd, she saw D-Minus and Genya having an animated argument. After a while, Svetlana came out of her corner to take the referee's other hand, refusing to meet Gravity's eyes. Boca had done a good job of cleaning her face, but there was a streak of blood across her biceps.

The referee lifted Gravity's arm way up high before stepping away and sweeping the two girls together into an awkward, sweaty hug.

Because of the height difference, Svetlana's face was pressed to Gravity's neck. She could hear the hiccups there as her friend tried not to cry.

As they stepped apart, Gravity murmured, "Good fight," but Svetlana was already turning her back, golden braids whipping over her shoulder.

Gravity followed her back to her corner, where she did all the things a good winner does—hugged Boca, held the ropes apart for Svetlana—but she knew that something about their friendship was permanently altered. That first time they had sparred, Svetlana could have been mean, but she hadn't. She had been kind. And now Gravity had taken all the lessons she had learned and used them to beat her.

Fatso held her hand as she walked down the ring stairs, her thighs trembling. All at once she felt very tired and very hungry. A few people reached out to shake her gauze-wrapped hand. Genya, having apparently lost the argument, was sulking as he handed D-Minus a ten-dollar bill.

"That's grimy," said Genya. "She's my sister."

"That's boxing," said D-Minus.

Chapter Eight

At six the next morning, all twenty-four Trials boxers slouched in their rows of folding chairs in the hotel conference room, half awake and awaiting their turn on the scale. Gravity could feel the difference from yesterday morning's initial weigh-in, when everyone had been more or less on an equal footing. One day in, half of the girls had been shunted to the losers' brackets. It was a small room to hold all that drama, and the recirculated air was thick with tension.

Gravity decided to bite the bullet and say good morning to Svetlana, who looked pretty much recovered from last night, only slight bruising visible on the bridge of her nose. She was sitting in the back row, chatting with her roommate, Wendy, who had also lost her preliminary match. When Gravity greeted her, Svetlana stared straight ahead, as though she wasn't even there.

Gravity thought she had not heard, so she spoke louder: "We missed you at dinner last night! Your nose looks great! I watched that girl May, and she's got nothing for you."

But Svetlana kept up the I-can't-hear-you act.

Wendy gave Gravity an awkward half smile, clearly unsure of what to do.

Gravity decided to let it go. As she went to sit down next to her roommate, Chantal, she mentally recited some lines from an old samurai poem that Fatso had taught her:

I have no parents: I make the heaven and earth my parents.
I have no friends: I make my mind my friend.

That poem always made her feel better. Svetlana would get over herself. And maybe Gravity would make new and better friends once she was on the national team. She glanced longingly at the front row. Kaylee Miller, a blond California flyweight who had won last night by stoppage, was making Sacred Jones crack up by imitating a pirate. The last time Gravity had seen Sacred Jones on TV was at the ESPYs, in a spectacular gown of peach satin. Gravity thought the great champion looked even better like this: no makeup on her warm brown skin, in a dinosaur headscarf and sweats. She and Kaylee were laughing so loud that a few girls cast resentful glances in their direction, but Gravity wished she could be a part of their conversation.

Her opponent for that night, Paloma Gonzales, was sitting all by herself at the end of Gravity's row, staring into space with her headphones on. Gravity tried to catch her eye but could not.

"A bronze isn't bad, but I plan on winning gold," Gravity said to Chantal. She said it loudly, hoping Paloma would hear and take offense, but she just kept listening to her music.

Chantal said, "I heard she didn't even deserve to go to London. My coach said *she* shoulda won." She nodded to the front of the room, where Aaliyah Williams was stepping on the scale, topless and in boxer briefs. Aaliyah had a spectacularly muscled physique and was tattooed all over.

"One hundred and thirty-two even," announced the female fight doctor.

"One thirty-two for Aaliyah Williams," repeated the female official, writing it down.

Aaliyah stepped off the scale, pulled her jeans back on, and accepted the congratulations of her friends.

It was Paloma's turn next. Gravity watched as she stripped to bra and panties, noting the efficiency and aggression of her movements. A large tattoo of the Olympic rings stretched across her tan, muscular back, and her dark hair hung down in a long braid almost to her knees. Gravity thought it was creepy to have hair that long. Plus, it must add at least an extra pound.

The doctor announced, "One hundred thirty-one point eight pounds."

"One thirty-one eight for Gonzales."

Nakima, a nice middleweight from Newark, leaned over to Gravity and whispered, "USA Boxing loves Paloma 'cause she gets all the sponsors and press. If you wanna beat her, G, you gotta *beat* her. They won't give you a close decision."

"I'm not afraid of Paloma Gonzales," Gravity said quietly. "Everybody goes down if you hit them right. And Aaliyah Williams gasses out. I can outwork her."

Nakima remained silent at that. Probably she thought Gravity was all talk. Paloma and Aaliyah were nationally known, and she was just some kid from Brooklyn. That was all right. By the end of the tournament, everybody would know who she was.

Chantal made 112 with two ounces to spare, and Gravity gave her a high five. Then it was her turn. She pulled off her Cops 'n Kids jersey and bent down to strip off her sweatpants. She took off her bra and socks, too, because she didn't want to give up an extra ounce, and you only got one chance to make weight.

Stepping onto the cold metal square, she balanced on the balls of her feet and thought about light, fluffy clouds. The display flashed with double zeros. After a moment, it settled on 131.7. She exhaled with relief.

As she stepped off and bent to pick up her clothes, she caught Paloma Gonzales watching. A flare of delight went off inside Gravity's heart. She stood up very straight, still bare-chested and in her lucky pink thong, holding Paloma's gaze.

"What are *you* looking at?" she said loudly, lifting her chin in the air.

Sacred Jones and Kaylee went, "Ooh!"

D-Minus had been in the fitness room last night, and he said Paloma was running her mouth about how easy the field was in this year's Trials. Apparently, she had said Gravity would be light work because she was only sixteen. Well, Gravity might be young, but she was the only undefeated fighter in the whole tournament.

Chantal said, "Yo, G, chill!" but she kept on staring. It was fun.

Paloma looked way less intimidating in person. Like Svetlana, she was on the small side for lightweight. She had a button nose and pouty lips, and there was something brittle about her brown eyes that made her swagger seem like a lie.

"All right, ladies, knock it off," said the fight doctor, but she sounded mildly amused. Weigh-ins were kind of a drag, so everyone appreciated a little action. Gravity held Paloma's gaze as long as she could, then snapped her eyes away and left the room, filled with the triumph of having decisively won the pregame.

Chapter Nine

The hardest part of a fight was waiting for it to begin. The staredown with Paloma left Gravity so hopped up on adrenaline that she couldn't make herself eat breakfast, which threw off her entire rhythm, and the day went downhill from there.

At lunch, she was unable to stop herself from eating a chicken burrito the size of her head, after which she fell into a deep carbohydrate coma, emerging just in time to catch the shuttle to the sports center. She would have missed it entirely if not for Fatso, who always took the precaution of banging on his fighters' doors if they did not text him back.

Gravity was in such a rush that she forgot to bring socks or a cup to the venue. She did without the socks—Tyson had never worn them—but a cup, though optional for women, took some of the sting off body blows, so she borrowed one from Nakima. It was so big that Fatso had to tape it all around, and it stuck up out of the waistband of her trunks, making her look like a dork.

D-Minus was fighting right before her in the same ring, so Fatso was working his corner instead of warming Gravity up. She shadowboxed by herself in a quiet part of the cavernous sports center, trying to get a good sweat on, but she felt exposed and anxious. Normally, Svetlana would have been by her side, feeding her a steady stream of positivity until the time came to make her ring walk. There had been some indication of a thaw between them. Svetlana had won her fight that night against Hawaii and had silently accepted a hug afterward, but Gravity missed her friend's presence at her side. Alone, she had no buffer from the uncertainty that kept creeping into her mind.

Had she made a mistake that morning? She had felt so certain of herself when she called Paloma out, but what if she couldn't back it up? Coach was always telling D-Minus, "Don't let your mouth write checks your ass can't cash."

She glanced up into the ring, but D seemed to be taking care of business. His opponent was a light-punching kid who thought he was slicker than he was. As she watched, D switched southpaw, his body language broadcasting supreme confidence.

She needed some of that confidence.

She caught sight of Lefty in the crowd around the ring and dashed over to him. He had on huge silver Beats and was bopping his head in time to the music as he divided his attention between D-Minus's fight and the little pocket notebook in which he scribbled his rhymes. Gravity smelled beer fumes radiating off him.

"Are you okay?" she asked.

Lefty was due to fight the world youth champion tomorrow. He probably should not have even come out tonight, much less been drinking.

"Chillin'," Lefty said. "You fighting tonight?"

"Of *course* I'm fighting."

"Sweet!" He pulled out his phone and tried to take her picture but took a burst of selfies by mistake. She shook her head.

"Lefty, do you have Coach Thomas's phone number? Can you call him for me? I would do it myself but I'm gloved up."

Once you got the official ten-ounce competition gloves on, you weren't allowed to take them off, which was why it was so important to pee before you went to the glove table. Lefty stared at her in confusion for a moment, then bent over his phone. Gravity looked back up into the ring just in time to see D-Minus's opponent stagger backward from a big right hand, drawing an eight count.

She yelled, "That's it, D! Beautiful!"

"Here," Lefty said, holding the phone up to her face.

She cupped a glove over her other ear, blocking off the cacophony of the three simultaneous rings.

"Coach?"

"Champ! You okay?"

Something in her relaxed when she heard his deep, gravelly voice.

"Hi, Coach. I'm okay." She hadn't planned anything to say and felt suddenly shy. Lefty was standing so close to her, studying her with his sexy vampire eyes.

But Coach seemed to understand, because he said, "You're about to go in against Gonzales?"

"Yeah."

"You all warmed up?"

"Not really." Every part of her body felt tight and cold. Her mouth was dry. Her head throbbed.

"Do twenty jumping jacks right now," he said.

"Okay." She looked up and saw Fatso climbing down the ring stairs with a euphoric D-Minus. "D just won. I'm up next." Her stomach lurched. She didn't want to get off the phone.

"Listen to me. Paloma Gonzales boxes to please her father. You box to please yourself. That's why you'll win." Gravity considered this. She had never thought about it before, but maybe it was true. Coach erupted in a fit of coughing. When it was over, he wheezed, "You have already defeated all your enemies."

She let that sink in. She didn't understand what it meant, but it sounded good.

"Thanks, Coach."

She nodded to Lefty, who took the phone away and hung up.

"Left . . ." She hesitated. "You've got a tough fight tomorrow. I don't think you should be drinking."

He smiled at her, but his eyes stayed sad. "Let's be real, G. I can't beat that kid. You know it. I know it. Everybody knows it. Might as well enjoy the night and the fights and the music." He put his headphones back on.

Gravity had never in her life heard a boxer talk like that. Then again, something about Lefty had always been different. It was like he was always hearing music in his head.

Then Fatso found her and said, "Come on, baby, we're up."

The New Jersey head coach, who everyone called Sergeant Slaughter because he was so mean and always dressed in camouflage, followed with the spit bucket.

They pushed their way through the crowd toward ring two, where the round timer sounded like a fire drill siren, and she was through the ropes before she could ask Fatso what the game plan was. Everything went very quickly after that. The mouthpiece, the final drink of water, the bows to the judges. Dark eyes boring into hers, dread blossoming in her belly, the fire drill siren, and Paloma running at her full speed, like a bus into a bicycle.

Paloma ran over Gravity in center ring, forced her to the ropes, and ran her over again in each of the corners. It was the worst thing that had ever happened to her in the boxing ring. The next thing she knew, the fire drill siren screeched again and Paloma went away. Gravity staggered back to Fatso, who grabbed her and plunked her down on the stool. Sergeant Slaughter clapped a bag of ice on the back of her neck.

Fatso told her to breathe and she breathed. He told her to drink and she drank. He gave her some instructions, but it sounded like someone talking at her from very far away.

Then he was gone, and Gravity watched, frozen, as Paloma came running from across the ring. She turtled up immediately and took the opening barrage on the shoulders and the backs of her hands. Paloma was relentless. Every time Gravity thought it was her turn to get off, Paloma would pivot and start over from a different angle.

The first standing eight count was bullshit, called after a flashy triple hook that Gravity totally deflected on her forearm. She spent the first few seconds arguing with the referee, even though that was pointless. By the time she remembered to look at Fatso, Paloma was back on her.

She got low, and a three-piece combination sailed over her head, but when she tried to pop back up with a hook, Paloma threw a straight right inside it.

Bright, sharp pain shot through her left cheekbone, just below the eye. Gravity heard as though underwater the oohing of the crowd and Paloma's father cheering in Spanish from the corner. It was an awful feeling. With difficulty, she lifted the gloves back to her face to convince the referee that she wanted to continue.

The siren sounded, and Fatso came to her, grabbing her by the rib cage.

"I forgot to do the twenty jumping jacks!" she gasped, seized with despair.

"What?" he said.

"I forgot . . ."

She doubled over, no air to spare for speech.

"You forgot to throw punches is what you forgot," Fatso said. He steered her back to the stool and pushed her down. Sergeant Slaughter put ice on her cheek.

As Fatso's eyes met hers, he looked calm and almost amused. That made her furious.

Did he think this was funny?

"I didn't warm up," she snapped. "You *weren't there*."

He laughed. "Well, you're warm now."

Sergeant Slaughter hooked his hands under her armpits and lifted her back onto her feet.

Was the break over already? She wanted more time. She wanted to sit back down on the stool.

Fatso shoved the mouthpiece back in.

Someone yelled, "Seconds out!"

Just before he left the ring, Fatso grabbed her headgear and yelled, "Last round, baby. Don't get mad at *me. I'm* not the one beating the shit out of you. Let your motherfucking hands go. If you don't throw punches, I'm stopping it."

Gravity teetered on her boots. That was the meanest Fatso had ever been to her. In the five seconds before Paloma was on her, a host of emotions passed through her: hurt that he would speak to her like that, humiliation at the thought of him throwing in the towel, anger at Fatso, anger at herself, anger at Paloma.

Yes, that's it. She was supposed to be angry at *Paloma*.

She seized on that thought as the beating began again. And she *was* angry, but it wasn't the kind of anger that did any good. It was a slow, heavy, resentful kind of anger. It reminded her of something.

Gravity could see Paloma's father over her shoulder, gesticulating passionately from his stool. A knife twisted in an old wound, and Gravity was filled with self-pity, because her father would never be in her corner, and she always thought she was over it, but she would never get over it. She looked down at Paloma's boots—white on white—and knew she should just accept that she was the loser because she always broke everything sooner or later and *that* was what it reminded her of. It reminded her of life.

She was dimly aware of some contradiction in her logic, but the punches were coming so fast she couldn't think. As she stood there, panting, her vision crystallized and she saw everything with incredible clarity. The banners on the walls of the sports center. The wrinkles in the forehead of the referee as he watched her with concern. The intensity on the faces of D-Minus, Lefty, Boo Boo, Genya, Monster, and Svetlana as they watched from the front row, hands cupped to their mouths, screaming something in unison.

Svetlana. Svetlana was rooting for her too.

She looked over at Paloma. Her mouth was open, and her hands were at her sides. A wet strand of dark hair had escaped from her braid and clung to the hollow of her neck. She must have been tired too. She had thrown a lot of punches in the first two rounds. Maybe too many.

"Box!" commanded the referee.

Gravity figured out the mistake in her logic. She had been angry at Paloma for beating her, but Paloma hadn't won yet. There was still time left in the round, and that made this different than all the other messed-up things in life. Victory was still possible.

She bit down on the mouthpiece. Just as Paloma came within punching range, she made out what her team was screaming. Svetlana's voice, more piercing than the rest, floated to her over the crowd: "Q Train!"

It was an old code from Cops 'n Kids. Boo Boo's dad started it: a system of combinations based on this street fighting style 52 Blocks. Gravity remembered Q Train because it had always been her favorite—a strange feint with the left, then a short right to the body, half step back, right uppercut, left hook, right hand. She had spent rounds throwing it over and over on the stationary wall bag until she could make it shake with the final cross.

Paloma still had her hands around her sides, lulled into complacency by how badly Gravity had been fighting. She was a sucker for the feint, and the short right to the solar plexus made her double over, presenting a perfect target for the uppercut. Gravity grinned as she half-stepped back.

So what if Paloma had an Olympic bronze? She didn't have Gravity's heart.

The uppercut lifted Paloma's head for the tight little hook that followed. But that was just a way to bring Gravity's weight back onto the rear foot for the big finish. She threw the right hand straight and strong, just like Coach taught.

Paloma looked surprised to find herself on the canvas. She blinked up at Gravity, her legs splayed, her feet flopping out to the sides, like a scared little girl who had fallen on the playground.

Gravity's heart sang.

The referee started to count.

Back when she had first gotten her USA Boxing passbook, Coach had taught Gravity two things about competition: to bow to all the judges when she entered the ring and to get up slowly if she ever got knocked down. They had practiced the knockdown part. D-Minus spun her around until she was so dizzy she fell over. Then he counted in a loud voice while Gravity got her feet underneath her and rose on six, making eye contact with D-Minus to convince him she could continue.

"In the amateurs they take any excuse to call off a fight," Coach had warned her.

Despite all her international experience, Paloma had no idea what to do when she found herself on the canvas. She tried to pop up immediately and lost her balance, staggering sideways.

Gravity smiled when she saw that.

The referee shook his head and waved his hands in the air. It took a moment before Paloma understood she had lost. When she did, she ripped off her headgear and threw it to the canvas.

True knockdowns were rare in women's amateur boxing—it was Gravity's first—and although Paloma Gonzales was popular with the sponsors and press, she was not loved among her fellow boxers. Gravity got a huge cheer when they raised her hand.

Chapter Ten

That night, they had dinner at Denny's with a few of the New
Jersey kids and coaches. Jersey fielded a big team with male
fighters in every weight class. Gravity and Svetlana sat at one
end with Nakima, who had fought bravely that night but was
sent to the losers' bracket by Sacred Jones.

"It's not fair," said Nakima, pointing at Monster with her
fork.

All three of the women boxers were eating avocado and
chicken Caesar salads (dressing on the side). Monster was
plowing through a country-fried steak, a salad, onion rings,
fried mozzarella, and an Oreo milk shake. That was life as a
superheavyweight.

The night had been a great one for Cops 'n Kids. In addition to wins by D-Minus, Svetlana, and Gravity, Genya had
avenged his loss to Jack Riebel. Monster had gotten a bye,
which was what they called it when you advanced automatically without fighting. Superheavyweights were increasingly
rare. Coach said it was because football and basketball lured
the big men away to easier money. There were only five other
men in Monster's class, so if he won his next fight, he would
qualify for Trials.

Nakima sighed and poked at her lettuce. "I wish I was a
superheavyweight."

Gravity eyed Monster's enormous arms. She wasn't so

sure she'd like to be a superheavyweight and get hit by arms like that. Besides, what was the point in coming all this way for just two fights?

"Can I get some dessert?" Monster bellowed, trying to flag down their server. "Why'd they sit us way back here?"

Nakima ran a finger over the dark skin of her arm and gave him a significant look.

It was true that Gravity's party looked very different from the rest of the Denny's patrons, who were all white, and who periodically shot nervous glances in their direction. The hostess had seated them in a dark corner in the rear of the restaurant, which they were rapidly destroying. Lefty had spilled raspberry lemonade all over the table as soon as they arrived. D-Minus was throwing sugar packets across the room, and the light heavyweight from Camden kept trying to get the waitress's number.

Fatso, Boca, and the Jersey coaches were at an adjoining table, generally ignoring the chaos, although whenever D-Minus used the n-word, Fatso made him drop and do fifty push-ups. Some of the boxers said please and thank you, but most of them acted like the server was some kind of slave and Denny's was their personal trash can.

Gravity hadn't really experienced racism until she left New York. When she was by herself or with her mom and brother, people usually assumed she was white. Sometimes they might look at her frizzy hair and naturally tan skin and ask where she was from in that weird, searching way, and she would answer, "Coney Island," even though she knew that wasn't what they meant. But most people in New York had better manners than that. There were lots of people like her who didn't fit neatly into any one box.

It was only when she had started traveling for boxing that

94

she felt it. When they walked into stores in small towns in upstate New York, Gravity and her friends would be shadowed by security. In restaurants, they set off ripples of anxiety. People moved their handbags closer. Servers asked if they were sure they could afford the food. Sometimes Gravity wished her boxing friends would act more calm and quiet and like they belonged in nice places. Then again, how could you act like you belonged if people treated you like you didn't?

She heard laughter behind her and saw that D-Minus had removed himself from their table and sat down with one of the elderly white couples he had hit with his sugar packets. He was autographing their napkins and inviting them to the tournament. Gravity watched as the old man took off his baseball cap, which was beaded with a Native American design, and set it on D-Minus's head.

Gravity flinched, because D-Minus hated to have his hair messed with—he went to the barbershop before every tournament to get his name carved in the back of his head—but D just smiled and shook the old man's hand, and then he did the most surprising thing of all. He trotted back to their table to get the teddy bear he had won from the claw machine at the casino, which he had been bragging about giving to some flyweight who had a tongue ring, and set it in the old lady's lap. She blushed like a teenager and promised to come watch him box.

Gravity met Svetlana's eyes and they both smiled and shook their heads. D-Minus was always a surprise.

Gravity sank back into the booth and let her eyes close. The adrenaline had worn off and now she just wanted to go back to the hotel and fall asleep under the crisp white sheets. She got tomorrow off. What a wonderful feeling. That was the reward for being in the winners' bracket. She was trying not to act too happy around Sveta and Nakima, who had one loss apiece.

Svetlana would have to fight Paloma tomorrow. Gravity snuck a peek at her friend and noted the slight bruising still visible on her nose and the shadow beneath one eye. Paloma would murder her. Gravity wished Svetlana would get sick or something, so they would not have to fight. There was something subdued about Svetlana's manner, as though she had already accepted, somewhere deep down, that she would lose again.

Gravity recalled Coach's words to her: "Paloma boxes to please her father. You box to please yourself."

Maybe Sveta was a little like that too; maybe Kostya wanted it more than she did.

Gravity closed her eyes again and returned to the warm glow of her victory, replaying the knockdown in her head. Her teammates' voices washed over her until the uncomfortable moment came to pay the check.

The server dropped it on the coaches' table, where the adults eyed it like a pile of sweaty handwraps. Finally Fatso sighed and dragged it toward himself with one fingernail, at which point a lengthy discussion began among the coaches. They passed it along, without comment, down the kids' table, where the boxers produced various excuses, wrinkled piles of singles, and stacks of change. Gravity's salad cost $7.95, so she put in a ten-dollar bill.

Her mother was very strict about restaurants. She never let them order anything but water because sodas cost too much, but she always made sure they put in a tip. Mom had waited tables back when she was studying to be a nurse. She said waitresses made shit money and that if you could not afford to tip, you should not eat out.

When the check made its way back to the adults, Sergeant Slaughter stood up and bellowed, "All right, you little ass-holes. We're still sixty-four dollars short. Pay up!"

The check made its way around again, and Gravity put in two more dollars and Nakima put in seventy-five cents. The light heavyweight from Camden threw in a napkin with his cell phone number scrawled on it. D-Minus, who hadn't paid anything the first time around, told Genya to lend him twenty bucks. Genya told him to stop smoking crack. D-Minus called Genya the ugliest white boy he'd ever seen, and the two began slap boxing viciously, overturning an-other glass of raspberry lemonade.

"Enough!" roared Sergeant Slaughter. He counted up the change and announced that they were now fifty-one dollars short. The coaches, after a brief huddle, laid some more bills on the table and hurried everyone out of the restaurant.

"Well, there's another Denny's we can never go back to," said Fatso.

"Plenty more where that came from," said D-Minus. He took a selfie in his new baseball cap.

February 13, 2016
Women's Olympic Trials Results, Day Three

SPOKANE, WASH.—The six undefeated boxers got a day off today to roam the Vision Quest, while the challengers' brackets battled on. After three thrilling days of competition, half of the competitors have now been eliminated. Tomorrow's action moves from the Spokane Sports Center to the Vision Quest's ballroom.

Flyweights
Chantal Thompson of Cincinnati stopped Chicago's Eve Stotland at 1:18 of the third round. Austin's Marisol Bonilla edged Sharmila Rao of Providence, Rhode Island, in a close tactical battle. Bonilla and Thompson square off tomorrow in what should be a classic matchup of boxer versus puncher.

In tomorrow's winners' bracket final, we'll get another look at the entertaining southpaw Kaylee Miller of Venice Beach, California, who has a tough assignment in defending champion Aisha Johnson of Washington, D.C. Johnson, who went from homeless to representing her country in the London Olympics, has won all five of the pair's prior meetings.

Lightweights
Defending champion Paloma Gonzales scored a unanimous decision over game Brooklyn southpaw Svetlana Mamay,

whose nose bled throughout their brutal war. The skillful Luz Ortega of Albuquerque won unanimously over the army's strong-punching newcomer, Jay Allen. Gonzales and Ortega clash tomorrow.

But the match we're licking our chops for is the winners' bracket final, in which the unstoppable force of Brooklyn's young Gravity Delgado takes on the immovable object of Seattle's Aaliyah Williams, four-time national welterweight champion and longtime *Boxing for Girls* favorite. See our extended interview with Williams for an account of her harrowing childhood sexual abuse and activism with fellow LGBTQ assault survivors.

Williams will have the crowd behind her, fighting so close to her hometown. Can the undefeated young phenom out of Cops 'n Kids pull off her second big upset of Trials? Watch the USA Boxing livestream here or check our Twitter feed for live updates from ringside.

Middleweights

Two words: Sacred Jones. Everyone else in this weight class should just pack up and go home.

Chapter Eleven

Gravity woke up refreshed after her day off and eager for her showdown with Aaliyah. She made weight easily. The weigh-ins got quicker as the tournament progressed and more girls were eliminated.

Three of her teammates were still alive in the men's competition: D, Genya, and Monster. Monster's win last night over the army kid—if you could call it that—had secured his place in the Men's Trials. Genya and D needed to win one more fight to qualify. D had been fighting great so far, but tonight he would run into Tiger Biggs.

The only ones she saw at breakfast were Monster and Lefty. Avoiding Monster's table, she went to say hello to Lefty, who was hanging with his cousins from the New England team, all of whom had already been eliminated. They had bloodshot eyes, smelled like weed, and appeared to be testing the upper bounds of the all-you-can-eat buffet.

Lefty had actually gone the distance last night against the world youth champion. He had lost every round but never quit, not even when a cut opened under his left eye. When Gravity approached his table, all the boys stood up. One of them gave her a long-stemmed rose, which confused her for a moment until she remembered that today was Valentine's Day. Another slid a foil-wrapped chocolate heart across the table to her and said, "I can see why my cousin is always talking about you." Lefty told him to chill.

Gravity was surprised. She had never realized Lefty thought much about her one way or another. She headed to the buffet to get oatmeal, but as she was bringing it back, Monster yelled, "Hey, Gravity!"

She went reluctantly to where he sat, slouched in a booth, wearing a T-shirt that said "This is what a feminist looks like" and poking glumly at a mountain of eggs. There was swelling over his right cheekbone from all the army kid's jabs last night. Across from him sat Andre Vázquez, his laptop open on the table. He had worn his Vision Quest robe to breakfast, and the neck flapped open, revealing a thatch of dark chest hair.

The minute she slid into the booth, Andre got up and went to schmooze with more important people. Andre had never paid any attention to her. He focused exclusively on the men and mostly on the heavier weight classes, who earned more money as professionals. When Gravity had complained to Coach about it, he had laughed and said that was like a gazelle complaining that the jackal never noticed it.

Gravity chewed her oatmeal slowly, trying to avoid eye contact with Monster. She knew what he was going to ask her, and she wished he wouldn't.

"G? What did you think of my performance last night?"

She swallowed, then took a sip of water.

"You hit him with a really good right hand in the second."

"Be honest."

She stole a glance at him. His big brown eyes were wide as a puppy's.

"Well . . . you could've let that right hand go more, not

101

load up so much. He was initiating most of the exchanges. And when you got close, you were letting him tie you up."

He was silent. Relieved, she went back to her oatmeal, but then she heard a strange sound.

"You think I lost," he said, his big head hanging to his chest. A tear rolled down his bruised cheek and landed in his eggs.

"Stop it!" she hissed, looking around the breakfast buffet, but nobody was watching.

"It's okay," he said. "I know I lost. I told Seamus that last night."

Seamus was the army fighter's name. That was really nice of Monster to tell him that. Gravity liked to think she would do the same thing if she ever got gifted a decision. Seamus had boxed the shit out of Monster, but Andre Vázquez had strolled in right before the bout, handing out PLASMAFuel swag and palling around with the creepy old president of USA Boxing, and maybe that had nothing to do with the split decision going to the wrong man, but maybe it did. Like Rick Ross said, there was more to boxing than what went on in the ring.

"I didn't want to win that way, G."

"I know, Kimani."

She put her hand on his forearm, marveling at the thickness and strength of it, and at how a man could be 250 pounds and so humble, while D-Minus, who was only 123, had an ego the size of a skyscraper.

"Wanna go for a walk after we digest?" she asked him. "I think we're all going a little crazy just being in the casino all the time."

"I can't," he said. "I have to do a photo shoot for the USA Boxing website."

"Oh," she said, trying to ignore her pang of jealousy. This was the first she was hearing about any photo shoot.

Andre came back to the table, clapping Monster on the shoulder and saying, "All right, son, let's get you that massage so you can be nice and rested for the cameras."

Just hearing the word "massage" made Gravity's entire body cry out. She had never had a real massage before but always wanted one. She headed back upstairs to her room, where she put the long-stemmed rose in a water bottle and looked at the chocolate longingly before throwing it out.

"Who gave you those?" asked Chantal.

"A couple of Lefty's cousins," Gravity said. "I think they bought them in bulk."

Chantal giggled. "Lefty cute, though."

"Yeah, he is. His rhymes are good too."

"He raps?"

"Yeah!" Gravity went on his SoundCloud and found that boxing song to play for Chantal. "This track's called 'The Battle of the Little Giants.' Lefty's rapping like he's Wilfredo Gómez, and this guest Mexican rapper is Salvador Sánchez."

"Who's Wilfredo Gómez and Salvador Sánchez?"

Gravity hid her disapproval. Wilfredo Gómez was one of the greatest Puerto Rican boxers ever, and Salvador Sánchez was one of the greatest Mexicans. She could not imagine getting this far in boxing without knowing your history, but Melsy always told her not to be so judgmental of people who weren't as intense as she was.

"They're old fighters," she said, hitting Play.

The way the song started, you were rooting for Gómez, and it was sad when he got TKO'd. The next verse was even sadder, because you thought Salvador Sánchez was going to be this great champion, but he got hit by a truck and killed when he was only twenty-three. The last verse was about how we should all live in the moment, because we never know when our time will come. In the end, Salvador Sánchez looked down from heaven at Wilfredo Gómez, who was getting high in the bathroom of the Boxing Hall of Fame. That gave Gravity a funny feeling in the pit of her stomach; she would have to ask Lefty about it later.

She looked at Chantal, who said, "It's aight. Kinda boring, though."

Gravity sighed and opened Instagram. The picture of her beating Paloma had 153 likes. Melsy had commented with a string of hearts and muscles, then commented again, "You Beat Her Up! You Can Do It, I Love You Big Sis, This Is Tyler Delgado." Auntie Rosa wrote, "Goddamn, niecey, you fierce! <3<3 We are all here rooting for you! <3<3" Even her science teacher had commented: "You are so strong and we are so proud of you! Remember, gravity is one of the four fundamental forces in the universe! :)"

Gravity grinned; Ms. Laventhol was such a nerd. She replied to her comment, "Yeh but you said Gravity was the weakest of all those forces." Ms. Laventhol must have been online, because she replied instantly, "Glad to see something sank in during all those naps! ;) Yes, it's the weakest, but on the planetary level, it's the only one that matters."

As she was hitting Like on that, another comment popped up, making her heart flutter:

keestothekingdom: I see you, boo. Happy <3 Day. Stay undefeated.

She liked it and turned off her phone.

No time for that now, she told herself. *Eyes on the prize.*

But the memories flooded in. Keeshawn was the first boy she had ever really kissed. Well, technically the *only* boy. Not that she hadn't had other chances, but there was always so much else going on.

Gravity closed her eyes. Just one time. She would think about it once, because it was Valentine's Day, and then she would put boys out of her mind.

She had met Keeshawn at the track in the park by Broadway Junction. The first few times she saw him, they had just nodded and checked out each other's moves. He was a sprinter who lived uptown but had family in Bushwick. He had long dreadlocks and legs that went on for days. When he hit full speed on the straightaways, Gravity held her breath for joy.

The first time they had spoken was the day she brought her agility ladder. She had laid it on the grass and gotten lost in the patterns. When she paused, panting, before the third set, she saw him at her elbow. She still remembered what he was wearing: a solar-yellow tank top, little navy shorts, and tube socks that stretched over his powerful calves. He flashed her a million-dollar smile and asked if he could work it with her.

It had been six months since he moved to Miami with his mom, but he was always leaving little positive affirmations on her workout pics, sometimes with eyeballs or hearts at the end.

She wallowed in sweetness as she remembered that last workout. The way he had stretched her out at the end. The way he had kissed her, finally, pressed up against a pole in the subway station, waiting for his train to Inwood and hers to Far Rockaway. Many A trains had come and gone while they kissed goodbye. Even though it was her first real kiss, Gravity had known just what to do.

Before he left, Keeshawn pulled back to look at her, his

strong arms still wrapped around her waist. He said, "The way you work is beautiful. It's like your religion."

She had wanted to tell him how beautiful he was too, but her brain was on the ropes. She felt his kisses everywhere in her body.

His last words to her were: "Don't mess around with these young boys. They'll only drag you down."

She smiled at that. Kee was only a year older than her.

Sexy Keeshawn. He gave her sweet dreams.

Chapter Twelve

Casinos were weird places. They went on and on, and the lighting stayed the same, night and day. The slot machines emitted a constant stream of electronic burbling that floated through the cigarette and vape fumes. Gravity had excellent lung capacity and could hold her breath for the entire two and a half minutes it took to reach the ballroom, but she couldn't avoid imbibing the misery: All those elderly and obese people, pressing buttons like zombies. The drunks, who made Gravity cringe with shame, thinking of her mother. The craps players, who made her sad, thinking of Tray.

D-Minus's brother had gotten killed at a dice game. Boo Boo had told her the story. It was a cee-lo game up in the Bronx, and Tray hadn't even been the one playing. He had just been hanging on the corner.

Boo Boo said Tray was more calm than D-Minus, but he had the same zero-tolerance policy toward disrespect. When a gangbanger came swaggering down the sidewalk and walked straight through the dice game, Tray said, "Yo! What's up with that?"

Those were his last words. The kid pulled out his gun and shot Tray three times in the chest. Just like that.

"And the fucked-up thing?" Boo Boo said. "That's exactly how D's pops died: three bullets to the heart. Only *he* got shot by cops."

Gravity often thought back to that very first time she had seen D-Minus. He had ridden into the gym on his bike, done a wheelie, and given her that smile like the sun coming out from the clouds. And Tray had died just one week before.

How could D have smiled like that? It was impossible to know. He had the best game face of anyone she knew.

When she pushed through the ballroom doors, she spotted him immediately, working pads with Fatso inside a circle of admirers. It was customary to warm up where your opponent's corner could not watch you and analyze your moves, but D-Minus had stationed himself right next to the Chicago crew, whose stony-faced coaches made a great show of ignoring him.

His opponent, Tiger Biggs, was shorter than D and had thick legs with veins that popped out of his calves. That made Gravity nervous, because Coach always said power came from the earth and that it was more important to have strong legs than strong arms.

One of the Chicago coaches, a beefy white man in a tank top that said "Beast Mode," nodded to her. He gestured at Tiger with his stopwatch.

"He does the same dynamic warm-up every time," he announced. "Research shows that consistency breeds confidence."

Gravity had never heard a boxing person talk about research before. The man's booming voice sounded vaguely familiar. His skin was this weird orange color that looked sprayed on.

"It's a jungle out there," he said. "Evolve or die! Journal articles, conferences, seminars, webinars! I've listened to over a thousand TED Talks this year!" Without warning, he blew his whistle.

"Ow!" Gravity clapped a hand to her ear.

"Pain is weakness leaving the body," he said.

Now she realized why his voice sounded familiar! "You're Rick Ross, aren't you? 'Pain Is Weakness Leaving the Body' was the title of one of your podcasts!"

He lifted his mirrored shades and winked, then reached into his fanny pack and gave her a business card. One side had a glossy photograph of him in a Speedo that made Gravity kind of uncomfortable. The other side said:

Mr. Rick Ross, B.S., C.P.T., C.S.C.S., R.D.
STRENGTH AND CONDITIONING EXPERT
FOR <u>ELITE ATHLETES</u> AND <u>CELEBRITIES</u> ONLY
ROSS IS BOSS!!!!!!!!
FOUNDER AND CEO, BEASTMODE™, ULTRABEASTMODE™, BEAUTYANDTHEBEAST™
SOLE AUTHORIZED NORTH AMERICAN DISTRIBUTOR, MITOCHONDRIA MILK™
ASK ME HOW TO MAKE YOUR JUICE OR SMOOTHIE MIGHTY WITH MITOCHONDRIA MILK™!!!

Gravity put the card in her pocket.

"Just look at them," Rick Ross said sadly, gesturing with his stopwatch at D-Minus and Fatso. "They probably still do back squats and run in plastic suits. I feel bad for that kid, because you can tell he's talented, but talent without technique is like a gun without bullets."

"What's wrong with plastic suits?"

Gravity had run five laps around the casino yesterday in hers. She'd lost a whole pound.

"If you're dehydrating this late in the game, you're not in shape. I've had Tiger on weight for two weeks now. His diet is strictly Paleolithic, plus performance-enhancing smoothies."

Gravity watched with concern as D-Minus, having worked up a sweat on the pads, emptied the dregs of a bag of Cool Ranch Doritos into his mouth. She said goodbye to Rick and went to join her teammates, who had taken up seats on the first row of bleachers.

D came out fast at the bell and stood in center ring, glaring at Tiger with hostile glee. Gravity had never seen him look so handsome. The blue NY Metro tank top hung loosely on his lean frame. He wore his trunks low over his cup, "RIP Tray" embroidered in royal blue across the waist. Sweat silvered his shoulders and the high shelves of his calves.

The two bantamweights began a dangerous game of feints. Tiger flicked his left, and D-Minus slipped a jab that never came. D-Minus twitched a shoulder, and Tiger tightened his guard. Tiger did a little stutter step, and D-Minus retreated, spooked.

"Quit playing!" hollered Genya. "Let your hands go!"

But Gravity loved this part of a boxing match: the delicious tension before the real fight broke out. It started with a corny shoulder feint from Tiger that even Gravity could see through. D-Minus just laughed and stuck out his tongue, and before the referee could reprimand him, he hurled a lead right that connected with the sweet spot at the tip of Tiger's chin. Tiger's sturdy legs wobbled. If there had been a hook behind it, he might have gone down.

Gravity leapt to her feet.

It was the kind of punch—thrown with contempt and abandon—that changes the whole night. Suddenly D-Minus's handspeed and timing seemed entirely out of Tiger's league.

Gravity screamed, "Body, body!"

But D was on it. He found a place beneath Tiger's right

floating rib that made the other boy freeze with pain. Before D could follow up, the referee thrust his arm between them.

It was a standing eight count!

"That's what I'm talking about!" yelled Svetlana.

But the bell rang before D had time to press his advantage. Tiger staggered back to his stool, while D-Minus danced to the corner. Instead of sitting down, he did an Ali shuffle.

Gravity frowned. They didn't like showboating in the amateurs. Fatso must have felt the same way, because he pushed D-Minus down onto the stool, where he gripped the sides of his headgear and began yelling angrily. D acted like he was paying attention, but the minute Fatso turned to rinse the mouthpiece, he jumped off his stool and leaned over the ropes toward Carmen Cruz, who sat ringside.

"Write about that body shot!" he yelled.

Carmen laughed and yelled back, "The fight is just beginning."

She was right. They had worked some kind of magic in Tiger's corner, because their fighter ran out for the second round on steady legs and fired a strong one-two. D-Minus blocked the jab and slipped the right, but Gravity's stomach sank. When someone takes your best shot and recovers, it does something bad to your confidence. Gravity could tell that D-Minus and Tiger both felt it. The momentum had shifted.

The first two times Tiger backed D-Minus to the ring's edge, D spun off as soon as his calf touched the bottom rope, but the third time, it was the corner, and Tiger cut off the angles. D's torso was a blue blur as he slipped and rolled, but every tenth punch or so, Tiger would connect. Then the blur would resolve itself into a snapshot of her friend, drops of sweat frozen in the air around him, his handsome face transfixed with concentration and pain. Finally the bell rang, ending what Gravity thought might have been the worst three minutes of her life.

Fatso leapt into the ring, moving with astonishing speed for a man of his size. He grabbed D beneath the armpits and steered him back to the stool, where Boca emptied an entire bottle of water down his tank top while Fatso knelt on the canvas, frantically rubbing his thighs.

During the terrible third round, Gravity recalled something Coach had said once, when they were watching Larry Holmes versus Gerry Cooney: "The longer the fight lasts, the more the truth comes out."

The truth was that D-Minus was the more beautiful boxer. He switched southpaw and rolled with Tiger's punches with a desperate grace, the white fringe that ran below the waistband of his trunks always in motion. As she watched, Gravity saw his heart. She also saw all those mornings he had slept in instead of doing roadwork, all the nights he had hung out late. She winced as he ate a big right uppercut that made his head snap back. It got an eight count.

"That's all right!" she yelled. "We'll get it back."

Her team had gone silent, as people will when their friend is losing badly. Svetlana wore the stricken expression of someone watching a house burn down. Monster had pulled out his cell phone. Genya and Lefty were snickering and making jokes about muggings, which was just their way of coping. At the final bell, the only ones still cheering were Gravity and the elderly couple from Denny's.

When they raised Tiger's hand, D-Minus acted like he

didn't care. He hugged Tiger and touched gloves with the corner, but he did it like he was sleepwalking. Gravity hated seeing him that way. She rushed to ringside to tell him—well, she wasn't sure what she would tell him—but he brushed past her like she wasn't there.

Chapter Thirteen

Gravity left the ballroom and held her breath as she strode between the slot machines and gaming tables. She had at least forty-five minutes before she needed to get warmed up for Aaliyah, and she wanted to clear her mind. When she got to the lobby, she saw the familiar figure of Carmen Cruz, who must have also needed a break from the action. Carmen was standing in front of the mural of the Kalispel Tribe, studying it intensely and scribbling in her little notebook.

When Gravity came to stand beside her, she did not even say hello, just gestured to a photo of a young Kalispel woman in traditional dress.

"Look how beautiful," Carmen said.

The woman's eyes were like lasers. Gravity wondered what her life had been like to give her eyes that fierce. Gravity stood beside Carmen and took her time reading the text. It talked about the tribe's history, hunting and fishing across the Pacific Northwest until the whites came and confined the Kalispel to a tiny reservation on the Pend Oreille River. The reservation looked beautiful—there were even buffalo—but poverty, illiteracy, and alcoholism were widespread. The display said the casino money was helping revive the tribe's dying language, which was called Salish.

Gravity got so lost in the story that she almost jumped when a voice said, "Well, hello there, ladies!"

A stout man in a Vision Quest baseball cap stood beside them, twinkling.

He said, "How do you like our historical display?"

"It's wonderful, Francis!" Carmen said. "Very moving."

"I wish the other journalists were as interested as you, Carmen," he said.

Gravity studied the man. His laughing eyes and round cheeks made her think of Santa Claus, but he didn't have a beard.

"Are you one of the Kalispel?" she asked.

"Francis, tribal elder." He gave her a warm handshake.

"Francis has been to all the fights," Carmen said. "I think we've converted him to a boxing fan."

"My people have fallen in love with the boxers, especially you young ladies," he said. "Watching you fight for recognition is very spiritual. The Kalispel love underdogs."

Gravity glanced back at the photo of the young woman with the fierce eyes. "Are there Kalispel warriors?"

Francis laughed. "We're lovers, not fighters. But things get pretty intense when we play the stick game."

He told them some great stories then about a jingle dress, an old canoe, and his first eagle feather. Francis spoke in a way that was very smooth, but he was different from Carmen Cruz, who was smooth because she was always writing things down in her head, or Andre Vázquez, who was smooth because he was always selling something. Francis was smooth like a politician. Not like he was lying or anything, but like he knew that he was representing a lot of people and that Carmen was taking notes.

"It must have been hard, growing up on the reservation," Gravity said.

Francis said, "It was. There was one phone line for the

whole tribe. The well water was orange. You could make green Kool-Aid, and it would still come out orange." He shrugged. "But what do *I* know, really? I don't have anything to compare it to."

Gravity nodded. That was like growing up without a father. She thought it was hard, but she had nothing to compare it to. Maybe things would have been worse with Dad around. She looked back at the mural and sighed. Everybody had such a sad story. D-Minus. Her opponent tonight, Aaliyah Williams. The Kalispel. She supposed somebody might even think *her* story was sad, if they didn't understand how boxing fixed everything.

"I have a question," Carmen announced. She paused, like a boxer loading up for a power punch. "Your display says that alcoholism has devastated your community."

Francis nodded gravely. "I saw many of my friends destroyed."

"Then why do you make your living in this way?" Carmen asked, waving her notebook toward the casino.

Gravity looked at Carmen in surprise. Gravity had wondered the same thing, but she would never have asked Francis, for fear of coming across as rude.

But he did not seem to take offense. He answered carefully, "At first, when we opened the casino, we did not serve alcohol. The elders who came before me forbade it. There were many conflicts among us, but in the end we needed the profits to help our people." He spread his hands. "I am not proud of it, but it was a necessary evil."

A necessary evil. Gravity thought of what she had done to Svetlana, of what she hoped to do tonight to Aaliyah. Life was hard sometimes. That was one reason she liked boxing:

It was like life. You played basketball or football but nobody *played* boxing.

She glanced across the lobby at the clock.

"The young lady has somewhere to be," Carmen said.

"I have to fight soon," she said, feeling a wave of excitement rise up inside her.

"I have a feeling you're going to win!" Francis said.

Gravity laughed. "Me too!"

He laid a warm hand on her shoulder. "Come, I'll walk you back."

Chapter Fourteen

Gravity slid between the ropes of the big ring like she was sliding into a warm bath. A calm had come over her since her talk with Francis and Carmen. All boxers believe in luck, and Gravity felt that her meeting with the tribal elder was a sign. She knelt in prayer and said the Shema. She thanked God for making her a boxer. She thanked Him for letting her get this far. She asked for fair judging and safety for herself and Aaliyah. At the end, she said, "And let it be the fight of the night."

Aaliyah's cheering section took up half of the stands. The dockworkers from her union screamed when the announcer called her name, waving rainbow signs that said "EMPRESS AALIYAH." To Gravity's irritation, she saw that her roomie, Chantal, was among the loudest boosters.

The nerve! Gravity had cheered for Chantal all week. Now she was glad Marisol Bonilla had kicked her ass.

But Gravity had fans in the room too. All her teammates screamed when they called her name. Genya had won his fight, qualifying for Trials, and was bouncing all over like a big puppy. The New Jersey team was cheering for her too, along with Lefty's Connecticut cousins. The old couple from Denny's, whose names were Doug and Rae Ann, held a hand-painted sign that said "LET'S GO, DOOMSDAY!"

She skipped out to center ring to meet the eyes of her opponent. Aaliyah was an imposing presence up close. Tattoos covered the tawny skin of her arms, which were cut like a bodybuilder's. Her simple cornrows highlighted the beauty of her face, somewhere in between pretty and handsome. Gravity lifted her chin, threw back her shoulders, and stared.

She saw something she liked in Aaliyah's hazel eyes. A tiredness, maybe, or a blankness. The sense that she wasn't fully there, not the way Gravity was.

When she went back to her corner, Gravity hugged Fatso over the ropes and told him she loved him, which seemed to take him by surprise. It took her by surprise too. She wasn't sure what had come over her. Maybe it was Francis's story about the eagle feather. Or maybe the Valentine's Day spirit. She felt filled with love for everybody, filled with love for boxing.

Fatso said, "I love you too, baby. You go show her how we do."

She danced out at the bell and started circling left, thinking they were going to feel each other out, but Aaliyah stepped straight at her with the jab. It was a stiff jab, perhaps the stiffest she had ever felt from a woman. The right that followed also landed, but Gravity rolled, diminishing its impact. Their bodies smashed together, and Aaliyah walked her to the ropes and held her there, attempting to work the body but smothering her own shots.

Gravity felt herself absorbing information, felt Aaliyah's tremendous physical strength pressing against her. *This* was what Coach meant by "woman strength." As the youngest fighter in the division, Gravity was at a disadvantage against older opponents who had grown into their power. But she felt something else, too: Aaliyah's overreliance on brute force.

Paloma had been better in the clinch. She had known little tricks to make room for her punches. Gravity was in no danger this close with Aaliyah; it was like the eye of the hurricane. She sagged, letting the bigger woman expend energy trying to muscle her around.

Gravity took the openings where she found them, sliding to one side or the other to dig left hooks to the liver or right uppercuts to the ribs. Body shots were like money in the bank.

When the bell rang, Gravity trotted back to the corner. Fatso and Boca moved with their usual composure, but she could feel their worry. Fatso told her to keep her left hand high to block Aaliyah's right.

Boca said, "You lost that round, G. Stop running and stand your ground."

She took some water, rinsed, and spat.

"Never ran, never will," she said.

Fatso laughed. "All right, Brownsville. Whatcha gonna do?"

"She's almost done, I swear," she told him.

He swiped more Vaseline across her lips. "All right, baby. Just don't wait too long. You got six minutes."

Someone called, "Seconds out!" and Boca took away the stool.

"Finish everything with the hook," Fatso yelled as he left the ring.

She bounced on her boots and gazed across at Aaliyah. It was strange. Somehow, she just knew she could not lose.

Of course, she would probably have to beat Aaliyah twice, because it was double elimination. But one thing at a time. Tonight, she would send her to the losers' bracket.

Tomorrow, she would enjoy another day off. Then she would beat her again, or Paloma, or whoever else battled back. She felt certain of it, with an almost religious faith.

Aaliyah started every round aggressively, so Gravity held back, moving laterally along the ropes to draw her in. When the old champion complied, her hazel eyes glazed with fatigue, Gravity spun her, landing a right-left to the body, then danced back out to center ring.

Aaliyah rushed in again, missing with the right. Gravity dug for another two-piece downstairs, and that was when it happened: Aaliyah stumbled. Not enough for anyone else to notice, but Gravity understood. Her legs were shot from all that good body work and all the needless wrestling.

Time to shine. Gravity drew her weight back like a slingshot. She had long arms, and Coach had taught her to throw very straight, to maximize her reach and power. The lead right hand made a beautiful sound as it connected with Aaliyah's cheekbone, and so did the left hook that struck her temple. Aaliyah looked stunned, so Gravity followed with a jab-cross-hook combo, rolling left.

She didn't hear the eight count until the referee yelled at her to go to the neutral corner.

The bell rang on "seven," ending the round.

"*That's* what I'm talking about," said Fatso.

She waved away the stool, too hyped up to sit. She opened her mouth and drank the water Fatso offered. She drank in his joy, too, the sense of having pleased him. Past his shoulders, she saw D-Minus and Genya taunting the D.C. Headbangers, who were rooting for Aaliyah.

Svetlana and Nakima were on their feet, hands cupped to their mouths. Their voices came to Gravity's ears: "Good round, G!"

The bell rang again, and the real fun started. At Cops 'n Kids, Gravity was considered a puncher, not a boxer. Stylists like D-Minus and Boo Boo made her look crude. But the advantage to being outclassed on a regular basis at your home gym was that you were actually pretty slick compared to the general population.

Gravity boxed that last round against the hard-hitting Seattle dockworker at a level she had never before attained. She knew it was special as it was happening. In the spacious sense of time that she experienced, she found herself recalling Svetlana's advice, back in their tiny locker room: "Take control of the rhythm."

It was like she was catching some basic pulse that spiraled over the square canvas and deep down into the earth. She risked strange combinations that she had written in her journal but never tried. She danced to the right. She threw as she moved. Her hands found all the open places, and she felt so filled up, like she had more power than she could ever use.

February 16, 2016
Meet Your 2016 US Women's Boxing
Olympic Trials Champions

SPOKANE, WASH.—Twenty-four women came to Spokane dreaming of Olympic gold. After a week of magnificent battles, three leave with the right to represent their country in Rio.

But their tickets aren't booked yet. They will still have to qualify for the Games with top finishes at the Women's World Championships this May in Qinhuangdao, China.

Before that, the US will send a full team to a warm-up tournament in Ontario, the Americas Continental Championships.

And before *that,* we will dance and drink champagne.

Flyweight Kaylee Miller, 23, Los Angeles: This sunny southpaw picked up boxing as cross-training for track and field while earning her B.A. in communications at UCLA. Undaunted by her five prior losses to London Olympian Aisha Johnson, Miller fought ferociously in the winners' bracket finals, losing a split decision. She battled back through the grueling challengers' bracket, defeating the delightful Marisol Bonilla to earn her rematch with Johnson. This time, Miller used her superior reach to triumph decisively.

She is used to bucking the odds. All her life, Miller has struggled with obsessive-compulsive disorder. She says she hopes her success will empower others to recover from mental illness and chase their dreams: "It's about being happy. That makes the bad thoughts go away."

Lightweight Gravity Delgado, 16, Brooklyn: This tall, whip-thin puncher shocked the field in Spokane. The youngest competitor in the tournament, Delgado put on a boxing clinic to frustrate and outpoint the bigger, stronger Aaliyah Williams. Williams battled back, decisioning Luz Ortega—who, in another upset, had eliminated defending champion Paloma Gonzales—and Delgado faced Williams a second time. Picking up right where she left off, Delgado deconstructed Williams more thoroughly than I would have thought possible.

"I always loved to fight," said the teen, who is a junior at William E. Grady High School in Coney Island and spends her spare time studying classic fighters like Marvin Hagler, Alexis Argüello, and Mike Tyson. "I guess I just have this anger inside me. Those nine minutes that the fight lasts? I wish all of life was like that."

Middleweight Sacred Jones, 21, Detroit: Back in 2012, Jones was the Gravity Delgado story: the teen phenom who stormed through the field. Now she's boxing royalty, with an Olympic gold medal and a four-year winning streak. Jones won every round of every fight this week. When I wished her luck, she grinned and said, "I don't need it. Give it to somebody else."

She is still seeking the commercial success she hoped would attend her historic medal, but with a documentary in theaters now and another gold in Rio likely, the word seems to be getting out.

Chapter Fifteen

Gravity wore her gold medal to the disco. Underage boxers weren't supposed to get in, but Sacred and Kaylee went in first and Kaylee came out five minutes later with Sacred's bracelet for her. Gravity took it with wonder, still getting used to the fact that she and Sacred Jones were going to be teammates, maybe even friends.

All around her, the same operation was taking place between various boxers: Gravity saw Monster and Nakima slipping their bracelets to Genya and Svetlana. Lefty did not need one because he had his brother's fake ID, and D-Minus did not need one because he had somehow gotten a VIP press pass that let him in everywhere.

Inside, it was dark and hot. The bar was at the back, three people deep. In front were the DJ booth and dance floor, pulsing in a pool of lasers and fog machine smoke. She and Kaylee pushed through the crowd by the door and made their way to the corner of the bar where Sacred stood, looking like a sexy sci-fi heroine in her skintight gold jumpsuit.

"Thank you!" Gravity yelled over the music, passing back Sacred's bracelet.

"Ahoy, matey!" yelled Kaylee, who was always making pirate jokes. "How's the briny deep?"

Sacred lifted her glass of orange juice to indicate the area on the dance floor where a gorgeous Jamaican superheavy-weight was dancing in a pool of light.

"Too bad he can't fight," Sacred yelled.

Kaylee said, "Maybe he can do other things."

She grabbed one of the free bottles of PLASMAFuel off the bar and made a gesture so obscene that they all broke up laughing. Sacred laughed so hard the orange juice went up her nose.

"How about them?" Gravity cried, pointing to the sharp-dressed sons of a famous boxer from Omaha. Identical twins, one competed at lightweight, one at light welter. They stood out from the dance floor like a special effect.

"Hot," Kaylee said. "*And* they can fight."

"Nah." Sacred shook a finger. "Too tiny. I never go below junior middle."

They laughed again. Gravity looked from Kaylee to Sacred, letting it sink in that she would get to travel around the world with these two. She could not remember ever feeling this happy.

"Speaking of tiny, *your* boyfriend is sexy," Kaylee said.

She nodded toward where D-Minus was holding court in the middle of the bar. Gravity was positive he had seen her come in, but he was refusing to meet her eyes.

"He's not my boyfriend," she told Kaylee.

Why did everyone think she and D were an item? At the moment, he wasn't even speaking to her. She maneuvered herself closer until she could catch the end of D's rant: "Fuck the amateurs. I'm turning pro."

"Yo, they *violated* you," Genya said.

Boca took a swig off his Corona and said, "They always screw us. They *hate* New York fighters here."

Gravity sighed. Incredibly, the story among her team now

126

seemed to be that D-Minus had deserved the decision against Tiger Biggs. Gravity had refused to join in with that bullshit. As a result, everybody was giving her the cold shoulder.

None of them had even come to watch her fight that night. It hurt her feelings, but beating Aaliyah the first time had been the hard part; tonight had been like walking in tracks already stomped down in the snow. She touched the gold medal hanging against her chest and told herself it didn't matter. She worked her way back to Sacred and Kaylee.

Lefty had joined them. His white guayabera glowed under the black light as he leaned back against the bar sipping an enormous goblet filled with blue liquid, sliced fruit, and a plastic monkey. Gravity expected him to ice her out like the rest of the team, but instead he lifted his drink and yelled, "There she is! Great fight, champ!"

Gravity was surprised. "You saw it?"

"*Claro!* How'm I gonna write songs about you if I don't do research?" He extended the glass to her. "Here, have a Screaming Orgasm."

Gravity was tempted to ask if it had alcohol, but she didn't want to look like a nerd in front of everybody. She was touched that Lefty had come out to support her when everybody else was being so lame.

Sometimes, right before she broke things, she got a premonition of disaster. This was not the case with the Screaming Orgasm. Even after the plastic monkey stabbed her in the pad of the thumb, she still thought she could recover, but the sides of the goblet were slick with condensation, and she was still fatigued from her fight. The cocktail made an impressive sound as it smashed against the club floor.

Everyone stared.

"You a mess," Sacred said, laughing.

Kaylee asked the bartender for napkins so she could swab the deck.

Gravity rummaged in her pocket so she could pay Lefty back, but he told her to chill. He pulled a silver flask out of his back pocket and took a swig.

He winked. "Always have a Plan B."

"Come on, let's dance," said Sacred.

Kaylee had already started to shimmy in place in her ruffled yellow sundress.

"Wanna dance, Left?" Gravity asked.

"Not yet," he said. "I'll just stay here and admire your beauty."

Sacred led them out into the sea of fog and disco lights. They danced over into the circle formed by Marisol Bonilla, Aisha Johnson, Aaliyah Williams, Nakima Fanning, and Kiki Mailer. Everybody smiled and parted to admit them. Gravity felt a little awkward seeing Aaliyah again so soon after their two battles, but the other woman smiled at her warmly and reached across to clasp her hand, yelling, "Good fight, baby."

Gravity was glad Melsy had told her to pack nice clothes. She had on her cutest pair of jeans, the ones with the rhinestones on the butt, and a gold wrap sweater that left her stomach showing. All the boxers looked beautiful. There is no dance floor in the world better than one filled with boxers and trainers after the fights are done.

Aisha Johnson, in a hot-pink minidress and platform heels, stepped into the center of the circle and started twerking. The silver medal bounced against her chest and everybody cracked up and cheered. She danced her way back out, pointing at Gravity.

This was a tough act to follow, but Gravity shimmied to

the circle's center and closed her eyes, waiting for the music to find her feet. Dancing was the one thing both sides of her family enjoyed. Her mother danced by throwing her hands in the air and jumping up and down like a kid in a bounce house. Tyler imitated robots. Auntie Rosa could dance salsa and bachata really well. Melsy preferred EDM. The one thing Gravity's whole family had in common was that they danced like nobody was watching.

That was why it was such a surprise to find out that someone was. When she danced her way back out, tagging in Marisol, someone hugged her from behind and whispered in her ear, "Nice moves. Got any Puerto Rican in you?"

It was Lefty, who knew she was Dominican, so she didn't understand why he was asking that.

She said, "No."

He said, "Want some?"

"Ew!" She pulled back and narrowed her eyes at him. "Don't be gross."

He laughed. "Sorry. It's just, that's the worst pickup line I ever heard. I always wanted to try it. Your turn."

"My turn for what?"

"To try to pick me up with a terrible line."

"What if I don't want to pick you up?"

"Then it's a good thing it's terrible!"

She laughed. "Okay. If I told you that you had a beautiful body, would you hold it against me?"

"Nice one!" He gave her a high five. "If I told you that *you* had a beautiful body, I'd be telling the truth. Do you know why southpaws make better lovers?"

"Why?"

"Come find out."

She laughed.

Lefty moved his eyes up and down her body. "Look at you, all grown up and winning everything."

Gravity blushed. "Stop."

"What?" he said. "A man can't look?"

So she looked too. The disco lights glistened off the diamonds in his ears. Next to his right eye, a butterfly bandage covered the cut he had gotten in his brave stand against the puncher from Kronk. It looked cute there, like a little kiss.

The DJ put on some Marc Anthony.

Gravity's body felt so soft all of a sudden. When Lefty hooked a finger through one of the belt loops on her jeans and pulled, she let him. They stood like that for five heartbeats, their bodies almost touching.

She could smell his cologne beneath the sweet smell of whatever he had in his flask. He took a half step back and, with incredible gentleness, guided her left hand to his shoulder and clasped her right in his. With his other hand on her waist, he began to move her body with the music.

"You don't know how to salsa," he said.

She tried to pull away, embarrassed, but he wouldn't let her. "Shh. Just follow."

It was harder than merengue but not that bad if she looked down and mirrored the motion of his Vans. Lefty counted softly in her ear. She glanced over his shoulder to see if D-Minus or anyone else had noticed, but as soon as she looked around, her feet got messed up.

Lefty scolded her and pulled her close. He slid his hand from the side of her waist to her hip bone. She slid her hand from his shoulder to the nape of his neck, where his hair was buzzed close. He reached around toward the back pocket of her jeans.

Maybe he *would* write a song about her. It would mostly be about boxing, but there would be romance in it too.

"Here."

He slipped something into her hand. She looked down and saw that it was the flask. A bit of liquid sloshed around in the bottom.

"What is it?" she asked.

"Just drink."

He had salsaed them off into the darkness and relative quiet at the back of the dance floor. Gravity sniffed at the mouth of the flask. It smelled like dessert. She put it to her lips and sipped. It was delicious.

"Good, huh?" said Lefty. "Amaretto."

"Tray's drink," Gravity said.

"How did you know that?" He looked at her with surprise and sudden sadness.

Lefty had been best friends with Tray. Boo Boo said he had taken his death really hard, maybe even harder than D.

"From your tribute song 'Brother's Keeper.' I liked that part where you talk about how, when you were little, you could only afford one pair of gloves, so you wore the left one and he wore the right one, and you sparred inside a chalk square on the stoop. It felt like I was there." She blushed, remembering the part about how Lefty and Tray would make love to different girls side by side in the same bed.

"Dang, Gravity. Thanks."

His eyes were so dark and sad. Gravity looked down at her flats. She always wore flats, because she was taller than a lot of boys her age. Lefty was exactly her height, though, so they were eye to eye, and she was afraid to gaze at him too long. It was like a staredown in the ring, only something other than a fight was going to break out.

She wished she could think up an excuse to touch him again. Some girls were so good at that. Melsy was always touching everyone. She would laugh and set her hand gently on your arm in a way that made you feel special. Gravity didn't know how to do that. She tried to remember how it had started with Keeshawn that one time in the subway.

She said, "I always wanted to ask you. At the end of your song about Salvador Sánchez, I get this funny feeling in my stomach, thinking about Wilfredo Gómez doing drugs in the bathroom of the Boxing Hall of Fame. It's, like, kind of funny? But it's sad at the same—"

He kissed her. Gravity was so surprised that she tried to back away, but he had her in the corner, so there was no place to go.

"Irony," he said. "That's called irony."

A thousand pleasures and a thousand worries battled in her mind—Had she remembered to brush her teeth? What would Fatso think if he knew? What about D-Minus?—but then Lefty moved his hands from her rib cage downward, and she lost all the strength in her legs. She let out a little whimper and reached out for him, and he held her there, pinned to the wall, his knee between her legs and his tongue between her teeth and his warm hands everywhere.

After a while, she felt a sharp object pressing the seam of her jeans. When she looked down, she saw it was a keycard.

"Western New England went home," he whispered. "But their rooms are booked through the end of the tournament."

This feels better than boxing, she thought.

Then she stopped thinking altogether.

Chapter Sixteen

Gravity sighed and rolled onto her side. She pulled a braid across her nostrils and inhaled his cologne, which still lingered in her hair. She reached over onto the nightstand for her gold medal and lay there, just holding it and basking in the quiet and the sunshine coming through the sheer drapes.

Once they had gotten their clothes off, she'd told him, "You're prettier than me."

He hadn't argued; she hadn't minded. Each of his tattoos had a story, and he told her all of them.

She had told him it was her first time, and he seemed happy about that. It only hurt a little, right at the beginning.

Putting the medal on so it lay heavy between her breasts, she felt a delicious laziness all over. Coach told his male fighters, "Women weaken legs." He said if they had sex before a fight, they would go in vulnerable. Gravity wondered if that applied to females, too.

It was true that something felt loose in her quadriceps. She didn't feel like fighting or doing roadwork. Rolling out of bed, she padded over to the bathroom mirror.

She looked just the same, apart from the gold medal. She wasn't sure what she'd thought would be different. Her eyes maybe. Maybe she should look more sexy or grown. Like a woman, not a girl. But she was still the same old Gravity: the black-brown eyes that were too small and squinty; the gap between her two front teeth; the broad nose that was good for boxing, because it never broke and hardly ever bled. Her hair was fuzzy now at the scalp where it escaped from the braids. High on her left cheekbone was a tiny bruise from the bout against Paloma, and there was a new mark on her right eyebrow from the rematch with Aaliyah.

She smiled, remembering how Lefty had kissed it and said it looked pretty.

No, it wasn't that she looked any different. It was that she *felt* different. On the inside. More alive.

As she headed down to the buffet, she was halfway hoping everybody would have already eaten and left. The sight of them lingering over empty cereal bowls set her heart pounding. She had no idea what to expect.

Would Lefty ignore her and act like nothing had happened? Worse, would he have gossiped? Would they all slut-shame her?

Everyone was there: D-Minus, sulking; Svetlana, bent over her cell phone; Genya, wearing his own gold medal and holding an ice pack to his neck; Monster, editing photos on the new laptop Andre had given him; Fatso, reading *The Book of Five Rings*; Boca, reorganizing his trainer's bag; and, leaning back in his chair with his long legs stretched out, Lefty.

When he looked up at her with those dark eyes, Gravity felt an ache beneath her gold medal, as though he was squeezing her heart. For all the time they had spent together, she felt like she understood less about him than before. She wanted to learn what made his eyes so sad and what his family was like and where he got the ideas for his songs.

"Hey, boo," he said. "I saved you some Cap'n Crunch."

He uncrossed his legs and indicated that she should sit in his lap.

Gravity was stunned. Of all the things he could have done, this was the least expected. She couldn't help glancing across at D-Minus. He met her eyes with a glare of such intense hatred that she froze momentarily. All the other boys were studiously avoiding her eyes, but Fatso lifted up his tiny reading glasses and studied her, a look of mild distaste on his face. Gravity wanted to turn around and go back to her room, but then Svetlana looked at her and smiled encouragement.

Gravity crossed the room in a kind of trance and sat down in Lefty's lap. She tried not to let on how good it made her feel.

Fatso said sarcastically, "How'd you sleep, champ?"

"Good."

He slid the milk in her direction. Gravity studied Fatso's face, trying to think of some way to get back whatever status she had lost, but she could not come up with a game plan. Lefty wrapped his hands around her waist.

She supposed Fatso would get over it. They all would. Everyone had accepted Svetlana and Boo Boo being a couple.

"Don't take too much time to celebrate," Fatso told her. "You have Continentals soon."

Gravity shoveled cereal into her mouth, suddenly enormously hungry. "I know. I'm gonna stay on weight."

Lefty whispered in her ear: "Eat up. We got that room for three more hours."

Chapter Seventeen

Gravity stood before her apartment, keys in one hand, luggage in the other. She unzipped her jacket so the gold medal showed. As the national champion, she would get a monthly stipend of two thousand dollars. Her life was going to be better and different from now on.

She took a deep breath and unlocked her front door. Inside, it was dark, and it smelled bad, like rotting food.

"Mom? Ty?" she called.

Gravity went to switch off the television, and that was when she saw her mother, lying on the floor next to the sofa, unmoving. The baby quilt Auntie Rosa had made for Tyler stretched across her face.

For a moment, blind terror seized Gravity. Then her mother snored.

"Mom?"

Gravity shook her gently, then more vigorously.

"Mom! I'm home! I won!"

More snores. Gravity glanced around the apartment, noting the empty vodka bottles and Chinese takeout containers scattered across the coffee table. A half-full jug of Gallo burgundy next to her mother's head held a drowned cockroach.

Gravity pulled out her phone to text her cousin that she

was home. She cracked a window and began to clean, deliberately banging the wine jug down on the counter and letting the cabinet doors slam, but her mother did not stir. She dragged all the trash into the hall, held open the wedge-shaped door of the trash chute, and stared down into it.

When she was a little girl, that chute had fascinated her. She'd had fantasies of climbing inside it with Tyler and sliding way, way down to land softly in a big pile of trash. And then a truck would come and take them to a boat, and the boat would take them somewhere their mother could never find them.

She let the chute fall closed and went back inside, where she knelt down to scoop her mother up off the floor. Recoiling at her sour breath, she slid her onto the couch, smoothed her hair back from her face, and tucked the quilt in around her.

"Well, Mom," she said bitterly. "I did it. I'm the national champion. See?"

As she shook her medal in front of her mother's closed eyes, Gravity was seized with an almost uncontrollable urge to strike her. One sharp smack across that milky skin. Those long, delicate eyelashes snapping open in shock. Paying attention, for one split second, to the fact of Gravity's existence.

A lot of moms would feel lucky to have a daughter who was the best in the country at something. Boo Boo's mom was making Svetlana a whole big barbecue, and she hadn't even won.

Gravity stood before the living room window, pulling out the dead leaves in her mother's spider plants, then went back and forth from the sink to the window until they all got enough water. She stared out the window at the dull courtyard of their apartment, thinking about Sonny Liston.

One time, when Gravity had complained to Coach about her mother never coming to her fights, Coach had said that if Gravity thought she had it hard, she ought to feel lucky she wasn't Sonny Liston. Sonny's dad had twenty-five kids and beat them so hard they got scars. Coach said Sonny had gone to jail and knocked heads for the Mob and that all the pain in Sonny's heart came out the hammers of his hands.

Together they had watched the YouTube video of Sonny Liston's demolition of Floyd Patterson to win the heavyweight championship of the world. The fight was in Chicago in 1962. On the plane home to Philadelphia, Sonny rehearsed the speech he had written for all the people who would be there when he landed to congratulate him. It was a speech about the American dream.

The plane landed at the airport and Sonny stepped out, ready to address the crowd. Except there was no crowd. The runway was bare. People didn't want a black heavyweight champion who had been to jail. That wasn't *their* American dream.

When Gravity dropped off her luggage in her bedroom, she saw her empty trophy case. It was bare. All of it was gone: her Silver Gloves trophies, her PAL Nationals cup, even the plaque she had gotten for volunteering every Thanksgiving at the food pantry. For a moment, her vision went starry, and she clutched her gold medal until it dug into the flesh of her hand. When her sight returned, all she could feel was rage.

She was going to *kill* her mother.

She was going to kill her with her bare hands.

Her phone chirped. It took her a moment to hear it through the pounding of her blood. She pulled it out of her pocket and blinked at it, her hands shaking so badly it was hard to dial in the passcode: 1009, Tyler's birthday.

It was Melsy.

Hey cuz welcome home!!! Come asap we have pizza.

Gravity had started to reply when another text came in.

Don't freak out, we have your trophies. Hurry pizza getting cold.

Gravity took a long, shaky breath and slid the phone back into her pocket. She walked through the living room, keeping her eyes averted from her mother, and straight out into the night. Past the Cyclone roller coaster and the kiddie rides at Luna Park, she lingered on the boardwalk a moment, breathing in the cold sea air and willing herself to be calm.

Her phone chirped again. This time it was Lefty, who had gone to Boo Boo's barbecue and was texting party pictures. She scrolled through them, feeling sorry for herself and jealous of Svetlana, until she got to the last picture and almost dropped the phone. It was a dick pic. It looked like he had taken it in Boo Boo's bathroom.

Gravity stared at it, shocked, before deleting it. Then she went to the deleted pictures and stared at it some more. He was holding himself in one hand, hard, while he took the selfie with the other. In the background, you could see Boo Boo's little brother Nigel's action figures lined up on the side of the tub. Lefty had added the caption Thinking of you and a heart-eyes emoji.

Why would he *do* that?

She closed her eyes and remembered the smell of it, like baby powder and musk. The feel of it in her hands, surprisingly hard yet so warm and alive. The feeling of it inside her, filling her up. Then she opened her eyes and looked at it again.

It was just kind of *weird*-looking. The hottest part, actually, was his hand. Maybe if he'd cropped out the bath mat? Or made it black-and-white? Everything looked better in black-and-white.

That made her think of what Monster had said, about how all the boxers in her gym looked better in black-and-white except for D-Minus, who could pull off color. She smiled as D's face came to her imagination: those high cheekbones, those changeable eyes. She knew what Monster meant: D was just drawn in brighter colors than the rest of them. Then she felt embarrassed, because it was weird to think about D-Minus while looking at Lefty's dick. She emptied the Recently Deleted folder and jogged to the subway.

Chapter Eighteen

Her auntie lived in a tiny, bright one-bedroom in Washington Heights, high up on a winding street by Fort Tryon Park. It was an hour and a half by subway. Totally worth it when she saw what her family had done for her.

"Surprise!" yelled Melsy.

"Surprise!" yelled Tyler.

They leapt from the sofa when they saw her and started blowing noisemakers and jumping up and down. There were homemade banners taped up all around the living room that said "Welcome Home, Champ" with screen grabs printed out from the livestreams of her fights that showed her landing shots on Svetlana, Paloma, and Aaliyah.

And "pizza" had been an understatement, because in addition to two enticingly greasy boxes from Como, Gravity saw a stack of pupusas from the Salvadoran place, a roast chicken, yucca with onions, her auntie's famous coconut rice, a Caesar salad, Krispy Kremes, a platter of cheese cubes and grapes, a butterscotch pie, and a bowl of shrimp cocktail.

Ty barreled into her so hard that she staggered backward, laughing, and bonked her head on the door. Next came Melsy, smelling of honey and melting into her arms. As her cool, soft cheek pressed against Gravity's, she murmured, "You can start your diet tomorrow."

"Is that pizza?" Gravity said. "It better have black olives and onions!"

"Ew, gross!" yelled Tyler. He had this thing about black olives looking like cockroaches, and he viewed onions as a personal insult.

"I got one with black olives and one with sausage," said Melsy diplomatically. She opened the boxes and slid succulent greasy slices onto paper plates.

"Why'd you take so long!" Tyler said. "The food got cold and Auntie Rosa fell asleep!"

"Sorry." Gravity stroked his hair, which was buzzed on the sides into a subtle Mohawk and felt crisp with styling gel: clearly Melsy's influence. "I just needed to straighten up a little at home."

Everyone was quiet for a moment as they attacked the pizza. Gravity double-fisted her slice with a pupusa while working in occasional cubes of Swiss cheese. All her big talk about staying on weight melted in the face of this onslaught of deliciousness. Tomorrow was another day.

Midway into Auntie Rosa's famous coconut rice, Tyler blurted out, "Melsy made me stay here the *whole time* you were away. It's a *long ride* to school."

Gravity looked at Melsy, who mimed gulping from a bottle.

"That was very nice of Melsy and Auntie Rosa to let you stay," Gravity said.

"They *made* me," Tyler insisted, turning on the PlayStation. "But I made them take all your trophies so Mom wouldn't steal anything else."

Gravity laughed. "Good boy."

"Come on, Gra Gra, play with me," Tyler said, passing her a controller.

She slid onto the couch next to him and they began a game of *Hell Slayer 3*.

"Remember about the asps," she warned him.

"Duh," he said.

He always played the Paladin, and she played the Barbarian; they made a good team. The undead asps slithered across their path, and Tyler took them out with his flying knives. The same thing happened with the wave of wraiths and then the killer bats.

Gravity didn't see the swamp ghoul until it had taken a huge bite out of her thigh.

"God*damn*, cuz!" said Melsy.

Blood spattered across the screen as her stamina dropped to eight percent, but Tyler stormed over, killed the ghoul, and cast a healing spell. The PlayStation chimed with a happy little tune.

"Wow," Gravity said. "You got so *good*, Ty Ty!"

"I practiced."

"It's, like, all he ever does," said Melsy. "That and polish your trophies."

They were almost at the main boss, Sabado. When he was little, Tyler used to wake Gravity up in the middle of the night and want to cuddle because he had nightmares that Sabado had come to life. Now he didn't seem scared at all. It was like he'd grown up overnight. He leapt over the drawbridge with a showy front flip and marched across the moldering carpet that led to the throne of bones. Gravity didn't even have time to go into a battle rage. At the perfect moment, Tyler threw a dagger at Sabado's midsection, right where a boxer would throw a left hook to the liver.

One of the best features of *Hell Slayer 3* was the death throes. First Sabado's brain exploded. Then his body rotted away into maggots and flies. At the end, all that was left was his bone ax and a pile of rings from the fingers in his hair.

Tyler let out a whoop of triumph as he and Gravity materialized in Level Two, the Citadel of Chaos.

There was a stirring by the bedroom, and Gravity looked up to see Auntie Rosa in the hallway, smiling and watching them. She was wearing a silk kimono. Her hair was up in rollers and her sleepy eyes were full of kindness. Rosa had the same kind of beauty as her daughter, but softer and more world-weary. She had to get up very early for her job as a Starbucks barista and was always sleepy.

"Welcome home, Gra Gra," she said.

Gravity said, "Thanks for all the food, Auntie Rosa! Thanks for making coconut rice. I know how much work that is."

Gravity went over to her aunt and hugged her gently. Rosa always felt so soft, like there were no bones at all in her body.

"We watched every fight," she said, pulling back to cup Gravity's face in her hands. She traced a finger along Gravity's cheek, lightly touching the tiny bruise that remained on one cheekbone. "It's hard sometimes, mi vida. To see you get hit. Does it hurt?"

"Nah," Gravity lied.

Considering how tough the tournament had been, she had come through without much damage. The headache after her bout against Paloma had only lasted an hour, and her neck was almost back to normal now.

"Gravity's tough," Tyler announced.

Auntie Rosa smiled. She picked up a pupusa and looked at it. "You get that from your father."

"Was our dad tough too?" Tyler asked.

Gravity blushed, hearing the hunger in his voice. She and Tyler had given up on trying to get Mom to talk about Dad. The only thing she would do was insult him. Auntie Rosa was also generally closemouthed on the subject of her brother, but she would give them useful information sometimes: sweet little tidbits like the fact that he had played semipro baseball in Santo Domingo, was a great cook, and could fix almost anything.

"Oh yes," Rosa said. "Your father . . . he stuck to his guns. Your mother is stubborn, too. So . . ." She spread her arms and a sad look came over her face.

Gravity always got the sense that Auntie Rosa thought the breakup had been Mom's fault. Certainly their aunt had a better way with men than their mother. Melsy's dad was still in the picture, and Rosa had various boyfriends who came over with little gifts and sat around drinking coffee and fixing things in the apartment. These men always filled Gravity with a vague longing. It would have been so good for Tyler to have a male role model. But Mom was so volatile that nobody stayed around for very long.

Tyler was sitting up very straight on the couch, the controller forgotten in his lap, hoping for more information, but Rosa glided across the living room to pull a cardboard carton from underneath the coffee table. She extracted a T-shirt from the box and shook it out.

Gravity felt her heart melt. Auntie Rosa was really creative. There was hardly any kind of art she didn't do: she made stained-glass boxes, and pottery, and she had a silkscreen machine for making personalized T-shirts. This one was black with "Gravity 'Doomsday' Delgado" in white lettering on the front in a cool retro font. Underneath it was a picture of Gravity's face, drawn like she was a comic-book character. There was a little Star of David on one sleeve and the Dominican flag on the other and a big American flag on the back with a rainbow arcing over it and the words "Olympic Trials Champion." Instead of a pot of gold, the rainbow ended in the Olympic rings.

"It's beautiful, Auntie!" Gravity exclaimed, kissing her soft cheek.

"I made a lot," said Auntie Rosa, yawning. She tossed Tyler a size small and Gravity a medium. "You can sell them to raise money for Rio."

"I need to qualify first," Gravity said, feeling a tiny ripple of anxiety.

"Oh, you'll qualify," said Melsy. "And I'll wear my shirt in Brazil when I watch you win gold."

Auntie Rosa sank into the purple armchair and fell back asleep, the pupusa still in her hand.

Tyler whined, "I want to know about Dad."

Gravity rubbed his back and said, "We'll ask her later, okay? Now why don't you go brush your teeth and get ready for bed? Paladins need sleep so they can kill more zombies tomorrow."

He looked like he wanted to argue, but Gravity gave him her sternest stare and said, "Don't make me go into my battle rage," and he stomped off to the bathroom.

After he had gone, Melsy launched into a state of the union address about her love life. Gravity made herself focus so she could stay up to date.

"My current fave is Colin. He's so generous. He took me to the opera the other night, and there was an elephant onstage! Although maybe that's cruelty to animals."

146

Gravity smiled politely. She thought Colin was bougie, and he talked too much about his mother.

"Then there's always Corey. He's my break-in-case-of-emergency guy. He's *so* sweet."

Gravity blushed. Her cousin had told her some extremely intimate details about Corey. He was a vegan personal trainer, and Melsy said he was proof that animal protein was not necessary for superior performance.

"Jerome and Earl are always in the running, of course, but they're both so flaky. If you want to get with me, you have to return my texts within the hour. I don't know what's with these young boys and their nonchalance. That's why college men are better."

Gravity didn't remember Jerome or Earl. "I can't keep track of all your boys," she said.

Melsy sighed theatrically. "Sometimes I can't either. That's why I never yell out a man's name during sex. I might get it wrong, and that's embarrassing. You can't go wrong with papi."

They both giggled.

"What's so funny?" Tyler demanded.

Gravity and Melsy stopped laughing, guiltily, and looked at him. He was just about the cutest thing in the world, with his square little-man face and pudgy belly. He was wearing his *Cars* pajamas, and his short, dark hair, still crispy with styling gel, was all mussed up. His eyes were red at the corners.

"I wanna know," he said.

"*You* are!" Gravity said. She tackled him in a hug and lifted him up in the air, staggering a little under his weight. He was almost too big now to lift. "You're the funniest kid ever."

He squirmed. "Am not!"

"Are too." She set him back down and went in for the tickle, right where it always got him. Melsy joined in, and soon he was wriggling with delight on the couch, yelling, "Stop! Help! Auntie Rosa! Make them stop!"

Auntie Rosa opened her eyes and told them to turn out the light. Tyler yawned and laid his head down in Gravity's lap. Melsy flitted about, gathering cups and putting the left-over shrimp cocktail in the fridge.

When she was very sure that Tyler had fallen asleep, Gravity told her cousin about Lefty.

Melsy quit straightening up and came and sat next to her. She took Gravity's hand.

"Wow. Congratulations, cuz," she said. "I'm surprised, though. I always thought you and D . . ."

"No!" Gravity said, blushing furiously. She thought of how mean D had been to her in Spokane, how he had glared at her when he saw her with Lefty.

"So?! Ya dime, G. How was it?"

Gravity closed her eyes. "It was great. He was . . . great." She opened them again and looked at Melsy shyly. "I feel like it's all I want to do."

Melsy nodded. "Join the club. They say boys think about sex more than girls, but I don't see how that's possible."

They both laughed.

Tyler's eyes popped open. "What's so funny?"

"Go back to sleep," Gravity said, stroking his cheek.

His eyes stayed stubbornly open. "Show me the pictures," he demanded.

"Oh, I left them at home, Ty Ty. Here, I'll pull them up on my phone."

"Mom will steal them!" he said with alarm, sitting upright.

"Shh, shh." She pulled him back to her and showed him the first one, of their father cradling her in his arms. "Why would she steal them? They're not worth anything to anybody except me and you."

He sniffed. "And *Dad*. They're worth something to Dad."

"Yeah. And Dad."

" 'Cause he loved us so much. That's why he's smiling at me like that. But I'm crying 'cause I pooped."

She chuckled. "And here you are at the zoo."

Melsy looked confused and bent over the phone. "But that's not—"

Gravity silenced her with a reduced-strength boxing glare.

"Dad and I loved to go to the zoo together," Tyler told Melsy. "Our favorite animal is the lion because the lady lions do all the work and all he has to do is make cubs and roar."

"Sounds like feminism needs to come to the lion kingdom," Melsy said. She gave Gravity a long, disapproving look.

Gravity looked down at Tyler and back up at her, shrugging, as if to say, "What can I do? You see how happy it makes him."

Melsy shook her head.

"And here you are playing video games. That must be why you're so good at them. You started young."

His eyelids fluttered as he gazed at the picture. "Was Dad cheap like Mom?"

Gravity cocked her head. That was another new one. Mom said Dad owed her a hundred thousand dollars in child support, but Gravity remembered the pockets of his leather jacket being deep, filled with colored rubber bands for her hair, silver dollars, and butterscotch candy. He had shown up at Gravity's eighth-birthday party with so many toys he could barely knock on the door. She felt that old familiar ache inside her, like a wound that would never heal.

"Oh no," she told Tyler. "He was very generous."

But he was already asleep.

Chapter Nineteen

Coach bellowed, "There she is! My champ!"

Gravity felt her heart pound with love as she scooted behind the timekeeper and the bell and the judges to the end of the first row ringside at the Barclays Center, where Coach always parked his chair. Nobody ever challenged his right to sit there, even if his actual ticket was for way up in the stands. He was a rolling VIP section.

When she bent to kiss his cheek, her gold medal banged against his chest and he laughed and grabbed it, holding her there for a moment and thumping her back with his jabbing hand.

When he let her go, he said, "What did I tell you, eh?"

"Yes, sir," she said, glowing.

"Light work!" he proclaimed.

"Light work," she said, laughing, because it had not been light work at all. It had been the hardest work of her life.

She knelt down next to his chair, glancing up at the bleachers, where Auntie Rosa and Tyler were sitting in the free seats Mr. Rizzo had given them. Lefty, Sveta, and their families were a few rows over. Sveta was especially dressed up tonight, since Boo Boo was fighting.

A passing usher scolded, "Miss, we can't have you blocking the aisle like that."

She stood up, apologizing, but Coach cleared his throat.

"Coach!" The usher knelt down on the stadium floor. "I'm so sorry! I didn't see you there."

"How are you, Herbert?" Coach asked.

"Another day, another dollar. Got anyone tonight?"

"Boo Boo trains with us. Red corner in the co-main."

The usher gazed up at the illumined ring and said dreamily, "That coulda been me."

Something about his voice made Gravity sad, but Coach just shook his finger at the man. "None of that, Herbert. Regrets are like roaches. Exterminate them before they multiply."

The usher nodded. "You oughta see my son shadowbox. How old they gotta be to train?"

"Old enough to listen," said Coach softly. Gravity thought maybe he was a little sad too.

The usher rose slowly to his feet and patted Gravity on the shoulder. "You stay there as long as you want, miss." As he walked off to help more patrons, he turned back and said, "Oh, and Coach? I leave D-Minus be because I know he's one of yours, but can you please tell him not to keep hitting on the ring card girls?"

Coach shook his head and murmured, "Such a waste of talent." At first Gravity thought he was talking about D, but then he said, "Herbert could have beaten any heavyweight in the top ten right now."

"What happened?" she asked.

"He got married."

"Oh."

Gravity didn't see what that had to do with anything. If she married Lefty, it would be good for their boxing. He could work her corner and travel with her to tournaments. Not that she wanted to get married, but still. Thinking about it gave her a warm feeling.

"Would you like bout sheets, Mr. Thomas? *Campeona?*" said a musical voice.

The emerald ring glinted on her finger as the proprietress of *Boxing for Girls* handed Gravity and Coach pieces of paper listing all the fighters' vital details, down to the color of their trunks.

"Oh, there's women fighting!" Gravity exclaimed.

"*Claro!*" said Carmen. "That's why I flew in. And to cheer on José David. I know him from back home in Bogotá."

BOUT SHEET
February 19, 2016

Bout 1: 4 Rounds, Middleweights

KENDER SAINT-SAVEUR	STEVE ZEHNTNER
156 lb/6'/20 yrs	155 lb/5'6"/28 yrs
Brooklyn, NY	Des Moines, Iowa
Red/White	Silver
Pro Debut	0-2

Bout 2: 4 Rounds, Heavyweights

LONNIE SIAKI	SAM VENTURA
246 lb/6'5"/21 yrs	272 lb/5'11"/33 yrs
Brooklyn, NY	Des Moines, Iowa
White/Blue	Leopard
Pro Debut	1-5, 1 KO

Bout 3: 6 2-Min Rounds, Female Bantamweights

SHERIKA HILL	ERIN SROKA
118 lb/5'5"/26 yrs	118.5 lb/5'3"/33 yrs
New York, NY	Durham, North Carolina
Gold/Black	Pink/White
5-1	2-6, 1 KO

Bout 4: 8 Rounds, Bantamweights

JORDAN CRUZ
119 lb/5'5"/19 yrs
Bronx, NY
Red/White/Blue
9-0-2, 6 KOs

PEDRO SOSA
118 lb/5'2"/22 yrs
Mexico City, Mexico
Purple/Gold
10-12-3, 7 KOs

Bout 5: 8 Rounds, Jr. Welterweights

JULIAN DE LA ROSA
140 lb/5'8"/24 yrs
Newark, NJ
White/Red
12-0, 8 KOs

TRUCK JACKSON
140 lb/5'9"/28 yrs
Mobile, Alabama
Black
3-6-1, 3 KOs

Bout 6: 10 Rounds, Cruiserweights

ISHMAEL HURLEY
192 lb/5'11"/25 yrs
Trenton, NJ
White/Red
15-1-1, 9 KOs

JOSE DAVID RUIZ
185 lb/5'9"/35 yrs
Medellín, Colombia
Yellow
3-6-1, 2 KOs

Bout 7: 12-Round Co-Main Event, Light Heavyweights
ABC Topaz World Championship

CLARENCE "BOO BOO" HARRISON JR
174 lb/6'/22 yrs
Brooklyn, NY
Blue/White
12-0, 10 KOs

SAMUEL ADESOGAN
175 lb/5'9"/22 yrs
Lagos, Nigeria
Yellow/Black
12-0, 3 KOs

Bout 8: 12-Round Main Event, Jr. Lightweights
ABC World Championship

JIMMY O'DONNELL	YOENIS MENENDEZ
130 lb/5'6"/25 yrs	129 lb/5'10"/34 yrs
Dublin, Ireland	Miami, Florida
Green/White/Orange	Red/White/Blue
25-1-1, 19 KOs	19-0, 6 KOs

"Boo Boo trains at your gym, I believe?" Carmen said, pulling out her little notepad. "Have you seen the opponent?"

"Of course I've seen him. I coached his trainers."

Carmen winked at Gravity. "I think your coach has trained everybody in New York except the Statue of Liberty."

Coach furrowed up his eyebrows, but Gravity could tell he was enjoying himself. Carmen was so beautiful tonight, in a little red dress with patent leather pumps. Coach always complained about the press, but everybody loves being interviewed. It's fun when someone asks you questions and writes down your answers. It's only afterward, when you read what you said in print, that you wish you had been more careful.

"The Nigerian is tough," Coach said. "But I expect Boo Boo'll stop him."

"It's a big step up in competition for them both."

Coach snorted. " 'Bout time. These days they don't put kids in with anybody who's got a pulse until their twentieth fight. How they supposed to learn?"

Gravity knew what he meant. Boo Boo's fight and the main event promised to be good matches, but the rest of it was garbage. The professional game was different than the amateurs. Everyone in the red corner, which was the left column on the bout sheet, was a prospect. They had managers and fans to support them and they got paid just to box. When she and D-Minus went pro, they would be like that, because they had Coach and Mr. Rizzo in their corners.

The fighters on the right side of the sheet were called journeymen. They worked as security guards and bouncers, took fights for chump change at short notice, and traveled far, sometimes without a trainer. It wasn't fixed, exactly, but it wasn't fair, either.

"Keep your eyes open in bout four," said Coach mysteriously.

"What do you mean?" Carmen leaned in, but Coach stabbed a finger at the notepad.

"This is off the record."

When you tell a writer that something is off the record, they aren't supposed to write about it. Carmen looked disappointed. She put the notepad back in her patent leather clutch.

Coach said, "That little Mexican is better than his record. He fights under a couple different names. Fatso saw him knock out an undefeated kid last month in Guadalajara."

A bell rang.

Gravity had seen the first fighter, Kender, sparring with Genya and Boo Boo. You could tell it was a mismatch just from looking at his opponent, Steve "The Iowa Chainsaw" Zehntner, who had a roll of flesh that hung out over the waistband of his old silver trunks.

"Send him home in a body bag!" yelled a red-faced man who had taken the seat next to Gravity.

She scooted closer to Coach, who was gazing into the ring serenely, as though watching a slightly boring nature show. Kender was pretty good. He was patient, and he mixed up the levels. At the end of the first round, Steve Zehntner's right eye was almost swollen shut.

During the break, a stunning blonde in a bikini printed all over with beer bottles walked around the ring in heels holding up a card that read "Round Two." The red-faced man next to Gravity whooped.

The blonde exited the ring and took a seat next to two other ring girls.

"Hey, cuz! Hey, Mr. Thomas!" Melsy waved at them, beaming.

"Well! Hello, young lady!" called Coach, waving back. "Well, now, doesn't she look sweet! You never told me your cousin worked the fights."

"It's her first time."

Someone from the promotional company had apparently found Melsy on Instagram and offered her three hundred dollars cash to be one of the ring girls tonight. Melsy had asked Gravity's permission, which was sweet, and Gravity hadn't seen how she could refuse.

Next to Coach, Fatso was regarding Melsy with the same look of distaste he had given Gravity at breakfast in Spokane when she sat in Lefty's lap. Fatso's wife wore a hijab, and Gravity had heard him deliver many lectures about modest Muslim dress.

Gravity had mixed feelings about ring card girls. On the one hand, they reminded you what round it was. On the other hand, it was kind of sexist. It wasn't like there were men in Speedos holding up the cards when women boxers fought. Of course, Melsy was gorgeous, and if she could make money off her gorgeousness, she should. But she had a lot of other things going for her too, and Gravity did not like the idea of her being on display for drunk douchebags.

Kender was taking his time breaking Steve Zehntner down, and soon Melsy was on. The heels were so high that Gravity held her breath, worried she would trip, but Melsy ducked through the ropes flawlessly and made a graceful round, holding the card aloft at each of the sides. The beer bottle bikini looked great on her, and she had gotten her hair done in big waves that hung down her back and gleamed blue-black under the lights. When she got in front of Gravity, she stuck out her tongue.

"She looks like a feisty one!" said the red-faced man.

Gravity went to sit with her auntie so she wouldn't get ejected for fighting in the stands.

Chapter Twenty

The plaza outside the Barclays Center was lit from below by spotlights set into the concrete and from above by the blue glow of the electronic billboards. As they streamed out of the arena, the boxers and fight fans lingered in raggedy packs, discussing the evening's violence.

The Cops 'n Kids crew posted up in their usual spot. Gravity kept one eye on D-Minus, who was showering Melsy with exaggerated compliments on her ring card skills, and the other eye on Tyler, who was playing with Boo Boo's kid brother, Nigel. The boys had two tiny Lego boxing figurines, one in red and one in blue, and they were running all over the plaza, making loud sound effects as they reenacted the evening's bouts and bumped into people.

The main event had been a snooze-fest won by the Miami Cuban, who was a prospect of the mysterious multi-millionaire manager Brian Jones, but Boo Boo's fight had been a thriller. He had pulled off a spectacular knockout that still had everyone talking.

"You look beautiful tonight, Gravity," said Boo Boo's dad, puffing on a victory cigar. "You should wear your hair like that more often."

"Thanks!" Gravity had taken out her cornrows, and her hair was like a lion's mane. Melsy had convinced her to bleach a few streaks and dye them bright red.

Mr. Rizzo caught Tyler and Nigel, who were pretending the little Lego boxers were Boo Boo and his opponent, just before they barreled into Coach's wheelchair.

"They need a Lego ref," he remarked dryly, turning his kind eyes on Gravity. He pressed some bills into her palm. "Here. Take a cab home. Your aunt looks real tired. She fell asleep in there for a second."

Gravity pocketed the bills. It felt like at least sixty dollars. "Thanks, Mr. Rizzo!"

Next to Mr. Rizzo, Boo Boo's mom was delivering a passionate tirade against the judging in amateur boxing. Auntie Rosa was pretending to be interested, but her eyes were fluttering open and closed. She had to be at Starbucks in Harlem tomorrow morning at five. Hopefully she would stay awake until they got in the subway. (Because they would definitely take the subway; Gravity never wasted the cab money Mr. Rizzo gave her on cabs. Sixty dollars bought a lot of groceries, and she still hadn't gotten her first stipend check from USA Boxing.)

Then Boo Boo arrived, and all other conversation stopped. He was beaming, surrounded by Boca, Genya, Svetlana, Kostya, Andre Vázquez, and Monster, who was taking pictures of everything.

Boo Boo was tall and powerful, but when he was happy, he grinned like a little boy. Gravity watched as he made the rounds with Boca, shaking everyone's hands and accepting their congratulations. He invited Melsy to feel his muscles, kissed Auntie Rosa's hand, and bent down over Coach's wheelchair for a hug.

"Good fight, young man," Coach said warmly. He put one of his big hands on Boo Boo's shoulder and looked over at Boca. "He did good."

Boca made his humble face.

Before Gravity had gotten to the gym, Boo Boo had trained with Coach too, but then he got lured away by Boca's swag, just like Monster and most of the other elite competitors. Gravity and D-Minus were the only serious fighters who had stayed loyal. Boo Boo always treated Coach with respect, though, and his face was eager now as he asked, "How'd I look in there, sir? That right hand was pretty good, huh?"

"Oooh-wee!" said Coach, swiping his hand through the air and breaking into a laugh. "Yes indeed. That was a *right hand*."

Everybody talked about Boo Boo's right hand. The Nigerian boxer had hurt Boo Boo badly in the first round and then again in the second. Thank God they hadn't stopped it, because Boo Boo had recovered and coldcocked the guy in the third. It was the kind of punch where you knew instantly that the fight was over. Boo Boo's dad said it was like a Riddick Bowe right hand. But Coach said no, it was more like Joe Louis.

Dreamy silence fell over their group at the mention of the great Joe Louis. When Coach was in a reminiscing mood, he would tell Gravity stories about what it had been like to spar the Brown Bomber; how mean his coach, Jack Blackburn, was; and how it felt to be on the receiving end of a Joe Louis jab: "Like a red-hot poker. You could feel it in the soles of your feet."

Melsy broke the silence to ask if Boo Boo's opponent was going to be all right, and Boca told her not to worry. The fight doctor had cleared him, and in the dressing room he had been walking and talking just fine.

"Shit," said D-Minus. "I hope he still remembers how to find Nigeria on a map."

Genya laughed and gave D-Minus a pound, and it was on. Gravity grinned. Watching those two mock the opposition was always a highlight of the evening.

"My man Africa went down like he was shot," said Genya.

"Word," said D-Minus. "He stayed down so long they set up a GoFundMe."

Genya doubled over in laughter. He said, "He needs humanitarian aid and shit."

"This was you, Boo Boo," said D-Minus. He mimed winding a right hand way up and then punching Genya in the face, yelling, "BAM!"

Genya dropped to the concrete, clutching his head and howling, "Mama! Mama! That big black man took my lunch money!"

D-Minus started laughing so hard he fell down on the concrete. He and Genya rolled around in hysterics. Every once in a while, one of them would say a new thing, like that Boo Boo's opponent had lost precious childhood memories or that he was going back to Africa in an ambulance, and they would both start howling again.

Soon everyone was cracking up, even Coach and Mr. Rizzo. Just when they had all finally stopped and D-Minus and Genya had gotten back up, Boo Boo's mom said, wonder in her voice, "That man did go down *hard*, though. He made a *loud sound* when he fell."

D-Minus and Genya hit the concrete again. Everybody cracked up, and Gravity laughed so hard her stomach hurt. Finally D-Minus sat up on his elbow, clutching his stomach in pain, and said, "Seriously, though, Boo Boo, you fucked that n—— up."

"Demetrius!" yelled Mr. Rizzo. "Language, please." He

spread his arms to indicate Nigel and Tyler, who were gazing at the big boys, wide-eyed.

"My bad," said D-Minus. He gave Nigel and Tyler high fives. "For real, though, Boo Boo. You fucked him up."

Mr. Rizzo sighed and shook his head.

Gravity watched D return to Melsy, a sweet smile on his face. Even though it was annoying that he was pushing up on her cousin, she was glad he was in a joking and flirting mood so soon after losing Qualifiers. His Olympic dream was over, and it made Gravity terribly sad for him, despite what a dick he had been to her in Spokane. She could not even imagine how he must feel. He was a better pure boxer than her. He was the best pure boxer of any of them.

The delicious smell of curry shook her out of her reverie. Fatso had returned from the roti truck with the traditional postfight snacks.

"She sold out of shrimp, so I got you boneless chicken," he said, handing one to Gravity.

It was heavy in her hand and big enough to feed both her and Ty. Roti were like the burritos of the Caribbean, with layers of spice that unfolded in your mouth like a long story.

"You gave me the wrong thing," complained Coach.

"No, that's yours," said Fatso nervously. "Channa and kale."

"What the hell is channa and kale?"

Fatso was avoiding Coach's eyes. "Channa is chickpeas. They're good for your pressure. Kale is a leafy green."

"It's good for endurance!" Melsy chirped.

"Get me meat and salt!" Coach roared. He pounded the side of his wheelchair so hard that Auntie Rosa, who had nodded off next to him, woke up with a start and yelled, "Grande soy latte!"

163

Fatso headed back to the roti truck, grumbling, "Don't blame me when you have a heart attack."

Tyler tugged on Gravity's wrist and whispered something in her ear.

She smiled. "Boo Boo! My brother wants to ask you something."

Tyler kicked her.

"Ow!" She rubbed her ankle. "What did you do that for?"

"*You* ask," he whispered.

"Go *on*," she said, pushing him toward Boo Boo. "He doesn't bite."

Tyler swallowed. He held out his program in both hands, craning his neck to look upward. "Can I please have your autograph, Mr. Boo Boo?"

Boo Boo grinned. "Of course, big man. Who's got a pen?"

Andre Vázquez produced a gold pen from inside his suit jacket, handing it to Boo Boo with a flourish. "Be careful, champ. That's a Montblanc. It cost five hundred dollars."

"Wow." Boo Boo took the pen carefully and signed Tyler's program. Then he said, "Hey, big man, don't you want everybody's signatures? You got the best team in New York right here!" Boo Boo counted off on his fingers. "One Women's Olympic Trials champion, two Men's Olympic Trials participants, and how many Golden Gloves champions— six?"

"Seven," said Lefty, appearing behind Gravity and murmuring in her ear, "Wanna sleep over?"

"I gotta get Ty and my family back to Washington Heights," she whispered back.

He touched her nose. "We'll drop them off on the way to the Bronx. My cousin drove the Escalade."

"Okay."

She watched Lefty walk away, a warm, wonderful feeling coming over her because she would get to be with him that night. She could not wait to see what his house looked like and lie with him in his bed.

As Tyler's program made the rounds, he kept his eyes on Boo Boo, at one point reaching out to touch the back of his hand with a fingertip, as though testing to see if he was real. When Boo Boo responded by ruffling Tyler's hair, her brother gazed up at him like a heart-eyes emoji.

Gravity had learned to hide her longing, but Tyler looked for dads everywhere. He preferred men who drove large vehicles like backhoes and bulldozers, but sometimes he branched out to athletes or men in uniform. It could get embarrassing, but not around her teammates. Most boxers were from broken homes, so they didn't judge. Even the toughest of them were gentle with little fatherless boys.

Gravity signed and gave the program back to Tyler, who immediately opened it up and looked at Boo Boo's signature, enraptured. It made her laugh. She walked over to Andre to hand back the gold pen. She felt a little sorry for him for having spent so much money on something so stupid, so she said, "It sure is heavy."

As he slid it back inside his suit jacket, he winked and said quietly, "My cock is heavy too, but I don't take it out and pass it around."

She blinked at him in astonishment. She looked over at Melsy, but she was busy taking a selfie with D-Minus. Andre met her eyes blankly, as though he hadn't said anything out of the ordinary. Gravity edged away from him and went to stand by Coach.

The pleasant warmth that had come over her was gone. She felt kind of cold inside. She pulled her winter jacket closer around herself.

Andre showily passed the pen to Monster and said, "Why don't *you* keep it, champ. You'll need it to sign that contract. Next time, that'll be *you* in the Barclays."

Everyone oohed and aahed over the generosity of the gift.

"What contract?" asked Coach sharply.

"Oh, didn't you hear?" said Boca. His voice was exaggeratedly casual. "We're going pro right after the Olympics. Andre here will be Monster's manager."

Coach let out an almost imperceptible laugh. He glanced at Monster and said, "Show it to a lawyer before you sign, young man."

Silence fell over the group. Gravity still had a gross feeling in the pit of her stomach from what Andre had said to her. Suddenly she just wanted to go home.

Finally Mr. Rizzo said, "Don't worry, Jefferson. I'd never let one of my kids sign anything without running it by my lawyers."

Coach grunted. He liked Mr. Rizzo; everyone did.

Andre cleared his throat and said, "How about that steak dinner, gentlemen?"

"We out!" announced Boca, waving his arm.

Svetlana kissed Gravity good night. Boo Boo gave Tyler a hug. The Bocacrew shouldered their PLASMAFuel duffel bags. To Gravity's horror, she saw Carmen Cruz emerge from the media door in her red dress and heels to take Andre's arm as they headed off into the night.

"I *hate* that guy Andre," Gravity said.

"Aw, he aight," said D-Minus.

"He is *not* all right," Gravity said. She wanted to tell them all what he had said to her, but she felt too ashamed.

"They'll ruin Monster," said Fatso.

"Bah," said Coach. "He'll do okay till the crossroads. They'll build him up easy, then cash him in."

Her phone chirped. It was Lefty, telling her to meet him across from Shake Shack. She woke up Auntie Rosa and collected Melsy and Ty, and they all piled into the Escalade.

Chapter Twenty-One

Gravity leaned back into the pillows, adjusting the plate of chicharrones so it did not interfere with her sight line.

"Babe," she said. "Scroll back like thirty seconds. I want to see that uppercut again."

Lefty kissed her cheek as he reached for the laptop. She sighed, watching him stretch across the bed, and ran a hand over the back of his bare thigh. He turned to look at her and grinned.

"You good, mami?"

"Mmm."

She had never in her life felt this relaxed. She and Lefty were in the bedroom he shared with one of his brothers. Lefty lived alone with his brothers; their mom was back in Puerto Rico and he never mentioned his dad. The brothers had been out all night, and she and Lefty had fucked on each of the beds, plus the floor.

Lefty hit Play and she snuggled into him, smelling his skin. They watched Alexis Argüello, the great Nicaraguan, in his old-school blue velvet trunks with his impossibly long limbs—his nickname was the Explosive Thin Man—lob a brutal uppercut to the midsection of Aaron Pryor.

"God*damn*," said Lefty.

Gravity took another bite of the garlicky, greasy chicharron. It was hard to believe she had gotten hungry again after splitting that huge roti with Ty, but she and Lefty had burned a lot of calories. She moved her eyes from the computer screen to him.

He was looking right at her.

"You still hungry?" he asked.

"Not for food."

He took her plate away and pressed her back into the tangled sheets, and they shared a garlicky kiss while Pryor and Argüello kept trading blows and Lefty's latest track played on endless repeat. Just as he was sliding his hands inside her shirt, his door burst open and two boys came in.

"Yo, what's up?" Lefty said, pulling his hands away from her breasts without seeming embarrassed. She tried to imitate his nonchalance.

" 'Sup?" said the bigger of the two, nodding to her.

They were obviously Lefty's big brothers. They had his same handsome baby face, but on them it looked harder. Lefty introduced her as his girlfriend, which gave her a rush of pride.

The bigger one, whose name was José, set a package of cigars on the nightstand and plopped down next to them on the bed.

He peered at the laptop. "So. What are we watching?"

"The first Pryor-Argüello," she said.

"The Hawk!" said the other brother, Edgar, rising in Gravity's estimation by knowing Aaron Pryor's ring nickname. He crowded onto the bed too. Lefty put his arm around her.

Aaron Pyror was boxing behind the jab now. He circled beautifully, light on his tasseled boots. The change of tactics seemed to confuse Argüello.

"Aaron Pryor is slick," said Lefty.

"Yeah, he is," she agreed.

Gravity had watched this fight countless times. Both fighters were admirable for different reasons. Pryor switched directions, and his right cross drew blood. She looked away. She never liked to watch Argüello bleed.

"Smell this," said José, holding out an open baggie of marijuana.

Lefty whistled and said it was good shit.

Gravity thought it smelled like a dead skunk. José broke up the buds with his fingers so they made a stinky mound on the newspaper he'd laid across his lap. The boys leaned in over it, discussing the features of this particular strain. Their enthusiasm was a total mystery to her.

"Boxers aren't supposed to smoke," she said, looking at Lefty.

He lifted his sad eyes to hers. "I'm not a boxer, boo. I'm a artist."

She frowned. She wasn't so sure it was good for artists, either, but that was between him and his rhymes.

José sliced open one of the cigars. "You never smoked before, mami?" he asked her.

"No."

"Gravity's a good girl," said Lefty.

He sounded proud of her, which made her happy, but it was weird that he was proud of *her* for not smoking but thought it was okay for *him* to smoke. José scooped up the green hill and funneled it into a thin line down the middle of the gutted cigar.

"My brother rolls the best blunts in the Bronx, Gravity," Lefty said. "You're in the presence of greatness."

"Mmm," she said. "I'll just sit in the other room while you smoke, okay?"

She didn't want to be rude, because it was their house,

but she couldn't afford to take any chances with USADA. She got randomly drug tested now, and you could get disqualified just for taking the wrong kind of cough syrup. But Edgar and José waved her off.

"Nah, nah. We'll go to the roof."

With a jingle of chains and snapping shut of folding knives, the brothers gathered their things and left, kissing Gravity on the cheek on the way out. She watched Lefty debate whether he wanted to remain with her or follow the weed. It looked like she won by a split decision. She ignored the tendril of fear that snaked through her: if there was a rematch, she would lose.

On the laptop, Pryor and Argüello were still battling away. Gravity forgot all about Lefty as she lost herself in admiration for the two legendary warriors. The crowd at Miami's Orange Bowl roared as the tall Nicaraguan advanced, landing a hard right just before the bell that ended round thirteen.

She settled back into Lefty's lap, keeping her eyes on the screen. This YouTube upload cut away from the corners during the round breaks, so you couldn't see the famous water bottle incident, but she had already watched it many times: Aaron Pryor's trainer, Panama Lewis, yelling at one of his seconds, "Not *that* water bottle! Get me the one I mixed."

Nobody knew what was in that bottle. A year later, Panama Lewis got caught taking stuffing out of one of his fighter's gloves. The opponent in that bout went partially blind.

Gravity didn't like to think about things like that. Life was crooked enough. She preferred to believe that boxing was fair, that the reason Aaron Pryor came out screaming for round fourteen was that, sitting on his stool, he had searched deep inside himself and found some higher gear. Whatever it was, it was too much for Argüello. The Explosive Thin Man staggered back against the ropes, defenseless. Gravity hid her face against Lefty's chest. She could never bear to watch the end.

March 20, 2016
US Women's National Team Set in Box-Off

COLORADO SPRINGS, COLO.—This week in Colorado Springs, six boxers who were unsuccessful at the US Women's Boxing Olympic Trials moved up or down in weight to clinch titles in the non-Olympic classes.

For those just joining us, only three women's weight classes are represented in the Rio Olympics, as opposed to ten weight classes for men. (Why? Because sexism.) Although these six women will not be eligible for Rio, they will proudly represent the US at the Women's Continental Championships next month in Cornwall, Ontario, and the Women's World Boxing Championships in Qinhuangdao, China, in May.

Meet your new US team:

Light flyweight (106 lb) Marisol Bonilla, 22, Austin, Texas. It's all in the family for Bonilla, who began training at age 8 at her father's gym. A fast, defensively minded boxer, Bonilla cites the great "El Finito" López as her inspiration: "I want to prove to people that women can box as technically as men."

OLYMPIC WEIGHT Flyweight (112 lb) Kaylee Miller, 23, Los Angeles. See our coverage of the Olympic Trials for more on this courageous scholar-athlete.

Bantamweight (119 lb) Aisha Johnson, 26, Washington,

173

D.C. A bob-and-weave brawler, Johnson found boxing five years ago while living at a women's shelter in Baltimore. She represented the US in the London Olympics. Johnson says, "Boxing is life or death to me. I always fought to survive."

Featherweight (125 lb) Paloma Gonzales, 25, Sacramento. The most famous name on this roster, the bronze medalist from London has served as an inspiration to young Latina athletes everywhere and used to boast a list of corporate sponsors longer than her knee-length brown hair. Just a few have stayed with her after her upset loss this year at Trials. A well-rounded boxer-puncher, Gonzales should be a powerhouse at featherweight and a top contender for hardware in China. Says Gonzales, "The refereeing and judging at Trials was bullshit, but I'm not going to let down my fans. The best is yet to come for Paloma Gonzales."

OLYMPIC WEIGHT Lightweight (132 lb) Gravity Delgado, 16, Brooklyn. This protégée of the legendary boxing sage Jefferson Thomas <u>pulled off the upset of the Trials</u>.

Light welterweight (141 lb) Aaliyah Williams, 32, Seattle. Owner of one of the best jabs in the women's game, the powerful Williams boxed beautifully at this higher weight. Williams is a proud member of the Seattle Dockworkers Local 21 and volunteer counselor at Strong Heart, a center for LGBTQ sexual abuse survivors. She says, "I'm not just fighting for me but for all the women who never got the chance."

Welterweight (152 lb) Nakima Fanning, 26, Newark. Fanning was a starter in basketball at Rutgers but dropped out after a knee injury ended her athletic scholarship. Now waiting tables at IHOP and attending night school for speech pathology, Fanning picked up boxing just three years ago: "I was really down after I had to quit playing ball. Boxing gave me hope."

OLYMPIC WEIGHT Middleweight (165 lb) Sacred Jones, 21, Detroit. <u>The magnificent middleweight</u> has not lost a bout in four years.

Light heavyweight (178 lb) Kiki Mailer, 26, Philadelphia. Mailer is imposing at this higher weight. One of the best infighters in the women's game, she trained alongside the great Bernard Hopkins and always has a trick up her sleeve, picked up in the legendary gyms of Philly. When we asked Mailer for a quote, she replied, "I got nothing more to say. I said it all in the ring."

Heavyweight (178+ lb) Bettina Rosario, 33, San Diego. Rosario won the box-off unopposed. Women heavyweights are rare, and she has only managed to have six amateur bouts in four years of boxing. She says she often drives five hours for sparring: "I hope I get some fights in Canada and China."

Chapter Twenty-Two

Gravity's eyelids fluttered open as Ms. Laventhol said her name.

"People think gravity is just this glue holding us on to the earth," she was saying. "But it's not. Gravity is *not* that things fall down."

Ms. Laventhol tucked a strand of her dark, limp hair behind one ear. "See, we *feel* stuck to the earth, but that's only because the earth is so much *incredibly more massive* than we are!" She spread her arms as wide as they could go, and her dangly earrings jingled.

On the blackboard was a diagram of an inclined plane with a little cart rolling down it. She had written "$F = ma$" above it, and there were arrows going in different directions, labeled with Greek letters and words like "sin" and "cos" that Gravity was pretty sure nobody in class understood.

Sometimes Ms. Laventhol taught stuff that went way over their heads, but that was okay because she never tested them on it or anything. Her tests were always really easy: plugging things into equations and matching words with their definitions. But every once in a while, she would get kind of emotional and go off on some topic like black holes or the Big Bang.

"What people don't realize about gravity," she said,

stabbing the blackboard with her chalk, "is that *everything* pulls on *everything*. *Everything* falls toward *everything*. We are all just drifting through space, slowly falling toward each other. And the closer we get to each other, the faster we go. That's the universal law of attraction!"

A hand shot up.

Ms. Laventhol smiled and pointed with the chalk. "Yes! Nevaeh?"

"Can I have a bathroom pass?"

Ms. Laventhol's shoulders slumped.

Gravity felt bad for her sometimes. She probably should have been teaching at Lincoln or somewhere else more academic.

She gave Nevaeh the bathroom pass and picked up an apple off her desk. She held it up. "The *universality* of gravity was the breakthrough that Newton had. When the apple fell on his head, Newton was like, 'Oh, snap!'"

A few kids giggled. Sometimes Ms. Laventhol tried to use slang to relate to them, but it just sounded funny. She ignored this and forged on.

"He was like, 'Dude! It's *not* just a property of *planets*. It's a property of *everything*!' And *that* was a breakthrough. It was a unification and a simplification, a property independent of the quality of the objects."

A property independent of the quality of the objects.

That reminded Gravity of Coach's advice to her before her very first fight: "Everybody goes down if you hit them right." Coach had told Gravity to run to the other girl as soon as the bell rang. Just run as fast as she could and start punching her in the face. Gravity had done that, and the other girl had done it too. But the other girl had closed her eyes, whereas Gravity kept hers wide open. That made all the difference. Gravity smiled, remembering how good it had felt to win that first time.

Ms. Laventhol met her eyes and smiled too, exclaiming, "It's just so elegant!"

Gravity heard a snicker behind her and turned to see Brandon and Bart, two knuckleheads who barely ever came to school, cracking up. Brandon was making a V with his fingers and wiggling his tongue in the middle of it.

Gravity shook her head and turned back to the front of the class. Some kids made fun of Ms. Laventhol because she was married to Ms. Lee, who taught gym, and neither of them made any attempt to hide it. Gravity didn't see what the big deal was.

When Gravity had left the casino disco that night with Lefty, Aaliyah Williams and Aisha Johnson had been making out in one corner. And Nakima was going out with one of the flyweight girls who lost in the prelims. You couldn't get very far in women's boxing if you had a problem with stuff like that.

Last year, Gravity had stood up for Ms. Laventhol when some dumb sophomores were telling nasty jokes in the lunchroom. Ever since then, everybody thought Gravity was gay. This was irritating, but whatever. It wasn't like she wanted to date the guys from school anyway. Nobody was as cute as Lefty or D-Minus or Boo Boo, and a lot of them made dumb comments about her boxing, like saying, "Ooh, don't beat me up!" or asking what happened when she got punched in the breasts.

"What happens when you get punched in the breasts?" was the most common question men asked her about boxing.

The fact was, the chest wasn't a big target area, not like

the face or the liver or the solar plexus. Some girls wore chest protectors, but Gravity found them bulky, and her breasts weren't that sensitive anyway. It was just a nonissue, but the first few times she had tried to explain this, she realized that the men who asked this question were not really interested in her answer. They just wanted to bring up breasts to her. It turned them on. Or else maybe they felt it cut her down to size. Boys were so stupid sometimes.

She put her head down on her desk and dozed until the bell.

After school, she headed home to pick up some more clothes and see if the stipend check had arrived yet for March. She was hoping her mother would be out for happy hour, but to her dismay, she could hear through the door the Curtis Mayfield album blasting on her mom's old turntable. The LP must have warped in the sun, because Curtis's voice was swaying nauseously in a way that made Gravity want to crawl out of her skin.

She let herself in and stood in the doorway, surveying the terrain. Her mother was lounging on the couch in a peach satin robe, leafing through a high school yearbook from the fancy school she had gone to in Shaker Heights, Ohio. Light slanted in the window and lit up her auburn hair. On the coffee table were a half-empty bottle of vodka, a can of V8, and a jar of pickles. The house was neat, and something smelled good.

"Hi, Mom," she said uncertainly.

Her mother smiled and sipped from a mason jar. "Gravity Lynn!"

Gravity stepped inside. Her mother only used her middle name when she was in an excellent mood. She smelled the air again. Was it possible?

"Did you bake *bread*, Mom?"

Her mother rose from the couch, swaying only slightly, and carried the drink with her into the kitchen, from which she emerged with a thick slice of challah, smeared with butter. Gravity took it, despite the carbs. She could not remember the last time her mother had baked challah. She took a bite and paused, then chewed and swallowed. It took a second to identify the problem: she had forgotten the salt.

"And how are your culinary studies proceeding?" her mother asked.

"Um, okay. We've been learning about health department inspections and—"

"*I* should have gone to culinary school," her mother said, flopping back down on the couch. "I would have been quite good. Look at this!"

She held up the yearbook, open to a page labeled "Domestic Goddesses." It had pictures of girls in their home economics class. Everyone was white, and they all had this innocent, happy look. Her mother's portrait was blown up in the middle of the page. Her hair was her natural brown, in a short bob that turned up at the ends.

"You look beautiful, Mom."

Gravity wondered, as she always did with the old photos of her father, what had gone so terribly wrong.

Her memories of the golden days when her mother and father were together were as scarce and faded as those old Polaroids. Gravity tried not to call them to mind too often, because the more she thought of them, the less vivid they became. Soon they were no longer real memories at all but stories about memories she used to have.

She let herself go back now, to one of her favorites. It was a Saturday, because she and Mom had gone to synagogue.

Gravity had paid extra attention, because the sermon was on Ruth. There weren't that many stories in the Bible about women doing exciting things, but Ruth was different. She was brave and loyal. Even though she lost her husband, she stuck with her mother-in-law and traveled with her to another country. And when they got there, Ruth met this rich guy who owned the wheat field where she went to work, and he fell in love with her, and everybody lived happily ever after.

After the services were over that day, Mom had taken out the Bible and read Gravity the exact words Ruth spoke to Naomi:

Entreat me not to leave thee, or to return from following after thee; for whither thou goest, I will go, and where thou lodgest, I will lodge. Thy people shall be my people, and thy God my God.

Gravity memorized that because it was so beautiful. Dad had just reappeared, and he was trying hard to win Mom back, and that afternoon he had taken them out on a Circle Line cruise around Manhattan, which was the kind of touristy thing that real New Yorkers never do. Gravity loved it.

When their boat passed the Statue of Liberty, Dad had pointed and said, "Mira! The third most beautiful lady in New York."

It had taken Gravity a second to figure out who numbers one and two were supposed to be, but Mom laughed right away, and she and Dad kissed a really sexy kiss. And Gravity had thought that it was just like in the Bible, that Dad would never leave them now but would go where they went and lodge where they lodged.

Gravity tried not to taint the memory with the bitterness of her present knowledge, but she felt some of the sunshine drain out of that old afternoon. So she put it carefully out of her mind.

Dad hadn't loved them that much. It was okay. That was just the way things were.

Whither thou goest, I will go, she thought, bringing Lefty to mind. *She* would be loyal like that.

Her mother had drained the rest of the mason jar. She let out a theatrical sigh and said, "I should have been one of those chefs on TV! I would have been a natural. Do you know, Mr. Baird told me I had the kind of voice Broadway shows are made for? Look!"

Gravity smiled. It had been a long time since her mother had been in such a good mood. She had forgotten how pretty she looked when she was happy. She watched her leaf through the old yearbook, her shiny auburn hair falling in a wave across her smooth cheeks. She stopped at the section on the school plays and gazed adoringly at the photo of herself from her high school performance of *The Miracle Worker*, tracing one finger along the line of her dress and reading aloud the caption: "Eileen Berman thrills the crowd as Annie Sullivan."

She looked up at Gravity abruptly and barked, "Look at all the great things I used to do!"

Gravity tried saying, "You still do great things, Mom!" but her mother just let out a bitter laugh and reached for the vodka.

"I was always gifted," she said. "Daddy said I had the finest mind in the family." She filled the mason jar halfway with vodka, added a splash of V8, and stirred it with a pickle.

Gravity stood there a moment, waiting for her mother to ask about Spokane or Tyler or why Gravity had come home, but her mother remained bent over the book. She rocked rhythmically in time to the warped Curtis Mayfield, moving her lips as she whispered the captions. It was a little frightening.

"I won't be here long," Gravity said, backing away. "I just came to grab some stuff. I have to go to Canada in a couple weeks."

Her mother waved her hand toward the bedroom. "Help yourself."

"Did any mail come for me?"

"Just junk."

Gravity went over to the recycling bin and sifted carefully through the circulars and discarded bills—her mother generally threw bills out until they said "Final Notice"—but there was nothing from USA Boxing. It was irritating. She was supposed to have gotten the check three weeks ago.

She hurried into her and Tyler's room, where she threw random stuff into a garbage bag, eager to get out before her mother's mood worsened. When she had accumulated enough of her own clothes, she went to her brother's drawers and cleaned them out too, because she wasn't sure when they would be back. Then she grabbed the photos of their father from under the bed.

On her way out, she stopped again in the doorway and looked back.

"Bye, Mom. Can you please call or text if I get mail?"

"Sure. Take care." Her mother did not look up.

"Auntie Rosa got Tyler glasses. I think he was having trouble seeing stuff on the board. We went to his parent-teacher conference and they said it was a big improvement."

"Stay at Rosa's as long as you want," her mother said, waving a manicured hand. "I'm fine here."

Gravity took a deep breath and gazed out the window, pushing down the anger that threatened to rise. The spider plants on the windowsill looked thirsty again, the tips of their leaves papery and brown. She ought to water them, but one more look at her mother convinced her to go. She couldn't save everything.

Chapter Twenty-Three

Before she left for Cornwall, Gravity had sent an email to USA Boxing to complain about not getting her stipend check for March and to ask if they could maybe send one big check for both March and April. She also asked—now that she knew you could request roommates—if she could room with Kaylee or Sacred. She was happy to learn from Bonnie Rosario, who picked her up at the airport, that they had listened.

"I made sure they put you in with Kaylee, honey," Bonnie told Gravity as she barreled down the Ontario expressway, her enormous breasts bouncing beneath the T-shirt that said "Most people wait their whole life to meet their favorite boxer. I raised mine."

"*Pendejo!*" Bonnie shrieked, leaning on her horn. "These Canadians! They drive worse than they box."

Bonnie was the Olympic team manager. That meant that she would travel with them to China and Rio, which made Gravity happy. She was the mom of the heavyweight champion, Bettina, but she treated all the boxers like they were her daughters. She had insisted on rescuing the Honduran featherweight, Miranda, from the airport, where she was stranded without her luggage.

"Kaylee is a good girl, just like you, honey," Bonnie said, patting Gravity's hand. "Like I always tell Bettina, you gotta stay clear of drama on the road. Don't let any of these petty bitches drag you down."

"No bitches! No drama! *Entiendes?*" Bonnie hollered into the backseat at Miranda. When Miranda shook her head, Bonnie translated heatedly. She kept up a steady stream of bilingual gossip and advice on the drive to the sports center.

That car ride would be the most Gravity would see of Cornwall, Ontario. The entire tournament took place inside a big sports center that the fifty-three women competitors— all national champions from North, Central, and South America—hardly ever left. Everything they needed was inside the vast complex: dorm rooms, a cafeteria, weight rooms, the auditorium in which the fights took place, even little lounges with televisions that broadcast a weird selection of Canadian stations.

When Gravity arrived at her room, Kaylee was already there, standing up on her bed, a towel spread underneath her feet to prevent germs, to hang a skull-and-crossbones flag on the wall. Kaylee's blond braids and peaches-and-cream complexion reminded Gravity of Svetlana, but Kaylee was longer and stronger, and she had that something extra that marked her as a champion.

She turned to greet Gravity with an "Arrr! Ahoy, matey! Ready to set sail aboard the USS *Beatdown?*"

"I guess so!" Gravity said.

Kaylee hopped down from the bed. She grinned and said, "You'll get used to me and my pirate ways. I'm glad we're bunkmates. You kicked ass in Trials." She handed Gravity a button with a skull and crossbones on it, and they headed to the cafeteria, which Kaylee called the mess hall.

The whole team was there, spread out between two tables

with Bonnie and Coach Shorty. Everybody looked up and said hello when they arrived. Ruben "Shorty" Feliciano was barely five feet tall, with little glasses and a thin mustache above a permanent smile. Boca said Shorty had only gotten where he was because of political connections. Fatso just shrugged when his name came up and said, "He's from Wisconsin. You ever heard of a great boxer from *Wisconsin?*"

Hopefully he would be a good head coach. You could never really tell what someone was like until they worked your corner.

Shorty caught her studying him and winked.

"Boricua?" he asked.

Gravity knew that word. It was Spanish for "Puerto Rican." She replied with one of the few complete sentences she knew: "Mi padre es dominicano."

"Oooh!" Shorty replied. "Dominicana!" He raised both hands in the air like she was dangerous and might shoot him.

She laughed politely.

He then launched into a rapid speech in Spanish that forced her to use one of her other complete sentences: "No hablo español." It was a little embarrassing, being half Dominican and not speaking Spanish, but Gravity couldn't help it. Rosa and Melsy always spoke English with her, and Spanish class at Grady was just too boring.

Shorty had a way of laughing that didn't make her feel like he was laughing *at* her. He just patted her hand and said, "One day you learn, champ."

Gravity could tell which of her teammates had moved up in weight and which ones had moved down by the amount of food on their trays. Aisha and Aaliyah were giggling as they fed each other strawberries. Kiki kept going back for more baked chicken and broccoli, and Bettina was eating like it was her job.

The girls who had cut weight to qualify looked miserable to varying degrees as they stared at their carefully measured starches and proteins. Paloma had always been sulky, but it was a real change to see Nakima so drawn and quiet. Poor Marisol was still a pound over and not eating anything at all.

Around her, the cafeteria buzzed with champions. Carmen Cruz was flitting among them, hugging the boxers and scribbling notes. The sight of her made Gravity think of Andre. She had shoved his creepy comment way down into the back of her mind, like spoiled milk she could not face dumping out. How could Carmen be friends—or more—with someone like that?

Gravity knew from Carmen's tournament preview that Brazil and Canada were the only other nations besides the US to field full squads. The Brazilians brimmed with fighting spirit, their musical Portuguese echoing through the cafeteria as they laughed and ate. They were a rainbow of skin tones and hairstyles and sizes, but all wore the same crisp navy-blue tracksuit that said "BOXE BRASIL." Gravity got excited just thinking about fighting them.

The Canadians were sitting nearby. Gravity peered at each woman, trying to figure out who was their lightweight. They looked just like Americans, except that all of them were white and some were speaking what sounded like French. This was surprising to Gravity, and she nudged Kaylee and asked, "Are we near France right now?"

Paloma heard this and laughed.

Kaylee, who was in the process of cleaning all her silverware with sanitizing wipes, said, "Matey, France is in Europe, across the stormy seas."

Gravity said defensively, "I thought I heard French." She had never been very good at geography.

Kaylee pulled up a map of Canada on her phone as Paloma continued to snicker. She showed Gravity where Quebec was and told her that a whole part of Canada had French as its first language.

"Your opponent is from there," Kaylee added.

"Which one is she?"

"Annie. Blonde, second from the right."

Gravity watched Annie eat. She remembered from Carmen's tournament preview that she was a policewoman and mother of two. There wasn't any footage of her online.

"Is she any good?"

Paloma broke in, saying, "She's tough but old and slow."

"Oh. Thanks."

Paloma went on, her voice like a parent lecturing a child, "Argentina and Puerto Rico are skillful but they can't go toe to toe. Mexico is strong but crude. Brazil is the one to beat."

Coach Shorty stood up to address the table, flashing them all his signature grin. "Ladies! Trial scale is in the fitness room. Get good rest and we see you at the weigh-in at seven sharp. Conference room E."

"Do not be late!" Bonnie added. "I *will* come to your rooms and dump a bucket of ice on you."

Chapter Twenty-Four

"Fuck!" Gravity stared at the scale in despair. She was 133.5.

"Shit!" said Kaylee. "Lemme try."

She took Gravity's place. They both stared at the blinking digital display until it resolved. Kaylee was 113.4.

"Fuck!" Kaylee said. "I was on weight when I went to bed!"

"Are you sure it's accurate?"

"I checked it against the trial scale last night. I was a hundred and twelve point two on both."

"Could it have, like, broken overnight? Or maybe the floor in here is slanted or something?"

They looked at each other miserably, then back at the scale.

"I'll run down and check again," Kaylee said.

"Okay," Gravity said. "In the meantime, we should start spitting."

She grabbed an empty water bottle off the dresser and began to work up saliva, then spit it inside. By the time Kaylee came back, Gravity had managed to fill the bottle a quarter of the way. Her mouth felt cottony. She looked at Kaylee hopefully, but her roommate shook her head.

Gravity had already taken a shit that morning. She did not need to ask Kaylee if she had gone, because her roommate had used up two entire rolls of toilet paper. It must have been an OCD thing.

"Should we tell Bonnie?" Gravity asked.

"What's *she* gonna do? Plus, she'll just tell Coach."

Everyone wanted to impress Shorty and get on his good side. The thought of making a first impression with her new coach as an overweight slacker was horrifying.

"Let's make a sauna," Kaylee said.

They dashed into the bathroom, where they turned on the hot water in the shower and the sink at full blast and put towels under the door.

"Do you have a plastic suit and Albolene?" Kaylee asked.

"Of course."

They rifled through their luggage until they found their plastics. After they had stripped, slathered themselves with Albolene, and layered up, they went back into the tiny bathroom, which was already filling with steam. Since the light was connected to the fan, they shut it off and sat on the edge of the tub in the darkness, sweating and spitting into bottles.

"We're lucky they have good hot water," Kaylee said. "In Russia it was cold showers."

"What was Russia like?"

"Honestly? It sucked. The beds felt like wooden boards. The girls were really tough, and we didn't get time to recover from the jet lag. We all lost except Sacred."

"Sacred is amazing."

"She's a beast," Kaylee said. "I love her to death. Usually we room together, but Bonnie said you requested me and I wanted to get to know you better."

"Wow! Thanks, Kaylee."

Despite her anxiety about the weight, it was kind of fun

just sitting there in the pitch dark and talking. It made Gravity think of being a little girl and building pillow forts with Melsy. They would lie inside them for hours, listening to music and gabbing.

"Most of the girls on the team now are cool," Kaylee said. "And Bonnie and Shorty are great. The only one you have to watch out for is Paloma. She'll stab you in the back if it would benefit her career."

"I kinda got that feeling."

"Last year? Paloma asked Aaliyah to help her get ready for the duals with Germany and Kazakhstan. Paloma *promised* Aaliyah one of her fights in the dual. Aaliyah flew out and gave her great sparring, then, when the time came, Paloma kept all the fights for herself. That's why Aaliyah and Aisha can't stand her."

"Wow."

"And it's why they like you. Everybody likes you 'cause you finally beat her."

Gravity laughed, adjusting the elastic of the plastic suit where it dug into her stomach. Mingled sweat and condensation dripped down her forehead and off her nose. She spat some more in her bottle.

There was a light as Kaylee turned on her phone.

"It's six-thirty," she announced. "We need to stay in here until the last possible second. It takes five minutes to get to the conference room. I can dry off and change in three."

"Me too."

They sweated silently for a while, then Gravity asked, "Do you mind if I pee?"

"Go ahead."

Kaylee held up the phone for her so she could find the toilet. It was a little hard to pee with someone else in the room, but Gravity managed. She washed her hands and shook them out into the sink since there were no more clean towels. Kaylee used up a lot of towels, too, which must have been another OCD thing. Gravity sat back down and said, "Can I ask you a personal question?"

"Sure."

"I read on Carmen's blog about your OCD."

"Yeah."

"What's it like?"

"Well, it's an anxiety disorder. I have this thing about germs. When I was in middle school and high school, it was really bad. It takes up a lot of your time. Now it's better." She was silent for a moment, and they listened to the sound of the shower. "I used to be on meds, but I think it depends on your life and how happy you are, just the happiness of knowing who you are. After a while, I didn't need the drugs, because boxing made the repetitive thoughts go away."

"I know what you mean," Gravity said, thinking of how Coach's voice in her head always silenced the angry words of her mother and the ache in her heart about her father.

The phone illuminated Kaylee's red, dripping face. "Avast! It's six-fifty. Let's do a high-knee run for the last sixty seconds, matey. Just be careful not to slip."

They did the interval, sloshing around in their suits, and then they turned off the water and dashed back into the bedroom, where the cold air gave Gravity goose bumps. Kaylee had hoarded a towel, but Gravity had to dry herself off on a pair of sweatpants. They were still 0.2 over on Kaylee's scale, but they spat their hearts out on the way to the conference room, got on the scale buck naked, and made weight on the dot.

Chapter Twenty-Five

Gravity sat in between Aaliyah and Kaylee in the half-empty auditorium, cheering as Marisol Bonilla took the ring. The announcer introduced her twice, once in French and once in English. Five of them were fighting that night, in size order. Gravity had the St. Lucian champion in bout eight.

She gripped the PLASMAFuel bottle in her gauze-wrapped hand and took a deep swig, instructing the molecules of liquid to flow down into her rubbery legs and up into her pounding skull. She could not remember ever feeling this awful before a fight.

Wake up, she told herself. *You are about to get in the ring.*

After making weight, she and Kaylee had gone to the cafeteria and pounded smoothies with protein powder, then collapsed in shuddering heaps in bed, but Gravity's headache had made sleep impossible.

She had gone down to the cafeteria again. The line was closed, but there was milk in the machine and she sat and drank it slowly at one of the tables. Two girls had come in, chattering and laughing and looking at her sideways. They had pretty headscarves and looked like identical twins. Gravity had the feeling she had seen them somewhere before.

"You Gravity?" one of them said in a lilting Caribbean accent.

"Yeah, hi."

The girl lifted her chin. "I'ma teach you something about your name tonight!"

Her sister laughed and said, "The bigger they be, the harder they fall."

"Okay, then," Gravity said, taking another sip of milk. Something about the way the girls held themselves marked them as novices.

"I'm Honor and this is Truth," the first girl said. "Truth fights Paloma tonight."

"And Honor fights you," Truth said. "You are in for a big surprise, Gravity."

"I look forward to it," Gravity said.

Gravity's refusal to take offense seemed to confuse them, but she didn't have the bandwidth to trash-talk. They took two apples from the line and headed off, staring daggers at her and whispering behind their hands. Gravity finished her milk and went back to her room. She still couldn't sleep, so she called Coach, who repeated his mysterious advice from Spokane: "You have already defeated all your enemies."

Gravity still did not understand what that meant, but the last time he'd said it to her, she had won all the marbles. She took two Advil PM and conked out until Kaylee woke her to go down to the fights.

She didn't know if it was the Advil or the dehydration or her period coming on, but she had the chills and put on a double layer of thermals beneath her warm-ups just to stop from shaking. She did not let on to anyone how bad she felt. Kaylee must have known, though, because she kept her hand on the back of Gravity's neck through much of Marisol's bout, gently rubbing her nape.

The Brazilian champion was very aggressive, and she won the opening round, but Marisol kept it moving, circling the ring on her fast legs until the Brazilian hit her limit. Gravity joined her teammates in cheering on their littlest member's win.

The Dominican and Argentine light flyweights had a clinch-filled contest won by Argentina, and then Aisha Johnson was up, facing a Colombian. Kaylee led everyone in a cheer of "U-U-USA!"

Gravity saw Carmen Cruz rise from the press row, gathering her pashmina around her, and dash across the auditorium to stand by the small Colombian team and join her voice to theirs, but the Colombian champion had no answer for Aisha's power.

Aaliyah turned to Gravity and said, "She looks good, right?"

"She looks *great*," Gravity said, giving her a pound.

"You okay?" Aaliyah did not let go of Gravity's hand but grasped it strongly, fixing Gravity with her soulful hazel eyes.

"Yeah."

Aaliyah cocked her head. "Don't lie to me, youngster."

She sighed. "I feel like shit. I dunno. Maybe I have the flu."

Aaliyah nodded. "Doesn't matter. You got an easy draw."

"Yeah. They were talking shit to me in the cafeteria, but I get the feeling it's an act."

"Those who know don't talk. Those who talk don't know."

Gravity smiled. That sounded like something Coach would say.

Aisha gave her opponent an eight count and Aaliyah leapt to her feet, screaming, "That's my baby! *Beautiful* hook! She don't like that!"

After the ref raised Aisha's hand, Gravity rose to begin her warm-up.

Paloma was taking the ring to square off against Truth

Hickson, the lighter of the St. Lucian sisters. The first exchange convinced Gravity that she and Aaliyah were correct: the St. Lucians were beginners.

She did some stretches she had learned from sexy Keeshawn, trying to banish the bone-deep fatigue. Thinking of Keeshawn made her think of Lefty, which made her think of Coach's words about women weakening legs. Sex was supposed to be bad for a boxer.

What if Lefty had stolen her strength? This was her first fight since losing her virginity. That thought scared her, so she put it out of her head. There was a cheer from her team, and she looked up to see the ref raising Paloma's hand. Aaliyah came over and put her strong arm around Gravity.

She said, "Paloma beat the shit out of the sister. Your girl will be shook."

"Thanks."

Aaliyah grinned and went back to cuddling Aisha. Maybe sex didn't weaken legs after all, because Aisha and Aaliyah were sharing a room, and Aisha could not have looked stronger. Unless it was different for women. Or maybe Aaliyah and Aisha waited to have sex until after the tournament.

"Okay, champ!" Shorty said to Gravity. "We on a roll! You gonna keep it going!"

The official at the glove table inspected her wraps and signed them with a Magic Marker. Shorty gloved her up and gave her a round of pads. He was okay, but nothing like Fatso. Gravity went through the motions, willing her body to wake up.

As they prepared to take the ring, Shorty said, "You look tired."

She looked at his tiny, bright eyes behind the little glasses. "I'm fine," she lied.

He laughed. "Start strong and you stop her. She greener than a dollar bill."

"Okay."

As Gravity walked past her team, everyone cheered and reached out to touch her glove.

"Arr," Kaylee said. "Make her walk the plank!"

Sacred yelled, "Do you!"

Their love raised her morale, and as she stepped through the ropes and onto the firm canvas, the same magic thing happened that always happened: she felt happy. Despite the weakness that still hung over her limbs, she felt a sense of being exactly where she belonged. She looked down with wonder at the "USA" on her chest. This was the first time she had fought on behalf of her country.

Across the ring, the St. Lucian was shadowboxing all crazy, yelling with every punch.

Gravity got on her knees and sang the Shema. She thanked God, with all her heart, for easy work on this day when she felt so drained. She prayed that she might not hurt Honor and that Honor would not mess around and head-butt her or something. She prayed for fair judging, although she was not planning on leaving it in the judges' hands.

In the staredown, Honor's almond-shaped brown eyes bored into Gravity's with a hostility that bordered on insane. When Gravity extended her gloves, Honor slammed hers down on top of them. Despite Gravity's fatigue, she grinned around her mouthpiece.

Back in the corner, Shorty hugged her through the ropes. His head barely came up to her neck.

"She gonna come wild," he said. "Don't worry. One good right hand, and boom."

"Yeah."

She shuffled out at the bell, keeping her guard high, and caught Honor's shots on her gloves and forearms: arm punches, lacking proper leverage. Gravity's mother hit harder than that. She waited until Honor was done and then fired back a single jab.

It pushed her back, so Gravity followed with a hard right to the chin. Honor closed her eyes and halfway turned away. Gravity took a deep breath, slid out to the right to get distance, and threw two more straight right hands, both of them at the head. The second one dropped her.

Gravity backpedaled to the neutral corner as the referee gave the count and Honor rose bravely, shaking her head. Gravity turned off the part of her that liked this girl. Because she liked Honor a lot: her swagger, her game, the fact that she had a twin. Twins were lucky.

She looked into the bleachers to where her teammates were cheering her knockdown. They looked like an advertisement for feminism in America: all of them on their feet, yelling with joy, even Paloma. Aisha and Aaliyah were holding up a big American flag, and Kiki, all gloved up and ready to go in next, had stopped shadowboxing to cheer.

Sacred's loud voice floated to her ears: "Make us proud!"

Gravity shuffled out again, hands high and elbows tight. She knew Honor would rush her, trying to prove the knockdown hadn't mattered. Once again, she let her say her piece, catching the shots on her guard. When Honor was done, Gravity got the last word.

The referee was watching carefully. All Gravity had to do was give her an excuse to end it. She took a little strength off and put it into speed, landing the kind of showy five-punch combination that D-Minus excelled at. The ref stepped between them, waving it off.

Honor was so angry she ripped off her gloves and threw them to the canvas, then jumped up and down. The referee, a glamorous Dominican with an Amazon's build, watched with amusement, arms folded over her chest.

"Are you through?" she said at last.

Honor nodded.

When the ref raised Gravity's hand, Kaylee led the team in a chant of "Doomsday."

April 8, 2016

US Continues Strong on Day Two of Continentals: Miller, Gonzales, Delgado Advance; Fanning Eliminated

CORNWALL, ONTARIO—The US went 3–1 on the second night of exciting action in the American Continental Championships. Although this tournament is nonadvancing, it gives the fighters vital international experience and the chance to test themselves in preparation for next month's World Championships in China.

In the Olympic flyweight class, Kaylee Miller won unanimously over Gisela Suarez of Argentina, who boxed well but lacked the power to stand up to Miller's aggressive onslaught. The rest of the flyweight bouts were mismatches in which strong champions from Canada, Puerto Rico, and Brazil blew out novices from Mexico, Ecuador, and the Dominican Republic. The women's amateur programs in many of these countries are still developing.

The 119-pounders made a strong argument for the opening of more Olympic weights. Carolina Berenbaum of Argentina put on a boxing clinic against the game Dominican Arisleyda Martinez. Aisha Johnson, fresh off last night's victory over my countrywoman Ileana Santos—good fight, Ileana!—squared off against Toronto's excellent Kathleen Glynn. Johnson won the close, strategic match by split decision. In the final bantamweight contest, Brazil took a lopsided decision over the lone Jamaican here.

The Olympic lightweight class was up next, featuring some of the strongest fighters in the tournament. Reigning Pan American champion Nydia Tapia of Puerto Rico handily outboxed Ecuador. Tomorrow she will face Brazil's fearsome puncher Ariana Leite, who advanced unopposed when Barbados withdrew due to injury.

Brooklyn phenom Gravity Delgado, who got a soft touch last night in Honor Hickson of St. Lucia, looked uncharacteristically sluggish as she eked out a narrow unanimous decision over Quebec City's workmanlike Annie Bervin. The final lightweight bout had the sparse crowd on their feet as Mexico's Sylvia Rosalba Sánchez pulled out the split decision over Argentina's Maria Suarez. The two Latina warriors never stopped trading in this punch-fest fought in a Canadian phone booth.

In the sole welterweight bout of the evening, Manitoba's powerful Amanda Ross outboxed talented newcomer Nakima Fanning of Newark by unanimous decision. Action continues tomorrow in the fly, bantam, feather, light, and middleweight divisions, featuring the return to the ring of reigning Olympic champion Sacred Jones.

Chapter Twenty-Six

Gravity was lying in bed ogling Keeshawn's Instagram to wash out the bad taste in her mouth from reading Carmen's description of her as "uncharacteristically sluggish" when the ominous text from Melsy came in.

Hey cuz I wanna ask u something

She texted back:

What's up?

Melsy wrote:

Ever since the fights your boy Demetrius keeps texting me being all cute. You mind if i hang with him?

Gravity felt the wind go out of her, as though she had been hit by a good body shot. She must have made some sound of distress, because Kaylee said, "Are you okay?"

Kaylee was sitting cross-legged in bed, rolling up a pair of handwraps, her blond hair up in a messy topknot. She was the perfect roommate, despite her ravenous consumption of towels and toilet paper. She always seemed to know when to leave Gravity alone and when to talk, when to be a goofball and when to get serious. And she boxed with such commitment.

"My cousin is asking me if she can date this kid from my gym."

"Is he your ex or something?"

"No."

"So why's she need your permission?"

"She . . . she thought maybe I liked him. She's just asking to be considerate."

Kaylee cocked her head. "She sounds like a great cousin."

"She is." Gravity wished she could explain why it hurt so much, but she wasn't sure she knew herself. She bent over the phone, a dull ache still in her chest. She texted back:

Of course M, have fun!

She added some smileys and pressed Send before she lost her nerve. She was immediately seized with a terrible sinking feeling in her stomach.

The answer came right back:

You're the best G! Hey you did great last night!!!

Gravity wrote, Love you, cuz, then turned off her phone and went to drink some milk.

She had *not* done great last night. It had been one of the most cringeworthy performances of her career. Paloma had been right about Annie Bervin—she was tough but past her prime and had never been a world-beater—yet Gravity had been behind at the halfway mark and had needed a strong rally to win.

And now she had her period and had to fight that Mexican. Gravity had watched Sylvia Rosalba Sánchez battle the Argentine champ. She was the kind of fighter Mexico was known for: relentless forward motion, all aggression, lots of body-head combos. Gravity felt tired just thinking about it. If only she could have had a single night off.

When she got to the cafeteria, she saw that Honor and Truth were in there again, playing cards with a deck printed with the St. Lucian flag. Gravity nodded as she passed them, and they murmured something to each other. She ignored it, filled up a mug with milk, chugged it, and filled it up again.

She tried to carry the milk to a table by the window, but Truth yelled, "Hey, Gravity!" in her singing accent, beckoning her over.

Gravity approached, bracing herself.

The twins rose. They had the same short, natural hair, bleached to a canary yellow. It would have been hard to tell them apart, but Honor, having bulked up, had the fuller face. Truth had cheekbones sharp as knives.

"It was an honor to fight you," Honor said.

"You are a true champion," Truth said.

Their demeanor was so completely changed that for a moment Gravity thought they were making fun of her. She looked from twin to twin, but they returned her gaze earnestly.

"Thank you," she said. "You did good, both of you. You really hung in there."

Honor nodded gravely. "We underestimated you."

Truth said, "We were in deep water out there."

Honor said, "We were at the top of the mountain, and that's where the eagles are flying."

Gravity grinned. "If you keep training, I'll bet you could make it to Tokyo 2020. You're lucky to be twins. You always have someone to spar!"

"Sit and visit with us," Honor said, and they dealt her into their game.

They turned out to be from Brooklyn. *That* was why Gravity had thought, when she first met them, that she had seen them before. They trained at Smiley's with Tiffany Clarke, one of the few women coaches in New York, but they were born in St. Lucia and had persuaded the country's boxing federation to let them be its representatives. They were worried they had let St. Lucia down by their performance, but Gravity tried to convince them this was not so.

"St. Lucia is such a beautiful country," Truth said, gathering up the cards. She handed the deck to Gravity. "Here. Take that as our gift."

Honor said, "It's small, but it's not the size of a thing that matters. I'd rather have a small box with a diamond ring than a big one that is empty inside."

Gravity pondered that as she walked back to her room, but it only made her think of D-Minus. How he had a heavyweight's heart packed into a bantamweight frame. She turned her phone back on and went onto his Snapchat. When she saw what he had uploaded, she put a hand against the wall to steady herself.

In the middle of his usual montage of shirtless selfies and sparring clips was a picture of Melsy in her bikini in the Barclays Center. D had written "mood" across it followed by a bunch of heart-eye emojis and flames.

Next was a video. They were in Cops 'n Kids, and they must have asked someone else to film it. Melsy was listening to D talk, her head tilted to catch his voice over the sound of the music and the bell. D had a medicine ball under one arm, and his bare chest gleamed with grease. As Gravity watched, he reached out to touch a lock of Melsy's hair. Their eyes met. A lazy smile spread from his lips to hers.

Gravity turned the phone off. She laid her palm against the spot where it hurt in her chest, just beneath the left breast. She was with Lefty, so what did she care? D always went for girly-girl types like Melsy.

She *didn't* care. It was just pain, and Rick Ross said pain was weakness leaving the body. Maybe Melsy was doing her a favor. Now she would be a better girlfriend to Lefty. She nodded to Kaylee as she flopped onto the bed, curled into a fetal position, and mentally recited more lines from that samurai poem Fatso had taught her:

> *I have no parents: I make the heaven and earth my parents.*
> *I have no friends: I make my mind my friend.*
> *I have no enemy: I make carelessness my enemy.*
> *I have no armor: I make benevolence and righteousness my*
> *   armor.*
> *I have no castle: I make immovable mind my castle.*
> *I have no sword: I make absence of self my sword.*

She slept as though she had fallen into a deep, dark well. When Kaylee woke her to go to the fights, she sat up in terror, unsure where she was.

"Damn, girl!" Kaylee said.

Gravity pressed her fingers to her temples. "How are you feeling, Kay?"

"Great! Arr! Can't wait to get me gold!"

Gravity smiled weakly and grabbed a PLASMAFuel gel with caffeine. She sucked it down as they headed to the auditorium.

Kaylee went to warm up for her bout against Canada, and Gravity took the empty spot next to Sacred Jones, who was bopping her head to her music. When Gravity sat down, Sacred pulled out an earbud, called her "little champ," and asked if she was ready to put on a great show.

"I hope so," Gravity said.

"You hope so?" Sacred said, recoiling in mock horror. "You better *know* so. Let's try that again. Are you ready to put on a show?"

"Hell yeah," Gravity lied.

"That's what I'm talking about," Sacred said. "Fake it till you make it."

Gravity could make out the sound of gospel music coming out of her earbuds. Sacred always looked happy, but tonight she was positively radiating joy at the prospect of finally getting to fight after two nights of sitting in the stands. Gravity couldn't wait to watch her win. The great thing about cheering for Sacred was that you never feared she would lose. She was 68–1 and on a four-year win streak.

Sacred said, "I see you having a tough time. You and Kaylee both. Weighing in buck naked. What were you doing, running around Canada in sauna suits?"

Gravity looked down at her boots. "Something like that."

"Listen. This tournament don't mean shit. This is a learning experience. You can beat that Mexican girl. You got better leverage than her. You just gotta keep punching and never stop."

Sacred put her earbud back in and kept nodding her head in time to the gospel.

They both rose to scream for Kaylee in the leadoff bout. The Canadian girl was fast and smart and had good angles. They battled for superior foot position through the first two rounds.

"Who's winning?" Gravity asked Sacred at the top of the third.

Sacred said, "I think Kaylee got it. She's stronger than that girl." She broke off to yell, "Hook there, Kay! Hook when she roll right!"

At the final bell, Gravity still did not know who won. To her delight, they gave it to Kaylee.

Soon it was time to root for Aisha, who lost to a tough Brazilian, and Paloma, who boxed circles around the Mexican.

Then it was time to get ready, and Gravity glanced over to the opposite side of the auditorium, where Sylvia Rosalba Sánchez was throwing punches in the air. She was orthodox, average-sized for lightweight, and did not look like much when she shadowboxed. It was her conditioning that wore people down.

Sylvia was the first boxer Gravity had ever seen who was fighting in a skirt. It looked unflattering. There had been a whole big thing about skirts in the last Olympics. When AIBA had first announced that women's boxing would finally be added to the Games, they had proposed that skirts be mandatory, so people would be able to tell the women apart from the men. They had quickly dropped the idea, but Gravity still remembered the angry article Carmen Cruz had written about it in the *LA Times*. It was where she had learned the word "misogyny."

Shorty came to get her, his friendly banter and permanent grin now a familiar presence in her corner. Gravity bowed to the judges and knelt down in the corner, pressing her face to the post. She sang the Shema with everything she had.

Please, God, she prayed, and she asked for something she had never asked for before in her prefight prayer: *Give me strength.*

She wasn't sure if that was cheating, but she couldn't help it.

She rose to her feet, hugged Shorty, and met the Mexican at center ring. Sylvia gazed up at her blandly, dark eyes eerily calm in her pale, broad face. Like it was just another day at the office and Gravity was just another unlucky customer. They touched gloves politely. At the bell, they both came out swinging.

The nine minutes that followed were the most grueling

of Gravity's life. Halfway into the first round, she was more tired than she had ever been in any of her twenty-three previous fights. Sylvia was not a particularly hard puncher nor outstanding in any way, but as Gravity parried her unending barrage, she sensed behind it a will that would not give.

Gravity's lungs burned and her neck ached as they stayed there in the pocket and grimly traded blows. The close range negated her reach advantage, but she had nothing to spare for side steps or rolls. She bent her knees, leaned in, and kept throwing, and it was like climbing up a mountain that went on and on.

Once, she thought she saw a look of surprise light up Sylvia's eyes at a particularly brutal looping right. She risked opening up then, to try to get the eight count, but Sylvia caught her with a straight hook and forced her back, and a hot line of pain shot down her spine.

Gravity punched until she could not punch anymore. Then the bell rang, and Sylvia went away. Then it rang again, and Sylvia came back, and Gravity made herself punch some more. At the round breaks, she was too tired to do anything but sit and breathe. Bonnie iced her neck while Shorty rubbed her legs and told her she needed to pick it up.

Twice she spat her mouthpiece to the ground so the ref would break the action. She had learned that trick from D-Minus. But she was afraid to get a point deducted, so after that she bit down and went on punching.

That was when she understood what it really was to have heart. Every second, she had to choose not to lose. She did not know where the strength came from, but it came when she needed it like the answer to her prayer. When the final bell rang, she spat out her mouthpiece one last time, ran to her corner, and puked in the bucket.

Bonnie rubbed her neck, and Shorty rinsed her mouth. She could barely stay standing long enough for the ref to raise her hand.

She forced herself to stay awake to watch Sacred's beautiful display of the sweet science. The poor Brazilian middleweight had once been a world champion, but Sacred was entirely out of her league. When the bell rang to end the brutal first round, the Brazilian looked back at her corner with the expression of a frightened child. Gravity could almost see the thought bubble over her head saying, "Coach, I wasn't ready for this."

She went the distance, though. By bout's end, her braids were loose and her cheeks and shoulders were covered with marks, but she kept coming forward into Sacred's punishing combinations.

"Brazilians are tough," Gravity remarked to Aaliyah, who was sitting beside her, icing her knee.

Aaliyah said, "*Women* are tough."

Gravity nodded. She rose to her feet and cheered as they raised Sacred's hand.

April 10, 2016

US Is Golden at Last Day of Continental Championships

CORNWALL, ONTARIO—The last night of competition at the Continental Championships was a triumphant one for the US women, who captured the Best Team trophy with a total of six gold, two silver, and two bronze medals. Second place went to Brazil, third to our generous Canadian hosts.

Light flyweight Marisol Bonilla of Austin kicked off the action with a graceful victory over Claribel Martinez of Argentina. Bonilla dedicated the medal to her younger brother Alexis, a promising amateur boxer who was tragically murdered last year in a robbery at their family's home. Bonilla always boxes with his name on her trunks.

California's Kaylee Miller edged Brazil's Emilia Matos in a well-matched flyweight final. Miller is boxing strongly and seems in good position to qualify in China.

Heavy-handed bantamweight Clelia Bosco captured the first gold for Brazil in an entertaining slugfest with Argentina's Carolina Berenbaum.

London medalist Paloma Gonzales continued her domination at featherweight, dissecting Argentina's Leonela Benavidez.

"That shoulda been me," said Gonzales, pointing to teammate Delgado, who snatched Gonzales's spot on the US Olympic team last month at Trials. "But Paloma Gonzales will come back stronger than ever."

Young Gravity Delgado's tournament performance here in Cornwall bears out Gonzales's skepticism. Having barely squeaked by Canada and Mexico, Delgado got a gift this evening in her split decision win over Brazil's powerful Ariana Leite. Although Delgado landed more punches, Leite's were the harder and more damaging. Delgado will have to step up her game in China if she wants to qualify for the Summer Games.

Maribel Silva, another heavy-handed Brazilian, took the split decision against Seattle's Aaliyah Williams in the all-action light welterweight final.

Amanda Ross of Manitoba claimed the first gold medal for our host nation with an easy win over Barbados's Keri Brathwaite. The Canadian team lifted Ross up on their shoulders and carried her around the ring.

Sacred Jones continued to show the crowd why she is considered by many to be the greatest female boxer ever, with a physical and psychological dismantling of former world champion Susan Marshall of Ontario.

In the moving light heavyweight final, Philadelphia's Kiki Mailer outpointed Armelle Miville-Deschênes of Montreal. Miville-Deschênes, who is deaf, reads her coach's lips at the round breaks.

"We just let the refs know," said Canadian head coach Simone Boulanger, "because she can't hear them say 'break' and she can't hear the bell."

The mood of the crowd lightened as American heavyweight Bettina Rosario and Brazil's Victoria Freitas squeezed between the ropes and faced off like two battleships. The two tired after about 30 seconds. Freitas dug deep and pulled out the win.

Chapter Twenty-Seven

Gravity was still seething about Carmen's blog post when her flight touched down at LaGuardia. As soon as she had cell service, she texted Kaylee and Svetlana to complain and Melsy to make sure she and Auntie Rosa were still picking her up, and to ask if they had room for two more passengers.

Svetlana texted back:

Fuck Carmen she don't know shit about boxing

Kaylee texted back:

Don't worry about it, matey. Fuel for the fire.

Melsy texted back:

We're at Terminal A arrivals with mofongo. You know the ark always has room for two more lol

Gravity multitasked, retrieving her luggage from the overhead compartment and texting Kaylee:

Fuck Carmen! She doesn't know shit about boxing

She staggered as the luggage hit her face. It was a little hard to move around right now, because her neck was half frozen from the fight with Ariana Leite. Gravity could rotate it to the left, but when she wanted to see anything on the right side, she needed to swivel her whole body like a robot.

Kaylee texted back:

Um, ok, lol!

Gravity texted:

What?

Kaylee forwarded an old text Gravity had sent her:

So glad CC is here!!! She's the only sportswriter who cares about the women's game and she always calls it like it is

Gravity glared at her phone. She texted Kaylee back:

You thought i won right?

The phone was silent.

She texted Svetlana:

You thought i won right?

Svetlana texted back:

I'm so sorry g I didn't watch,,I had a date w Boo,,,but I'm sure you won,,you always win,,,FUCK CARMEN SHES A HATER! plus a string of muscles and boxing gloves and a hand painting a fingernail.

Kaylee still did not reply, so Gravity shouldered her luggage and waited in the jet bridge for the St. Lucian twins, who cheered up immensely when Gravity offered them a ride back to Flatbush. It wasn't too far out of the way on the drive to Coney Island.

Gravity would have liked to keep staying at her auntie's, but sleeping on the foldout sofa with Ty hurt her neck. Plus, Auntie Rosa and Melsy deserved some space after all the time they had spent looking after Ty. Once Gravity finally got that fucking stipend check, she would be able to rent a room for the two of them.

They found the Ark at arrivals just as Kaylee's reply came in:

It doesn't matter what I think.

Gravity texted:

It matters to me

Kaylee texted:

U and Ariana are the only ones who know who won.

Gravity felt her face flush at that, thinking of the fierce, thick-necked Brazilian who, alone among Gravity's twenty-four opponents, had seemed immune to her power. When they had raised Gravity's hand at the end, Ariana had made no protest, but a look of profound contempt had come over her handsome face. All throughout the medal ceremony, Ariana had worn that contempt like armor. Gravity still felt the force of it, and it hurt worse than her neck.

"Easy, easy!" she told Tyler, laughing, as he dashed out of the Ark's backseat and launched himself at her with full force.

"You good, cuz?" Melsy asked, kissing her cheek.

"Yeah," Gravity said, waving at her phone. "Just some bullshit."

"You spend too much time on that thing!" said Auntie Rosa, walking around the Ark to envelop Gravity in her arms.

"I know, Auntie."

Auntie Rosa must have come right from work, because she smelled like espresso. She pulled back and studied Gravity's face, then planted a kiss on the tiny red bruise on her left cheekbone from an Ariana Leite right hand.

"My tough little baby. It's too much!" Auntie Rosa turned to the twins. "Look at you two, so beautiful! I bet your aunties can't stand to watch either. Why couldn't you girls play soccer or something?"

The twins laughed.

Gravity said, "Auntie Rosa, this is Truth and Honor. They stay right by Brooklyn College."

"No problem," Rosa said. "Just move all the junk out of the way and squeeze in."

Somehow the Ark was slightly bigger on the inside than it

216

was on the outside. They wedged their bags in the trunk next to the folding chairs and silkscreen supplies, put Tyler up front on Melsy's lap, and piled into the back. Rosa pumped up the volume on Hot 97 and passed back two Tupperware containers, one with the mofongo and one with the broth. Melsy handed out packets of plastic cutlery.

As Rosa piloted them out of LaGuardia, she interrogated the twins about where they were from, who their family was, if they were dating anyone, if they had ever been to the DR, and their personal history with mofongo. Gravity's mother always said to forget about solar power, that the world energy crisis could be solved by a generator hooked up to Auntie Rosa's mouth—when she wasn't napping, that is.

Gravity steadied her hand against the back of the passenger seat as she poured the savory broth over the mashed plantains, took two big bites, and passed the dish to Honor.

As with everything she did, Auntie Rosa added her own artistic flair to her mofongo, mixing in fresh herbs along with both fried pork rinds and garlic shrimp. She refused to reveal the secrets of the broth to anyone, but Melsy had caught her straining out the solids once and said she saw a turkey wing in there alongside the traditional marrowbones.

"Why she drive like that?" Honor asked, passing Truth the mofongo.

Now that they had hit top speed on the BQE, Auntie Rosa had her window rolled down and was driving with her head stuck all the way out, like a dog. There were little pinging sounds as her hairpins fell out and hit the side of the Ark.

Rosa pulled her head back in and said, "When I'm very tired, the force of the wind helps keep my eyes open."

Honor went a little pale, but Truth said, "I love it! It's like a video game!"

Gravity told them not to worry. Auntie Rosa had never fallen asleep at the wheel.

"Give them pamphlets," Rosa yelled.

Melsy reached in the glove compartment for two of Auntie Rosa's famous self-published pamphlets on how to avoid getting traffic tickets. She had made some money off them in the nineties.

"The science of it is called SCAB," Rosa explained as she wove in and out of traffic. "There's four important steps to SCAB. The first is Stickers." She pointed to the small badge on the dashboard that said "NYPD Benevolent Association." "I've got two more on the bumper. My niece gets them from that cop who runs her gym."

Honor made a face. "We hate cops."

"Black lives matter," said Truth, raising a fist.

Melsy raised one too.

"Everyone hates cops," said Auntie Rosa, whose Facebook page was approximately twenty-five percent cat videos, twenty-five percent family photos, and fifty percent videos of unarmed people of color getting tased by police.

"Well, I wouldn't say *everyone*," Gravity mumbled. If it weren't for Mr. Rizzo, she never would have become a boxer. Neither would a lot of other kids at their gym.

"Your Officer Rizzo is the exception that proves the rule," said Auntie Rosa. "I want everyone in this car to understand one thing, especially you, Ty Ty. There's a time and a place for pride, and it's not when you're dealing with the NYPD. Do you understand me?"

"Yes, Auntie," Tyler said.

"Now, step two of my patented system is Cry."

Melsy pulled down the sun visor of the Ark's passenger seat to show the bottle of eyedrops hidden there.

"Keep the lid off the bottle," Rosa explained. "You need to be weeping profusely when the cop approaches the vehicle. Step three is Apologize. Make sure you say 'Officer' a lot. It's very submissive and cops love that shit. If you do the first three steps right, you probably won't even need step four: Beg."

Rosa's voice trembled realistically as she whined, "Officer, p-p-please don't give me a ticket. I p-p-promise I've learned my lesson."

Gravity felt uncomfortable. She could tell Truth and Honor did too; they were looking out the window at the passing houses of Crown Heights. It was hard to watch a grown woman grovel, even to an imaginary cop.

"You can make shit up," Rosa added. "Like, say your man will beat you if you come home with a ticket."

"But that doesn't work with female cops," Melsy cautioned.

"Female cops are a challenge," Rosa agreed. "The safest bet is to play the single mom card." She indicated the faded baby photo of Melsy taped to the Ark's dash. "Tell them you're raising your kid on your own, can't pay for Pampers, blah blah blah. Most of them are single moms too, because who wants to be married to a lady cop, am I right?"

"True," said Honor.

With a screech, Rosa made a hard right turn onto Avenue D. She brought the Ark to rest in front of Flatbush Gardens.

"Is this right?" she asked.

"This is good," they said in unison.

Gravity opened the door and they all tumbled out of the Ark with relief. She rubbed her neck as the twins retrieved their bags and thanked Rosa.

"It was educational," said Truth.

"And delicious," said Honor.

The twins had tied their headgear to the outside of their duffel bags like bragging rights. Gravity hugged them and made them promise to pass through Cops 'n Kids for sparring, and they made her promise to come by Smiley's to train with them and Tiffany. Gravity watched them walk off, side by side.

She polished off the mofongo while they drove to Coney Island. That was when Melsy told her the news. She said it so casually that it went in one of Gravity's ears and out the other.

"Wait a minute. What did you just say?"

"D-Minus. He's going to Rio."

"What do you mean?"

Melsy explained what he had told her over cheesecake at Junior's. Genya and Monster had gone to Memphis, where they had both lost at the US Men's Trials, but D-Minus— never one to take no for an answer—had done what the St. Lucian twins had done. His parents were both born in Haiti. Mr. Rizzo had helped him apply to the Haitian federation for permission to be their bantamweight representative.

Gravity had to explain to Melsy that this did not mean he was automatically going to the Olympics. Like Gravity, he now had to qualify by placing in the top of his weight at the World Qualifiers, which for the men would be in Azerbaijan. It would be difficult, but he still had a fighting chance.

Gravity's joy for him was so great that nothing could kill it, not even the thought of him and Melsy eating cheesecake together, or the sight of her mother sprawled out on their sofa back home with her latest disgusting hookup, who looked like a homeless lumberjack. They were drinking vodka with

220

Coke and watching porn, which they did not even bother to turn off when Gravity and Ty walked in.

"Oh look," said the lumberjack. "It's the boxer!"

Gravity told Tyler to go to his room.

"Do you mind turning the volume down?" she asked them. "We have school in the morning."

Her mother rolled her eyes. She hit the volume control with one polished toenail, turning it down imperceptibly.

"Did any mail come for me, Mom?"

Her mother yawned. "No."

"You're sure?"

Gravity went to the recycling bin, but there was nothing inside it except a few cardboard boxes.

What the fuck was up with USA Boxing? She had just won them a Continental gold! They owed her four thousand dollars by now. She pulled out her phone and sent another email, cc'ing Bonnie this time.

"Don't beat us up!" said the lumberjack, which was the stupidest joke in the world.

Chapter Twenty-Eight

Gravity whistled to herself as she turned the corner onto the little alley that led to Cops 'n Kids, her new Continental gold medal swinging from her chest. There was nothing like taking time off from the gym to make you miss it. Every detail of the street looked sweet to her, from the litter gathered by the curb to the cans of gourmet cat food Coach had left congealing by the dumpster.

It was chilly, but the air had a whiff of spring. The feral tabby had had three kittens. One of them, a tuxedo, was friendlier than the rest. He skittered alongside Gravity, meowing until she bent to pet him, then ran away and disappeared beneath the dumpster.

Monster was leaning against the gym door, a camera around his neck, talking on his cell phone. She waved to him and he motioned for her to hold still.

"I'll call you back," he said.

He hung up the phone and took her picture.

"You look great in that light, with your medal on and the dumpster behind you." He reached out to adjust Gravity's hat and smoothed her hair down. "Think about winning that gold out there in Canada."

Gravity thought about Ariana's arrogance, about Carmen saying she would have to step up her game.

"No! Not so serious!" Monster said. "All right, think about sex."

Gravity laughed. When she'd left Lefty's that morning, he'd said he'd be by the gym later.

"That's better," Monster said.

He took a few more shots, went and adjusted some of the trash that was spilling out of the dumpster into a shape he liked better, and snapped a few more. Gravity smiled into the lens.

"I heard about Trials, Kimani. I'm sorry."

He shrugged. "Andre says it's for the best. He's lining up a pro debut."

"Really? When?"

"Who knows. I wish I could just take photos all the time."

He scrolled through the pictures, saying, "You look great. Hold on a sec." He plugged a little box into the camera. It hummed and flashed and printed out a tiny Polaroid. Monster waved it back and forth in the air and handed it to Gravity.

It was in black-and-white. Gravity was smiling, hiking her gym bag up one shoulder and gazing at the sky. Her skin looked soft against the cold black metal of the dumpster. In the background, the tuxedo kitten had slid halfway out of a cardboard box and was peering at her with shining eyes.

"Wow," Gravity said. "It looks like a movie."

Monster said they would shoot some more later on. "A reporter is inside from the *Daily News*. They're doing a piece on the gym and on you and D both trying to qualify for Rio."

"Cool, thanks!"

Press wasn't uncommon at Cops 'n Kids, but this was the

first time she was part of the story, and that put her in an excellent mood. She couldn't wait to see Coach again and give him the red-and-white Boxing Canada hoodie she had gotten him in Cornwall. But as soon as she got inside and caught a glimpse of him, she could tell he was in a foul mood.

He was rolling toward the back corner of the gym, muttering under his breath. Boca sat on the apron of the larger ring with Andre, holding court for the reporter, who held his phone in front of the three of them to record everything. Various members of the Bocacrew were circling around, Snapchatting the interview.

Coach came to a halt in the opposite corner, as far away from Boca as he could get while still being in the same gym. Gravity tried to surprise him with a hug, but he stiffened at her approach and barked, "Where have you been?"

Gravity grinned. It was Wednesday. She had only taken two days off to be with Lefty and catch up on sleep. Everything about the gym today felt sweet, even Coach's grumpiness.

She bent to kiss his wrinkly old cheek and said, "I missed you."

He grunted. "Gym's been open all week."

"I just needed a couple days off, but I'm back! And I did my roadwork this morning."

"Bah," he said. "What do you want, a medal or a monument?" He waved a hand across the gym at the big blue ring, where D-Minus was shadowboxing. "Gear up. You're going in with D and Boo Boo."

"I don't feel like sparring today," she said.

He lifted his eyebrows and fixed her with a bloodshot glare.

"*I don't*," she said weakly. "It's my first day back. I'm tired."

With a speed that belied his age, Coach shot out a hand and snatched the Polaroid from her grasp.

"Hey! Monster gave me that!"

"You'll get it back after you spar. This is a gym, not a modeling studio. Gear up and get your fat, lazy ass in the ring." He rolled away from her toward the PLASMAFuel vending machine.

"I am *not* lazy!" she grumbled as she stalked off to the locker room.

She wasn't about to say she wasn't fat, because then he might make her get on the scale, and she didn't want to know her current weight. Her ass and boobs felt pretty big.

She stopped to say hello to D-Minus. He had on a cup and sparring gloves, trunks made out of a Haitian flag, and a creepy mask like out of the *Purge* movies.

"Mazel tov," she told him. "Melsy told me your good news."

"Thanks," he said, baring his mouthpiece in a smile.

It was hard to interpret his mood because of the *Purge* mask. The smile could have been a sign that he was happy about his positive career news and therefore ready to forgive her for dating Lefty and thinking that he lost to Tiger Biggs. Or it could have been an evil smile because he knew they were going to spar and was looking forward to humiliating her.

"Hurry!" Coach bellowed.

Gravity headed to the girls' room. Svetlana was already in there, taking her time getting changed. They hugged and Gravity quickly peeled off her jeans.

Svetlana said, "Coach Thomas is in a bad mood. You . . . you weren't here Monday. . . ."

"I know." Gravity pulled on a tank top Lefty had given

her that said "$outhpaw: All Is Fair in Love and War." If her photo wound up in the *Daily News*, that would give his music free publicity.

"I gotta hurry," she said, aware that her friend wanted to talk but not wanting to get into anything and give Coach the excuse to get even madder.

Back on the gym floor, Monster had set up lights, and everyone had gathered around the ring to watch. Coach laced her into the sparring gloves and waved her into the ring. She barely had time to get her mouthpiece in before D-Minus rushed her, his mask replaced with headgear and his smile now clearly of the evil variety.

After the first brutal body shot, he walked her to the ropes and whispered in her ear, "What's my name?"

She wouldn't say it.

To be fair, she couldn't say anything, because all the oxygen felt like it had been surgically removed from her body. D held her to him long enough for her to recover, then whirled her off the ropes and thrust her back into the center of the ring, where he could have more fun.

His jabs were like strokes of a whip to the point of her nose, the cheekbone, the chin, the solar plexus. Gravity gritted her teeth and stared through the involuntary tears.

"Why you crying?" he asked, loud enough for the whole gym to hear. It got a few chuckles.

She kept her hands high and her eyes on his shoulders because that made it marginally harder for him to sucker her with feints. Whenever she could, she jabbed. Not out of much hope of landing, but just to show that she was still trying.

There was only so far D-Minus could reasonably go. To actually beat a girl up would have looked bad. He walked the line, hurting her in private little ways. At one point, he spun her into the corner and threw an uppercut to her ass, right where the sciatic nerve connected. Her entire leg zinged with pain and then went numb.

She looked outside the ropes for Coach, but he had rolled off to the bathroom, so she grabbed on to D-Minus and did a sweep with her good leg, dragging him onto the ground.

All the gym rats whooped with delight.

"Yo, Gravity's on some judo shit!" cried Boo Boo.

Everyone watching called out the names of their favorite pro wrestling moves while Gravity and D-Minus rolled around on the canvas. D wound up on top in the mount and tapped her softly in the face with his open glove, pretending to ground and pound.

"Say my name!" he yelled.

Gravity felt a delicious ferocity rise up inside her. D-Minus looked adorable perched there on top of her belly, but he had no idea how to fight on the ground. Gravity's old shotokan sensei had a blue belt in Brazilian jiu jitsu, and he had taught her a thing or two, because he said all girls should have one submission move in their pocket for self-defense.

She went limp for a second to feign fatigue. When she popped her hips, D-Minus shot up off her, looking even cuter in his surprise. She spread her legs and put him in the guard, hooking her ankles together around his waist.

Genya yelled, "Yo, D. Watch out for the arm bar!"

Too late. She scissored one leg around his neck and arched, stretching his elbow joint.

"Ow!" he howled. "Yo, what the fuck?"

She spat out her mouthpiece and said, "Tap out."

"Yo, D, tap!" yelled Genya.

Gravity pressed her boot to the canvas. She felt his elbow start to hyperextend.

"You better quit, bro!" yelled Boo Boo.

"Say you quit," she said through clenched teeth.

D-Minus groaned in pain. He said, "Fuck you!"

"Enough!" roared Coach, who had come out of the bathroom and was zooming toward the ring at top speed.

Gravity rolled off to the side, irritated. She'd have to work more on her triangle so next time she could choke him out.

Monster made them pose in front of the ropes with their arms around each other, smiling.

D whispered in her ear, "How'd those body shots feel?"

She whispered back, "How's your elbow feel?"

He replied, loud enough for everyone to hear, "All I'm saying is, that's the weakest I ever seen you box. You and your ugly boyfriend musta gone twelve rounds this morning."

All the gym rats snickered.

Gravity blushed. She still hadn't figured out what D's beef was with Lefty. She said, "I coulda broken your arm if I wanted."

D reached below his chin to unbuckle his headgear and pulled it off. He smiled at her. It was the first kind of smile now, his sunny smile, no meanness in it anywhere. He hugged Gravity loosely around the neck, pulling her sweaty body into his, and when his lips reached her ear, he whispered, "It was worth it to get between your legs."

That was the picture that made the *Daily News*: Gravity looking at D, cheeks flushed and eyes wide, sweaty tendrils of hair escaping from her headgear like a lion's mane. D was eyeing her sideways, his arm draped lazily across the back of her neck. The light gleamed off his shaved head, and his brown eyes shone with laughter.

Growing up is weird because you never notice it happening. One day you just wake up and you can't make featherweight anymore, no matter how much Albolene you use. When she saw that photo in the newspaper later, Gravity felt, for the first time in her life, like a woman.

She tried to follow D-Minus out of the ring, but Coach rolled to the bottom of the stairs and blocked her path.

"Where do you think you're going?" he said.

"I thought I could hit the bag a little."

Something was different between her and Coach. Every limb of his big, old body bristled with rage. It scared her.

"Give me that mouthpiece," he snapped.

She handed it over. He rinsed it out and shoved it back in her mouth.

"Get back in that ring," he said. "You're done when I say you're done."

Gravity turned and trudged back up the ring stairs. Her quadriceps felt like Jell-O, but she knew better than to argue.

"You looked like shit in Canada," Coach snapped. "We're picking it up from here on out. No days off. No bullshitting." He waved Boo Boo over and told him to get into the ring and give Gravity six rounds.

"Six rounds!" She looked at him in disbelief.

"Oh, that's not enough for you?" Coach said sarcastically. "Give her eight, Boo Boo. We go at the next bell."

Gravity stared across the ring in misery. D was right. She should not have had sex with Lefty that morning. Her road-work had been shitty enough; she had nothing left for the gym. Now she knew for sure that the old maxim "Women weaken legs" applied just as well to men. Lefty had drained her like a sex vampire.

Somehow she got through the rounds. Not with dignity. Not with grace. But with that native stubbornness that made it impossible for her to call it quits, short of total loss of consciousness. It helped that Boo Boo did not have a mean bone in his body. He batted her around like a big dog playing with a puppy.

Coach remained silent throughout the ordeal, allowing Boca to give them water and advice. Whenever she dared to look down at him, he stared fiercely back from underneath his furrowed eyebrows.

"Had enough?" he said finally, after the eighth awful round.

"Yes, sir."

Boo Boo held the ropes apart and gave her his arm as they went down the stairs.

"I'm sorry I wasn't good work today, Boo," she said.

"Don't sweat it, G," he said. "I was tired too."

"Some of us were more tired than others," Coach said.

He grabbed Gravity's right glove and peeled off the tape. His face looked like he had been sucking a lemon, but some of the anger had gone out of him, and everything might have worked out very differently had Lefty not chosen that precise moment to saunter into the gym. Chocolate-brown Cleto Reyes gloves swung from his neck like a mink stole, and he rapped along to his own track as it blared from the inset speakers in his futuristic Bluetooth hoodie. As he passed her, he planted a kiss on her cheek, saying, "Mmm, baby! You look good enough to eat."

If Gravity thought Coach had been mad before, she hadn't seen anything yet. He backhanded Lefty with such force that his hoodie quit playing music.

Lefty stumbled backward, eyeing Coach reproachfully.

"I want *none* of that bullshit in my gym!" thundered the old man. "Do you hear?"

He yelled so loud that everybody paused their workouts

and glanced nervously in their direction. D-Minus sat down nearby and started eating popcorn.

Lefty mumbled, "I'm sorry, sir."

His voice cracked a little and he looked down at the floor. It made Gravity think of something sad he had told her, while they were holding each other after sex, about how his father used to get drunk and hit him.

Gravity looked at Coach's face, all wrinkled up in frown lines like a prune.

"You're so *mean*," she said.

He raised his eyebrows dangerously. "Excuse me?"

D-Minus laughed.

"We have *nothing* to apologize for," she said, her heart pounding.

Coach remained silent, studying her. The bell rang. She felt suspended, like those cartoon characters who run off a cliff without knowing it and stay there awhile, legs windmilling, before they make the mistake of looking down.

"It's okay, G," Lefty said, touching her softly on the shoulder.

"It's *not* okay," she said. "We have *every right* to date who we want to."

"Not if you're *my* fighter, you don't," Coach said. "I will not have you acting like a little whore in my gym."

The word "whore" struck Gravity in some weak spot she hadn't known she owned. She swayed on her feet for a moment, heat flooding her whole body. Then she ripped off the sparring gloves and threw them in Coach's lap, hating him, hating herself, hating the words as they came out of her mouth:

"Then I guess I'll find another coach."

Chapter Twenty-Nine

"I'm gonna kick so much ass in China," she told Lefty. "I don't need Coach. It's all about conditioning at this point. I just need to stay on weight and find good sparring."

"I feel you," he said.

It was the day after her fight with Coach, and she had come straight to Lefty's after school for some therapeutic sex. They had fucked twice, and now he was doing hits out of a bong shaped like a cheeseburger while they watched the third fight between Sugar Ray Leonard and Roberto Durán.

Gravity reached for another chicken wing. His brothers had left them money for dinner, and they had gotten takeout from the Chinese place across the street. She had thought about asking Lefty if there were healthier options, but once they had sex, she forgot.

It would be okay. She would just up her mileage on the roadwork and wear plastics for a while. Next week she would go to Smiley's and find a new trainer. She had thirty-five days left before China. Gravity fixed her eyes on the laptop screen, calming the anxiety that threatened to rise at the thought of the ticking clock.

She loved a great boxing trilogy, but Leonard-Durán sort of let you down at the end. The two boxers were post-prime and much heavier and slower compared to their first two fights.

"Ooh, look at that right hand!" Lefty said. "Manos de Piedra!"

"Ray blocked that punch," she said.

"*Hell* no."

She hit the space bar and scrolled back. "See?"

"You're crazy! Durán knocked him back!"

She tried to scroll back again, but Lefty wouldn't let her. She sighed in frustration, replaying the last exchange in her mind's eye. Sugar Ray's gloves were *totally* in front of his face. He had stepped backward because his feet were square, but it wasn't a scoring blow.

Gravity tried to watch fights objectively, seeing what she could learn from each boxer. Lefty watched like they were superhero movies. His heroes were always the Latino fighters. If it was two Latinos, he would always root for the Puerto Ricans, then the Dominicans, then the Cubans, and so on down to the Mexicans, who were his last choice, because there was a bitter historical rivalry between Puerto Rican and Mexican boxers. At any given time, in some boxing gym somewhere, a Mexican and a Puerto Rican were beefing.

"Durán just seems like such an asshole," she said. It was good to punch with bad intentions, but he radiated them like a toxic cloud. "He only won the first fight because he insulted Sugar Ray's wife and got him off his game."

"So? It worked, didn't it?"

"And what about the second fight? How can you root for Durán after he said, 'No más'?"

Lefty got a blasé look on his face. He was in denial about the fact that his hero had given up in the middle of the rematch, and he refused to even watch that fight with her. Gravity liked to watch trilogies in order, and skipping Leonard-Durán 2 was like going right from *Star Wars* to

233

Return of the Jedi without giving the Empire the chance to strike back.

Lefty took a big hit from the cheeseburger, and the bong water bubbled so loudly that for a moment neither of them heard the knocking on his front door.

"Who is it?" Lefty called, in a cloud of smoke, out the window.

They both giggled until Mr. Rizzo's voice came back: "Is that you, Lefty? Gravity's aunt told me she might be over here."

"Oh shit," Lefty whispered, opening the window wider to fan out the smoke.

He mouthed, "Spray!" to Gravity, pointing to his dresser, atop which sat every fragrance of Axe known to man. Gravity picked up Apollo and Dark Temptation and sprayed them around the room, then began sneezing furiously.

"Gravity, is that you?" said Mr. Rizzo.

Lefty made a throat-cutting signal, but Gravity couldn't lie to Mr. Rizzo. Especially not if he had come all the way to the Bronx.

"I'll be right there!" she yelled.

Lefty gave her a fierce look. He used a box of condoms to sweep up the loose weed from his nightstand.

"Keep him in the living room," he whispered. "And get rid of him before my brothers come home. If they know I let a cop up in here, they'll kick me the fuck out."

Gravity nodded, an unpleasant revelation sinking in about why Lefty and his brothers always had money for food and new clothes and why there was always so much weed around. She left him there, squeezing Visine in his eyes, and went to open the five locks on the apartment door.

Mr. Rizzo wore a rumpled polo shirt and khakis and

held a plastic bag. She couldn't remember having seen him in glasses before. Beneath the thick frames, his eyes looked tired. Gravity switched on a lamp, feeling awkward. Nobody ever hung out in Lefty's living room. She gestured to the plastic-covered couch.

"Would you like to sit down? Can I get you, uh . . ." She didn't know what they had besides leftover fried rice and maybe some Tropical Fantasy. Lately the tap water at Lefty's had been coming out brown.

"That's okay," he said. "Here, bring these home to your brother." He set a box of Girl Scout cookies down on the coffee table.

"Wow, Samoas! Thanks! That's his favorite kind."

He smiled. "I know. My granddaughter is selling them. She's gonna bankrupt me."

The bedroom door squeaked open and Lefty emerged, exuding Axe from every pore. Mr. Rizzo was no dope; Gravity saw him roll his eyes.

"How *are* you, Lefty?" he said, handing him a box of cookies.

"Chillin'," Lefty said. "Hey, Thin Mints. That's my favorite kind."

"I know." Mr. Rizzo put a hand on Lefty's shoulder. "We miss you at the gym."

"I'm just taking a break. My brothers needed some help around the house." Lefty shrugged off Mr. Rizzo's hand, tore into the box of cookies, and ate three Thin Mints at once.

"And how *are* your brothers?" said Mr. Rizzo, a slight edge in his voice.

Lefty shrugged. "Working."

Mr. Rizzo took off his glasses and rubbed his eyes. It

looked like he was debating whether or not to say something, then decided to say it: "We went by the cemetery last week for Tray's date. They did a real nice job with the stone. You should go see."

"Sure," Lefty said.

Gravity could tell he had no interest in going. Mr. Rizzo must have known too, because he pulled out his phone and showed Lefty a picture of a polished gray tombstone surrounded by yellow flowers. A pair of boxing gloves was carved on one side of it and a crucifix on the other. The inscription read:

Trendon Saint-Amand
Sunrise 2/11/1993
Sunset 4/7/2012
Oh, what a wonderful world!

"He always liked that corny song," Lefty said, handing back the phone. His eyes brimmed with what might have been tears, but maybe it was just Visine.

"The retrial is next month," Mr. Rizzo said. "There's still time to change your mind, you know. Your testimony would—"

"I'm not changing my mind," Lefty said.

Mr. Rizzo's pale face reddened. "So you're just gonna let that sonofabitch walk? Really, Lefty?" As he spoke, he grew angrier than Gravity had ever seen him before. "You're gonna sit there on your hands while the bastard who shot your best friend *in front of your face* goes free?"

Gravity flinched.

Lefty was there at the dice game?

Nobody had ever told her that part of the story. The puzzle pieces clicked into place in her mind. He was there at the dice game and watched Tray die. *Now* she understood what D-Minus had against him. Why D was always talking shit about him and beating him up in sparring. Lefty could have put D's brother's murderer away, but he refused to take the stand!

"I ain't no snitch," Lefty said. He tucked the cookies under his arm and stomped off, slamming the bedroom door.

Mr. Rizzo sighed. He turned his tired eyes on Gravity.

She glanced away, embarrassed by Lefty's behavior and suddenly conscious of how she must appear to Mr. Rizzo, there alone, at this hour.

"What's this I hear about you leaving Coach Thomas?" he said.

She looked back at him. He did not look angry, just sad.

"I can't train with him anymore," she said, feeling sad too.

"Why not?"

"He . . ." She didn't want to talk to Mr. Rizzo about her relationship with Lefty. "He disrespected me."

Mr. Rizzo sighed again. "He's old, Gravity. And he's not well. He has old-fashioned ideas about things."

That made her mad. Just because Coach was in a wheelchair, that didn't give him a free pass to call her a . . . she didn't even like to think about what he had called her.

She had overheard guys at the gym saying a lot of misogynistic things. But this was different. This wasn't some teenage hoodlum or sleazy PLASMAFuel rep. This was her *coach*. Sometimes she had even pretended he was her father. She had trusted him.

"That old man loves you, Gravity," Mr. Rizzo said. "It kills him that he hurt you. I swear, I've never seen him like this before. Go back to him. Please. You need each other."

"If he's so sorry, how come *you're* here and not him?"

Mr. Rizzo remained silent.

Coach knew how to send texts now too; D-Minus had taught him. He could have checked in or said he was sorry if he had wanted to, but he hadn't. She felt sorry that Mr. Rizzo had come all that way and brought cookies and everything, but it was impossible for her to go back. That would be like saying that the way Coach had treated her was okay, and it wasn't.

"What will you do?" Mr. Rizzo said. "Want me to talk to Boca for you? He's a great coach too. I know he'd love to have you."

Gravity shook her head. As mad as she was at Coach, she would never disrespect him by staying at the same gym and training with his rival.

"I'll probably go to Smiley's."

Mr. Rizzo grunted. "Well, there's lots of action there." He rose slowly and picked up his plastic bag. "Any coach would be lucky to have you. Take care of yourself. If you wanna know if someone's a scumbag, you can always call me and I'll give you the police report."

"Thanks, Mr. Rizzo."

"You can come back to us anytime you want. And if you have trouble paying for tournament travel, let me know. I might be able to do something."

"Thanks, Mr. Rizzo."

She thought of all the things he had done for her over the years, all the things he did for everybody at the gym. She wanted very badly to hug him, but suddenly that felt too awkward. She wasn't a little girl anymore.

As soon as he had gone, Lefty opened the bedroom door. Gravity walked in to face him, dizzied by her new knowledge. How could he have watched Tray die and do nothing?

Lefty did a bong hit, said the words "Manos de Piedra" in a cloud of smoke, then paused to cough and drink some Tropical Fantasy. She watched as if through a pane of glass. He was an entirely different person than she had thought. She had thought he was brave, that he told the truth in his music.

He went on, "Manos de Piedra did not quit. He *chose* not to go on, because Ray made a *mockery* of the sport. Ray shoulda manned up and fought Roberto instead of dancing around the ring like a big pussy."

Gravity's anger at Lefty about Tray shifted instantly into irritation at his use of the word "pussy." How could Lefty use the word in such a sweet voice to talk about her body and then turn around and use it as an insult? And how come everyone always said "man up" when they meant "be brave"? Women were braver than men. If she had watched Tray die, you would have had to kill her to keep her from taking the stand.

"Leonard was *way* braver than Durán," she said.

Lefty laughed.

"He *was*. The proof is that he stood there and slugged in that first fight when slugging wasn't his game. It's brave to take a stand, even when it's not in your best interest. Even if you might get hurt or lose."

She gave Lefty a significant look, hoping he would understand that she was not talking about boxing anymore, but it went over his head so fast she almost felt the wind. So she came out and said it.

"You ought to say what you saw. Tray was your best friend. He was D's brother."

Lefty's face hardened. "I ain't no snitch."

She thought of Coach. He must have known Lefty was there at the murder too. Now his disapproval of their relationship seemed more understandable, and she felt a sharper pain in her heart, thinking of all Coach's wisdom, now inaccessible to her.

The girls she would fight in China were inside their gyms right now, around the world, training. She was sitting on her ass, eating fast food and breathing secondhand smoke. She hadn't gotten on a scale since Cornwall. She was probably light welterweight by now.

"What time is it?" she said, looking around for her coat.

"Time to take off your panties."

"No, I gotta get home. I want to . . . jump rope or something."

Lefty laughed and pulled his T-shirt over his head, revealing his smooth, fragrant chest. "That rope'll be there tomorrow."

His handsome face looked squinty and sleepy with weed. Despite everything, he still had a hold on her, and she wished she could convey to him the urgency she felt. The rope would be there tomorrow, but her will might not. She had already wasted so much time. He reached out a hand for her, but she slipped it like Sugar Ray.

"I'm sorry, Lefty. I gotta go."

Chapter Thirty

The most famous boxing gym in New York City occupied an airy old printing house near the Hudson River. Sunlight poured through the huge windows and drenched the four rings, in which professional champions shadowboxed side by side with bankers training for adventure races and movie stars practicing for action roles. Everything about Smiley's was the opposite of Cops 'n Kids. It cost a lot of money. It had showers, a weight room, and a favorable human-to-cockroach ratio.

A small man in a rumpled business suit sat behind the front desk, reading an old magazine with naked ladies on the cover. He had an eye patch and a miserable expression on his face.

"Hi, Smiley," Gravity said.

The man set down the naked ladies and glared at her through his single eye. "Who's that?"

"I'm Gravity Delgado," she said, holding out her hand.

He stared at it for a while as though unfamiliar with this odd custom. Finally he gave her a limp, clammy handshake. She was positive he knew who she was. Smiley's Gym often hosted the Metropolitan Championships, which she had won three times. He had personally given her trophies.

"I was hoping to sign up here. I used to train at Cops 'n Kids."

"Hmph," Smiley said. "One of Rizzo's charity cases. I suppose that means you can't pay dues."

Gravity fingered the sixty dollars in her pocket. Ms. Laventhol had insisted on giving it to her when Gravity told her about breaking up with Coach. Gravity smiled, remembering how concerned Ms. Laventhol had been. It was nice to have a teacher on her side.

Gravity was hoping not to have to waste the sixty dollars on dues. That way, she could save it for trainers' fees, if the coaches wanted to charge her, or—even better—for food. She still had not received any money from those assholes at USA Boxing. Mom had actually gone food shopping that week, but Tyler was growing fast and consumed alarming amounts of cold cuts.

She said to Smiley, "I just got back from Spokane, where I won Trials at a hundred and thirty-two pounds, and the American Continentals, where I took gold. Lightweight is an Olympic class for women, so if I qualify, I could go to Rio."

"Mazel tov," he said dryly.

"I was hoping . . ."

There was an unspoken rule in boxing that really good amateurs didn't have to pay to train. Somebody like Gravity was good for business. Then again, maybe he didn't need more good publicity. She looked behind him at all the banners hanging on the walls of the palatial gym, advertising past and current champions. She had begun to pull out her cash when somebody called her name.

"Gravity! How are you, champ?"

It was Tiffany Clarke, one of the few three-star AIBA coaches in New York. She was a tiny, tough Jamaican lady who held the record for being the oldest woman to ever win

242

a world title. She glanced at the cash in Gravity's hand, then at Smiley, pursing her lips.

"Don't tell me you're *charging* her?"

Smiley glared at Tiffany with his one good eye. She stared back, folding her arms across her chest.

Smiley returned to his dirty magazine, grumbling, "You're gonna put me out of business."

"Thank you," Gravity said, following Tiffany onto the sunny gym floor.

Tiffany patted her on the back. "Don't mention it. I watched the livestream of Canada. You hung tough! I won't lie, I thought that Brazilian edged it. But you're coming along."

Gravity hid her irritation. Why was Tiffany telling her that? She didn't need negativity right now.

They paused beside the nearest ring, where Tiffany had a group of little girls doing a bob-and-weave drill underneath clotheslines stretched across the ropes. Truth and Honor worked next to the ring, hitting the human-shaped punching bag called BOB. The twins paused, panting, and gave Gravity sweaty hugs.

"You look big," Truth said.

"Yeah," said Honor, prodding Gravity's belly with one glove.

"Look who's talking," Tiffany said, laughing. "Back to work now. Gimme that double jab, right hand, left uppercut, right hand, left hook." She glanced up into the ring. "Ella, don't cross your feet! Violet, bend your knees more! Come on, Ariana! Don't stop working when I stop looking!"

Gravity set her bag down on the ring apron and fished out her jump rope.

"You sparring?" Tiffany asked. "The twins are done, but my one twenty-five could use the work. Is Coach Thomas coming?"

"He . . ." Gravity hesitated. Boxing was a small world, and soon it would be all over the gyms that she had left Coach. "He's not the right trainer for me anymore."

Tiffany raised her eyebrows. "Don't you have Worlds soon?"

"Yeah."

China was in thirty-one days. Gravity scanned the gym, noting the half dozen trainers spread throughout. There was the old Panamanian who had gotten famous from *Million Dollar Baby*, but Gravity hated that movie. The cranky Irish guy who always told the press that women shouldn't box. That nice man who had started Boo Boo off, but he was one of Coach's old fighters and would not want to step on his toes. A muay thai trainer, a pro wrestling teacher, a group of men in tracksuits that said "Kazakhstan," and a few new faces she did not recognize.

Boxing gyms were like school lunchrooms: every clique had their own table, with hidden alliances and hostilities between groups. She hadn't realized until now how worried she had been about finding her place here.

She turned back to Tiffany, who was studying her with a frown, and blurted out, "Would you coach me?"

Tiffany sucked her teeth. "Jefferson Thomas had you since you were knee-high to a grasshopper. You best go back and talk it out."

Gravity shouldered her bag, cheeks burning. If Tiffany didn't want her, somebody else would. She headed to a quiet corner by the locker rooms, where mirrors stretched across the wall and a few boxers were jumping rope.

Her phone rang with a call from Tyler. Melsy and Rosa had gotten Ty a cell phone for his eight and a halfth birthday, which Gravity had been opposed to at first, because it would give him more of an excuse to spend all his time playing games. But it came in handy for moments like this, because it meant he could reach her without having to go through Mom.

"Hey," she said, blocking off her other ear from the bell.

"Hi, Gra Gra." He sounded unhappy. Gravity thought she heard sex noises in the background.

"What's going on?" she asked. "Is that a movie?"

"Mom is watching it with a man."

"Listen, Ty Ty. Go in your bedroom and lock the door and watch *Naruto* until I get home and make us dinner."

"But that's not fair. He's about to fight Konohamaru. You won't know who wins!"

Gravity smiled. "Let's make an exception just this once. I leave in a month for China, so we have a lot of episodes to get through. I want you to watch it and find out who wins and tell me why, okay?"

He sniffed. "Okay."

"I'll be there soon. Lock the door and watch."

When she hung up, she saw with surprise the familiar hulking form of Monster, climbing into the nearest ring with one of the men from Kazakhstan. Monster wore an "Autism Awareness" T-shirt and sleek new sparring gear that said "PLASMAFuel XXXtreme." Boca and Andre were leaning up against the ring ropes. Gravity felt a flush of embarrassment as Boca's eyes met hers, but he just smiled and kissed her cheek, like it was totally normal to meet her there.

He said, "Coach Thomas is too controlling. You're not a

little girl. How's he gonna tell you what to do on your own time?"

"Yeah," she said, his words cheering her up. "It wasn't like me and Lefty were bringing it in the gym."

"You work harder than any of the boys," Boca said. "I see you."

"Thanks." Gravity blushed. Boca had never said anything like that to her before.

Then Andre ruined it by saying, "You left that old man in the wheelchair? Good for you! He's a dinosaur."

She gave Andre a dirty look and began jumping rope. She didn't like hearing anybody insult Coach, especially not that sleazebag. Coach had *forgotten* more about boxing than Andre would ever know. And dinosaurs used to rule the earth.

She channeled her irritation into double jumps and banged out forty before tripping, then slowed to a basic jump as she watched Monster try to handle his stocky opponent. Normally, she jumped at least four rounds straight through, but today she allowed herself to rest on the breaks. The twins were right; she *was* big. She could feel the extra weight with every jump.

After three rounds, Gravity was gassed. So was Monster. The Kazakhstani fighter's class revealed itself slowly, like that little Polaroid that Monster had taken of her outside the gym last week, which, she realized with a pang, Coach had never given back. Gravity had never given him that Boxing Canada hoodie, either. The thought made her sad. She draped the jump rope over her shoulders and went to stand beside Boca.

"Who is that Kazakhstan guy?" she asked.

"World cruiserweight champion," Boca said. "Niyazimbetov or something. He defends his title next week at the Garden."

"Wow."

Cruiserweights were under two hundred, which meant Monster outweighed the guy by forty-some pounds, but Niyazimbetov or whatever was controlling everything. He was neutralizing Monster's right by keeping his own left high and jabbing relentlessly at Monster's shoulder.

After the fifth round, Boca yelled, "That's it for us."

Gravity and Monster worked the heavy bags side by side. He was barely even throwing his right hand, so she knew all those shoulder punches had hurt him. She was having an equally hard time. By a silent agreement, they both quit after four rounds and slumped down on the apron, where he clutched his shoulder, grimacing. Gravity pulled out some arnica balm and rubbed a thin layer over his stony deltoid.

"How's my champ?" said Andre. He patted Monster hard on the injured shoulder.

Monster shuddered and said, "Great."

"Glad to hear it! The other kid's team was real impressed."

"Yeah?" Monster looked over at the Kazakhstani coaches. "They said I was good?"

"They said I had a future world champion on my hands," Andre said proudly.

It suddenly came back to her, what Coach had said that night they all watched Boo Boo kayo the Nigerian: that Boca and Andre would build Monster up until the crossroads and then cash him in. She had meant to ask Coach more about that but she hadn't. Now she wouldn't get the chance.

She hoped Monster would be okay and that he could retire from boxing early with his faculties intact. It was a jungle out there. There were always sleazy people waiting to take advantage of trusting boxers.

Andre said, "All right, champ, I'll see you next week!"

"Okay, Andre! Thanks for the new gear!"

Andre smiled. "Like we say at PLASMAFuel: label first."

"What does that mean?" Gravity asked.

Andre looked at her with surprise and annoyance, as though one of the spit buckets had piped up with a question. He said, "The label tells people what to think. It's more important than what's in the bottle. If we want Monster to be a champion, we have to package him as one."

Gravity thought that sounded wrong. She said, "I thought you weren't supposed to judge a book by its cover."

Andre laughed. "Nobody reads books anymore."

As soon as he was gone, Monster moaned in pain.

"Do you want some Advil?" Gravity asked.

"Thanks. My head is killing me. That guy hits hard."

She slipped two Advil into his enormous palm. She couldn't imagine the size of the headaches he must get. She got headaches sometimes. After the fight with Ariana, she'd had trouble sleeping. Every boxer she knew got headaches, but they rarely spoke about them. If your coaches found out, they were supposed to keep you out of the ring.

She glanced at the old journeyman hitting the heavy bag near the locker room. Jimmy had a record of ten wins and thirty-seven losses, but he still loved boxing. The slushy way he said his s's was like how Tyler had said them before he had speech therapy, and sometimes he paused a long time before he found the right word.

That was the other reason you didn't talk about headaches: you didn't want to turn into Jimmy. You might joke about it, like if you forgot the combination to your locker, you might say, "I'm getting punchy." But you couldn't think too hard about it, because if you thought about that, you wouldn't be able to keep going.

"Can I show you something?" Monster said shyly.

"Sure."

"It's a new series I'm doing on ring card girls. Some are of your cousin."

Gravity looked at his phone reluctantly, expecting boobs and asses, but what she saw surprised her. The gym went away as she lost herself in the images.

A French-manicured hand gripping a card that read "Round Seven," the cords of the wrist popping, as though the hand's owner was terrified to let go.

A stiletto heel precariously balanced on the metal grating of the ring stairs.

Another immaculately manicured hand, draped in an unenthusiastic manner over the shoulder of a man in a business suit.

Two pairs of feet, crossed at the ankles, one dark-skinned, the other pale, in identical stilettos.

The pale feet again, red where the straps dug into the flesh and bowed at the ankles as though about to topple from exhaustion.

Hands holding a Hello Kitty cell phone.

Hands adjusting a bikini strap.

Hands lighting cigarettes.

Hands counting money.

She gave him back his phone. "These are amazing, Kimani."

"You really think so?"

"Yeah! When you look at their hands and their feet, you see how tiring it is to keep looking beautiful." She struggled to put it into words. "It made me feel kind of sad but also kind of . . . like I was inside their world."

"Empathy," he said. "That's called empathy. Those girls

fight their own fight, just like you and me." He looked at her searchingly. "You really left Coach?"

"Yeah."

"You two seemed so good together. He was like a father to you."

She sighed. Why was everybody trying to make her feel guilty about moving on?

"I had to. He disrespected me. Besides, I'd have to break up with Lefty, and I could never do that to him."

She had been thinking a lot about Lefty, and the more she thought about him, the more she regretted having gotten so angry. She should have had empathy. It must have been incredibly hard for him to go through that with Tray. He had to be feeling pulled in two directions now, between his own family and D's. She had been wrong to judge him so harshly. They had not spoken all weekend, although she had sent him a few texts checking in.

When she looked back up at Monster, he was studying her with those big solemn eyes of his.

"I hope Lefty appreciates you enough."

"Thanks, Kimani."

Boca came striding across the gym floor, yelling, "All right, Monster. We out."

Monster hugged her, and Boca gave her a kiss on the cheek. She watched them go wistfully and finished her workout alone.

Chapter Thirty-One

She got the email on the subway ride home:

April 18, 4:57 PM
From: gnagesh@usaboxing.org
Re: Stipend Checks
To: heavyhandz1999@gmail.com

Dear Gravity,

I just received a call from your team manager, Bonnie Rosario, who brought to my attention the matter of your missing stipend checks. I am sincerely sorry nobody from the office replied to your earlier queries. It's been extremely busy here and emails to our general information mailbox sometimes got lost in the shuffle. Please feel free to call or email me directly in the future.

According to our records, we mailed your March stipend of $2,000 on 2/29/16 and your April stipend of $2,000 on 3/31/16. Both checks were cashed at a Western Union on Coney Island Avenue in Brooklyn. I have attached a scanned image of the backs of the canceled checks so you can follow up on your end.

I'm sorry to say that we cannot reissue the monies. Going forward, I suggest we set up a direct deposit that could go right into a checking or savings account. I have attached the forms to this email. If you need help filling them out or setting up a checking account, please let me know.

Very best of luck in China, and congratulations on your Continental gold!

All best,

Gautham

Gautham Nagesh

Athlete Liaison

USA Boxing

One Olympic Plaza

Colorado Springs, CO 80909

Gravity did not need to click on the canceled checks to understand what had happened. The only mystery was how she could have been so stupid and why she and Ty had not packed up their things and left for good long ago. Her mother had already stolen her Golden Gloves necklace and gift certificates. Why wouldn't she take the stipends, too?

Gravity flashed back to that time when she had found her mother in that unusually happy mood, drinking Bloody Marys and baking challah and reading her old yearbooks. At the time, Gravity had thought it was just Mom trying to pull herself together. She should have known better. She had just been happy about stealing the first check. And she had lied about it to Gravity's face.

She ached for that four thousand dollars. There was a nice little studio in Auntie Rosa's building that was only fifteen hundred dollars a month. She and Tyler could have been moved in by now.

She stalked from the subway to their apartment in a fog of rage. When she arrived, she found her mother on the couch, watching porn and drinking vodka with Coke, her legs entwined with a new man's. The guy who looked like a homeless lumberjack had stopped coming around. This new one looked like a homeless leprechaun.

Gravity noticed certain details of economic prosperity that had escaped her before: the fact that her mother was drinking Grey Goose rather than her usual Popov, her salon-fresh red hair, her manicured hands and feet.

"Oh look, it's the boxer!" said the leprechaun. "Hey, don't beat me up!"

He and her mother giggled.

"Wow, I never heard *that* one before," Gravity said.

"Really?" said the leprechaun.

"No, not really." Gravity stared him down. "Everyone makes that same stupid joke and it isn't even funny. You would never say that to a male boxer. You say it to me because you think I can't do it, but I could if I wanted."

Her mother narrowed her eyes dangerously and said, "Watch your mouth." She turned up the volume on the sex scene they had been watching, in which a woman dressed as Dorothy from *The Wizard of Oz* got gangbanged by the Tin Man, the Scarecrow, and the Cowardly Lion.

Gravity's hands balled into fists and she began to tremble. The rage that rose up inside her was so endless that it scared her.

Tyler appeared at her side, crying.

She looked down at him. She took a breath. Slowly, the anger receded enough that she could unclench her hands. His tear-filled eyes glowed bright in the light of the television, and Gravity wished with all her heart that he could unsee all the bad things that he had seen. She took his little hand in hers.

Coach always said that some fights were not winnable. Part of being a champion was knowing which ones they were. That four thousand dollars was gone forever. It just about killed her to think about it, but maybe it was a bargain. You could not put a price on freedom.

She said, "We're going to Rosa's, and we're never coming back."

Her mother acted like she had not heard.

It was cold outside, and they had left without their jackets, but Gravity refused to go back. She hurried Tyler past Luna Park, which was still closed on weekdays this time of year and looked like a ghost town. They stopped to use the public restrooms before the long subway ride uptown, shivering in the cold sea air on the boardwalk.

Tyler looked so miserable on the subway that Gravity offered to take him back that weekend and go on any of the rides he wanted. She promised to buy him cotton candy and Nathan's hot dogs, but he called her a liar and began sucking his thumb.

"You're getting a little old to suck your thumb, Ty Ty."

He took it out of his mouth and said, "I only do it when I'm mad," then stuck it back in.

"That's okay," she said, ruffling his hair. "I'm mad at Mom too. But we won't stay with her anymore. We'll stay with Rosa and Melsy until I go to China." By then, she would have qualified for Rio, so her stipend would go up. "Then we'll get our own nice place together where Mom can't bother us."

"I'm not mad at Mom. I'm mad at *you*."

He would not tell her why until they were halfway to Washington Heights. Then he demanded, "Show me the pictures."

She pulled them up on her phone, but they did not seem to comfort him the way they usually did. He did not ask any of his cute questions, merely glared at each photo in turn and said "Next," until she got to the last one, the one of her playing video games with Dad. Then Tyler pointed at the little console in the picture and yelled, "*You* told me Dad wasn't *cheap.* That's a *PS1!* If Dad was generous, he *never* would've gotten me that. It would've been *really really old.* So I asked Auntie Rosa about it and she told me that's *you* in the picture." He pushed the phone away.

"She said that's you in *all* the pictures. Dad didn't love me and take me to the zoo. You *lied* to me, Gravity. Dad *hated* me and *I hate you!*"

He got up, walked to the other end of the subway car, and sat down, sucking his thumb furiously.

Gravity walked across the car slowly. She tried to sit next to Tyler, but he got up immediately and moved, this time across from her.

"I'm sorry," she said.

He ignored her.

"Ty Ty, I'm really sorry. I was wrong to lie to you. I was just . . ."

She was just trying to make him feel okay. The old wound of longing throbbed inside her. She didn't want Tyler to hurt the way she hurt whenever she saw a happy father and daughter together. Or when she saw the kids at the gym who came in with their fathers, even when their fathers were hard on them, like Kostya with Svetlana and Genya. At least Kostya showed up.

Because the truth was, their father *didn't* love them. If he did, he would have come back around. She wrapped her arms around herself, shivering. She wished Lefty were holding her. She wished he would at least text.

"I was wrong," she said again.

Tyler kept ignoring her and took out his cell phone.

She did a set of pull-ups on the subway handrail, but he just rolled his eyes.

She said, "I wonder who won between Naruto and Konohamaru."

He set his jaw stubbornly.

"I bet Konohamaru knocked him out."

"He could never!" said Tyler, outraged.

"So Naruto won?"

Tyler narrowed his eyes at her. "Konohamaru won."

"Really?" She sat down next to him. "How did he win? He's such a wimp compared to Naruto."

"Naruto wasn't paying attention when they explained the rules and he used an illegal jutsu."

"*Aha!* So Konohamaru won by DQ!"

"What's DQ?"

"Disqualification. Like when Tyson bit Holyfield's ear."

"Oh." He was silent for a second, sucking his thumb. "How come Dad left?"

"I don't know."

She put her arm around him and they stared at their reflections in the subway window.

"He was there when I was real little. That's when those pictures are from. The first time he left I was two or three, so I barely remember anything. Then he came back on my eighth birthday, and he was around for seven weeks. That's when Mom got pregnant with you, and then he left again."

She was quiet for a moment as the train brakes squealed.

"Mom said he went back to Santo Domingo, but I don't know why. Maybe he just couldn't deal with Mom anymore. But sometimes I feel like Rosa is mad at him too. Nobody ever wants to talk about him." She took a deep breath, aware that Ty was hanging on every word. Their father was always there between them, an unspoken presence in every room. She wished she had more to give. "I don't remember them fighting. And Mom wasn't drinking too much back then. Maybe he just came around to make us, and then he had other things to do."

Tyler blinked, and two perfectly round tears dropped from his eyes. "Maybe he didn't love me."

"Shh," she said, hugging him to her. "Everybody loves you."

At this hour, the subway car was mostly empty, but an old lady sitting nearby met Gravity's eyes and smiled. She rose from her seat, holding on to the poles as she teetered across the shaking car and pressed a pocket pack of Kleenex into Gravity's hand.

"Bless you, child," she said.

Some people thought New Yorkers were mean, but when you lived there, you understood they could be the kindest people in the world. Gravity loved traveling for boxing, but the best part of traveling was always coming home.

Chapter Thirty-Two

When Gravity walked into Smiley's the next day after school, she saw a familiar figure lounging on one of the massage tables, eating a protein bar.

"Champ!" exclaimed Rick Ross. "I didn't know you trained here."

"I switched gyms," she said.

The conditioning guru looked aggressively fit, gleaming with the unnatural orange hue that accentuated the veins in his neck and arms. He wore mirrored shades and a tank top that said "#GetSwole."

"Who trains you?" he said, glancing around the half-full gym. All the coaches were drinking coffee and preparing for the rush at 5:30 p.m., when the white-collar clients rolled in.

"I'm unattached at the moment." She tried to sound nonchalant, but it was like admitting you didn't have a date to prom.

Rick Ross looked ecstatic. He leapt up from the massage table, draped one rock-hard arm around her shoulder, and said, "Well! You're with me now."

Gravity felt a rush of pride as he led her across the gym floor. All the trainers cast sidelong glances at them, including Tiffany, and Gravity felt Rick's protection over her register with them. She thought of all the conditioning podcasts she had listened to on the long subway rides to Cops 'n Kids.

And now he would be her trainer, right when she needed someone the most! It seemed almost too good to be true.

He led her to the ring by the back wall, where a tall, muscular brunette in muay thai trunks and an elaborate sports bra was doing plyometric warm-ups. Rick looked at the brunette, then back at Gravity.

"I've got a great idea," he said. "Why don't you get warmed up. I'll be right back."

She pulled out her jump rope, in a trance of happiness. Finally something was going right, after all this drama with Coach and Mom and Lefty, who still had not replied to her texts. That afternoon, in an act of horniness and desperation, she had sent Lefty a topless selfie snapped from a stall in her school bathroom. She had never done anything like that before, and she grinned as she thought about her boldness. Hopefully he would invite her over that night.

She put him out of her mind as she began to skip rope, watching as Rick conferred with the brunette. When he returned to Gravity, he was beaming.

"Well, this is our lucky day," he said. "Jenna Petrone came in looking for sparring, and when I told her we had a national champion in the house, she jumped at the chance."

Gravity had not been planning on sparring that day. She had barely slept the night before and had jogged five miles in plastics that morning to start cutting weight. But Rick looked so happy about it. The brunette came to the side of the ring and leaned on the ropes.

"You ready to work?" she asked.

"Um, sure," Gravity said. She looked at Rick. "So you coach her, too?"

"Jenna and I go way back," he said.

Jenna laughed.

"How much do you weigh?" Gravity asked her.

"I fight at feather," she said.

Gravity looked Jenna up and down. She looked a *lot* bigger than 125. Then the muay thai trunks made her think of something. "Wait, you *box* at featherweight?"

"I fight MMA."

Gravity didn't know the weight classes in MMA. "Exactly *how much* do you weigh?"

Jenna shrugged. "I didn't weigh myself today. Probably one forty-seven, give or take."

That made Gravity nervous. "I fight at one thirty-two. I'll spar up to one forty-one if it's somebody I know."

Rick patted her arm soothingly. "Well, we all know each other here."

"I just want some tech sparring," Jenna said. "My strength is ground fighting and I'm going up against a real good striker in my next fight. Rick here said he could get me work against someone with hands."

Rick produced a pair of gloves and held them open, looking at Gravity expectantly. She pushed her hands into the gloves, which felt heavy and pillowlike. When he tied off the laces, she saw that they were eighteen ounces.

"I usually spar in fourteens," she said.

"These are good for conditioning."

Gravity sighed. She was a puncher. She preferred lighter gloves that let the opponent feel her power. Especially with a new girl she did not know. She studied the other woman. She was almost Gravity's height but broader-shouldered and thicker through the legs.

Rick headed over to help Jenna into her gear, then announced, "We'll go on the next bell."

Gravity climbed the ring stairs right before the bell and

went to touch up, which was when she noticed that Jenna, in addition to outweighing her, was in fourteen-ounce gloves. She was also, annoyingly, in one of those headgears with the bars across the face, the kind of headgear white-collar clients wore who were afraid to take a face punch. Fighters sometimes wore them if they did not want to get cut before a fight.

Gravity had been expecting a feeling-out process that led into a light, elegant exchange, but the first punch Jenna threw was a lead right that landed like a club on her temple, sending her staggering toward the ropes. This was not tech sparring.

Somehow, she got through it. At the round break, she walked dizzily back to Rick Ross, who was holding a phone up to the ring, recording. She stood in front of him, panting and waiting for him to give her water or instructions, but he just kept recording.

Tiffany, who had come over to watch, jumped onto the apron and said, "Come here, Gravity." She pulled out her mouthpiece, gave her water, and said, "You have to box. Keep moving. Don't stand there and punch with a big girl like that."

Gravity yelled across at Rick, "Jenna's in fourteens!" but he had turned the phone on himself and was recording his commentary on the first round. She heard him say her name and that she was the US national lightweight champion, which made her feel good, but she wished he would pay more attention to helping her and less to recording.

She tried to follow Tiffany's instructions and stay moving, but her quadriceps still ached from her long run that morning. She kept it going for the first ninety seconds or so, but then Jenna managed to trap her against the ropes and hit her with a heavy jab to the chest that pushed her back. Gravity slipped the right that followed, but Jenna followed through with her elbow, an illegal move that might not have been intentional. It hit Gravity's eye, and she held on in desperation, her vision blurry. Jenna was borderline dirty in the clinch, too, jumping up and down to dislodge Gravity's hold and banging the hurt eye with the side of her headgear.

At the second-round break, Rick Ross put down his phone long enough to give her water. She waited for him to tell her something to do, but he just stood there.

"What do you see?" she asked in exasperation.

He said, "We'll analyze the video later."

It was cowardly to quit before at least going three, but Gravity was so exhausted that she gasped, "I think that's enough for me. I can feel my eye swelling."

Rick cocked his head at her and said, "You quitting on me? I told Jenna we'd give her four rounds."

Gravity felt a pang inside. She did not want to let Rick down.

She looked around at the small crowd that had gathered. It was weird sparring somewhere other than Cops 'n Kids. It made her feel very exposed.

Rick patted her on the headgear and said, "You go out there and show me what you've got. Leave it all in the ring."

Gravity got back on her legs and boxed. Jenna had an open guard and fought with her chin too high, and Gravity was able to keep her on the end of the jab and catch her with a few good rights, but between the pillowy gloves and the closed-face headgear, it didn't have much effect.

Toward the end of the round, Jenna slid close, ducking to evade a hook. Gravity's left arm had slid behind her neck on the follow-through, leaving her body unguarded, and Jenna dug hard to Gravity's left floating rib, harder than you were ever supposed to dig in sparring.

The pain took a moment to hit Gravity's brain. When it did, she hunched over and crumpled to the canvas, watching the mouthpiece fall from her lips, trailing a line of spit. It was epic pain. It was the worst thing she had ever felt, as though her chest had been turned inside out.

Bells rang and people murmured and she stayed there on all fours like a dog, too agonized to even feel the shame.

She heard someone asking, "Are you okay?"

Tiffany was helping her to her feet, her strong little arm around Gravity's shoulders.

Her rib felt weird. She touched her left eye where it was swollen.

"Here you go, champ!" said Rick Ross, handing her a cold pack.

Tiffany snatched it from him, glaring. "What were you thinking, putting Gravity in with that bitch?"

Rick acted blasé. "Gravity can handle herself."

"Of course she can handle herself," Tiffany said. "She's a champion. But she shouldn't be having gym wars when she's got Worlds just around the corner. What's that supposed to teach her?"

"Grit," said Rick.

Gravity pressed the ice to her left orbital bone. The throbbing cold dispelled some of the pain. She let their voices wash over her. Trainers were always arguing about everything. She was grateful to Tiffany, but maybe Rick was right. Maybe she needed to toughen up.

Besides, Tiffany had blown her off. Rick was the one who had seen her and wanted her.

Gravity felt so tired. She just wanted to go lie down in Lefty's arms and forget about everything and let him make her feel better. He must have seen the sexy selfie by now.

"I gotta go," she told Tiffany.

She set the ice on the apron but Tiffany gave it back to her, saying, "Take that with you, and keep it on the eye as much as you can."

"Okay."

"And ice your rib, too."

"Okay. Thanks, Tiff."

Gravity waited for Rick to give her some parting words, but he was busy fiddling with his phone.

"What time do you want to train tomorrow?" she asked.

"Oh, I can't do tomorrow," he said vaguely. "I'm traveling."

"When will you be back? When do you want to look over the video of me and Jenna sparring?"

"Oh, that!" He laughed. "That was just for my records."

Her phone chimed.

"And I'll be gone until June."

Gravity felt her heartbeat accelerate. It was hard to figure Rick out. Why did he set up sparring for her and record it if he didn't want to use it to discuss her mistakes? And why had he acted like he wanted to be her new coach if he knew he would be traveling?

Her phone chimed again.

Tiffany said, "Listen, come train with us if you want. We start every day at four."

Gravity thanked her. As she picked up her gym bag, her phone made more sounds. Texts had come in from Lefty, Svetlana, and Melsy.

Her heart leapt when she saw Lefty's name, and she felt a rush of need and longing so intense the pain in her rib disappeared. But it came back doubled when she read his message.

Heyyy G! thanx 4 the pic;) your sweet but I think we r just not compatible:(

She stared at the phone in shock.

Was he breaking up with her? Over *text*?

The message from Svetlana said:

Left just posted pics on IG with Caroline from hempstead PAL,,,I was trying to tell you the other day,,he's been posting kiss faces and wet emojis on her pics for weeks,,FUCK HIM,,how's smileys?

Melsy's said:

Cousin. Demetrius told me he saw your boy making out w this skank from long island last night. Fuck him. Moms making coconut rice and we got you a futon to sleep on and a special neck pillow, come home.

Gravity's heart began to pound. She went to Instagram and saw it. Lefty, with his goofy postsex grin, draped over the shoulder of a big-boobed blonde. Gravity knew that girl. She fought at light welterweight and was terrible. Her dad owned a big car dealership on Long Island. She went to Lefty's Facebook page, furious, and saw that he had changed his status to "Married" and his cover picture to a cheesy montage of Caroline's shitty selfies.

Gravity texted Lefty, WTF?

She texted Svetlana, Good looking out. Smiley's kinda sucks tbh.

She texted Melsy a string of crying faces, then erased them and put a string of angry faces, then erased them and wrote, I love you cuz.

Lefty texted her back two question marks.

Svetlana texted back, Whos coaching you now?

Melsy texted back, did you luv him?

Gravity texted Svetlana, I thought Rick Ross but he's traveling so maybe Tiffany Clarke

She texted Melsy, I don't know.

She set the phone down and made her way to the shower in a daze. Smiley's had good water pressure; she winced when the jets hit her bruised face and left side.

How had everything gotten so fucked up? Everyone seemed to be working against her: Coach, Mom, Rick Ross and Jenna Petrone, and now Lefty!

She had thought she was in control of her life, that everything was going the way she wanted on a straight road to Rio. And now it was like she had taken one wrong turn and suddenly had no idea where she was.

She looked around numbly at the gleaming tiles of the shower stall, wishing she could be magically teleported to the claustrophobic girls' room at Cops 'n Kids with the busted mirror patched with duct tape; Tray's old locker covered with stickers; Svetlana scrubbing herself with wet wipes. It wasn't the number of rings or heavy bags that made a boxing gym. It was the people and the way they cared. She put a hand to her rib.

Coach never would have let anyone hurt her.

If only she could call him.

No, she thought, her longing giving way to resentment. She could not stand to hear him gloat.

Coach would hear that she and Lefty had split. Everyone would. They would all know that Lefty had dumped her for that other girl. She thought of D-Minus and Boo Boo and the rest of the boys, of what they must think of her now. Then she remembered the naked selfie.

Oh, God.

She got down on her knees and prayed: *Dear God, please don't let him show that to anybody, please please please.*

She watched the water run off her body and down the grate to wherever water went when it was dirty. She hadn't felt like a slut before, not when she thought Lefty loved her. But now that he had poured her down the drain, Coach's judgment no longer seemed unfair. She *had* been whoring around at the gym. And it had ruined everything.

She turned off the water and stood dripping until she began to shiver. It wasn't fair. Lefty could still go back to the gym anytime he wanted and swagger in like he owned the place. People would respect him *more* because he had slept with her.

She was the champion and the more loving one, and she had lost all her status. And she could *never* go back there now, not *ever*. She toweled herself off, hard, until her skin hurt. She wished she could scrub the entire layer of skin off her body.

She picked up her phone.

Melsy had texted: Are you crying?

She texted back, No.

Svetlana had texted: Tiff is cool but Be careful about that guy Rick,,,heard he gives people steroids

She texted Svetlana back, Thanks. It's hard training without you, and added some emojis of muscles and hearts and a girl with two blond pigtails and a boxing glove and a Ukrainian flag.

Lefty hadn't texted.

She stared in despair at the two question marks that were the last text from him. The curved shapes reminded her of their bodies when they spooned. She thought again with regret of how judgmental she had been their last time together, how he had wanted her to lie back down with him but she had hurried off. Maybe he didn't know how much she cared. Maybe that was what the question marks meant.

Her heart pounded as she texted, Lefty I'm so sorry if the last time we were together I came off as bitchy or something. Can we please talk about this in person? It's so hard over texts. I miss you. Please don't do this. I just wish I could touch you and look in your eyes.

She hit Send before she could lose her nerve, then pulled on her leggings and Team Boo Boo hoodie.

Svetlana texted back a funny GIF of a cat on a treadmill.

Melsy texted back, If you aren't crying, you didn't love him.

Lefty texted back, I had fun w u but I'm in luv w Somebody else

Gravity collapsed onto the bench. Coach always said that the punch that really hurt was the one you didn't see coming. He was in *love* with that girl? How could it be love? It had only been a few days.

It must have been going on a lot longer, then. But he had called Gravity his *girlfriend*. How could he have done that if he was with someone else?

She blinked, willing her eyes to produce tears, but they wouldn't. She just felt kind of dead inside. Was Melsy right? Was the fact that she couldn't cry proof that she didn't love Lefty? Then again, Gravity never cried. She could not remember the last time she had cried, not counting hard punches to the tip of her nose.

She reread Lefty's text. He had had fun with her. *Fun.* Like playing a video game or petting a dog. That was all it was to him.

She went back to Instagram and looked at the photo of the two of them again, hating Caroline with a thick, hot hatred. Caroline outweighed her by fifteen pounds, but she fucking sucked. They matched her lightly at her father's club shows because he always sponsored everything.

Gravity imagined taking the train to Hempstead, barging into the PAL, and challenging Caroline to spar in front of all her bougie Long Island girlfriends. She would only ask for one round. Nobody could say no to one round. That was all Gravity would need to knock her the fuck out.

Chapter Thirty-Three

When Gravity walked through their front door, Auntie Rosa said, "Finally!" and handed her three coconuts. "You're the best at breaking things."

"Ooh! Ooh!" cried Tyler, jumping up and down. "Can we do it the fun way?"

Gravity nodded. "Do you wanna pitch or catch?"

"Catch!"

Tyler dashed off into the elevator, and Melsy came and held Gravity in her arms, squeezing her tight and stroking her back.

"Aw, cuz," Melsy murmured. "You okay?"

"I guess."

"Let's do your hair!" Melsy said, taking one of Gravity's frizzy curls between her fingers. "I got some gold extensions that will look hot. We can try it out, and if you like it, I'll redo it for China."

"Okay."

Gravity tried to smile, but her face felt numb.

"Forget that boricua!" yelled Rosa from the kitchen. "He does not deserve you."

"Thanks, Auntie."

Gravity walked across the living room as though in a dream. She moved aside the enormous jade plant on the windowsill. Its shiny blue raku pot was one of the many pieces of her auntie's pottery that Gravity had broken as a child. She traced a finger down one of the lines of golden lacquer that shot through the blue, holding together the pieces. Somehow Rosa had repaired it so it looked even more beautiful for having been broken.

Gravity pulled the window up and raised the screen. Tyler was down there already, waiting patiently.

When he saw her at the window, he grinned and waved his arms.

"All clear down below!" he yelled.

Gravity let go of the first coconut. It hurtled downward, at some speed that Ms. Laventhol had taught them but she forgot—she had been half asleep—and hit the sidewalk with a satisfying crack. Tyler looked back up at her, his huge grin white in the night.

"That was a good one!" he yelled.

"That *was* a good one!" she yelled back, but she did not feel good. She did not feel much of anything.

She watched Tyler gather the pieces of coconut together and put them in the big pot Auntie Rosa had given him. He craned his neck to look up at her. It made her own neck hurt to see it. It was nice of Melsy and Rosa to get her a special pillow, but it would not help. Gravity would be seventeen in just a couple months, but she had the neck of an old lady.

"All clear down below!" he yelled.

Gravity let go of the second coconut and watched it fall.

It felt like her soul was not inside her body but somewhere impossibly far away, operating all the functions from a distance. She could smell the smells and see the sights, but she could not feel the feelings.

The coconut hit the pavement. Tyler inspected it.

"It broke a little bit," he yelled up. "That was an okay one."

She let go of the third coconut.

A moment after it left her hands, a little kid came from out of nowhere on a scooter.

Tyler screamed, "Watch out!"

But it was too late. Gravity could do nothing but watch in horror as the coconut hurtled five stories down, accelerating at 9.8 meters per second squared—a useless fact she suddenly recalled, her mind operating best in high-impact situations—on a collision course with the little boy's frohawk. His mother should have made him wear a helmet.

If Gravity had not already had faith in God, what happened next would have made her believe. At the last possible moment, a rat shot out from Auntie Rosa's garbage cans, making for the bodega across the street.

The little boy shrieked and veered off course.

The rat disappeared into the night.

The coconut broke against the concrete.

Gravity felt her soul land back in her body.

And nobody got arrested for manslaughter.

"That was a *great* one!" Tyler yelled, jumping up and down.

"That *was* a great one!" she said, giddy with aftershock.

As she closed the window and turned back toward her family, she could not stop laughing.

"What happened?" Melsy asked.

"A New York miracle," Gravity said.

Tyler came back with the pieces of broken shell, and they set to the hard work of grating. You could do it in a Cuisinart, but the Delgados had cooked and chomped many a pot of coconut rice, and the consensus was that hand-grating was superior. Melsy, Ty, and Rosa did it in shifts, on the special graters Rosa had brought back from the DR, while Gravity went to wash her hair.

She looked at herself in the bathroom mirror while she blew it out, studying her face: her squinty, dark eyes, the swelling around the left one already almost gone; the broad nose that was good for boxing; the annoying zits where her headgear rubbed her jaw; the thick, soft lips that Lefty had said were made to be kissed.

Nothing had changed. Nothing was broken.

One of Tiffany's white-collar clients was a physical therapist. He had said the rib was just bruised and would take three or four weeks to heal. China was in four weeks. Gravity would work hard and get better.

Fuck Lefty. Rosa was right. He didn't deserve her. It wasn't how many times you fell down, it was how many times you got back up.

"I am going to win an Olympic gold medal," she told herself, and she still believed it.

When she came out of the bathroom, Rosa was squeezing the coconut meat in cheesecloth. Tyler was playing *Hell Slayer 3*. Melsy was arranging the bundles of hair, rubber bands, and combs with the precision of a trainer preparing to wrap a champion's hands.

Gravity felt gratitude fill her to the brim. Mom could steal her money and her trophies, but she could not take their love away from her. She sat on the floor at Melsy's feet, let her eyes close, and surrendered to the wonderful feeling of her cousin's deft fingers. Melsy hummed as she worked, painlessly combing out the tangles and sectioning the hair into pieces. She made it just a bit too tight so the braids would last, and it always gave Gravity a headache, a different kind than the ones from the ring.

Pretty hurts. Gravity thought of the photos of the ring card girls Monster had shown her: the leather shoe strap cutting into the soft white flesh.

"What was it like for you?" she asked her cousin. "Being in the boxing ring."

She could feel Melsy smile behind her. "It was so *bright*."

"Yeah!"

"It was like a whole different world in there. The canvas was bluer than blue. Like my *quinceañera* dress. I could barely see the people in the crowd because the lights were in my eyes."

"You looked so beautiful," Gravity told her, inhaling the delicious fragrance emanating from the kitchen. Rosa was boiling down the coconut milk now until it caramelized like *dulce de leche*.

Melsy began braiding in the gold extensions. "At first I was trying not to fall in those heels. Then I got the hang of it, and I started listening." Her voice filled with wonder. "It's amazing what those coaches say. It's like a whole telenovela!"

"It is!" Gravity said.

"The ropes got kind of sweaty later on in the night. That was gross."

Gravity laughed. "I guess they do. I'm always so sweaty I don't notice!"

Next to them, Tyler let out a triumphant whoop. Gravity looked up at the screen. His little Paladin was dancing around the bloated corpse of a one-eyed giant.

"No way!" she said.

"Way!" Tyler was beaming.

"He beat the Bubonic Cyclops!" she told Melsy. "You don't even understand how hard that is!"

"I'm a *bad* man," Tyler said.

Auntie Rosa emerged from the kitchen, looking proud. "Okay, bad man, time for dinner."

She had fried up some red snapper and *tostones* and made black beans, but the coconut rice was the main event. It was past midnight now, because a good main event always takes time, and Tyler and Auntie Rosa started nodding off mid-meal. Gravity finished her rice, then started in on Tyler's, savoring the coconut's nutty sweetness.

"It came out real good," she said.

Melsy nodded. "Mmm-hmm. Now come let me finish before we fall asleep with your hair half done."

Gravity sat back down at her feet and gave herself up to Melsy's soft hands. After a while, she worked up the nerve to ask what she was wondering.

She tried to make her voice sound casual. "How's it going with you and D?"

Melsy snorted. "He's too little for me. Never date a man under six feet tall unless he makes six figures."

Gravity laughed. Melsy was probably five foot four if she was wearing her tallest heels.

"He might be little," Gravity said. "But he's big in the ring. He's got such long arms and good rhythm and distancing that he can outbox guys much taller. Like, remember Kimani? The really big one who was taking photographs the night you worked the fights?"

"Monster?"

"Yeah." Gravity tried to think of how to express it to her cousin, but it was hard. "It's like, Monster's a superheavyweight, right? But inside he's kind of insecure. You could psych him out if you knew what you were doing. But D . . . D's got, like, *infinite* potential. If there's *any* way to win, he'll find it."

She thought about D's loss to Tiger. "I'm not saying that he can't be beat, because he can. He's lazy and stubborn. You can beat him on conditioning alone." She laughed, thinking about the crap he ate. "He's like a fancy sports car running on cheap gas. But you can't outslick him or take his heart. Even if he loses, he'll go down punching."

"Oh. My. God," said Melsy, her hands freezing midbraid. "I am *so* sorry, Gravity."

"What?" Gravity asked.

She turned back to look at Melsy. Her cousin had tears in her eyes.

"You love him," Melsy said. "You *love* that boy, and I hooked up with him. I am *so* sorry. I never would have done that if I knew."

"I do *not* love him!" Gravity said, but she could feel herself blushing. Why was she blushing?

She just loved his *boxing.* And his sense of humor. And just the whole infuriating D-Minusness of him. And he had been right about Lefty. He was usually right about the important stuff. It was just that he was such a dick about it.

"You know what?" Melsy said thoughtfully. "I think he likes you, too. He talked a whole lot about you."

"Really?" Gravity searched her cousin's eyes. She was dying of curiosity but did not want to seem too eager.

Melsy understood. "He said you were the best woman boxer in New York. He said you were a little like him, because you had the devil in you. I could tell he meant that as a compliment."

"Hmm." Gravity tried not to show her disappointment.

She wanted to be the best woman boxer in the *world*—after Sacred, of course. And she had been hoping maybe he would have said something about her as a girl, not just as a fighter.

When she looked back at Melsy, her cousin was studying her intently.

"What?!" Gravity said. "I *don't* love him. He's too conceited."

Melsy nodded. "Oh yeah, he's conceited. But you gotta admit, he backs it up. And Demetrius knows how to treat a woman." She gave Gravity a mischievous look. "Don't believe what you hear about black guys not going downstairs. That boy stayed there for *hours*. I just about lost my mind."

Gravity gasped. She tried not to picture it, but funny questions kept popping up in her mind, like whether he had kept his hat on the whole time. Soon she was laughing so hard it made her sore rib twinge.

Tyler woke up instantly.

"What's so funny?" he demanded. "And who ate my rice?"

Chapter Thirty-Four

The remaining days until China flew by like a coconut falling from a skyscraper. Gravity woke up painfully early to do roadwork—there were beautiful runs uptown like the High Bridge to the Bronx and the winding paths of Fort Tryon—then she ate egg whites and oatmeal and slept on the endless subway ride to school with Ty.

She got a little more sleep in her classes. Now that she was in the running for Rio, all of her teachers had come around to Ms. Laventhol's way of thinking, and nobody minded if she sat in the back row and snoozed. Her teacher for culinary lab even looked the other way when she curled up in the supply closet.

Melsy or Rosa picked Ty up, which let her go straight to Smiley's and train with Tiffany. By the time she got home, she was so exhausted that she barely had the energy to eat the healthy dinner Auntie Rosa had prepared before she collapsed onto the futon—the special orthopedic neck pillow actually did help—and slept dreamlessly until it was time to drag herself out of bed and do it all over again.

Before Gravity knew it, it was her last training day at Smiley's.

"I have two surprises for you," Tiffany announced when Gravity entered the gym.

"Uh-oh," Gravity said. She was not so sure she liked surprises.

"Don't worry," Tiffany said, laughing.

"Good things come in twos," said Truth and Honor.

They were gloved up and waiting for her to spar. Tiffany had invited all of her clients to Smiley's that day to spar Gravity one round apiece, as a way to say goodbye. The white-collar clients were nervously waiting their turn. Even the kids from her beginning boxing class were there, looking cute in their oversized sparring gloves, like little puppies with big paws.

Gravity pulled her headgear over the tight new braids that Melsy had just put in that morning. She pushed her hands into the sparring gloves Tiffany held. They were her favorites, red, white, and blue, with gold piping. Shorty had given them to her in Cornwall, and Tiffany had written inspirational sayings on the linings in permanent marker. She did that for all her fighters. The left glove said "Arms too short to box with God." And the right glove said "If you ain't the hammer, you the nail."

Gravity climbed into the ring and the fun began. Honor came in first and got Gravity's legs warmed up by dancing around and making her cut off the ring. Next came Truth, who was more of a puncher than her twin. Truth had improved a lot since Cornwall; at her best, she could push Gravity, but nobody was trying to push her today.

The little kids came in, one by one. For some it was their very first time sparring, and they took it adorably seriously. Tiffany got in the ring to referee, hiding her laughter behind a stern face when they turned their backs or closed their eyes or tried to throw karate kicks.

A half dozen of Tiffany's top competitive fighters cycled through next, each showing her a little something of what they did best. The bodies came and went, different looks and shapes and sizes, different smells, different rhythms. It was like being passed from one partner to the next in a rough but affectionate dance.

Next came the white-collar clients: the nice physical therapist Johann, the annoying mergers and acquisitions lawyer, the kooky psychiatrist, the snobby yoga clothes designer, and the lady who bred designer dogs called Cavapoos. Gravity had to pay attention, because these were not seasoned boxers but just normal people blowing off steam from their stressful New York lives. As a result, they were either too aggressive (the lawyer and the designer) or too fearful (Johann and the psychiatrist). The Cavapoo breeder was just right.

Finally Tiffany came in to give her a round, and they went a bit harder. Tiff was a light-punching bantamweight, so her power was not a problem, but her superb defense gave Gravity fits. When they had first sparred, Gravity had found her impossible to touch, but today she managed three solid connects, which was a small victory. When the final bell rang, everybody cheered.

It had been twenty rounds, but Gravity felt energized rather than fatigued, and after downing some water and orange slices, she had plenty of energy for her first surprise, which turned out to be Fatso.

"I thought you might want to get in a few rounds of pads for good luck," Tiffany said.

Gravity was so happy to see him that she leapt up off the apron and into his enormous arms without even thinking about how sweaty she was, but he did not seem to mind. He patted her on the back and murmured, "All right, baby. Let's see how much you forgot."

Fatso had just returned from Hong Kong, where he had been training an action star, and he wore a spectacular black silk uniform embroidered with gold dragons. Soon he was drenched in sweat too, as he moved her through her paces, circling fluidly around the ring. He barked out numbered punch combinations and she threw them straight and true in the Coach Thomas tradition. They landed in his mitts with a satisfying thwack. Then he threw hard countershots, trying to hit her for real, but she ducked and slipped and blocked and pivoted while he said, "That's my girl."

Everyone gathered around to watch them work, even that old Irish guy who thought women should not box. She could feel their admiration. The first time Gravity had seen Fatso work, it made her think of this one tomcat. He was always sleeping in a sunbeam on the boardwalk, his big belly pooling around him, until the day a sparrow flew by. Then he lifted his head lazily and, without warning, jumped way up high—higher than Gravity's head—and caught the bird in his jaws. Fatso was explosive like that. You couldn't tell by looking at somebody resting how fast they could move.

It felt so good to be back in the ring with him. Tiffany was a good trainer, but she did not know Gravity as well. Her style was more defense-oriented, and it just wasn't the same. Fatso felt like family.

Gravity wanted to tell him how much she had missed him and Coach. She wanted to ask how D's preparations were going for Azerbaijan and what everybody was saying about her at the gym, but she knew that gossip was not Fatso's style. So they spoke through the pads, like they always had. When they were done, everyone applauded.

"Not bad," Fatso said. He took off one punch mitt, removed a dragon-embroidered handkerchief from his pocket, and mopped the sweat from his brow.

"Not bad?!" Honor objected.

Truth cried, "Gravity gonna teach them what her name means!"

"Not bad," Fatso repeated.

He took off the other mitt, carefully folded up the handkerchief, and put it back in his pocket. Then he set his heavy paws on Gravity's shoulders and fixed her with his cold, unblinking gaze. It went through her like a metal detector, and she squirmed in her boots, even though she was not hiding anything.

She was on weight. She had been running every day. There was nothing she could have done differently. Except go back in time and not fuck Lefty or spar Jenna or let Mom steal, but what was done was done. She would get in the ring in China without regrets.

"You'll do all right," he pronounced at last.

He hugged her to his enormous chest and thumped her back.

"And now for your second surprise," Tiffany said.

When Gravity got out of the ring, she saw that Johann the physical therapist had set up a whole kit of hot stones and aromatherapy oils around one of Smiley's massage tables.

A massage!

Sometimes Melsy gave her neck rubs or Ty walked on her back, but she had never had a real massage before. Her neck and shoulders cried out for attention as she hurried to take off her boots and tank top. She lay facedown, and the gym went away, replaced by the scent of lavender and the feeling of Johann's strong but gentle hands.

"Just relax," he said.

His palms traced warm furrows along her back and over her knotted shoulders.

It was not so easy to relax. Boxing was hard, and so was life. She was always a little tense, waiting for the next blow.

"Relax," he said again, placing warm stones at the base of her spine.

She almost cried, it felt so good.

BOXINGFORGIRLS.COM
THE WOMEN WARRIORS' WITNESS

Carmen Cruz, Independent Journalist

May 19, 2016
World Amateur Championships Brackets Set:
Tough Draw for US Women

QINHUANGDAO, CHINA—A total of 285 female boxing champions from 64 nations have traveled to this seaside city three hours' drive from Beijing. After a week of competition, 10 will emerge as new world champions. But the world's attention will be on the Olympic weights. This week determines which 36 women—12 flyweights, 12 lightweights, and 12 middleweights—will win the right to box in the Summer Games.

It is not true, as we have heard some boxers claim, that the top 12 finishers in each weight are going to Rio! A boxer must finish at the top of her weight *relative to other boxers from her continent* in order to qualify.

If you have questions about what this means for you or your boxer, feel free to email *Boxing for Girls*. Please note that due to slow, censored internet in China, we will not be live tweeting this event and will have only sporadic access to social media and champagne.

Flyweights

There are 49 boxers in this weight class, led by top-seeded Elsie Mortimer of the UK, the defending Olympic champion. California's Kaylee Miller comes in riding high off her gold medal finish in the Continentals. However, she has drawn an extremely difficult bracket, with a preliminary match against five-time world light flyweight champion and London bronze medalist Laishram Memi of India. Should she win, Miller will then face the second seed in her weight, Russia's Elena Petrova, who took gold this year at the European championships. Miller must finish as one of the top two flyweights from the Americas to qualify.

Lightweights

This weight class fields 47 boxers, including "Irish" Jean Sullivan, the defending Olympic champion considered by many the face of women's boxing. The undefeated newcomer Gravity Delgado of Brooklyn has drawn a fearsome opponent for her first match in Azerbaijan's Katarina Karimova, the former light welterweight world champion, who enters unseeded but is among the toughest in this class. Should Delgado pull off the upset there, she will face the hometown champion, third-seeded Du Li. Delgado must finish as one of the top two lightweights from the Americas to qualify, and she looked vulnerable last month in Cornwall. Keep in mind that this is single elimination: one loss and Delgado is out.

Middleweights

This class boasts 34 competitors, all hoping to unseat defending Olympic and world champion Sacred Jones. As the top seed, Jones snags an opening-round bye that will leave her fresh to demolish the winner of Tajikistan versus Germany. It seems unlikely that any fighter in this tournament can end Jones's four-year winning streak, but we expect strong showings from the Dutch, British, and Chinese champions. Jones must finish as one of the top two middleweights from the Americas to clinch her Olympic berth.

Chapter Thirty-Five

China was the strangest place Gravity had ever been. Everything about it was different from home: the smell of the humid and smoggy air, the taste of the food, the look of the squat gray buildings, the feeling of life being smashed together into a smaller space.

Outside of the tournament area, nobody spoke English at all. When she and Sacred had gone into a supermarket to buy toiletries, it felt like they had fallen off the edge of the earth. A tiny Chinese lady had rescued them and, watching their pantomime, led them to the aisle with the deodorant and shampoo. She refused to leave, trailing them to the cash register and then back to their dorm, until the male security guard, who was wearing a big gun, put out his cigarette and scolded her—the Chinese men always seemed to be smoking and scolding—and sent her away.

Before she left, the tiny lady had told them, "I love you. I love America," and taken a selfie with them.

Everyone wanted a photo, especially if Gravity was with Sacred or another dark-skinned teammate. The Chinese acted like they had never seen black people before. Sometimes they even wanted to touch their hair, but Sacred seemed used to it and was very patient. Gravity towered over nearly all of the Chinese people they met, even the men.

Despite all this strangeness, the boxing ring was the same.

Boxing rings everywhere were the same. When Gravity followed Shorty out into the brightly lit, echoey Olympic Sports Center—it had been built for the Beijing Games—and walked up the steps into the squared circle, she felt a calm come over her and the certainty that she had done everything in her power to prepare. All her life had been preparation.

As Gravity knelt in the corner and sang the Shema to herself, she felt serene. The team had gotten to China four days ago, so she had recovered from her jet lag. Making weight had been easy. Her longing for Coach had faded into a dull, distant ache like the ache in her almost-healed rib. And she did not give a moment's thought to Lefty, except to reflect that, by qualifying for Rio, she would prove how much better than him she was.

She rose and Shorty reached over the ropes to knead the nape of her neck in a comforting way. She was getting used to Shorty, although he did not know her like Fatso or Coach and his advice was hard to follow. She put that worry out of her mind as she locked eyes with Katarina Karimova.

The Azeri stood eye to eye with her, the first lightweight she had faced who was her equal in stature. She was dark-haired and very pale beneath her red headgear, and her grim black eyes revealed nothing. Gravity had the dim sense of hardness behind them: hard work, hard will, hard knocks in whatever places she had come from that had led her to that ring. Then the bell rang, and everything else went away.

Gravity leapt forward with a one-two to announce her presence, but the tall Azeri slipped and turned, slapping her with a hook. They reset, and Gravity tried again, but again Katarina evaded and countered with a cross to the nose and hook to the temple, both of which scored. Her shots were not hard, but they were quick and from unusual angles.

As they circled at center ring, Gravity studied her. There was something twitchy about Katarina's movements, something jerky and unpleasant. Her pale face was contorted with concentration as she leapt forward, feinting to Gravity's head and lobbing a one-two to the body that Gravity caught on her elbows. She tried to counter off the block, but Katarina tied her up on the inside, and she was skilled in the clinch, and Gravity could not free her hands.

A single, long buzzer sounded, and Gravity relaxed her arms, but that was the bell for ring B. Katarina seized the moment to land a flashy uppercut, catching Gravity with her mouth slightly open so that her jaw rattled with pain. Enraged by the cheers of the Azeri team, Gravity lunged after Katarina, who grinned as she slid back, slapping in a final hook right before the triple tone sounded that Gravity should have known—*What an idiot!*—was the bell for ring A.

Back in the corner, Shorty gave her water and told her to spit.

"You tired?" he asked.

She shook her head.

"Then pick it up! You need to close the distance, Gravity. Step *to* her with the jab. Punch in, don't rush in." He gave her water and told her to drink. "Use feints. Feint, then jab. Feint, then right hand. No one punch at a time."

She looked at his kind face, so serious behind the little wire glasses, and knew he was worried. He put the mouthpiece back in.

"You letting her tie you up on the inside. You gotta punch on the inside."

It was too much. Shorty was good at the physical work of cornering—he gave her just enough water, he had her rise just before the warning—but he gave too much information, and he let her feel his fear. She felt a sudden pang of intense longing for Fatso, who always knew just what to say.

She stared across at Katarina.

What would Coach and Fatso do?

As Katarina shuffled forward out of the red corner, grim and strong and awkward, Gravity closed her eyes for a split second and prayed. And God must have answered her prayer, because she heard Coach and Fatso inside her head, just as clearly as she could hear the Shema.

She knew what they would do: They would laugh. They would joke about the Russian villain from *Rocky IV.* It didn't matter that Katarina was not Russian. None of them knew where Azerbaijan was.

Fatso would say, "Shit! You gonna let that Drago bitch do you that way?"

And Coach would scowl and say, "I thought we had rhythm. I thought we worked off the jab."

She opened her eyes. You could win a fight with nothing but the jab. You could win a fight with rhythm. Something came over Gravity then, and she understood that her mistake had been in allowing Katarina to set the style, to make it an awkward in-and-out affair, like one of her mother's old LPs that was warped from the sun.

Gravity whipped out the jab and stepped left, marking the edge of one of many circles. There was a new kind of authority in it that Katarina felt at once, taking a tiny step backward and tightening her guard. Gravity switched directions swiftly, circling right now and mixing up levels: up, down, stutter step, then a double to the face, then a feint and a big right hand.

Katarina might have been her equal in height, but she did not have such long arms. This was why she was so skilled at moving in and out, stopping and starting. Gravity did not need to work like that. She could keep it in a very narrow groove, a range at which she could touch Katarina but Katarina could not touch her. It was all a question of keeping her own beat going, even in the silence between the punches, filling the space between them and making it her own.

Just before the bell, she tried something Boo Boo had taught her, suckering Katarina in with a slow walk to her right, her left hand low around her knees, a shiny lure that promised a false opening. It was a risk, but this was no place to play it safe.

Because of the angle, Katarina could not see the right arm, locked and loaded. At the right moment, Gravity spun, turning her foot, turning her hip, pouring all the weight from her right leg into her left and beyond, into her shoulder and arm and glove. Had she missed, she might have fallen, but she did not miss. She clenched her fist tight within its little gauze shell, and her first two knuckles met bone.

Red blossomed beautifully from Katarina's nose. The follow-through threw their two bodies together, chest to chest, headgear to headgear. When Gravity pulled free, her tank was stained with Katarina's blood. The bell made its triple chime. She danced back to the stool.

"Good round," Shorty said, pulling out her mouthpiece.

Gravity sank down gratefully. She had thrown a lot of punches the second round and felt exhausted. Shorty knelt at her feet and squeezed water into her mouth.

"Hey, Gravity!" Kaylee yelled from the stands. "Look!"

When Gravity looked over at them, all her teammates did the wave. She laughed.

"Beautiful right hand!" Sacred yelled.

"Do it again!" Kaylee added.

I will, she promised them, and even though she was tired, she could not wait for the bell to sound again so she could go back out there and keep fighting.

Shorty reached into the waistband of her trunks and pulled her abdominal protector away from her belly, giving her room to breathe. Bonnie held ice against her chest and neck. Gravity felt her heart rate drop.

It was a long round break. Shorty pulled the towel out of his pocket and mopped at the blood on her chest. Because he had his back to center ring, it was Bonnie who noticed it first. She let go of the stool and raised her arms in the air, whooping. The referee appeared at Shorty's side and said, "Congratulations."

"Wait!" Gravity said. "Why?"

She looked past him to the red corner, but she couldn't see Katarina, just the backs of her coaches and the ring doctor, bending in over her.

"Her nose is broken. She doesn't want to continue."

Gravity felt a sinking inside her. She wanted to keep fighting. This was supposed to have been a hard fight. She had just been hitting her groove. She felt like grabbing Katarina and shaking her to make her keep going.

"Congratulations, champ," Shorty said in his scratchy voice. "You fight a beautiful fight."

Bonnie hugged her to her enormous bosom.

Gravity peered anxiously at Katarina, who was sitting on her stool, clutching a bag of ice to her face. The doctor was moving a penlight in front of her eyes.

"Is she going to be okay?" she asked.

Shorty made a dismissive gesture. "She be fine. Girls are tougher than boys."

291

Chapter Thirty-Six

That night, she sat in the stands next to Sacred and screamed for Kaylee as she took the ring to box the Indian champion.

Laishram Memi was a legend. She had survived poverty and violence to win five world championships, one of them just months after giving birth to twins. Her best weight was probably 100 pounds, maybe 106, and when the referee brought her and Kaylee face to face in center ring, the size differential was enormous.

"Kaylee looks like a giant!" Gravity said.

"Yeah," Sacred agreed. "But she don't look right."

Gravity knew what she meant. Kaylee had been nervous ever since the draw and had not made any dumb pirate jokes all day. Although Memi only came up to her shoulders, the tiny Indian champion radiated dominance, and her intensity filled the ring.

"She'll shake herself out of it," Gravity said.

Memi came out fast. She was a southpaw like Kaylee but with a more awkward style. A bit like Gravity's opponent that morning, she liked to get in, get off, and get out. Kaylee spent the entire first round chasing Memi, who zipped around like a hummingbird.

In the second round, Memi began putting combinations together. She kept her hands too low and looped her punches wide, but she did everything with such fire that the technical flaws were immaterial.

A cheer of "India! India!" rose from the opposite stands.

"That's all right!" Gravity yelled as Memi scored a looping left that they could hear from the bleachers. "Let's get that back!"

"Work, Kay!" Sacred yelled. "Work!"

Gravity and Sacred watched the third round in tense silence. The Turkish woman referee was letting them fight through the clinches unchecked, and Memi was rough in there. She tied Kaylee up and continued to club away with whatever was free, and sometimes what landed was an elbow or a hit to the back of the head. It wasn't intentionally dirty, but it wasn't Kaylee's style. They say that southpaws confuse everyone, even fellow southpaws, and sometimes that made for ugly matches.

"She's so aggressive," Gravity murmured.

Sacred said grimly, "She wants it more."

Gravity did not see how that was possible. She thought of Kaylee in their makeshift sauna in Cornwall, of all the sacrifices she had made to overcome her OCD. How could *anyone* want it more?

"She let Shorty and them get into her head," Sacred said quietly. "They good coaches and all, but Kaylee was peaking. She had finally beat Aisha after six losses. Bad time to make changes."

Sacred's words confirmed Gravity's own vague sense of Shorty's limitations. Kaylee had been training full-time at the Olympic Training Center since Cornwall. She said the altitude had done wonders for her conditioning, but her boxing looked more tentative.

"You think they tried to change too much about her?" Gravity asked Sacred.

293

Sacred spread her hands. "You gotta remember where you came from and what got you here."

Gravity nodded. She never would have been able to beat Azerbaijan if she hadn't channeled Coach and Fatso. It was still hard to believe Sacred was her friend, that they were sitting there, talking shop. She wanted to ask her a million questions.

"So, what do you do when Shorty gives you advice?" Gravity whispered. "I mean, he's such a nice guy. . . ."

Sacred scoffed. "Nice don't pay my rent. Look, you gotta *pretend* to listen. Maybe sometimes you even *do* listen, if it's something worth hearing. But when that bell rings, you do you. Shorty ain't the one in there taking punches."

Gravity winced as Memi wrestled Kaylee down to the canvas, falling on top of her. When Kaylee got up, she was limping. She bent and straightened her left leg repeatedly.

"Fuck," Gravity said. "She blew out her knee."

"She's gonna quit," Paloma said loudly.

Gravity shot a dirty look in Paloma's direction and cupped her hands to her mouth. She yelled, "Let's go, Kaylee! Dig deep!"

When the ref called time in, Memi flew at Kaylee as though launched by a slingshot. Kaylee's weight was all on her front leg, and as Memi connected with a left cross, she crumpled backward into the ropes and lay there in evident agony.

"Must've torn her ACL," Paloma announced. "Or maybe the meniscus. That's gonna take a while to heal." She sounded almost happy at the prospect.

They stopped the fight and gave it to Memi. Kaylee could barely stand up for the decision.

She wasn't going to Rio. It had all happened so quickly that it was hard to believe.

The team headed back to the dorms, but Gravity stayed in the venue to wait for Kaylee. On the floor by the ring, two pretty young women with a camera were talking excitedly.

"Memi looked amazing," one of them was saying. "Oh, I'm so happy for her!"

"Let's get Carmen Cruz to do voice-over on the knock-down."

"Do you think Kaylee Miller would give us an interview?"

"Ugh, I doubt it."

"There's no way she'll qualify now, right?"

"No. She's out."

One of them looked over and met Gravity's eyes. "Hey, you're Gravity Delgado!" She smiled. "Great fight today."

Gravity nodded, unable to smile back. She had been on a high since beating Azerbaijan, but now she felt incapable of celebrating. The two women seemed to take in her mood and understand it.

"We're sorry for Kaylee," one of them said.

"She can fight better than that," Gravity said. "Today just wasn't her day. Your girl deserved it. She's tiny but she punches above her class." That reminded her of D-Minus. He was fighting in a few hours. If he won two more, he would make it to Rio.

"Hey!" The one with the camera hoisted it onto her shoulder. "Could you say that again for the camera? But first just say your name and who you are."

That made Gravity laugh. She wanted to say, "I ain't no snitch," but they wouldn't get the joke, so she just said, "Kaylee's my friend. I'm not gonna be in some other girl's movie."

By then, Kaylee had come limping out of the dressing rooms. Bonnie had her arm around her, and Shorty was trailing sadly behind, carrying his trainer's bag. Kaylee's face was red and blotchy, and she wore tape around her knee. Gravity could tell she was trying very hard not to start crying again, so she did not say anything, just reached out for her friend's hand and squeezed it. Kaylee nodded, her nostrils flaring. Bonnie rubbed her back and made soothing noises as they rode the bus back to the dorms.

After a while, Kaylee said, "I fought like shit."

"That's not true," Gravity said.

"I just . . . I dunno. I just didn't feel it."

"Yeah."

The hazy light coming through the bus window lit up Kaylee's teary blue eyes. Gravity wished she could say something to make her feel better.

"It would have been better to get outclassed," Kaylee said. "But when you know you could have done better, it really hurts. I should have stuck to the jab and the one-two."

Even though Kaylee was sad, she agreed to go to Pizza Hut. Sacred was the one who had discovered the Qinhuangdao Pizza Hut, tucked away in the large shopping mall where they had gone the first day to buy cheap electronics. The team spread out across two booths, and the friendly server came and took selfies with everyone and brought them about a million Veggie Lover's pan pizzas.

The team had been warned not to eat Chinese meat, because hormones in it could cause false positives on the anti-doping tests. After five days of nothing but fruit, soy sauce, eggs, and rice, the pan pizzas were just about the best thing Gravity had ever eaten.

Kiki had won her fight against the Hungarian champion, and everyone toasted to her and Gravity's wins. Kaylee kept saying she wished she could do it all over again, and everyone consoled her, except Paloma, who said, "Laishram Memi is a legend. When you fight a girl like that, you gotta leave it all in the ring."

Gravity hoped Paloma lost soon. She was the kind of person who could not stand to see others win. It was like she thought happiness was a personal pan pizza, and whenever anybody else took a slice, that was one less in her pan.

That wasn't the way happiness worked. Happiness was more like an all-you-can-eat buffet: the best strategy was to stuff yourself to capacity and steal what you could for your friends.

May 21, 2016

World Amateur Championships, Day Two: Boxing Love

QINHUANGDAO, CHINA—The second day of competition here at the Olympic Sports Center saw the bantam, feather, light welter, welter, and middleweights battling it out in preliminary round action in two simultaneous rings. But the real action was in the stands.

Bantamweight Aisha Johnson, whose incredible life journey has taken her from the mean streets of Baltimore to the bright lights of the London Olympic ring, dropped a hard-fought unanimous decision to Stoyka Asenova of Bulgaria. As Johnson emerged from the dressing room, her girlfriend, Aaliyah Williams, dropped to one knee and proposed.

The US women lifted the happy couple up in the air and carried them around the stadium.

"I was going to wait for a more romantic moment," said Williams, "but I figured, Why waste time? I've had the ring in my pocket for weeks."

London medalist Paloma Gonzales of Sacramento, now campaigning at featherweight, enters as the third seed in her weight and advanced on a bye. Pronouncing the competition "disappointing so far," she said: "The only ones I'm worried about are Italy and Kazakhstan." Gonzales faces Ukraine tomorrow.

In the evening session, light welterweight Aaliyah Williams

celebrated her new engagement with a triumphant third-round stoppage of Alina Hajiyeva of Azerbaijan.

"This one's for you, boo," Aaliyah yelled to her fiancée as the referee raised her hand.

It's been a tough tournament thus far for the Azeri team, what with Gravity Delgado's dismantling of their lightweight champion yesterday. Delgado looked outstanding. Let's hope she can keep it up for tomorrow's outing versus China.

In welterweight action, Nakima Fanning of Newark met her match in Germany's Vera Weber.

"I've learned so much, just from being here," said Fanning.

Sacred Jones, entering as the top seed in her class, also enjoyed a first-round bye. She sat in the stands cheering on her teammates and watching the other middleweights with interest.

"I hope some of them can push me a little," she said. "I want to give the crowd a good show."

Chapter Thirty-Seven

Gravity was feeling great until she stepped through the ropes to fight Du Li. Then she looked across the ring and saw him, orange biceps bulging in his Team China T-shirt.

She turned to Shorty in a panic. "What is Rick Ross doing here?"

"He coaches China," Shorty said. "They pay good money, better than the US."

Rick flashed his bleached teeth at her, and she felt all the strength go out of her legs. Seeing him there across the ring, buckling on Du Li's headgear, was like learning that someone had gone through her underwear drawer and read every page of her diary.

Now she understood why Rick Ross had recorded the sparring that day at Smiley's. He must have brought the footage back to China so they could pore over all her weaknesses. Shit, he had probably set the whole thing up on purpose to get her hurt!

Of course he had. The knowledge made her sick to her stomach. Nobody in their right mind would make a fighter they cared about spar someone so much bigger so close to an important tournament. Her rib began to ache at the memory of Jenna Petrone's punishing body shot.

"He coached me for a second," she told Shorty.

"So?" Shorty grabbed Gravity's headgear and shook it lightly. "Come on, now. Get your head in the game."

She nodded and took a deep breath, trying to push down the self-hatred that swirled inside her. What an idiot she had been! Rick must have felt like he won the lottery when she walked through that gym door.

Numbly, Gravity turned to face the corner post and knelt in prayer, but her mind swirled with such anxiety that she could barely get through the Shema. She was tempted to ask for victory, for the first time in her life, but she stopped herself. Long ago she had vowed never to ask for that. She rose to her feet, feeling more agitated than when she had knelt down.

When she met Li in center ring, the shorter woman stared up at her with intense, burning eyes, looking like an angry child.

Right off the opening bell, Li went at her injured rib with ferocity, but Gravity had anticipated this and caught her with a crisp check hook coming in. Li was tough and sucked it up.

The Chinese champion was that dangerous thing: a southpaw with an educated right hand. She began stabbing the right jab to the body and head, then hooking off it, up and down. She had fast feet, and whenever she scored with the hook downstairs, she dug in, right where she knew Gravity was vulnerable.

So that's how it's going to be, Gravity thought, tying the girl up and staring over her shoulder at Rick Ross, who was sitting, smug and orange, on the arena floor. She wanted to climb out of the ring and scratch out his eyes.

"Lead right, left hook," Sacred cried, and it was good

advice, but by the end of the first round, Gravity was hurting so badly that all she could do was hold.

Shorty acted like he was sleepwalking through the round break. Maybe he thought all she needed was water and the stool, but she needed confidence and energy. She longed for Fatso to smack her across the face and ask her what her problem was!

Wake up, she told herself as she rose from the stool and gazed at Li's stocky form and burning eyes. *You are in the ring. Wake up. Fight.*

But it was like her mind was awake and her body was asleep. The second round was a blur. She tried to keep Li on the outside, but she could not muster the power to get the girl's respect. The body shots were cumulative. She felt a burning pain in that bad rib, and she found it hard to make herself jab. Her body wanted to keep the left arm pinned to her side, like the wing of a hurt bird.

At one point, she even switched southpaw to get the rib farther from Li, but she was a terrible southpaw and never trained that way and immediately got drilled with a left. She wobbled in the unfamiliar stance and felt something she had never felt before in the ring: fear.

Sacred cried, "Don't do that!"

She switched back to orthodox. Li rushed her then, dark eyes burning, and Gravity held on so hard the ref warned her again, more sternly this time.

Shorty yelled at her after that round, and she wanted to yell back at him. She wanted to yell at him for not being Fatso, for not being Coach, for not having some kind of magic answer. She sat there in despair, and when the bell rang for round three, it was the first time in her life that she did not want to be in the boxing ring.

She felt betrayed, disgusted. What was the point in trying your hardest if the people around you did not fight fair?

The first standing eight was from a body shot that dropped her to her knees. It was very hard to rise, but she made herself do it.

The second standing eight was a left cross to the head, and by now, Gravity was not trying to win anymore. She was just trying to go the distance. That was a small, bitter victory, but it was something: they could beat her but not stop her.

At the end, when they failed to raise her hand and she lost all hope of Rio, she turned away in disgust and walked out of the ring, without bothering to embrace the Chinese girl.

Fuck Du Li.

Rick Ross had softened Gravity up and recorded secret videos. It was cheap and dishonorable, and Du Li did not deserve Gravity's respect. Gravity would rather lose all the marbles than win like that.

Chapter Thirty-Eight

Gravity paced the dormitory courtyard beneath the gray Qinhuangdao sunset, muttering to herself and reading Sacred's Bible. She had the urge to Skype Coach, but what would she say? That she missed him terribly? That she was sorry she had let him down?

She was staring at her phone in despair when Kaylee came to drag her to Pizza Hut.

"I don't feel like it," Gravity told her.

"Arr! Captain's orders."

"I'm not hungry."

Kaylee stepped to Gravity and stared up into her eyes. Gravity stared back, willing the full force of her anger to drive her away, but the smaller woman held her gaze, unblinking. They had never sparred before. Gravity was surprised at the strength of her game face.

Many communications passed silently between them. Kaylee's eyes, gray-blue in the dusk and red around the edges, testified to her own anger and grief. Gravity remembered how Kaylee had come out with them after her loss, bravely showing her face at the table. And Kaylee was out of Rio for good, and her knee would take months to rehab, whereas Gravity had heard rumors that she might still be in the running, and her rib was only bruised. She felt ashamed of herself then. She looked down at the concrete and hugged the Bible to her chest.

"Okay. I'll go."

Kaylee put her arm around her. "Pizza's on me, matey."

The conversation at the Hut that night centered on Aisha and Aaliyah's engagement. Aisha held her hand out so everyone could see the ring: apricot gold, with two boxing gloves meeting in the center at a sapphire crown. She pulled it off and passed it around so everyone could read the inscription: "Empress of my heart."

Kaylee offered to officiate the ceremony aboard a pirate ship, but Aaliyah said they were going to do it in Seattle next spring, inside a boxing ring, and everyone was invited.

"Even you, Paloma," she said.

Paloma snorted and went back to her cell phone.

"You too, Carmen! Come to my wedding!" Aaliyah yelled across the restaurant, beckoning to Carmen Cruz, who stood near the hostess stand with some shady men from the amateur boxing commission of Uzbekistan.

Carmen waved at them, looking very serious and journalistic with her pantsuit and press credentials but still sporting stiletto heels. Gravity watched as she sashayed across the restaurant to their table.

"Ladies!" she said. "How are you all this evening?"

Everyone said, "Great," except Gravity, who studied the photographs of sausage pizza on the laminated place mats. She could not wait to get home and eat meat again. To her annoyance, Carmen slid into the banquette directly next to her. It was such a tight squeeze that Carmen's dark, glossy hair fell across Gravity's shoulder. It smelled like roses.

"I am sorry for your loss," Carmen told her.

"Thank you," Gravity said, gazing across the restaurant. She had not spoken to Carmen since her coverage of the tournament in Cornwall. What she had written about Ariana Leite having deserved the win still hurt.

"You were magnificent defeating Azerbaijan," Carmen said. "I thought you would pull out the win today. Du Li is not half the fighter you are."

Gravity turned to glare at her. Why was she saying these things? To torture her? To gloat? But to her surprise, Carmen was studying her with a pained expression. Her dark eyes brimmed with tears.

"Excuse me," Carmen said. "It's just . . . sometimes I feel things so deeply when I watch you girls box." She pulled a lace handkerchief from the pocket of her jacket and dabbed at her eyes and nose. "When you got in the ring today, I had the funniest feeling. Like someone had hurt you very badly before the fight even started. I wondered if you had heard some bad news from home. You fought like you had lost your faith."

The pizza arrived. Sacred Jones and Marisol Bonilla bent their heads in prayer. Gravity watched the grease sizzling around the edges of her crust.

Carmen said, "Forgive me, Gravity. Sometimes I make up stupid stories." She let out a little, bitter laugh and twisted the emerald on her finger.

Carmen's hands were long-fingered and elegant, but she had a prominent callus from writing, and there were ink smudges on her thumbs. Gravity thought of the photos Monster had shown her of the hands and feet of ring card girls, of how he had said they all fought their own battles.

"It's not stupid," Gravity told her. "You're the only one who writes what really happens." Something clicked inside her, and she accepted Carmen's judgment of her bout against Ariana. It would have been nice to rematch Ariana. She sighed. Now she wouldn't have the chance.

"Do you want some?" Gravity said, pointing to her Veggie Lover's.

Carmen smiled. "Never pet a dog while it's eating, and never take a boxer's food. You might get hurt."

Gravity laughed. It was true that she was starving. She slid a piece of pizza out of the pan and into her mouth.

"You do understand that you may still go to Rio, don't you?" Carmen asked.

Gravity blinked at her, chewing. She had heard rumors but had not understood them. There was always so much misinformation in boxing. She could not allow herself false hopes.

"How can I go to Rio if I lost in the prelims? They're only taking twelve lightweights. I didn't even make the top sixteen."

Carmen pulled out her notebook excitedly. "Mira, Gravity! It is not simply the top twelve. The Olympics use continental quotas to ensure geographical diversity." She showed Gravity a table she had printed off the AIBA website and pasted into her notebook.

"The top four lightweights from Europe will advance, plus the top three from Asia, the top African, the top Australian or New Zealander, and one Tripartite Committee selection that nobody understands—that's what I was trying to interview those gentlemen about." She gestured to the shady-looking men from Uzbekistan, who had taken a table in the corner and were eating calamari.

"And from our American region, they take the top two, and *all of you* lost today." She showed Gravity her bracket sheet, which she had been filling in by hand. "Your Ariana Leite lost to the great Jean Sullivan of Ireland. Annie Bervin fell to Russia. Puerto Rico lost to the UK, Mexico to South Korea, Argentina to Gabon."

She tapped a fingernail against the last fight. "That was a very exciting upset. It's a travesty, the conditions in which most of the African fighters train. The Gabonese fighter told me she goes without food after training so her son can eat. You would think AIBA would put money into development instead of spending it on bullshit like the World Series of Boxing."

She shook her head. "Anyway. All of the Americas' champions lost! That means your final rankings will be determined by the rankings of the women who beat you. You can still go to Rio if Du Li does well enough, and her draw, I must say, is auspicious. You need to start rooting for China."

Gravity looked at Carmen in shock. "I'm not rooting for that—" She stopped herself before saying the word "bitch." "I'm not rooting for Du Li." She cupped another veggie slice in her hand and started chewing it fiercely.

Carmen raised an eyebrow. "What happened in that ring today, Gravity?"

Gravity finished her pizza, slurped down the rest of her Diet Coke, and sat back in the booth. She reached for a napkin and wiped the grease off her hands.

Then she told Carmen the story. All of it. About Lefty, about leaving Coach, about how she had thought Rick wanted to help her when he was just setting her up to get hurt, about him recording her and taking the tape back to show Du Li. It felt good to get it off her chest. But then she saw that Carmen had started to take notes, and she felt panicked.

"You won't write about that, will you? I mean, I *hate* Rick

Ross, and I hate Du Li. But it's over. What's done is done."
She did not want to be like Paloma, giving Carmen bitter quotes about it afterward. That was not the behavior of a champion.

"I won't write about it if you don't want me to," Carmen said, putting away her notebook. "But in the future, you must always tell a writer beforehand if something is off the record."

"Okay."

"Du Li is a beautiful person. You can be sure she had nothing to do with it. This was all Rick. So many sharks in boxing, sniffing for blood."

That made Gravity think of Andre Vázquez and the gross thing he had said to her outside the Barclays Center.

"I want to tell you something else off the record," she said.

Carmen looked at Gravity expectantly.

"Are you and Andre Vázquez . . . you know . . . dating?"

It was weird to ask a lady Carmen's age about her love life, but Gravity had seen the way Carmen had taken his arm that night at the Barclays Center in her sexy red dress. Hearing his name now, Carmen flinched. It was like a boxer hearing the name of someone who had defeated them.

She said, "We . . . were never dating. And whatever it was that we were doing, we are not doing it anymore."

"Because *he's* one of the sharks," Gravity said. She told Carmen about Monster, how kind he was and how talented as an artist and how she was worried that Andre was just using him to make a quick buck. Then she lowered her voice and repeated what he had said to her that night: "My cock is heavy too, but I don't take it out and pass it around."

She told Carmen how Andre had acted like nothing had

happened and how it had made her feel, just for a second, so ashamed. And then she had to see him at the gym all the time, rolling in like he owned the place.

Telling all of this to Carmen made her feel the shame afresh, but afterward she felt better. It was like taking out the spoiled milk she had shoved to the back of the fridge and finally pouring it down the drain and throwing out the carton.

"Oh, mi niña," said Carmen. "Let me hug you."

Carmen held her in her arms for a while, and Gravity inhaled the roses of her perfume. It made her miss Melsy. As she thought of Melsy, Gravity let out a little sob. She would have to tell Melsy that she had lost. She would have to tell Tyler and Auntie Rosa and Ms. Laventhol and Keeshawn, who always hit her up on Instagram and told her to stay undefeated. She wasn't undefeated anymore, and soon everyone would know. Everybody back at Cops 'n Kids. Coach would be so disappointed.

Carmen pulled back and laid her hand on top of Gravity's head. "Do not despair. If you despair, that means Rick Ross and Lefty and Andre Vázquez won, and you don't want them to win, do you?"

Gravity sniffed. "No."

"I won't publish what you told me about Andre," she said. "But I won't forget it, either. I used to be a pretty good investigative reporter. A man who talks like that to a sixteen-year-old girl does other things, too."

She rose from the table, taking out her notebook and smoothing down her hair. "Okay, Gravity, keep your head up. I have to go interview those Uzbek thugs."

Chapter Thirty-Nine

Gravity was sitting in the cafeteria alone, staring at the half-moons of honeydew on her plate, when Marisol Bonilla slid into her booth and said, "Hey, G!"

The little boxer was round-cheeked and rosy. She looked like an entirely different person than the twitchy, ravenous 106-pounder she had been upon arrival in Qinhuangdao. The contrast shook Gravity out of her gloom.

"Holy shit, Marisol! How much do you weigh now?"

Marisol beamed. "One twenty!"

They both laughed.

"Nice one," Gravity said.

"I know, right? My dad's gonna freak, but whatever."

"How'd you manage that on fruit and rice?"

"No, no, I started eating the meat, 'cause I'm not going to the Olympics or anything. The chicken's really good! It's so *salty!*"

Gravity looked across to the hot-food line. God, that sounded good. All the fruit and rice had made her stomach sick of sweetness. She wanted to eat greasy meat and gnaw the bones. Then she wanted to lie down in bed and pull the covers up over her head where nobody could find her.

She had not told anyone about her loss, and people kept emailing her to wish her luck or ask how she was doing. Du Li had won again last night. Tonight she fought South Korea

311

in the quarters. Carmen had said Du Li's draw was "auspicious," and Gravity had looked that word up and it meant "lucky." It was true that Du Li's part of the bracket was the least dangerous. She would not have to run into the strongest girls—the Russian or "Irish" Jean Sullivan—until the finals.

"Wanna train?" Marisol asked. She was so cute, with her pug nose and fishtail braid and bangs that hung down into her eyes.

Somewhere deep inside herself, Gravity fought an internal battle. Part of her wanted to get up and get happy. Part of her wanted to stay sad, to punish herself for losing.

She said, "Yeah. Okay."

They met Shorty down in the big warehouse gym, where he was setting up round-robin sparring for Nakima, Aisha, and Aaliyah, who had lost the previous night. The gym was buzzing, sparring going on in both rings as well as in taped-off squares on the floor. Gravity saw girls from the UK, Sweden, India, Canada, and France, and lots of Chinese women, not just the women in the tournament but other local boxers who had come in to get good work. It was like a big meat market, with trainers running back and forth between the girls to match them up. Gravity felt her heart start to pound.

When Shorty saw her, he said, "That's what I'm talking about!"

She started doing her stretches, and when she was wrapped up and warm, she looked across the gym and saw Ariana Leite, surrounded by the Brazilian coaches, her Mohawk standing straight up like a cock's feathers. She and Gravity locked eyes, and Gravity could not see anyone else.

She felt that same giddy rush of happiness and excitement that she had felt five long years ago when, in the middle of all the boys and men, little Svetlana had walked in the gym.

Someone for me, she thought.

She tugged on the sleeve of Shorty's tracksuit.

"I want to fight her," she told him, pointing at Ariana.

He looked across the gym at the Brazilian champion, who smiled like she knew something Gravity didn't, but Ariana didn't know shit. Gravity would show her a thing or two.

Shorty said something in Spanish and then started to translate, but Gravity knew that word by now.

"Claro," she said, "estoy lista."

You had to snatch your opening when you saw it. Who knew if she would get the chance to fight Ariana again? One of them might not qualify for Rio. Or they might qualify but lose before they faced each other.

When Shorty nodded and said, "Bueno," she was so happy she wanted to jump up and down.

She watched as he walked over to talk to Claudio, the enormous Brazilian coach. Claudio nodded. Shorty came back and helped her into her gloves.

"You go in there in three," he said, pointing to the ring in which a French girl was roughing up a Swede.

But Gravity could not wait, and so she skipped across to mess with Ariana. The fight started the moment you knew who your opponent was. Their conditioning coach, Igor, spoke English, so she grabbed him by the arm and dragged him over to translate.

Ariana cocked her head and eyed Gravity, a half smile playing on her lips. Gravity extended her gloves, grinning. Ariana touched them.

"Tell her three rounds wasn't enough," Gravity said to Igor.

He translated. Ariana replied, looking right at her as she spoke.

Igor said, "She says it was enough for you in Canada. She says you run from her the whole fight."

"Tell her I'm from Brownsville. Never ran, never will. What I did was called boxing. She should try it sometime."

It was possible this did not translate perfectly into Portuguese. Igor and Ariana went back and forth a bit in their soft, sexy language that made everything sound like a love song.

Finally Igor said, "She says she will show you how they fight in São Paulo. And now there are not judges to steal her joy."

Gravity grinned and touched her rival's gloves again. She skipped back to Shorty to get the mouthpiece. The French-woman and the Swede slipped out of the ring, and Gravity and Ariana took their place. The bell rang and they began.

Ariana came out hard, like she was still angry about losing the decision, and fired off three pistonlike jabs. Gravity cupped the first two and slipped the third, dancing to her left and snapping out her own double jab in return. Ariana caught it on her high, tight guard, then fired a one-two combo to the head. Gravity slid left and countered with a hook to the body. Ariana brought in her elbow for the block.

Gravity raised her eyes from Ariana's shoulders to her face. The Brazilian was scowling in concentration. But even with her brow furrowed and her Mohawk smushed down by the headgear, she looked beautiful and strong.

Ariana surprised her with a lead right hand. It was a good shot, thrown with all her weight behind it, and although Gravity blocked it, she was knocked back a little. So she did the same, slingshotting off her back foot to return fire

314

and catching Ariana at the sweet spot at the end of her right arm's extension. Then it was Ariana who took a step back.

They broke for water and instructions, and when they started back up again, Gravity was feeling lighter, and her feet on the canvas were nimble. Both of them began moving more quickly, letting their hands go, throwing threes, fours, and more.

"That's it!" Shorty yelled. "Punches in bunches!"

Gravity lobbed a left uppercut, right hand, double hook to the body and head, without any illusion that it would score. Ariana slipped and slid delicately and returned to her piston jabs. Gravity blocked easily. She threw some shoulder feints, hoping to get Ariana out of position, but the other woman was undeceived and, smiling around her mouthpiece, jabbed at Gravity's body.

In the third round, Ariana kept circling and leading with the jab, while Gravity blocked and countered with her own. She felt somehow wide open, amused, although her focus was intense on Ariana. They continued this dance for a while, circling each other, probing for weakness.

It made her sad in a way when she saw how to beat her. There it was: as Ariana tired, her right dipped low every time she jabbed, leaving her open for a counterhook. Coach had taught Gravity to hook two ways. One was more looping, thrown from close quarters to strike the side of the opponent's head. Gravity would throw the other kind, the hook that was long and straight and thrown from farther out, almost like a jab but twice as hard.

Gravity had gotten the feel by now for Ariana's jabbing rhythm, which mostly went in threes. She waited till the end of her next triplet and hooked with her, hard. When it landed, Ariana's eyes watered with pain. Gravity came back immediately with a double right cross, being disciplined and keeping her distance. She was longer than Ariana. There was no need to crowd or rush. The second right hand wobbled Ariana's legs, and she barreled into Gravity, holding on tight and panting.

From then on, Gravity had it all her own way. She lit Ariana up, picking her shots, having her fun. The best part was, at the end of the fifth, Ariana turned from her, shaking her glove in the air and taking out her mouthpiece.

"Não mais!"

There it was. Gravity had made a great champion quit. This was an indisputable victory, a private concession better than a medal on her neck. If only Carmen had been there to write it down.

Chapter Forty

Gravity did not particularly want to see the Great Wall of China, but Kaylee said, "Anchors aweigh, matey! The sea air'll be good for what ails ye," and kept making dumb jokes about booty until she agreed to go, just to shut her up. Nothing is worse than an optimist when you are trying to be depressed.

Yesterday's sparring had temporarily elevated her mood, but after the endorphin high wore off, it left her feeling raw. It had whetted her appetite for boxing again, and that made the thought of not fighting in Rio ache in her anew.

Du Li had won again last night, advancing to the semis against the UK's Tasha Newman. Gravity had not been able to find Carmen to get the scouting report on Tasha. The other semifinal was Jean Sullivan against the Russian Sofya Bulgakov.

Gravity was the last on the bus, and as she trudged up the steps, the Chinese man in charge of the outing scolded her for tardiness—Chinese men were always scolding her. She took a seat in the back and watched the factories roll by as they headed to the place called Laolongtou, where the Great Wall ended at the Bohai Sea.

There by the water, the exhaust fumes lifted, and she could smell the salt air beneath. The mixed group of boxers, coaches, and officials gathered on a broad plaza by a statue of some general. Gravity was unable to muster the energy to listen to the tour guide's speech about fortifications and dynasties. Little snippets floated to her ears:

"More than twenty thousand kilometers in length . . . the only man-made structure visible from space . . . Laolongtou meaning 'head of the dragon' . . . a gift shop we will visit at the end."

They walked along a raised pathway of square tan stones with brick walls on either side. The walls started out about the height of Monster and gradually got lower. One side had crenellations that you could lean into and look out over the rocky shore.

As they walked along this path to the water, Gravity kept waiting to see the impressive Great Wall. Then they went through a big stone pagoda-looking thing and emerged onto a small platform that overlooked the sea. And that was the end, and she realized this *was* the Great Wall; they had been walking on it the whole time.

"Say 'cheese,' mami!"

It was Shorty, in a cap that said "Jabbin' for Jesus," his usual grin beneath his thin mustache. She gave him a big fake smile, squinting into the sun. He took a selfie with her, then made her take a picture of him. Then they stood together side by side, looking out at the Yellow Sea.

"Amazing, all the places boxing take you," he said.

"Yeah."

She wasn't really feeling it, but Shorty was always so enthused about everything. She didn't want to rain on his parade. He patted her shoulder. His hand was square and stubby, big for how short he was: a puncher's hand.

"It's good you train yesterday, mami. Train and pray. That's your job now."

She sighed.

He cocked his head and studied her through his tiny wire-framed glasses.

"You no pray, mami?"

"Yeah, of course I pray. . . ."

She had talked to God for hours after the loss, lying there in her bed sleepless and dry-eyed—because somehow she still could not cry, could not remember the last time she had cried, although her heart was breaking—then pacing the dormitory courtyard beneath the moonlight and flickering fluorescents.

She had yelled at God, asking why He had done this to her when she always tried so hard, when she had done her roadwork and looked out for Tyler and endured all her mother's bullshit and Lefty's betrayal and not done drugs or alcohol. Then she had apologized to God for yelling. Then she had berated herself and contemplated all her failings; it was like picking at a scab.

Then she had found her favorite Psalm in Sacred's Bible. It was Psalm 144, the one that started with "Blessed be the Lord my strength which teacheth my hands to war, and my fingers to fight" and ended with everybody being happy in the streets. But there was a part in the middle about God coming down and delivering King David from the hands of strange people who lied. She thought of it now, as she leaned out over the thick stone and looked onto the implacable sea.

God had not done that. He had let her lose. He had let Rick Ross play her. And Lefty, too.

She turned back to Shorty, who looked so goofy, grinning at the ocean in his Jesus cap. She thought of his barrage of corner advice, some of it good, some of it useless. He had no idea what she was going through.

She said, "I talk to God, but I don't think He's listening."

Shorty said sharply, "How you know what God hears?"

"I don't. I just mean, God has better things to do than worry about me and my boxing. Who am I to ask Him for favors?"

Shorty laughed and shook his head.

The group was on the move, and so they turned away from the sea and walked together in silence back through the pagoda-like thing and along the wall toward the gift shop. After a while, he said, "Let me tell you something."

What he told her next was better than any piece of corner advice she would ever hear. Gravity had heard rumors about it. Coach had said something way back about how Shorty was a miracle, and Kaylee mentioned something about him being part of "that 1980 team." She said it like it was something special, but Gravity could not remember any medalists from that year. It was the 1976 and 1984 teams that were the most famous. But she had never been that great at history.

Shorty had been the light flyweight champion, the smallest of all the weight classes. The reason she had never heard of his team was that 1980 was the height of the Cold War, and the US boycotted the Moscow Games. The team flew to Poland instead for an international dual meet. Shorty's mother had driven him to the airport in Wisconsin for his flight, but he could not make himself get out of the car. As he told Gravity this, he stopped walking, removed his glasses, and dabbed at his tears.

Gravity stared at him in astonishment.

"I don't know, mami. Something stop me. God told me don't go."

The plane crashed over Warsaw. The entire US team died: fourteen boxers and eight officials.

Shorty put the glasses back on, and his face assumed its habitual serenity as he turned back to look at the Great Wall. Gravity looked at him for a moment, registering her new understanding of his smile. Then she followed his gaze to the end of the wall, where it jutted out into the sea. It really did look like the head of a dragon.

Shorty said, "God works in mysterious ways, mami. You say, 'Who am I to ask God favors?' But who are you *not* to ask? You don't get to decide for God."

She took that in.

"Pray as hard as you can," he told her. "Right now, that's your job."

BOXINGFORGIRLS.COM
THE GREAT WALL OF BLOGS

Carmen Cruz, Independent Journalist

May 25, 2016

World Amateur Championships, Day Six: Semifinals Preview

QINHUANGDAO, CHINA—As the tournament winds to a close, the remaining 40 undefeated fighters prepare to face off in tomorrow's semifinal sessions. Most of the quotas for Rio have now been claimed; the remaining slots will likely be finalized when the semifinals are over. Let's take a look at the four US fighters whose hopes remain alive.

London bronze medalist Paloma Gonzales has had a good run at featherweight, outpointing Ukraine in the round of 16 and yesterday squeaking by Mongolia. Gonzales will face a tougher test tomorrow against Kazakhstan's Dina Kyzaibay, who has the size to give her problems and has dominated thus far with two stoppages and one decision. Gonzales says, "I'm not worried about Dina. She's a strong girl, but she has the boxing IQ of a squirrel."

Brooklyn's Gravity Delgado, although eliminated by China in the preliminaries, will be watching tomorrow's lightweight semifinals with great interest. If Du Li of China defeats the UK's Tasha Newman, Delgado goes to Rio. If Li loses, Delgado could still go, but only if Newman then takes the gold medal in this tournament. This seems unlikely, as the other semifinal features the greatest star in the lightweight division, Olympic gold medalist "Irish" Jean Sullivan, facing the talented southpaw Sofya Bulgakov of Russia. Delgado says, "I am praying for China."

In the middleweight division, the inimitable Sacred Jones will do what she does best against Aya Moudden of Morocco, the only African fighter still alive in this competition. The other middleweight semifinal promises an interesting stylistic clash between the tall Swede Josefine Johansson and the hard-punching Ukrainian Gallia Kob.

The final US boxer still standing is heavyweight Bettina Rosario of San Diego, who faces Turkey's Canan Corus. The daughter of US team manager Bonnie Rosario, Bettina has stormed through the heavyweight field with big wins over Romania and top-seeded Russia.

When asked about her progress, Bettina shrugs and says, "I got better."

Chapter Forty-One

Gravity and her teammates let out a whoop as Paloma Gonzales took the ring. Teamwork makes the dream work. But the whoop was noticeably quieter and less enthusiastic than the whoop they later gave Sacred Jones, Bettina Rosario, and even Du Li.

Bonnie had arranged for takeout from Pizza Hut, and Gravity emotionally ate a slice as she watched Paloma win the first round. Du Li was up next, and she felt like she was going to crawl out of her skin.

The second round was hard to score. Paloma might have edged it on ring generalship, but you could make an argument for Dina Kyzaibay on aggression.

Kaylee yelled, "All right, Paloma! Great round!"

In the third, Kazakhstan came on strong, and Sacred, who was all wrapped up and ready to go against Morocco, led them all in a cheer of "U-U-USA!"

When the final bell rang and Paloma was struggling to stay standing as Dina Kyzaibay battered her, everybody let out a huge cheer of "Yay, Paloma!"

So it wasn't that they didn't cheer; it was that, by a quiet consensus, the worse Paloma did, the more enthusiastic they grew. The German team could have told them the word for this: *schadenfreude*, the happiness you feel at another person's misfortune, especially when that person has spent all week bragging about her spread in *ESPN*'s "Body Issue."

"Dina seemed pretty smart for a squirrel," Sacred said dryly.

But Gravity was unable to focus on anything but Du Li, who had come out of the red corner dressing room and was swinging her arms and rolling her neck as she made the walk to the ring.

"She looks good, G," said Kaylee. "She looks confident."

Marisol reached out to squeeze Gravity's shoulder.

Tasha Newman's father—one of the few parents to have made the trip to Qinhuangdao—hollered loudly from the upper bleachers as his daughter made the walk from the blue corner. Gravity had not paid much attention to Tasha, beyond noting her extraordinary beauty. She had long dreadlocks and green eyes and an accent that made everything she said sound cool.

"All right, Li!" yelled Sacred, pumping her fist in the air.

Bonnie led the whole US team in a chant of "Let's go, China, let's go!"

Gravity looked around at them gratefully. Everyone on the team understood what was riding on the match. When Tasha came out, Gravity saw that she was a southpaw too. Gravity clenched her hands into fists at her sides, praying Du Li knew how to handle another lefty. Tasha was taller than she was and boxed in a classic upright style. The first was a feeling-out round. Not much happened, although Tasha opened up a little at the end and scored with a big left.

Gravity felt her legs begin to shake uncontrollably.

In the second, Li began to come on. She was leading the exchanges and landed a big left to the body and a right hook to the head.

"Yeah!" yelled Sacred. "That's it, China!"

Li closed out the second strong. Gravity watched Rick Ross in the corner, smooth and smug and orange.

Tasha faded in the third. Her guard was open, and Li was landing hard shots down the middle. At one point, Li trapped her against the ropes and landed a good, clean one-two-three.

Kaylee hugged Gravity and said, "You got this, matey!"

But Gravity said, "Hush."

There were sixty seconds left in the round. Du Li could still get knocked out, or the judges could steal it from her. Gravity got down on her knees, squeezed her eyes shut, and said the Shema until the decision was announced. Sacred came and put a gauze-wrapped hand on her head, and Kaylee reached down to take her hand, and they stayed that way during the interminable wait between the final bell and the moment when the referee raised Du Li's hand.

Who would have thought Gravity would qualify for the Olympics on her knees?

She had done it. She was going to Rio!

Best of all, she would see D-Minus there! She had watched him win his quota spot earlier that morning in Sacred's room, on a livestream that kept freezing. His performance had been magnificent, but she had been too tense then to truly celebrate. Now all the happiness came raining down on her at once.

She leapt up and hurried to the stadium floor as "Irish" Jean Sullivan and Sofya Bulgakov took the ring for the other lightweight semifinal. When Du Li and her coaches headed back to the dressing rooms, Gravity stepped out and blocked their way.

Li was swinging her arms like a happy little kid. Her short, dark hair was mussed, and red blotches on her shoulders and cheeks testified to Tasha's power. When she saw Gravity, she looked up, uncertain.

Gravity smiled.

"Good fight," she said. She held up a fist and shook it.

Li did not speak English, but she must have heard that one before, because she smiled too.

"Thank you for helping me get to Rio," Gravity said slowly.

Gravity kept her eyes on Li. She refused to even look at Rick Ross, but she could feel him lurking there, like a podcast on pause. The Chinese coach translated what Gravity had said, and Li nodded and smiled again.

Carmen was right; she did seem like a beautiful person, once Gravity's ego was out of the way. Most boxers were beautiful people when you got to know them. Gravity spread her arms and, seeing the permission in the other woman's eyes, gave her the embrace she should have given her before.

Li was damp with sweat, but Gravity did not mind. The sweat from a fight was different than other kinds of sweat: cleaner somehow. Even pretty girls in evening gowns hug a sweat-drenched fighter. That's boxing.

Rick Ross laughed and put a hand on Gravity's shoulder.

He said, "See? I always hook it up for my girls."

Gravity stared at the hand there, its skin mottled, spilling from the thick cuff of his Rolex. She remembered a judo throw that started that way. She would just have to trap the wrist, then turn and break at the waist. She imagined him flying over her hip and hitting the concrete floor. But he took the hand away.

"You don't even know," she told him.

"What don't I know?"

327

She finally looked up into his beady little eyes. If he had really wanted to hook Li up, he should have let Tasha win. Then Puerto Rico would have qualified, instead of Gravity. He had just invited the new gold medalist to Rio.

She laughed and said, "You'll find out."

Then she went back into the stands to study "Irish" Jean Sullivan.

THE BODACIOUS BARD OF BRUISING

Carmen Cruz, Independent Journalist

May 27, 2016

World Amateur Championships Finals: US Team Heads Home with Three Medals, Two Quota Places, More Wisdom

QINHUANGDAO, CHINA—The US team celebrated Sacred Jones's gold medal with one last round of pies at Pizza Hut. Jones's unanimous decision over Sweden's classy Josefine Johansson improved her record to 74–1. This summer, the Detroit native is poised to become the only modern US boxer, male or female, to win two Olympic golds.

US head coach Ruben "Shorty" Feliciano said, "Sacred is an angel to coach but a devil to fight. That's what boxing is all about."

Heavyweight Bettina Rosario, silver medal bouncing against her chest, reminisced happily about her brawl with China's Shijin Wang, which she lost by a split decision. When the server approached, Rosario said, "F**k it! Bring me another large with sausage and meatballs."

All the boxers cheered. They had been cautioned off Chinese meat and—with the exception of the strict vegan Aaliyah Williams—are as eager for a return to American hamburgers as your humble blogger is for a proper glass of champagne.

Paloma Gonzales, who won featherweight bronze, chose to stay back in her dorm room.

Gravity Delgado leaned back in the booth, nursing a

Diet Coke and her own distant thoughts. Soon Delgado will celebrate her 17th birthday. Although she goes home medal-less, she won something more important in China.

"I want to thank God and Coach Jefferson Thomas," she said. "And everyone who helped me get here, including you, Carmen."

She squeezed a rubber chicken that she'd purchased from the Great Wall of China gift shop. It let out a mournful wail.

Boxing for Girls watched Delgado grow up on this trip, weathering her first loss, confronting her demons, and qualifying for Rio by the grace of God. Keep an eye out for this dark horse of a lightweight. Something tells us Gravity is gold.

Chapter Forty-Two

When Gravity touched down at JFK, her phone exploded with alerts and notifications. She glanced at the screen: Melsy, Ty, Mr. Rizzo, Boo Boo's mother, Ms. Laventhol, and a couple numbers that weren't in her contacts. She texted Melsy back, I landed. I'm just going to pass through the gym for a sec and then I'll come home. She turned the ringer off and put the phone away.

She couldn't deal with anybody's drama right now. She still hadn't posted anything to Instagram or Facebook, not about her loss, not about qualifying. Getting to Rio the way she had was not something to brag about. Everyone would know soon enough. Boxing gossip traveled faster than an Ali jab.

She was hoping Coach would have read *Boxing for Girls*. She smiled, thinking of the look of surprise that would come over his cranky old face when she strolled through the gym door unannounced and laid the rubber chicken in his lap. She could barely contain her impatience through the long wait for her baggage. It was only about an hour via the AirTrain to Cops 'n Kids.

Coach would not hold a grudge. He would see—even if he had not read Carmen's blog—that Gravity's loss had humbled her. He would laugh at the rubber chicken and smile at the Boxing Canada hoodie and kiss her on the cheek. They could start over fresh, training for Du Li and Jean Sullivan. It was better to ask forgiveness than permission, in life in general but in boxing most of all.

She had worn her nicest leggings on the plane ride home and blown out her hair before smoothing it back, but by the time she trudged through the late-spring rain to Cops 'n Kids, dragging her roller bag behind her, she felt like a wet dog. She turned the corner onto the little alley with a mixture of longing and dread. Everything looked the same. She spotted the tabby cat underneath one of the parked cars, mewling pathetically. A few cars down, the little tuxedo kitten emerged, also meowing, and shadowed her as she walked down the block.

She wiped her nose against her jacket and pulled her cap down lower. Maybe Coach would not want to train her again, but at the very least she would give him the gifts, shake his hand like a true champion, and thank him for everything he had taught her.

Gravity didn't notice that the electric gate was closed until she was right up in front of it. She stopped in surprise at the unwelcome sight of the corrugated metal. A paper was taped to the front of it, flapping in the wind. Without thinking, she reached out to straighten it.

The shock traveled up her right arm to her shoulder, sending her flying backward. The tuxedo kitten shot out of the way as her butt hit the sidewalk. He meowed at her reproachfully from under the dumpster. She winced and rotated her arm in its socket.

"You okay?" said a deep voice.

It was Monster. He must not have known the gym was closed either, because he was carrying a gym bag and wearing a pair of sparring gloves around his neck. He gave her his enormous hand and helped her to her feet, and she brushed off the seat of her pants.

She started to say she was fine, but then she saw what the sign said: "Closed for Funneral."

Monster followed her eyes.

"Damn," he said. "Who passed? I just got back in town."

"Me too," Gravity said, staring at the paper and thinking of all those unread texts on her phone. The rain kept falling and the cats kept meowing.

Monster looked at the tuxedo kitten and said, "He's hungry."

Monster must have gone somewhere with a lot of sun, because his dark skin glowed a shade deeper. Maybe he had been at a training camp. Gravity could just make out a fresh nick over his left cheekbone. His nose had changed in the years she had known him, flattening and spreading from all the blows.

Her vision had begun to crystallize the way it did in the ring at crucial moments, and strange things were happening to her sense of time. She remembered how intimidated she had been by Monster the first time she had seen him, back when he was still training with Coach.

She put a hand to her heart. Coach had taught Monster the best things he knew—that stiff jab and hard right hand—and every fight Monster had won was because of those fundamentals. But when Monster left him for Boca, Coach had given him his blessing. He had let him go and still cheered from the sidelines.

Coach was so generous. And she was so selfish. All she thought about was herself.

The kitten kept crying, and Gravity was grateful for the

rain because she was crying now too. She could not remember the last time she had cried, but the tears felt like they came from deep inside her, from something huge and frozen melting. Monster put his hand on her shoulder.

"The cat . . . is . . . hungry," she told him, sobbing so hard she could barely speak.

Coach always fed the street cats. It was the first thing he did when he got off the bus. He always left open cans of cat food lined up along the curb, but today the curb was empty.

And suddenly she remembered the last time she had cried. She had been eight years and seven weeks old. It was the morning that her father had not shown up to brush her hair for school. Her mother had told her that he had gone home to Santo Domingo and was never coming back. And Gravity had cried and cried and refused to go to school.

"He's never coming back," she said to Monster.

"Come on," he said gently.

He led her to the apartment building across the street, the one they used for GPS purposes, and they stood together under the awning and pulled out their phones. Gravity looked at her lock screen. Two more texts had come in: one from Svetlana and one from Fatso. Gravity dried her hand against the inside of her jacket.

Her finger hovered over her phone and her heart pounded. She looked over into Monster's solemn face, lit up by his screen.

Coach had told her that Monster's family had lost everything in a fire. He said that was why Monster trained so hard: because he had nothing more to lose.

But there was always more to lose.

Until she checked her messages, it was possible to believe anything. That the funeral was for some kid like Tray who

334

had gotten shot in the streets. Or for one of Mr. Rizzo's cop friends. Or somebody's sick grandma.

It was wrong to hope that someone else had died instead of Coach, but she hoped it. She did. If she had been brave enough, she would have prayed for it, but the fear of God was in her, bone-deep. She slid her finger along the screen and read the awful words.

Chapter Forty-Three

By the time they got to the funeral home, the service was almost over. Groups of men were clustered beneath the awning, smoking and drinking out of paper bags. As she followed Monster up the ramp, they reached out to touch her shoulder, calling her a champ and saying they were sorry for her loss.

She hung her head, feeling undeserving of their sympathy.

She and Monster signed the guest book that sat below an old television broadcasting a photomontage. Gravity paused for a moment to watch—Coach at the Olympic Training Center with "Too Fine" Hines, Coach hugging an eight-year-old D-Minus—but it made the tears come faster, so she motioned to Monster to follow. They left her suitcase by the coatrack and squeezed through the door.

It was hot inside the gathering room. All the chairs were full, and people were standing in the aisle. Gravity spotted Boca and Andre, Svetlana and her family, Mr. Rizzo with the NYPD boxing team, Fatso and Too Fine, dressed in all white. She could not find D-Minus.

A man in a purple suit stood on the dais, leading them all in a hymn. Half the room was singing, and a few women were weeping.

Leaning, leaning,
Safe and secure from all alarms;
Leaning, leaning,
Leaning on the everlasting arms.

Gravity knew it was supposed to be about God, but it could just as well have been about Coach. About those strong arms of his that had knocked men out cold and laced her into her first pair of gloves and turned the wheels that took him everywhere. Arms so strong they had fooled Gravity into thinking they were everlasting.

Oh, how sweet to walk
In this pilgrim way,
Leaning on the everlasting arms.
Oh, how bright the path
Grows from day to day,
Leaning on the everlasting arms.

But the path did not feel bright. Everything felt dark to her, even the road to Rio. She thought of the last time she and Coach had spoken, the terrible words they had exchanged. Then she thought, with greater agony, of how it had occurred to her in China, after her loss, to call him. But she hadn't. She had thought . . .

Oh, God. She had thought Coach would always be around. She had thought there would be so many other chances. What a fool she had been. Mr. Rizzo had tried to tell her. *Everyone* had. If only she could go back in time. She would have given it all—everything in her trophy case, everything she had—just to see him one more time.

She averted her eyes from the huge coffin lined with lavender frills. It sat beneath a half dozen enormous flower arrangements: one shaped like a PLASMAFuel bottle, one an NYPD badge with a boxing glove, one a US Marine Corps medallion.

All those flowers, cut and wasted. People competing for who could buy the biggest thing. They did no good now, just like her dumb Boxing Canada hoodie and her stupid rubber chicken. They should have given them to Coach when he was around.

She balled her hands into fists and dug the nails into her flesh.

"Gravity!"

It was Boo Boo's mom, standing with the family against the back wall. She wore a gray chinchilla coat, and Clarence senior and the boys wore dark, gleaming suits and Gucci shades. Something inside Gravity softened at the sight of them, all decked out for Coach, especially little Nigel, squirming in his formalwear, a WWE figurine gripped in one fat fist. He looked like he couldn't wait to destroy the suit by jumping into puddles; Gravity put the over-under at about five minutes.

Shelly enveloped her in a furry hug, and Nigel attached himself to her leg.

"We were *texting* and *texting*!" he said accusingly.

Gravity petted his head, suddenly wishing Tyler were there to cuddle. But then she would have to tell him Coach had died. The thought of that conversation filled her with despair.

"My phone was off," she told them. "I didn't . . . I didn't even know he was *sick*."

"Mr. Rizzo says he passed in his sleep," Shelly said. "Very peaceful. All the family was there."

Not me, Gravity thought bitterly. *I wasn't there.*

Clarence kissed her cheek and said, "He was a good man and a hell of a coach."

She nodded, unable to speak.

Boo Boo embraced her. He had always given great hugs, the best in the gym. She tried to pull away after what seemed like the right amount of time, but he put his hand on the back of her head and murmured, "Your coach had mad love for you, G. You made him proud."

That made her start to cry again, and she couldn't stop, but Boo Boo just held her in his strong arms as the sobs shook her body. After a moment, she felt Shelly's soft hand stroking the sleeve of her jacket. Then she felt something pressed into her hand. She pulled back and saw that Nigel had given her his action figure: a brawny, mean-looking white man in a black jumpsuit.

The sight of the little plastic wrestler made her laugh and cry at the same time.

"That's the Undertaker," Nigel said. "He rises from the dead all the time."

"Hush!" Shelly said, cuffing him.

Nigel started to cry.

Gravity wanted to comfort him, but it was rude to interfere in someone else's parenting. When she was a mom, she would never hit her kids.

"What did we talk about?" Shelly demanded.

Nigel said resentfully, "Nobody rises from the dead except Jesus."

Shelly rolled her eyes at Gravity. "He goes on and on about that wrestler."

"He's the Deadman," Nigel insisted. "Coach is lonely, so they could be friends." He tugged on Gravity's sleeve, and when she bent down to him, he whispered, "I know it's just pretend."

Up onstage, the man in the purple suit told everyone the order in which they should say their final goodbyes. Row by row, the mourners rose and trooped past the coffin. Gravity felt her heart pounding as her turn came.

She had only been to one funeral before, in Cleveland, for her mother's father. She was ten years old and Tyler was a toddler. Gravity had been confused by the way her rich suburban cousins acted toward her, as though she had a disease that might be contagious. Her grandmother had called her and Tyler urchins, and Gravity had memorized the word, because she was sure it must mean something nice, but when she looked "urchin" up later, it said "a mischievous and often poorly and raggedly clothed youngster."

That had made her very angry, because Tyler had made zero mischief at the funeral, and Gravity had not broken anything. And they had worn their best outfits—her mother had already started drinking heavily, so Auntie Rosa picked them out—a brown corduroy dress for her, a little sailor suit for Ty. Right after that, her mother's family had cut them off completely. Ever since, Gravity had associated funerals with feelings of judgment and shame.

As they made their slow circuit toward Coach's body, other mourners kept meeting her eyes respectfully or softly touching her arm, and even in the heaviness of her grief, Gravity was grateful. She, Mr. Rizzo, and Svetlana's family were the only light-skinned people in the room, but she felt more sense of family here than she had among her blood.

One thing Jews did better, though: no viewings. This was the first time Gravity would see a dead body, and she did not want to.

She watched to see what you were supposed to do. A few paces ahead of them was a woman from Coach's family in a white linen dress. She stopped beside the corpse for a long time, wailing and petting its cheeks, until two other women put their arms around her and led her off.

Next came an enormous man she recognized as that usher, Herbert, from the Barclays Center. He walked by the body quickly, nodding as though passing an acquaintance on the street. Next were Boo Boo's father, who ignored the body entirely, and Shelly, who crossed herself.

Gravity hesitated by the foot end of the box as Boo Boo and Nigel approached it. Nigel tried to put the Undertaker figurine into the coffin, but after a fierce, whispered exchange with his big brother, he took it back and stalked off.

She walked toward the explosion of flowers and silk at the coffin's head and looked inside. It was nothing like Coach. The deep brown skin, which had been so alive with rivers of wrinkles, looked powdery and cold. The lips were painted, the cheeks rouged like a woman's. Only the eyebrows seemed the same: those old bushy caterpillars, sleeping now. He looked strange in the suit and tie they had dressed him up in, but Gravity was glad they were burying him in one of his caps. This was the red, white, and blue one with stars on it from the Los Angeles Olympics.

She forced herself to touch his chest with two fingers. Even through the jacket and shirt, it felt hard as stone. Coach's body seemed somehow diminished, less tall and broad, as though his soul had taken up actual physical space. Ms. Laventhol had said that gravity pulled on everything. Gravity would have to ask her if it pulled on the soul, too.

Her tears had dried up, leaving her eyeballs aching.

"I'm sorry, Coach," she whispered. "I'm so sorry."

She shook her head. This was pointless. He wasn't there anymore. She took her hand back and left the coffin.

When she got outside with her suitcase, it had stopped raining. Men were still milling about with their bottles, talking more sloppily than when she had passed them going in. Boo Boo's father pulled cigars out of his suit jacket and passed them around.

Gravity asked about D-Minus.

"Demetrius didn't even go to his own brother's service," said Clarence.

"He doesn't like funerals, Dad," said Boo Boo.

"It's disrespectful," Shelly said. "Coach Thomas treated him like his own son!"

Gravity tried to imagine D there, in a suit, singing hymns.

No. D-Minus was a street cat, not a house cat. He didn't come when people called. She felt a sudden pull to go to him, wherever he was, to find out how he was mourning their teacher.

She pulled out her phone and texted:

Hey this is G. I qualified for Rio!!! Where are you?

She was positive he wouldn't respond, but the text came back right away:

Miami

"He's in Miami!" she announced.

"Word?" said Boo Boo, looking at her phone.

A series of selfies came in: D-Minus shirtless on the beach, D-Minus shirtless in the gym, D-Minus and a tiny, hard-bodied fighter, grinning, post-sparring.

"That's 'Finito' Bracero," Shelly said. "Flyweight champ. He's defending his title soon."

"They must've paid him to go down there for sparring," Gravity said, just as the next text came in:

342

I get $200/A Day

Gravity looked at the picture of D with the champ. He looked happy. A little over his fighting weight, but happy and focused. He had time to slim down before Rio. She searched for some trace of sadness in his eyes or his words, some hint that he felt the loss of their mentor, but his defense, as always, was airtight.

She texted, I'm at Coach's funeral. We miss you

He stopped texting back.

Chapter Forty-Four

It was hard to make herself go back to the gym. The first few days she just lay in bed, thinking it over and crying. Melsy came and went, with trays of chocolate milk and white roses. On the third day, Melsy's tray also held a card.

"That came in the mail," she said.

Gravity pushed herself up on one elbow and examined the envelope. Her first thought was that it might be from Lefty, that he was sorry for everything and wanted her back, but the return address was in Harlem.

"Drink the milk," Melsy said.

Gravity grimaced. Melsy had been guilting her into drinking several glasses of chocolate milk per day. Gravity had no appetite and was actually down to 130.5, the lightest she had been in years. She took a deep breath and downed the entire glass in one gulp, then put a hand on her belly, forcing herself not to puke.

"Good girl," Melsy said. "I'm gonna go pick up Tyler. Want a ride to Cops 'n Kids?"

"No, thanks."

"Or I could take you to the other one?" Melsy said. "What's it called? The one with Tiffany?"

"No, thanks," Gravity said, turning her face to look out the window and willing her cousin to go away. She felt Melsy hesitate for a while and then withdraw.

Gravity was relieved. It was too hard to keep it together around people. She preferred to be alone with her thoughts, which were like a rat on a wheel, spinning and spinning around her own regret.

She gave herself a paper cut opening the envelope. She stared at the tiny red line across the pad of her finger, waiting for the blood, but it didn't come.

The young heal fast. Coach had said that to her once, after she separated her shoulder in a hard sparring with D. It had been true back then. But she wasn't so young anymore. Her seventeenth birthday was right around the corner, and she felt impossibly old.

The handmade greeting card had a symbol she'd seen somewhere before: a black circle, painted roughly in a single stroke. The two ends of the circle did not quite meet; in the gap she could see the fibers running through the paper. She opened the card and read the scrolly, old-fashioned cursive that filled the whole inside:

Dear Gravity,

I'm sorry for your lost. Jefferson was like a father to you. To me he was a better father than my real one. I wanted to tell you at the funeral but you looked shook up, and like in the corner, its better to give advice when a fighter can listen. You were his favorite more than D or Too Fine. I seen you look at the clippings by Jefferson's locker back at Cops 'n Kids. You felt sorry for yourself because theres all Demetrius articles and my articles up and none of yours. Well one thing you never knew about your Coach is that he got kidney dialysis three days a week at this shit hole in East New York. He called dialysis A Living Death and he wasn't wrong. Well he had all your

*clippings up in that place starting back at that fathers day
card you gave him when you were a Pee Wee and going
to that little picture Monster took of you outside Cops 'n
Kids the last day you had come. He loved that damn
fathers day card, I tried to get it for you but those ass holes
threw everything away. I wanted you to know. He looked
at it for strength while they stuck the needles in. He called
you his Hundred Dollar Baby. We would laugh about it.
He said he got a discount because you were Irregular. You
know how he was Gravity. He had lots of sons but you
were his only daughter. To Allah we belong and to Him
we shall return. Champ don't waste any more time crying,
it's seconds out. Call me if you need a ride to the gym.*

Peace,

Mustafa (AKA Fatso)

Gravity set the card down.

The Father's Day card. She had forgotten all about it. She had given Coach a card that first year together, and she had signed it "I love you," and his response had been so gruff that she had felt ashamed. She had thought maybe she had been inappropriate, and she had never given him a card again. But it must have been okay, if he had saved it all those years.

Before she could change her mind, she grabbed her gym bag—it was still packed from before Coach's funeral—and headed into the subway. She could just make it there before they closed. There wouldn't be time to work out, but she could at least thank Fatso, if he was there. And if he wasn't . . .

Gravity wasn't sure what she would do. It was already June 1. There was a two-week training camp in Colorado Springs she was required to attend in a few weeks, and another in July. Maybe Boca would just let her work out by herself for a while, until she figured things out. She *did* like Tiffany, but she hesitated to go back to Smiley's. It just didn't feel the same.

She spent the long subway ride reading and rereading Fatso's card. By the time she got to Brooklyn, she could laugh a little at the "Hundred Dollar Baby" part. That was a good one.

The walk to the gym was hard, but she put her head down and moved forward, not allowing her gaze to linger on landmarks that he would never see again. When she turned the corner and walked down the little dead-end street, she felt an actual pain in her legs. It was all she could do to get through the gym door.

She paused inside, inhaling deeply the smell of unwashed boys and sweat-soaked leather. The whole Bocacrew was in there, scattered on stretching mats in the big blue ring and on the floor around it. Michael Jackson's "Man in the Mirror" was playing at top volume, and some little kid was hanging from the pull-up bar, singing along.

Gravity walked quietly to the logbook and signed in. Hers was only the third signature for the day, although there were dozens of kids in the gym.

The music snapped off.

She looked up in surprise as Boca's voice thundered throughout the gym. "See how Gravity signs in! How many times do I have to tell you little bastards the same thing! Go do it! Now!"

The boxers peeled themselves off their stretching mats and rolled out of the ring, grumbling as they slunk across the gym to her.

"Hey, Grav," said Boo Boo, giving her a pound. "I'm all sweaty."

"I don't care."

He hugged her, and then they all did, and they took the pen from her to sign their names, one by one, in little puddles of sweat in the book. When Fatso enveloped her in an enormous embrace, she murmured her thanks in his ear.

"Seeing you back in the gym is all the thanks I need," he said.

Boca was the last to come forward. He hugged her hard and spoke stiffly, as though reading from a script: "Your coach was a great man. I learned so much from watching him work with you. It was an honor to share the gym for so many years."

She was still thinking of how to reply when he handed her a jump rope and told her to give him fifteen minutes.

"Then get in the ring to work on your feet," Fatso said.

She glanced at the clock. "But aren't you about to close?"

Fatso laughed. "I think we can stay open late for the Olympian."

Boo Boo and Genya and several of Boca's pros had gathered around to listen. As Gravity looked into their eyes, she saw a new recognition.

They looked up to her now. It was hard to believe, but it was true.

"We're not gonna change her," Boca announced. "We're just gonna polish her up. We got two months to get Gravity in the best shape of her life."

And just like that, Gravity was in the Bocacrew. Somebody turned Michael Jackson back on, and Fatso told her to quit stalling and get to work.

Chapter Forty-Five

Gravity jogged through the Heather Garden, dodging a stroller and breathing the thick fragrance of early-summer flowers. It was a beautiful morning, and the Olympics were six weeks away. Her rib was fully healed, her weight was good, and her legs felt like they could carry her all the way to Rio.

She jogged down the steps cut into the stone and hit the straightaway along the water, way above the world in a canopy of trees. She had never thought she would find somewhere better than the Coney Island boardwalk, but Fort Tryon Park in the summer was her new favorite place to run. She picked up speed as she ran beneath a stone arch, letting out a whoop that echoed back, magnified.

She had learned a lot at the June camp at the Olympic Training Center. The nutritionist there had drawn up a custom diet plan, and she was sticking to it, no more plastic suits. It was easy now that she and Ty had their own place up here, near Melsy and Auntie Rosa.

The commute was a bitch, but that was life. She would graduate next year, and when Ty got into middle school, they would try to put him somewhere good uptown. For now, she used the subway time to listen to Carmen's new podcast.

When she got to the benches at the park's northern tip, she stopped to do the set of dips, incline push-ups, and squats that Boca had added to her morning routine. She liked training with Boca. She had been worried that it would feel like a betrayal of Coach, or that she would not jibe with Boca's style, but it had all happened so naturally.

At first, Gravity had not known what to make of Boca's sudden deference to Coach's memory, how to square it with Coach's rage at Boca, Boca's habit of poaching Coach's fighters, and the tension that had always filled the air between them. All that was gone now, and Boca spoke of Coach as though he was George Washington or some other historical figure to be cited as a distant ideal. But maybe that is how it is when someone dies. They go from being there to not being there, and the survivors get to tell the story. Surviving is the ultimate victory, and maybe that was what Coach had meant when he said Gravity had already defeated all her enemies. Whatever battle the two coaches had been fighting, Boca had won. That was why he could afford to be generous.

She marveled over this as she jogged back to the pathway that circled the Cloisters and looped south toward 190th Street. The Buddhist monk was walking in the Heather Garden again. She waved and he waved back, fat and jolly in his bright robes. He made her think of Clifford the Big Red Dog.

When she got back home, Tyler was still asleep. He slept so hard, and in the weirdest positions. Right now he looked like he had fallen from a great height. One arm was flung overhead and the other was stretched across his face, and his Thomas the Tank Engine pajamas were halfway off. Sugar had cuddled up inside his shirt, but when Gravity walked in, he opened his yellow eyes and meowed reproachfully.

"Yeah yeah yeah," she said. "Don't forget I saved you from a life on the streets."

She popped open a can of Fancy Feast and put it in the little pet bowl she had bought at the Olympic Training Center. He skittered over in his tuxedo to eat breakfast.

She stood there a moment, drinking it in: their own place, clean and drenched in light.

It was such a small studio that it did not need much furniture. Mr. Rizzo had signed the lease for her and insisted on putting up the security deposit, even though her stipend had gone up to three thousand dollars because she had qualified for Rio. Auntie Rosa had made gauzy white curtains and given them cuttings from her houseplants. They had gotten a cute little sofa bed from the Housing Works Thrift Shop. Gravity's trophy case sat against one wall, and Tyler's Xbox against the other.

Best of all, there was nobody there to yell at them. Nobody to keep them from sleeping. Only the bare minimum of cockroaches, and Sugar put the fear of God in them.

Gravity drank a tall glass of delicious New York City tap water. She put out the cereal and milk for Tyler and went to jump in the shower, kissing him on the forehead on the way. She liked to let him sleep until the last possible moment. He always woke up when she made her kale smoothie.

Chapter Forty-Six

As she turned down the alley that led to the gym, Gravity pulled her blouse away from her body and blew on her chest, trying to evaporate some of the sweat. There were camera trucks parked all along the street and reporters and random bigwigs milling about. D-Minus was back today. They were doing a press conference before they left for the international training camp at the OTC.

She tried to calm her heart at the thought of seeing him again, but everything was swirling around inside her like one of the snow globes at the Great Wall of China gift shop.

Melsy saying, "You *love* that boy."

D whispering in her ear after that last crazy sparring, "It was worth it to get between your legs."

Watching him win his Golden Gloves; watching him lose to Tiger; watching, in Sacred's dorm room in China, the magnificent performance in Azerbaijan that had clinched his spot in Rio.

All the precious days spent learning at Coach's side. D-Minus was the only one who really understood what she had lost. She felt she could not bear to see him again, but she could not bear *not* to.

She had only cried for five minutes that morning. She was going to keep it together.

"Hey, Gravity!" yelled a cameraman leaning against one of the trucks.

"Good to see you!" Gravity said, giving him a fake smile.

Melsy had told her to say "Good to see you!" when she could not remember if she had met someone.

"What's the address here?"

"We don't have one."

"What?"

"The gym has no address." She gave him the number of the apartment building across the street.

A woman in a suit passed her and stopped to shake her hand. "Ms. Delgado!"

"Good to see you!"

"How are you feeling?"

"I feel so confident about this exciting new opportunity!"

She and Melsy had practiced three generic responses that Gravity was going to keep in rotation: "I feel so confident about this exciting new opportunity," "I feel humbled at the prospect of representing my country," and "I feel grateful to God and USA Boxing for all the support they have given me."

Once the sidewalk was quiet, Gravity pulled out the cat food and set it on the curb. The feral tabby and her remaining brood slunk out from the dumpster and fixed Gravity with their Technicolor eyes.

"Sugar says meow," she told them.

"Gravity!" yelled Mr. Rizzo, holding the gym door open. "Go on up into the ring! We want to get a picture of you and D with the city councilman and borough president."

Gravity hurried inside—where it was cooler, thank

353

God—and through the crowd of press and family. She paused to kiss Boo Boo's parents, hug Svetlana, shake many hands, and say "Good to see you" many times.

D-Minus was already up in the ring, basking under the lights. This was the first time she had ever seen him in a suit. It was steel gray and very expensive-looking. All the politicians looked like extras in the movie of his life.

Gravity hesitated at the ring's perimeter, trying to master her emotions. She yanked down her pencil skirt to conceal the run in her stockings. Even though Melsy had helped her shop for her outfit and do her makeup, she felt like a child at a grown-ups' party.

D-Minus had replied to none of her texts of condolence, although he had, uncharacteristically, loved her Facebook video about Coach and commented on her Instagram post— a collage of old photos of the three of them training—with a single crying-face emoji, a flexing muscle, and a heart.

She would not cry. She would not. She was so confident about this exciting new opportunity.

D-Minus saw her and called her to him.

She said, "I missed you at the funeral."

He said, "I don't do funerals."

She found it hard to look in his eyes, so she looked over his shoulder at the mural of Coach. "The service was beautiful."

"*You're* beautiful," he said, to her utter astonishment. He draped an arm across her shoulder, turned to the borough president, and said, "This is the next lightweight gold medalist right here."

She looked at him from beneath his arm, trying to figure out if he was being sarcastic. He gazed at her with such warmth that she blushed and cut her eyes away.

The councilman said, "I heard she just had her first loss!"

Gravity stiffened, but D squeezed her shoulder and replied, "Ever lose an election, Councilman?"

The borough president snickered.

"You gotta lose to learn," D said. "Coach taught us that. She'll whip that girl's ass in Rio."

Gravity said, "I feel grateful to God and USA Boxing for all the support they have given me."

After they were done posing, D held the ropes open for her and gave her his arm as they walked down the stairs, and all throughout the terrifying schmoozing that followed, he kept her at his side. Gravity knew this show of favor might just be one of his passing moods, but she accepted it, because it was from him.

Mr. Rizzo had done a great job getting the word out, and the gym was packed. Boca had made it look festive by hanging bunting around the rings, along with little Haitian and American flags. Boo Boo's mom had brought trays of barbecued chicken, yams, and collard greens. Boo Boo's dad had brought soda for the kids and a mysterious beverage for the adults called a nutcracker, which Mr. Rizzo pretended not to see. And Kostya, who ran an extermination service, had the roach population down for the count.

The faces came and went with their congratulations and condolences and questions, and Gravity allowed herself to relax into the protective field of D-Minus's charisma. He carried her through the interviews the way he had so often carried her through sparring. The third time she said, "I feel grateful to God and USA Boxing for all the support they have given me," he slid his hand down her spine—her blouse had a cutaway back, because Melsy said it flattered her—and let it rest for a moment, cupping her ass. Their backs were to the speed bag wall, so nobody could see. Gravity's face flushed and she shivered.

Soon thereafter, the press began to disperse, and a delicious impatience rose up inside her. She and D-Minus were going to be together. She knew it, he knew it, and the anticipation was almost unbearable.

Carmen Cruz came to say goodbye, accompanied by Monster. Both of them were sipping nutcrackers and seemed to be hitting it off. Carmen stood between Gravity and D-Minus, putting her arms around them.

"Take our picture, Kimani," she purred. "Get their coach's mural in the background."

"Of course, Carmen," Monster said.

He reached out to brush a speck of dust off the front of her dress.

"Your magnificent coach is looking down from heaven with great pride," Carmen said, squeezing them and smiling for the camera. "Two Olympians! What are the odds? We will toast to him with caipirinhas when we dance the samba in Rio."

She turned to look at the mural of their coach. "It is a wonderful likeness. Who painted it?"

Gravity didn't know. She had never thought to ask. She looked at D-Minus, aware of a sudden tension in him.

"My brother Tray," he said. "Lefty did the lettering."

Gravity looked at the mural again, seeing it with fresh eyes. Of course Lefty had done the graffiti writing; she saw that now. It looked just like how he wrote "$outhpaw."

But Tray had been a true artist. What she noticed now was how little he had done. In a lot of places, it was just the wall showing through. But the way he painted tricked your mind into filling in the empty spaces.

Carmen said, "Is he here? I would love to interview him."

"Nah."

D's face was unreadable, but Gravity had noticed that Carmen often caught things that escaped other people. She did so now, switching into the past tense: "Your brother painted with his brushes. You paint with your fists."

Andre Vázquez had wandered over and was listening in on their conversation.

"Funny about the record," he said, looking at the mural with a know-it-all smirk that reminded Gravity of Paloma Gonzales. "Somewhat ironic for a fighter nicknamed 'The Truth.'"

"What do you mean?" Gravity asked.

Ironic was like at the end of Lefty's song, when Wilfredo Gómez got high in the Hall of Fame. Coach's record of 97–12 (80 KOs) wasn't ironic at all. It was amazing.

"Coach Thomas was a journeyman," Andre said.

"He was *not!*" Gravity said, appalled. "He was a top contender. If it hadn't been for how racist boxing was back then, he would have been a champion!" She turned to Carmen. "Tell him! You wrote about Coach!"

Carmen put a hand on Gravity's arm. "I printed the record he claimed," she said softly. "But that may have been his unofficial record."

"Or his *imaginary* record," quipped Andre.

He passed Gravity his phone, opened to Jefferson H. Thomas's BoxRec page. Gravity stared in disbelief. Coach's professional record was 20–25. For some reason, she had never looked Coach up on the site. She had just assumed the record on the mural was accurate. She tried to pass the phone to D-Minus.

"Nah, chill," he said.

Gravity handed the phone back to Andre, who said, "Amazing he still had his faculties, really!"

"Show some respect," Carmen snapped.

Andre smiled. "I'm a businessman, Carmen. I respect the bottom line."

Carmen said mysteriously, "Bottom lines have a way of changing."

"What's that supposed to mean?" Andre asked.

Carmen just smiled and sipped her nutcracker.

Andre turned to Monster and told him it was time to go, but Monster said he would prefer not to, because he and Carmen had plans to go to the Met and look at the Temple of Dendur. Andre turned very red and reminded Monster that they had trunk fittings that afternoon for his pro debut. Monster said he would not be needing trunks because he was not planning to turn professional but would be pursuing his true passion, photography.

D-Minus snickered. He opened a bag of popcorn and offered some to Gravity.

"Need I remind you that you're under contract?" Andre said.

"Which contract?" Monster said, reaching into his pocket and pulling out Andre's five-hundred-dollar gold Montblanc. "The one I didn't sign yet with your stupid pen?"

Andre looked like smoke was about to come out of his ears.

"It's such a coincidence," Monster said, "because I was talking to Carmen about that, and it turns out her daughter is an immigration lawyer. And we showed *her* the contract, and guess what *she* said?"

Carmen threw back her head and laughed. Monster laughed too. Soon they were both laughing so hard that Gravity and D-Minus joined in, even though they didn't know what they were laughing at. They just knew it was at Andre's expense, so it felt good.

Monster finally caught his breath and dabbed the tears from his eyes. He put the pen in Andre's pocket and patted him on the head as if he were a little boy. "She said a *horse* wouldn't even sign that!"

Everybody cracked up again.

"I didn't tell you to show it to a lawyer," Andre yelled. "I told you to *sign* it!" He stormed out of the gym.

When he had gone, they stayed there for a moment, looking at the mural of Coach.

He was a *journeyman*.

Gravity felt that sinking in. She looked at D, but he was posing for Monster now, his suit jacket slung over one shoulder and his hand on a heavy bag. D had the most uncanny ability to take only what he wanted from life. He could probably drink the water out of a bottle of PLASMAFuel and leave the electrolytes behind.

Carmen said, "I think it's harder to make champions than to be one, Gravity. Do not let this shake your faith. Nothing has changed."

"But . . . he called himself 'The Truth'! He said he could have been like Joe Louis or Muhammad Ali if it weren't for all the racism and corruption."

Carmen said, "And that may be true. What is truth, anyway? What is measurement?" She waved her red plastic cup at the mural, teetering in her stilettos. Gravity realized with alarm that Carmen had had one nutcracker too many.

"Hieroglyphics!" she yelled. "Marks scratched in stone tablets and gleaming from electronic screens!" Her dark eyes shone and her musical voice gained force. Even D-Minus stopped posing and listened. Carmen was on a roll.

"When Cassius Clay took the title from Sonny Liston on February twenty-fifth, 1964, afterward embracing the Islamic faith with the name Muhammad Ali, there were as many truths as there were seats in the Miami Beach Convention Hall, leaves of grass in Louisville, verses in the Koran!"

She tossed back the rest of her nutcracker and threw the empty cup in the spit bucket, where it landed with a noxious splash. Monster reached out an enormous hand to steady her.

"Boxing is the dirtiest sport in the world, Gravity. It is also the purest." Tears were streaming down her face now, but she seemed unashamed. "Fuck Andre Vázquez. Fuck all those . . . those . . . *suits* who think they can buy a ringside ticket to our lives. Truth is *not* something you know. Truth is something you *are*."

She entwined her small hand with Monster's. "Come on, Kimani, let's go see the pyramids."

Chapter Forty-Seven

Gravity had made herself the OTC-prescribed serving of chicken breast and broccoli. She ate it slowly, imagining it was the mofongo Melsy was eating across from her at the table. Gravity loved her new table. She had found it on Craigslist for only twenty-five dollars. It looked like something from an old-school diner.

Melsy was going out dancing tonight and was wearing a fabulous silver romper, but her hair was still up in curlers. She had on fake eyelashes lined with rhinestones, which made it sort of dizzying to look at her. Gravity had tried to explain her outrage about Coach's fake record, but Melsy, like Carmen, did not seem to think it was a big deal.

"It's like guys on the internet saying they're taller than they really are," Melsy said. "Or girls saying they're younger. It's just fake advertising." She reached for more broth to moisten her plantains. Gravity averted her eyes. There would be plenty of mofongo after Rio.

"Your coach was exactly who he said he was, G. He was your teacher. He needed you to believe in him, so he did what he thought was best."

"How is it *best* to lie?" Gravity demanded, growing angry again. She got what Carmen had said, back at the gym, about there being a lot of different perspectives to boxing, but you could take that line of argument too far. Anyway, Carmen had been drunk.

"So you never lied to someone to make them feel better?" Melsy said, an annoying know-it-all tone in her voice. "To make them feel more confident, more protected?"

Gravity followed Melsy's gaze to where Tyler lay stretched out on his bed. He had fallen asleep in the middle of his fractions homework, the pencil still in his hand. Sugar was curled up in a ball in his armpit.

Gravity scowled. She knew Melsy was talking about those pictures of their dad, how Gravity had lied and told Tyler they were pictures of him.

"That's different."

"Is it?" Melsy asked. "No offense, G, but boxers are like children. You all just want to be loved. Your coach knew exactly what he was doing. He wanted you to believe in him, and you did, and it worked. *That's* not a lie."

Gravity chewed her broccoli angrily. Melsy was always ambushing her. She tried to fool you by being a beautiful ring card girl, but then she came out with these deep insights. It was irritating. Gravity's phone chimed.

It was D-Minus, texting:

g wassup?

She set the phone back down, her heart pounding. They had not spoken or texted since she had left the gym after the press conference that afternoon. She could still feel his hand on her skin, sliding down her back, cupping her ass.

Melsy met her eyes. "How'd it go with D-Licious?" she asked, psychic as always.

Gravity said, "Okay." The phone chimed again. She glanced at it:

where u at?

She tried to calm her breathing.

"That's him, isn't it?" Melsy said. "I can hear you panting from across the table. What's he say?"

Gravity frowned and passed her the phone.

"Hmph," Melsy said. "Remember how you told me that there's two styles of boxing?"

Gravity looked at her, confused. "There's so many styles of boxing."

Melsy insisted, "You said there were two. Like Muhammad Ali and what's his name with the grill."

Gravity laughed. "George Foreman." She and Melsy had watched *When We Were Kings* together a bunch of times back in middle school. Melsy found the African fashions very inspiring. "You're talking about boxers and punchers. Yeah, Ali was a classic example of a boxer and Foreman was a puncher, like Joe Frazier and Sonny Liston."

Melsy blinked, flashing her rhinestones. "You also said that sometimes boxers had more heart than punchers."

"I never said that!" Gravity said, appalled. "Nobody had more heart than Joe Frazier. He would have died in that ring if Eddie Futch hadn't stopped him."

Melsy made the adorable face she made when she was concentrating very hard. "But you said something about how much punishment Ali could absorb. And how a lot of the toughest punchers, like Tyson, were actually fragile. Like glass."

"*Chin!* Boxers have better chins! I mean, not always, but sometimes."

Gravity paused, trying to think of how to explain it to Melsy. "Heart is, like, pushing through the pain to show everybody who you are. You can lose with heart, but people will always respect you." She smiled. Heart was a nice thing

363

to think about. "Chin is different. It's something physical. Your heart could make you want to keep fighting, but if you have a glass jaw, you'll go down if someone hits you right."

"Like Amir Khan," Melsy said sadly.

Gravity grinned. Amir Kahn was one of the very few fighters whose names Melsy could remember, because she thought he was so handsome. She had actually cried when Danny Garcia stopped him.

"Exactly. But Khan is a boxer, so he's an exception to the rule. Coach always said that the purest boxers *had* to have great chins, because they didn't have the punching power to intimidate the other guy."

"Don't overthink it, cuz," Melsy said. "I'm just trying to make a point about love." She extended her left arm in a cute imitation of a jab. "When it comes to love, I'm the boxer. I'm fast. I try not to let them get too close. I might get rocked, but I always keep it moving.

"You're the puncher, G. You look tough, but you fall *easy*. You fell hard for Lefty. You fell for Keeshawn the first time you two met at the track. And I think you straight up fell for that coach, too, the guy with the orange skin. Not sex-wise, but you just *gave* yourself to him. You're all in, all the time. It takes a lot of heart, but it's *risky*."

Gravity felt her face burn from the accuracy of this portrait. She had been such a fool to trust Rick Ross. She wished she could be more like Melsy, but maybe love was the same as boxing. It was hard to change your style once it was set.

Melsy went on, "You feel more deeply for Demetrius than you do for any of these boys. He's got even more power to hurt you. *Don't* let him in, cuz. Not until after Rio, when you can afford to get knocked on your ass. Handle your business first."

Melsy slid Gravity's phone back to her. Gravity felt a sinking sensation, because she knew her cousin was right. She wanted D. Saying no to him would be way harder than turning down mofongo.

"Aw, poor baby," Melsy said, patting her hand. "Can't have that dick till after the Olympics."

Gravity laughed. "Maybe he won't be into me, though, if I make him wait."

Melsy shook her head. "He'll be *more* into you. Boys are like dollars: you can never have too many, and when you put them away, they gain interest."

They both laughed at that.

Tyler woke up and asked what was so funny.

When Gravity's phone chimed again with another text from D, she turned it off and put it away.

Chapter Forty-Eight

Gravity took a deep breath and made her birthday wish. Monster snapped her picture as she blew on the glove-shaped cake, taking out the ten central candles in the initial attack, getting low to smoke the three on the bottom, then sweeping across the top to kayo the final four. All the gym rats applauded. The time in Colorado Springs had been good for her lung capacity.

"Does anybody have a knife?" Gravity asked.

A dozen boys produced switchblades. Mr. Rizzo rolled his eyes.

Boca turned the mariachi music back on, and Nigel and Tyler went back to their water balloon war, swinging from the heavy bags like Tarzan. Gravity watched them for a moment, feeling wistful. Coach would have hollered that the heavy bags were not a toy and to take those goddamn balloons outside. Boca just eyed them, the scar on his cheek twitching in a grin, and said, "When they fall on their asses, they'll learn." Then he picked up a water balloon and joined in.

She passed the first slice of cake to Mr. Rizzo, who passed it along to Fatso, who said he wanted a bigger piece and passed it along to Svetlana, who said she wanted a smaller one and passed it along to D-Minus, who said, "Nah, gimme one with more chocolate laces." He came and stood behind Gravity, taking her wrist to guide her hand.

She gave him a look like, "Don't push your luck."

He gave her a look like, "Who, me?"

She cut him a big piece and then stepped away. She was afraid she would slip if she kept her hands near all that sweetness.

Melsy had been right about D only getting more interested when Gravity practiced patience. Not that one piece of cake would make a difference, but it was a slippery slope. You always craved another bite. The next thing you knew, you were naked in bed eating chicharrones and you had lost all the strength in your legs.

She went outside onto the street, where all four of Sugar's relatives had emerged and were chowing down on their canned lamb. When the gym door closed behind her, they froze.

"Meow meow," she said.

They stared at her distrustfully, licking their chops. When she remained perfectly still, they bent back down and kept eating. Sugar was such an affectionate, playful kitten. It was funny how one cat could come out so different from the rest of the family.

She looked down the street and off into the distance, as far as she could see. Deep inside her, an old wound throbbed. She stayed there, watching and waiting, until the cats finished eating and slunk off. Still she waited, her eyes fixed on the place where her vision began to blur and the buildings blended into the sky.

Gravity felt distant from herself, as though part of her was standing there on the concrete and part of her was

367

hiding under the dumpster with the cats, watching the world through wild eyes.

The gym door burst open and Tyler and Nigel spilled out, covered with cake.

"What are you doing out here?" Tyler demanded.

Gravity kept her eyes on the horizon for a few more heartbeats. She had thought maybe this would be the year. Because of all the press and all the things she had won.

He had shown up without warning that day she turned eight, his arms full of gifts. Every birthday since, it was what she wished for when she blew out the candles.

"Nothing," she said, turning back toward the gym.

The door opened again and Mr. Rizzo came out, dragging a garbage bag filled with mismatched gloves. He pointed at Nigel and Tyler, who were now taking turns punching each other in the stomach. "I gotta get back to the precinct. Don't let those two maniacs eat any more cake. I don't want to see them on the eleven o'clock news."

He slipped her an envelope. "That's for Rio."

Gravity started to argue that she had her stipend now, but he said, "Don't argue! And here. A little something else." He pulled a tiny box out of his pocket and gave it to her.

Inside was a Golden Gloves necklace set with a diamond. Gravity turned the pendant over. The inscription on the back said "2016 Golden Gloves 132 lb women champion."

"Your little brother told me what happened," he said gruffly.

She turned to glare at Tyler, but Mr. Rizzo said, "Don't get mad at him! I pulled some strings and had a new one made. Put it on."

For some reason, her hands were shaking, so he helped her take it out and fastened it around her neck.

"Thank you, Mr. Rizzo," she said.

He headed off to his car, dragging the bag of gloves. She thought she saw movement on the street behind him, but it was just someone opening their apartment window and tossing out a Styrofoam clamshell. It fell on the ground in a puff of rice, tumbled down the incline, and came to rest by the gym door. Gravity went to get the broom and cleaned it up.

August 5, 2016

Rio Roundup: Auspicious Draw for Delgado and Jones; Reckoning for Ross and Vázquez; Postcards from Brooklyn

RIO DE JANEIRO, BRAZIL—All 36 women boxers competing in the Summer Olympics made weight yesterday, and the brackets are in.

Our middleweight muse, Sacred Jones, entering as top seed, enjoys an opening-round bye, after which she faces the winner of Finland versus Morocco in the quarterfinals. She will celebrate her 22nd birthday the day she fights in the semifinals, and Detroit already has a parade scheduled to welcome her home as the first US boxer to ever defend an Olympic championship.

When we asked Jones how things have changed for her since the London Games, she pointed to her teammate Gravity Delgado: "I look at Gravity and I think how young I was back then. I thought everything would change after I won gold. But change takes time.

"I didn't get big sponsors. Some people said it was 'cause I'm too rough. They said I shouldn't say the things I say, like that I love punching girls in the face."

She laughed. "This is boxing! I'm not gonna change who I am just to get sponsors and press. People love who I am, and they love the way I fight. But I think they love who I am even more."

Brooklyn's Gravity Delgado enters the lightweight bracket unseeded and drew New Zealand in the preliminaries for what should be an easy win. This sets up a quarterfinal clash with London gold medalist "Irish" Jean Sullivan.

Some would say this is an unlucky break for Delgado, but we are not so sure. Sullivan looked beatable in China, narrowly winning controversial split decisions over both Russia and China. At 30 and with hundreds of amateur bouts under her belt, the defending champion may be past her prime, and Delgado has the size and high-volume punching style to beat her.

US head coach Ruben "Shorty" Feliciano agrees: "We can beat that girl. I like the draw. Better to get her early, while we're fresh."

Delgado says, "Jean Sullivan has never seen anybody like me."

The lower half of the lightweight bracket should be owned by Russia's fine southpaw Sofya Bulgakov, although Brazil's Ariana Leite, fighting on her home turf, is one to watch, as is China's Du Li, who was almost disqualified after a positive test result for a banned diuretic. Li has since been cleared to compete, but only after the Chinese federation dismissed controversial conditioning guru Rick Ross. Ross declined to comment.

Speaking of the shady side of boxing, head over to *La Opinión* for our exposé on boxing manager Andre Vázquez, who recently resigned from his position at PLASMAFuel amid a storm of sexual harassment allegations. Vázquez and PLASMAFuel declined to comment.

Boxing for Girls wishes all of our readers a happy Summer Games. Please join us in sipping a caipirinha as we enjoy this photo essay from our newest contributor, Kimani Browne, on the formative years of US Olympian Gravity Delgado, Haitian Olympian Demetrius "D-Minus" Saint-Amand, and the team behind them at Cops 'n Kids in Brooklyn.

Chapter Forty-Nine

Gravity clutched her new Golden Gloves necklace in her hand as she watched the strange landscape roll by outside the bus window. Rio made New York look small. It rambled on and on, with beaches and cliffs and skyscrapers and the densely packed communities that twinkled with light up in the hills. People told scary stories about the favelas, but people always talked trash about places they didn't understand. If the favelas were anything like Brownsville, that was where all the best fighters were.

The bus let them out in a big parking lot near Maracanã Stadium. She and Sacred got off, followed by Bonnie and Coach Shorty and the six boys on the US team, and they joined all the other American athletes snaking through the buses into a dark tunnel that led inside the stadium.

Gravity loved their uniform: crisp white jeans with a striped sweater and crested navy blazer. There were even red,white, and blue loafers. She had spent her whole life feeling like she didn't quite fit, but here, in this river of athletes, she felt part of something bigger.

The closer they got to the stadium floor, the louder the cheers grew, until it seemed like the walls of the tunnel themselves were trembling. Sacred and the boys had their cell phones out, so Gravity pulled hers out too. It was still open to Carmen's blog, and she could not help scrolling one more time through Monster's seven snapshots. It was like a movie of their life.

Gravity and D-Minus sitting on the concrete ledge outside the gym after their first sparring, arms around each other, looking like little kids.

Fatso in the corner in Mobile, Alabama, yelling at a fifteen-year-old D-Minus, who looked exhausted but was about to rally and win the Junior Olympics.

Gravity hitting the heavy bag at Cops 'n Kids while Coach pointed at her stance, his face wrinkled with displeasure. She could almost hear him: "Fix your goddamn feet!"

Gravity winning the Golden Gloves, her eyes lifted toward the ceiling of the Barclays Center, thanking God for the victory, the referee smiling at her, the opponent looking away.

The shot of her outside the gym wearing her Continental gold, with Sugar peeking out from under the dumpster, waiting to be saved.

Later on the same day, the photo of her and D that had made the *Daily News*, right after he had whispered that dirty thing in her ear that made her realize he saw her as a woman.

Her face and D-Minus's lit up by candlelight as she blew on the glove-shaped cake. So what if she never got her birthday wish? All her other wishes came true.

The tunnel ended, and she came out into the open air, holding her phone up to record the scene as the announcer's voice proclaimed: "*Les États-Unis!* The United States of America!"

The crowd roared and the rows of bleachers sparkled with the flashes of thousands of cameras. Way up ahead, she could see Michael Phelps waving his huge American flag. Gravity put her phone away to pay more attention.

The stadium lights made the Brazilian night hotter, and the strangeness of it all made her feel very alive.

Sacred grinned and waved her American flag, her London gold gleaming against her chest. The tiny flag looked even tinier in her big, strong hand, which made Gravity think of the famous photo of George Foreman, handwraps still on, waving his little flag after winning heavyweight gold in 1968.

Fatso and Coach had liked to argue about that. Fatso called Foreman a sellout and said he should have given the black power salute. Coach said if you won the gold medal, you got to do whatever you wanted.

She looked upward into the night and saw a blimp high up, crossing the darkness. She wondered if Coach was somewhere up there watching, maybe alongside Muhammad Ali. They had died within a few days, so they must have found each other in heaven. Boxing people always found each other, and Gravity did not believe there were separate heavens for Muslims, Christians, and Jews.

"Look!" Sacred said. "The NBA!"

They had reached the far end of the stadium, and suddenly all the athletes were together. The tall, dashing figures of Kevin Durant, Carmelo Anthony, and the other basketball stars sent a ripple through the crowd as athletes from all nations crowded in for autographs. Sacred went to talk to Melo, who was a big boxing fan, and Gravity wandered alone, lost in admiration for the uniforms of the various nations.

If only Melsy could see! Gravity could not decide which was her favorite, so she photographed them all: the bright robes of the Liberians and Ghanaians, the buttery silk jackets of the Thai, the chic German pullovers, the cute Bermuda shorts. She was trying to get a good picture of the embroidered Tajikistani suits when a figure popped up, ruining her shot.

"Wassup?"

"D!"

D-Minus gave her the kind of hug that would have become a problem if it went on too long. He was simply adorable in the Haitian uniform, like a character in an old-time movie who might, at any moment, burst into song. The embroidered blue cotton of the peasant blouse hung tantalizingly on his lean frame, and he wore a big straw hat that said "Haiti," tilted at a rakish angle.

"I never even knew your folks were Haitian," she said.

"There's a lot you don't know about me," he said, offering his arm to lead her back to the buses.

"Like what?"

"Like I always get what I want in the end."

Gravity laughed. "Then I hope you want that gold medal. First you get the money . . ."

They said in unison, "Then you get the honey."

They sat side by side on the ride back to the Olympic Village, their legs touching whenever the bus bounced, and watched online footage of their opponents.

After the first round of Jean's gold medal bout in London, D pushed the phone away, saying, "That girl sucks."

Gravity smiled. "She's the face of women's boxing, D. She hasn't lost in a couple of years."

He scoffed. "She about to be the black eye of women's boxing. You just run right out there, hit her with that big right hand. You hit harder than any girl I know."

"Thanks, D."

D-Minus had drawn Uzbekistan in the prelims. The kid

looked strong: a straight-ahead puncher without any glaring weaknesses. Judging could be shady in the men's game, and Uzbekistan was on the rise. D would need to take the lead early so his dominance was indisputable. She watched him gaze out the window, his straw hat low over his eyes.

"Don't wait on that kid," she urged. "You're in shape to fight the whole nine minutes. Leave it all in the ring."

He winked at her. "You handle your bum, I'll handle mine."

Chapter Fifty

Bright lights twinkled down on D-Minus from the lofty ceiling of the Riocentro Pavilion. He looked happy, a cocky lurch in his step, and his arms shone with the sweat of a good warm-up. A volunteer marched before him, holding a sign that said "Haiti," and his coaches followed, carrying a bucket and towel.

When D had qualified for the Games, there had been a scramble to find someone to work his corner. Haiti didn't have any three-star coaches, and Fatso and Boca had never bothered to take the necessary clinics. Gravity had been the one to suggest Tiffany Clarke. She had been worried that D would bitch about being coached by a girl, but he had just shrugged and said, "She's a professional."

Tiffany sprinted up the ring stairs and stood at the red corner gazing calmly across at the Uzbekistanis. She was tight with the Barbadian coach and had enlisted him to assist. He held the ropes apart as D-Minus ducked through and bowed to all the judges.

"He looks good," said Tiger Biggs.

Tiger had won his bout against Australia, and Bonnie was sitting next to him, cutting off his wraps. He and D were friends for the time being. They would not meet until the semis, if they both kept winning.

"This kid strong," Shorty said as they watched Jonibek

Khotamov take the ring and bow to all the judges. Uzbekistan's bantamweight champion was long but solidly built, his pale arms striped with muscles.

"That don't matter," Sacred said. "D too fast for him."

They all rose to their feet and cheered as the announcers called D's name. Gravity popped in a stick of gum and began chewing fiercely. She prayed that Sacred was right and that D's speed would make the difference. Across the arena, the Uzbekistani team cheered for their champion and shook their flags.

She was happy D had the red corner. Ms. Laventhol had told her once that red had a slight statistical advantage. Apparently, the judges subliminally perceived it as more aggressive than blue. That was why the number one seed always got red. A lot of things could affect the judges, including crowd noise, which was why Gravity had come ready to cheer for D with every hit.

When the opening bell rang, D shot out of the corner right at his opponent, whipping out a blistering jab. Before Khotamov could get set, he changed directions and stabbed with a lead right.

"Beautiful!" Gravity screamed, rising to her feet.

D seemed to have gotten the message that he needed to start fast. He kept moving and did not let up the whole first round. The two were about the same height, but D had those long arms, and he knew just how to use them.

Gravity felt herself get hot when she thought about that, and she glanced at Sacred, who was looking right at her with a knowing smile. Gravity blushed and looked down. Sacred patted her knee. The two of them had had a heart-to-heart about boys back at the Olympic Village.

"First round in the bank," Sacred said. "He took that boy to *school*."

The second was even better. Just as Khotamov started to time D's jab, countering with a straight right on top, D switched southpaw. Gravity laughed at the beauty of the move. D was probably even better as a lefty. It threw the other kid off, and right away, D landed a left cross flush to the jaw. Khotamov wobbled into the ropes, touching a glove to the canvas.

Gravity and Sacred whooped in unison, leaping up from their seats.

If a boxer's glove touched the canvas, it was supposed to be ruled a knockdown. But the referee just brushed off Khotamov's gloves and gestured for them to continue, as though it was a slip. Looking back on the fight later, Gravity would realize that this was the first sign of something crooked.

D spent the third round dipping and rolling in a never-ending dance, punctuated with sharp counterpunching. It was a near-perfect performance, and Gravity thought wistfully of how proud it would have made Coach. Right before the final bell, he even got off a shoeshine: a flashy roll of body shots that was usually just for show. It made Khotamov look like a novice.

Gravity would always remember that shoeshine. D's eyes were wide and bright, his arms a dark blur against the canvas's blue. His beautiful face held a look somewhere between boredom and arrogance. That was his gift: to not only outclass someone but act like it was nothing.

He kept his perfect game face during the endless wait for the judges' decision—which, Gravity realized later, was the *second* sign of something crooked—and his composure did not waver, not even when they said it was a split decision and raised the opponent's hand.

But Gravity just about lost her mind. By the time Sacred and Shorty had wrestled her back down into her seat, her throat was raw from yelling "Bullshit!"

Chapter Fifty-One

Gravity cut her eyes away from the platters of fish and broccoli rice that the server set down on their table. None for her. She took a bite of salad and stared past the bustling tables and live band out into the night. The moon hung low in the sky over Copacabana Beach, streaking the ocean with gold.

She still felt blue about D's robbery, but the pressure of her own upcoming bout had begun to force all other thoughts from her mind. At least the decisions were fairer for the women. One upside to niche sports was that they weren't worth fixing.

Only two more nights, she told herself, squirming in her chair. The worst part of fighting was waiting for it to begin.

Carmen Cruz said, "Thank you for joining us, Gravity. It would be a shame for you to come all this way and not leave the Athletes' Village." She raised her glass and addressed the long table. "To Gravity! And to the memory of her legendary coach, who is with us every time she laces on the gloves!"

"*Saúde!*" cried everyone, clinking caipirinhas.

Gravity blushed and raised her water glass.

Carmen seemed to know everyone in Rio. Besides Bonnie and Tiffany, their party tonight included a rock climber hired to hang BBC cameras; Igor, the Brazilian conditioning coach; those two women documentarians making the film about Laishram Memi; the parents of an Argentine wrestler;

and a Brazilian student Carmen had met at a political protest. There was one empty seat at the table.

Bonnie and Carmen helped everyone to pieces of fish and spoonfuls of broccoli rice. The fish looked crispy and golden, and the broccoli rice was a creamy Brazilian invention that was way more delicious than it sounded.

Gravity took another bite of lettuce and tried to pay attention to the band. There was a guitarist who sang, plus horns and a flute and drums. The Brazilians at the restaurant were singing along softly in their musical language, which would have been annoying in America but seemed to be good manners here. The drummer was laughing as he played, and the flute player actually stopped at one point to kiss a waitress. It reminded Gravity a little bit of an amateur boxing show: everybody seemed involved in making it happen.

"The music is wonderful, yes?" The Brazilian student had scooted over to her. "I am Julia."

Julia had a pierced lip and eyebrow and was one of the prettiest girls Gravity had ever seen. She spoke in that poetic way people sometimes did when they had learned English out of books.

Gravity said, "I love it."

She had never heard music like it before. The band played a smooth rhythm that rolled like the waves on the beach behind them. The guitarist was an old man with a floppy hat who had this way of singing like he was talking in your ear. She struggled to find the words to describe it: "It's cool how the band sounds together, but if you listen to an instrument by itself, it's like it's playing its own song."

"Polyphony," Julia said, smiling. "That's called polyphony."

"What are the words about?"

"Ah. This is difficult to translate. This singer is very funny, also he is very political. This is a new song he wrote for the Games."

"Really?" The song did not sound like it was about the Olympics. The guitarist's face had an intense expression, almost like he was mad. "Which sport is it about?"

Julia shook her head. "It is about . . . the cost of the Games."

"Oh." Gravity listened to the flute play a slow descending line. "I guess it must have cost a whole lot to build the stadiums."

"It is not just money," Julia said. She took a pack of tobacco out of her knapsack, which was covered with stickers and buttons, and began to roll a cigarette. "Do you know the Olympic Village used to be people's homes? He sings about an old lady named Maria da Penha. When the government came to kick her out, she would not take their money, because money cannot buy the shade of her mango and avocado trees."

"What's *that* thing?" Gravity asked.

The drummer had picked up a handheld instrument that made a startling moan, something like a crying baby, except you did not want it to stop.

"The cuíca!" Julia said. "A samba instrument that reminds us of the sound of the empty stomach of the people." She took a long drag of her perfectly rolled cigarette, exhaling a plume of smoke that rose up into the night. "It recalls our black tradition, fighting against slavery, hunger, poverty, imperialism, and police violence. . . ."

They both fell silent as the song grew faster and louder. Some of the Brazilians had gotten up and started to dance. It made Gravity want to dance too.

"Maria watches the bulldozers destroy her home," Julia said. "And we call on all the Orixás, who are saints from the world of nature and spirit. We call on the fighting spirit of all the Brazilian people to action against the powerful castes that imprison them."

"Wow."

Gravity did not entirely understand what Julia was talking about, but it was impossible not to be swept up in the power of the music. It was one of the best things she had ever heard. She stood up and applauded at the end. So did Julia and Igor and Carmen.

As they sat back down, Gravity asked shyly, "So do you . . . hate the Olympics very much?"

Julia looked distressed. "Oh no! I *told* you it was hard to translate. Brazilians always see the best in a hard situation. Every year at Carnival, we leave our problems and just dance and are joyful. We do not hate the Games. I would not be here with you if we did." She gestured with her cigarette to indicate their table.

Gravity saw with surprise that D-Minus had appeared in the empty seat. She had not seen or spoken to him since yesterday's loss, but he looked completely recovered. In his white button-down and dark-washed jeans, he seemed to glow in the moonlight. He was bragging to the documentarians about his fight with Uzbekistan as though he had won the gold.

"Everything he did I let him do," D said, demolishing the remaining fried fish.

Tiffany said, "Save room for the steak."

D said, "I'm just warming up."

Igor felt D's biceps and asked him how much he could bench.

D said, "The only thing I lift is fat women."

384

"Who is that boy?" Julia asked Gravity. "He is very handsome."

Gravity felt her stomach swirl. She said, "He's . . . hard to translate."

D-Minus looked right at them and smiled, flashing a new gold tooth.

Carmen raised her caipirinha.

"Another toast!" she cried. "To yesterday's elegant pugilistic display by young Demetrius Saint-Amand! No bad decision can diminish his feat, for the true arbiters of boxing greatness are not the functionaries outside the ring but the warriors within it and all those who witness their truth!"

Bonnie and Igor began to drink, but Carmen stopped them, sloshing caipirinhas onto the table.

"I'm not done! *And* to Demetrius's burgeoning pro career, which he has kindly allowed me to be the first to announce. Felicidades! To the newest prospect of Brian Jones."

Bonnie, Tiffany, Igor, and Gravity gasped. D-Minus beamed. The rest of the table looked confused, because Brian Jones was not well known outside boxing circles. Few had actually laid eyes on the mysterious multimillionaire who was the top manager in the fight game.

Carmen explained that D-Minus's robbery had gotten everyone's attention. The blistering postfight interview he had given the press had gone viral. Brian's people were looking for new talent, and they had reached out to Mr. Rizzo to draw up the papers.

"I fight next month in the Garden," D said, looking in Gravity's eyes. "Save the date."

Chapter Fifty-Two

Gravity and Shorty had worked up a good sweat in the dressing room, and the bright lights kept her warm as she made the walk to face Jean Sullivan. She still had a little bit of neck pain from her bout against New Zealand. It had been an easy win, just like Carmen predicted, but nothing is ever *that* easy in boxing. She rolled her shoulders to loosen them. They would relax once she got punching. Her legs felt light and strong. Her lungs felt good.

She let the headgear work on her like a horse's blinders, tunneling her vision away from the crowd and the cameras so that all she saw was Shorty's back, very straight inside his USA Boxing jacket, and her own boots, marching across the field of play.

A high, small voice yelled, "Hey, Gravity!"

She looked up into the crowd. A few rows up sat a chubby little girl, clutching an American flag. Gravity waved.

The girl cried out, "Mommy, Mommy, Gravity *saw* me!"

All the pain left her body. Gravity thought of how, when she was very little, she used to watch the Olympics on television with her mom, especially the gymnasts and figure skaters.

Look at me now, she thought.

She paused at the base of the steps that led to the blue corner. She liked the red corner better—the color of blood and anger, the color with the slight statistical advantage—but that belonged to Jean Sullivan as the top seed. One day, Gravity would be where Jean was. For now, she would take blue—the color of water and the sky, the color of having the blues—and run with it. She had always been an underdog.

She finally knew what Coach had meant when he said she had already defeated all her enemies. Her mother and her father were not the enemy, although they had done their part to make life hard. Her enemy was not Rick Ross or Andre Vázquez or Lefty.

Certainly the enemy was not this great Irish champion, ducking into the red corner and raising her long arms overhead, even though the sight of her filled Gravity with something like hatred. A pressure, hostile and impersonal, had been building since the Olympic draw, and it both drew her toward the other woman and repelled her, making it impossible to occupy the same elevator, breathe the same air.

Gravity opened her mouth. Shorty squirted in water and slipped in the mouthpiece, his words of advice floating away over the crowd's roar.

Too late for that now, she thought. *I did all the work back home with Fatso and Boca.*

She scanned the jubilant crowd at the Riocentro Pavilion. Earlier that day, the Brazilian lightweight had outpointed Russia, and the Brazilian fans were still singing and waving their flags. She thought of the music she had heard on the beach and what Julia had told her, and as she knelt in the corner and said the Shema, she thanked God for their generous host nation. She asked that He protect them all: her, Jean, everyone in the pavilion, all the Brazilian people.

And let me shine, she prayed.

As she rose, she saw them in the stands, and she laughed

so hard she almost lost her mouthpiece. Athletes got two free tickets to each fight, but the flight to Rio was so expensive that only Melsy had come. She was holding up the "G" in "Gravity." D-Minus rocked the "R," Sacred had the "A," Tiffany had the "V," and it was a good thing D-Minus was such a hustler, because there are a lot of letters in "LET'S GO GRAVITY KICK HER ASS," and he had conned some poor US athlete or fan into holding each one of them. Even the apostrophe.

The ref was a woman, which struck Gravity as auspicious. She followed her into center ring to gaze into the Irishwoman's proud green eyes. They leaned in. Their gloves touched. They backed away.

She had no enemies. That was how she saw it. Fear, shame, and despair were her enemies, but she had defeated them long ago. If she had not defeated them, she would not be a boxer.

The center of the ring was empty and bright. It was the only place in the world for a woman like her. Beyond it she saw her opponent: a bouncing red blur, intolerable.

The clear tone sounded. She charged into the light. The closer she got to Jean, the faster she moved, and when she reached the sweet spot her arms knew so well, she let fly the straight right hand. It struck Jean full in the face like ringing a bell.

Gravity broke everything sooner or later. She would break this girl too.

Acknowledgments

I have a lot of people to thank for the material, inspiration, and support to write this book, which I researched over twenty years in and around boxing. When I was twenty-two and newly arrived in New York, my wonderful tai chi teacher, J. P. Harpignies, told me I was a little young and angry for such an internal practice as tai chi and ought to learn to kick and punch in real time. This book wouldn't exist without him.

Thank you to all the women I fought during my five years as a competitive amateur. The ones I remember are Patricia Alcivar, Teresa O'Toole, Jamie McGrath, Danielle Bouchard, Sandra Bizier, Gladys Alonso, and Betzayda Abreu, most of whom beat me up. Much love to my sparring partners, Stella Nijhof and Crystelle Samson Morneau, who also beat me up regularly.

Thank you to all my trainers: Mike Smith, Ghislain Vaudreuil, George Acevedo, Ray Velez, and the late George Washington of Bed-Stuy Boxing. And my Pilates teacher, Clarice Marshall, whose work helped me recover from all those punches.

Getting to stay at the MacDowell Colony was one of the greatest things that ever happened to me. I will always be grateful for the gift of that time, during which I wrote the first pages of this book. I also wrote while sheltered by the midwife Sarah Bay; my writing teacher, Steve Friedman; and my gracious yoga student and friend, Jai Apfel.

Thank you to all the Kickstarter donors who made it possible for me to travel to China and Rio. Special thanks to the extremely generous Heather Moran, Debi Cornwall, Daniel Mandil, and Jonathan Sharp. Even more than the financial support, just knowing I had so many friends who believed in me helped keep me going.

My deepest gratitude goes to Pat Russo for creating NYC Cops & Kids, the free community gym in East Flatbush, where I have coached and tutored young boxers for the past six years. Thank you to Teddy Atlas and his foundation for funding the program for many years and to everyone else who helps keep our doors open, including Dave Siev, Ronald McCall, and the New York Police Department boxing team. I am blessed to coach alongside Hilergio "Quiro" Bracero, Aureliano Sosa, Benny Roman, and Wayne Atkins.

I wrote this book for the "kids" of Cops & Kids: Bhopp, Shu Shu, Blake, Africa, Jersil, Earl, Nkosi, Nikita, Reshat, Alban, all the Jonibeks, Julian, Chiquito, Jon, Chris, Leon, Edwin, Cassius, Ruben, Hamza, Henry, Justice, Michael Jackson, Lucky, Willade, Aaliyah, Jay, Renaldo, Samuel, Amadou, Ibrahim, Deen, Chop Chop, Terrence, the Muñoz twins, Khalid, Clarens, Pryce, all the Elijahs, the point guards Lawrence and Stan, my star ASVAB students Alvaro and Brian, and everyone else who walks through our door with the dream of being a champion.

My greatest inspiration for this novel was Claressa Shields, two-time Olympic gold medalist and reigning world middleweight and super middleweight champion. Thank you, Claressa, for existing and for letting me tag along. All the fiercest parts of Gravity I stole from you.

It was an honor to watch all the boxers who contended in the 2012 and 2016 Olympic Trials: Alex Love, Marlen Esparza, Christina Cruz, Tiara Brown, Queen Underwood, Raquel Miller, Tika Hemingway, Franchon Crews, and many others. Mikaela Mayer and Virginia Fuchs were especially generous with their time and stories. Special thanks to Pat Manuel for sharing his journey as a trans athlete.

Thank you to the elite coaches Billy Walsh, Kay Koroma, Joe Guzman, Basheer Abdullah, and especially Jason Crutchfield and Al Mitchell, whose superb corner work was a privilege to observe. Thank you, Coach Israel "Shorty" Acosta, for your miraculous story. Thank you, Delilah Ponce-Rico, for being the mom of Cali boxing. Even a knife fight is fun with you.

I would not have survived on the road without my own Tripartite Commission: fierce photojournalist Sue Jaye Johnson, who produced the documentary *T-Rex*; Coach Christy Halbert, source of all my best pull quotes; and independent journalist Raquel Ruiz, who is the world's best *parcera*.

Thank you to the warm people of Spokane. The lovable glove table madman Rowdy Welch. Doug and Rae Ann, beaming love from the stands. Most of all, thanks to Francis Cullooyah, his daughter Taunie, Albert Thomas, and the Kalispel Tribe for inviting me and Raquel to tour their reservation and hear their story. Francis told me that the women boxers' struggle for recognition reminded him of the struggle of his people. I have tried to do justice to that conversation here.

Thank you to Pat Fiacco and Boxing Canada for being such great hosts at the Continentals in Cornwall and the Pan Am Games in Toronto. Thank you to the nation of Canada for producing the brilliant Corey Erdman, commentator extraordinaire. Thanks to Pan Am champ Mandy Bujold for letting me and Raquel crash in her apartment, with the affirmations stuck to the walls. Thank you, Cathy van Ingen, for doing such important work for domestic abuse survivors in the community.

In China: Thank you to all the boxers, staff, and volunteers at the 2012 Women's World Championships. Thanks to the UK's Tasha Jonas and her dad, he of the booming voice from the upper rafters, and thanks to the Liverpudlian documentary crew who taught me the phrase "handbags at dawn." Thanks to Igor, the conditioning coach, and all the beautiful fighters of Team Brazil. Thank you to documentarians Anna Sarkissian and Ameesha Joshi of *With This Ring*. Thank you to Regina, the server at the Pizza Hut in Qinhuangdao, and to Tony Liu for letting me teach his English class at Yanshan University.

In Rio: I cannot thank Red Sullivan enough for his hospitality. Thank you to Julia and all the other artists, students, and political protesters Sue and I met at the occupation of the Canecão. Thank you to João Bosco and drummer Kiko Freitas for the music and the words.

Thank you to everyone around the world who has ever let me train in their club: the generous Bruce Silverglade at Gleason's, the beautiful people at Kops Gym in Amsterdam, Lanna Muay Thai in Chiang Mai, Crossfit Crown in Rio de Janeiro, Sulem Urbina and Andrews Soto in Phoenix, and my Parisian boxing sisters, Elisabeth Alonso and Annie Bervin, who taught me so much about heart.

Before I knew this material was going to be a novel, I was lucky to work with wonderful freelance editors. Thanks to Chris Greenberg for publishing my earliest coverage in the *Huffington Post*, and Gautham Nagesh and Anna John for all their excellence at Stiff Jab. Thank you to my friend Eric Klinenberg for introducing me to Carlo Rotella, whom I think is the best living boxing writer. Thank you to Carlo and his wonderful coeditor, Mike Ezra, for including my profile of Claressa Shields in their anthology *The Bittersweet Science*. And thank you to Wendy Lesser of the *Threepenny Review*, because I probably would have quit writing long ago without her encouragement.

Thank you to all my colleagues at NBC for the 2012 Olympic boxing broadcast: Rob Dustin, DT Slouffman, Mick Lewis, Scott

Katz, Mike Canter, Laila Ali, and BJ Flores. Thank you to Michael Gluckstadt, Kieran Mulvaney, Brad Davis, and the team at *Inside HBO Boxing*; it was so fun while it lasted. Thank you to Steve Farhood and the crew at Showtime for their support of the women's game.

I tried to be as accurate as possible in my depiction of women's boxing, but I took a few liberties for the sake of the story. The tournament locations and qualification pathway I describe are a mash-up between the roads to London and Rio. At seventeen, Gravity would not have been old enough to compete at Rio, where the minimum age for boxers had been raised to nineteen. Women's amateur bouts used to consist of four two-minute rounds, but I have written all the fight scenes here with three three-minute rounds, which is what women and men amateurs now box.

Thank you to all the good people of USA Boxing Metro, who work to keep the sport of amateur boxing alive: Ray Cuadrado, Sonya Lamonakis, Elise Seignolle, Joe Higgins, Ernesto Rodriguez, and Jeff Friedman. Thank you to Bobby Jiles, Chris Cugliari, Stephen Johnson, Malissa Smith, and anyone who's ever worked a glove table or held a spit bucket.

This book would not exist without Christopher Myers, who reached out when I was aimless and gave me a target. It was a dream to partner with him on this. My literary agent, Alyssa Henkin, is a joy, and I was very grateful to be edited by Jenny Brown and Michelle Frey, whose belief in the project and careful eyes on the prose helped this to be a better book. Thank you to Sylvia Al-Mateen and the entire team at Knopf.

I am indebted to the chess and pool novels of Walter Tevis, which served as models for how to write about the psychological aspects of competition. The scene where Gravity spars with Ariana Leite is an homage to *The Queen's Gambit*.

Thank you to all my great readers: Shahirah Majumdar, Josh

Wilson, Pari Aryafar, Karen Naranjo, and Gordon Eriksen. Thank you to Richard Nash for mentorship, Jean Manon for friendship in the trenches, Mia Russo and Janine Amado for a glimpse into the world of ring card girls, the great Daniel Pinkwater for telling me to make enough for the bandits, and my math teacher, Paul Lockhart, for explaining how gravity works.

Thank you to my family. I love you, Mom, Dan, Gram, Donna, Nik, Melsy, Ty, and all the Greenwolds, Cartagenas, Roches, Greenes, Pompers, and Demings.

When I first heard women's boxing would be in the London Games, I said to my husband, "I feel like I should follow this story." I had been out of the sport for ten years and didn't have money, a byline, or a plan.

He said, "Go. I'm buying the ticket."

Thank you, Ethan Iverson, for being my best reader, partner, and friend. Thank you for always being in my corner and filling my life with music.